The Paper Man

by

Michael Frederick

Novels by author:

White Shoulders

Ledges

Missouri Madness

Shy Ann

Summer of '02

Autumn Letters

Places

Blue River

Different

Dedicated to my brother, John

September, 2009/1st printing/5,000 copies

Thanks, Tony, for your art.
Cover Design by Anthony Conrad

It wasn't long after Independence Day in 1995 that nine-year-old Josie was told by her Aunt Laura she'd be moving to eastern Nebraska before the new school year began.

"When does school start, Aunt Laura?" Josie lisped.

"Oh, August 23rd or so," Laura answered as she struggled to keep her emotions in check.

Josie watched the end of August approaching as she mentally checked off each passing day on the calendar. On the square for August 21st Uncle Walter had written "Macy" — the name of the village on the Omaha Indian Reservation Josie would call home. Josie wondered to herself, *What will my new school be like? What's Granny Tenna like? When will I see Aunt Laura, Uncle Walt and Dennis again?*

* * * * *

Thirty-two-year-old Walter Bird was Tribal Chairman of the Pine Ridge Indian Reservation in South Dakota. As he drove their white, 1980 Crown Victoria out of Custer's United Methodist Church parking lot, he and his wife, Laura, were praying the same thing: *Please let Josie feel her grief and begin to heal before that awful drive to Macy.*

The drive from church to Pine Ridge was familiar to ten-year-old Dennis Bird, as he held his cousin's left hand in his right hand, imitating his parents' joined hands resting on the front seat. Dennis began to draw something with his left index finger on the back of the car's front seat. Those bright, golden eyes of Josephine Ann Tenna followed his finger tracing a heart with a feathered arrow through its center. She smiled at the invisible tracing for a few seconds. Dennis called Josie "Golden Eyes" because the color of her eyes matched the gold crayon in his big box of crayons that he diminished day and night as he drew nature scenes from the old *National Geographic* magazines strewn in his father's office lobby.

Josie smiled at the invisible heart tracing for a few seconds, then replied by drawing her arrow-pierced heart with the number two to the right of the invisible heart on the backside of Laura's seat. Dennis returned her smile.

Dennis and Josie had a strong familial love instilled in them by Walter and Laura through massive doses of open affection and lots of playtime together. The Birds were that way with any child they encountered. Holding hands while walking into Sunday school or even just crossing a dirt road in Pine Ridge were as natural to Josie and Dennis as saying their bedtime prayers and washing their hands before supper.

Josie saw the big-toothed smile Uncle Walter gave Aunt Laura. It meant they would stop at the A&W drive-in on the eastern edge of Custer and get a small frosted mug of root beer.

"Are we getting root beer, Father?" Dennis asked.

"Yes, we are. You want to get some cold root beer, Josie?"

"Yes, please," Josie answered.

Walter lost his stoic composure. That lisp from her missing front tooth, her honey-red uneven bangs she had cut with dull scissors, the innocent sound of such a deserving angel, and the countless prayers on her behalf all made his chin quiver and his black eyes well. He averted his face to his left as he felt Laura's tender squeeze.

Parking next to one of the drive-up order boards in the A&W

parking lot, Walter shut off his car's air conditioning fan before turning off his engine. "Windows down," he smiled.

Before the root beer was slurped to the last drop, Dennis had to know, "Father, when can we visit Josie after she moves away?"

She caught her uncle's dark eyes behind his wire-rimmed glasses looking at Aunt Laura before answering, "Maybe Christmas."

"Can she visit us here, or will we go visit her?" his son asked.

"Oh ... I'm sure we'll visit her."

Laura and her husband held hands all the way from the A&W to Pine Ridge. Tighter and tighter their grip grew until that damned yellow garage under the shabby pines was dead ahead with its foreboding, dark-hole entrance. Walter hadn't parked inside it since mid-June — the day before the "accidental suicide" of Mae, Laura's half-sister and Josie's mother. Laura asked her husband to burn it down after Josie sprinkled her mother's ashes atop Sheep Mountain Table in the Badlands.

"After you kids get out of your Sunday school clothes, I'll set up the sprinkler," Walter said. He watched the kids run inside their small yellow Bird house as his wife waited in the car to talk privately, leaving her window up.

"How much did you say Granny Tenna will get monthly caring for Josie?" she asked, swishing back her black braided hair over the headrest.

"Including food stamps ... $545.00."

Laura thought for several moments before she said anything bad about anyone, especially an elder relative. "How will we know how she's treated?"

"When we visit at Christmastime. We'll know by then," he

assured her.

Laura looked into the dark, single stall ahead of her. The feeling of its cold dirt floor under her bare feet was just one of the memories forever burned into her senses the morning she found Josie's mother lying near the tailpipe of their Crown Victoria. She had been asphyxiated after sliding the garage door shut, starting the engine, and sitting on the dirt floor next to the car's exhaust. It was enough to get Mae Tenna out of this world before anyone knew she had left her twin bed in the room she shared with Josie. "I can't stay here with that garage, Walt. It has to go before Josie goes."

He smiled his big, even teeth out from behind his puffy lips, anxious to please his wife. He sat there behind the wheel thinking about the job ahead. "Tonight," he told her. "Tonight."

"And we will visit her at Christmas?"

"Yes, dear," he smiled.

About an hour after midnight, Josie could hear Dennis snoring in her mother's bed, his foot poking out from his bed sheets and hanging toes-down three feet from her head. She could hear pine cones exploding above the garage as her uncle hosed down the overhanging branches well enough to keep them safe from the flames. Earlier in the evening she had seen him going from house to house to tell his neighbors about the late-night torching he had planned. They all knew why.

Josie's eyes glowed yellow as she stared at the devilish flames with her nose pressed against her bedroom window. Then she cried. She thought of the morning her mother was found "asleep" in the garage, of Aunt Laura wailing in her room, of the blue-and-white ambulance from Hot Springs as it drove away. It all seemed like a dream to her now. She remembered standing with the Birds atop an isolated butte on Sheep Mountain Table at sunset in the Badlands. She wore the dress her mother liked — the dress with splashes of orange and yellow and a pretty sash that tied at the back. Her mother had said the dress made her eyes look like a firestorm.

She couldn't remember driving up to that spot or Uncle Walter handing her the porcelain jar with the tiny blue flowers painted on it that her mother liked so much. She did recall Uncle Walter telling her how the Badlands were made out of volcanic ash from the Black Hills and how the Badlands were constantly being sculpted by wind and water and erosion until one day they'd be gone.

She'd wanted to throw her mother's ashes — jar and all — into the patch of salt brush shrubs and grasses growing between cracks in the hard dirt along the empty Sage Creek below. The dry, never-ending westerly wind whipped her dress to her chin as she clenched her mother's remains tightly between her little brown fingers.

Dennis had stepped up to the edge beside her as his parents sobbed in the car. He told her how his body tingled thinking of their ancestors standing on this very spot as they watched for the savage tribes to invade from the western mountains. He was now her warrior, he assured her — a protector and witness of this ceremony that would bond them forever. But he knew in his heart that she would be gone soon. Perhaps never to return.

Her lips had moved as she inaudibly spoke her final goodbyes to her mother, sending tears plip-plopping onto Dennis's Buster Browns. He thought about how the sun would come up and go down sooner where Josie was going to be living. She would always know the day ahead of him by one time zone that had been created by the white man. She would be leaving Pine Ridge before he could tell her what it meant to him to spend his early years with her. She was his half-cousin since their mothers were half-sisters. But what made Josie different from him the most was her blood. Josie was only one-quarter-blood

Oglala Sioux. Like her mother's father, Josie's father was a white man. She was the product of a one-night stand her mother had outside a Rapid City bar on the front seat of a traveling salesman's car. But it didn't matter a bit in the Bird household that their Josie was three-quarters white.

Walter was all too familiar with his niece's loss. Being a reservation chairman, he was always around children who had lost a parent or had never even known one. He wondered what would become of her. *Will she become another fallen one, lost on the plains? Will she succumb to life's darkness? Will her life end up as barren and isolated as this wonder called the Badlands?* He watched as his son placed his fingers into Josie's partly closed left hand and smiled right into those golden circles with his shining black eyes. "I will always love you, Josie," Dennis had told her plaintively.

She had watched Dennis's sloe-black eyes fill with liquid, then saw the tears spilling over from the lower rims of his eyelids and trailing down over his Lakota cheekbones. She had concealed that she was hanging on. At that moment she could not feel his words any more than she felt the loss of her mother. *If I could only be like Dennis now,* she thought, *free to let go and show fear, I'd be shaking like an October leaf, out of control, doomed to fall ... alone now.*

"Let's go get some root beer," Walter smiled as he walked up behind the two children.

They put the Badlands behind them, leaving the overwhelming desolation and harsh beauty to the red-winged crows fidgeting on the first fenceline into Custer.

Monday morning the black ashes from the yellow Bird garage were still smoldering. Josie found their remains another harsh reminder of having to tell her mother goodbye in the Badlands. It was the beginning of their last week together in

Pine Ridge. The four of them, Walter and Laura on either side of the two children, walked the short block to the old Methodist church located right behind Pine Ridge's only grocery store. The old church was now a makeshift daycare where a patient Laura Bird watched over thirty poor Native American children while their parents (or, in most cases, their single-parent mothers) worked in Custer, Rapid City, or Hot Springs.

Josie felt safe and connected holding hands with Dennis and Aunt Laura. Uncle Walter led the way, escorting his family safely like a home guard before continuing on two more blocks to work behind his desk at the Agency. Dust clouds mushroomed from their footsteps on the unpaved reservation roads, leaving fresh dirt marks between and around their exposed toes peeking out from the handmade sandals they wore. Josie and Dennis would assist Laura with the interminable clean-up, chores and help that caring for thirty kids demanded. Laura paid them each a dollar a day during the summer to help her at the daycare.

"What flavor of pop will you get today, Dennis?" his father teased on their walk.

"Coke," he returned with a big smile, causing Josie to giggle with Laura. They all knew that the old pop machine outside the front of the little grocery store only dispensed Coke.

"Gonna be a hot one today, Mother," Walter smiled. His turquoise leather string tie jiggled against the buttons on the short-sleeved white shirt she had ironed before going to bed the night before. His comment reminded him that he wanted to have a look at the daycare's giant floor fan he'd made. Laura told him it had quit working. He hoped it was just a loose connection, since one of the kids had tripped over its cord the previous Thursday. *Too hot to be without a fan today,* he thought.

They cut across the dirt on the front yard of the church and onto the uneven and broken sidewalk where weeds and poverty grass grew between every crack. The one-story church was turning ash-gray after one more summer without fresh paint. Never was there money for such things. Church attendance was next to nothing. For three years the Indian Methodists had been without a preacher. On Sunday mornings maybe twelve people at the most, including Josie and the Birds, would get dressed up and stop in before going on to Custer to a temporary place to worship. They would walk through the never-locked double doors, push together three or four benches to form a near-circle, and meditate amidst burning sage grass on the "urgent things" they could do the coming week — fix the floor fan, get Josie a new outfit for her move, check in on old Mrs. LaVelle every day to see if she had passed on during the night, and pray for a new community center.

The lone headlight on the driver's side barely cut through the blowing dust. The Conoco station at Mission, South Dakota, seventy-three miles east of Pine Ridge on Highway 18, was their last call before Pine Ridge. Five miles short of their destination the dust storm hit. The Conoco station — a red-and-white harbor with two gas pumps, a café, and a full-service garage — was owned by a tightwad Czech who never bought anything a Sioux City salesman was peddling.

John Floyd Deason knew he was close to Mission. Instead of pulling over in his dilapidated, shivering, rusted-out white station wagon, he crept along Highway 18 at fifteen miles per hour, craning his grizzled neck over toward his cracked passenger-side windshield where fifteen-year-old Floyd Harvey Deason sat without a trace of concern. John cursed when his car's only working windshield wiper on the driver's side made visibility even worse by smearing a wide strip of yellow film from dead insects across the windshield.

"God, I know I'm askin' for some help here, but get me to that cheap Czech's station and I promise I'll sell 'im this time!" John laughed.

John Deason was a taker. He thanked God for every sale he made, and he scolded Him for the ones he didn't. He had been taking orders for the Silver Paper Company in Sioux City since he was thirty years old. Twenty-three years to date. His son Floyd accompanied him on trips when school wasn't in session as a sort of apprentice — learning the customers, back-roads and shortcuts in what would eventually become his delivery territory for his father's employer. John Deason had worked his territory hard in the '70s and started coasting in the mid '80s.

Yes, even in this isolated part of western South Dakota, a million times hard-working hands had reached for, used, and tossed away his sales of one-ply toilet paper and stiff paper towels that fit only into Albert Silver's tissue and towel dispensers. All a client had to do was sign the lease and take the key to the dispenser, and he'd be locked in to having John Deason pestering him for a reorder three or four times a year for as long as the nail or screw held the cabinet to the wall.

Dust was everywhere. A brown-gray maelstrom of blowing dirt, dust and gravel obscured the station wagon's glass. Floyd watched his skinny father somehow get them to their final pit stop before Pine Ridge on their way to Custer.

The twitch under his dad's right eye was just like his — except Floyd's twitch was under his left eye. It only twitched this much when he rode along with his old man on one of his Black Hills runs. He even noticed his father's right eye spasm during his sales pitches. That was the amazing thing about John Deason: he could take any negative, bring it to light and laughter, and make that twitch the only reason he left with a sale. "Look! Ya see that twitch?" John would bark to his potential customer, who would never admit he had seen it and was surprised as hell this toilet paper salesman from Sioux City would even mention it. "That little twitch," he continued, "means you just got yerself a five-percent discount. Ten percent if ya buy a couple cases of anything Old Man Silver stocks."

Floyd would watch his father from a chair ten feet away in the main room of a co-op grain elevator. There might be a farmer or two seated beside him feeling the slippery-slick oil-based sweeping compound under their boots that this even slicker paper man had sold the elevator's manager the last time through. They all listened to the veteran salesman take control of his prospect by keeping his mouth shut until his prospect said something. It didn't matter how long it took. John might light a Camel non-filter, or he might take his prospect's eyes down to his counter and onto Silver's five-by-seven product card that listed some two dozen items that were his main lines. The crafty salesman would never turn to notice someone walking in or driving by. Then he would hear the prospect's first words.

"How much ya get for a case of them towels that fits those dispensers I got?" they would ask.

Then look out! After the price was quoted, John kept after his client with bulldog tenacity, suggesting other wares he was peddling. "How ya doin' on them coffee refills I sold ya last time?" John Deason stayed on his prospect's heels, following him to a closet or storage room, staying with him step for step to see just what other things he could suggest. "Can ya use a half-dozen of them thirty-two-ounce cotton mop heads? I got some Silver Bowl and Glass Cleaner in the car. A buck-fifty a quart. Did I ever get ya to try 'em out?"

The prospect's head would shake out his negative response. Then came the pure beauty as Floyd would see his father "turn it." A "180" his dad called it.

"Can I bring in one of each? And next time I'll bet you'll go for a case when ya see how fast and easy yer toilet bowl and windows get clean."

More silence. Light another Camel. Keep very quiet until, "All right, then ... I'll try one of each. And give me a case of them towels for my dispenser, and a case of them coffee refills."

John would remove his order pad from his worn handleless sales case that he called Charlie. With twenty-five orders per pad, he could go through three pads on a good week. John would scour the man's time with suggestion after suggestion until he could push no more. His boss, Albert Silver, would always say, "He's no order-taker; that guy can sell!"

Parked close to the Mission Conoco, Floyd watched his father's hands under the dim dome light. Covered with big liver spots and tiny broken blood vessels, they trembled as he reached for his billfold in a back pocket and opened the old cowhide to find "his key" to that cheap Czech. Floyd was used to seeing his father's fingers trembling later in the day, but now he was seeing it in the mornings too. It was obvious his dad was going downhill — losing bone and muscle tone and his quick smile. They didn't laugh together like they used to. Floyd's mother had left him and his dad a year earlier, running off with a plumbing parts salesman from Kansas City. She had tried to get their son to go with her, but Floyd wouldn't leave his dad. She told him she'd visit him, but he told her not to bother. That was it. Before his wife left, John would drink vodka only at night. Now he drank it day and night.

"Stay here," John told his son.

"Dad, I have to piss."

"All right. We'll have to wait till this blows out, anyway."

The wagon's passenger door nearly blew off its dry hinges when Floyd opened it. His father's skinny legs looked even thinner in those wrinkled teal-blue polyester slacks he'd worn for three days in a row. The ugliness of his shirt, however, proved a suitable distraction from his pants. It was a royal-blue fishnet with yellow specks. A dime-sized blue ink stain from a pen marked the bottom of his shirt pocket.

The Deasons were nearly blown into the station's glass door. John's thin brown hair strands did not move at all, having been greased flat and straight back on his small simian head with a hair cream that smelled like Vitalis.

Pulska was the Czech station owner who for years refused to take Deason's checks. One time he did, though, when John gassed up in the winter with no cash on him. He told Pulska he'd been comin' in and callin' on him for years, so he could take his check. Pulska had relented, and the check cleared with no problem. That's when the paper salesman began asking around about the tight Czech. This time John was ready for him.

John could see the wary station owner looking at him from behind his register. No smile or greeting from Pulska to the man he knew stopped at least two or three times a year. The storm in the paper man's eyes was far more unpredictable, moving on the offensive with greater speed than the fiercest dust storm nature could produce. Pulska's eyes were defensive and stationary from years of having people and things assail him. The short, chubby Czech braced for the salesman's usual pitch by crossing his arms in front of his green overalls. As his oil-dirtied thumb rubbed his jutting chin, his mind told him to turn this huckster-peddler away as fast as possible. But this unpredictable, calculating paper man was months ahead of his Czech prospect. With Charlie riding his left hip, he palmed his surprise in his right hand on Pulska's counter. "Ya know, I was readin' the paper in Sioux City awhile back ... I came across an interesting little article."

Deason opened his smooth-fisted hand and watched Pulska's blue eyes swimming down, searching the small print of a torn newspaper clipping, seeing only the title word: "Dissolutions." This announcement about Pulska's ex-wife divorcing the Sioux City feed salesman she had run off with was not news to Pulska. He had heard about it two months earlier. But what Deason had to say afterward was: "I was sittin' on a barstool on lower Fourth Street in Sioux City. And this bartender was tellin' me about this salesman, DePrecio, who married yer ex. He gave me that. Said he knew the whole story about the little swine."

About that time Floyd came out of the corner john, knuckle-rubbing the dust in his eyes. Habitually inconspicuous while his dad pitched, Floyd Harvey Deason was listening and learning. His old man was on the hunt, ready to punish this man for a hundred rejections. John baited the Czech and waited, lighting a Camel and pretending not to notice all the resolute prejudgments and patterns of a man taught not to show emotion.

The paper man took another drag, even breaking his rule by turning his head to the blowing dust that hid his station wagon. He knew his prey's heart thumped hard behind the silver tire gauge clipped inside his overalls pocket. John knew if he spoke he would lose. So did his son. The loser spoke first. John knew Pulska's story, recalling the day the Czech had driven thirty-seven miles to a tow in Winner and saw his wife's car parked at the Shamrock Motel next to DePrecio's car. Pulska had gassed and scrubbed the windows on that car every three months or so for five years.

"What'd he say?" Pulska finally asked.

"He never got time to tell me. He got busy and I had to go. I told him I'd stop in and get the scoop someday. Didn't really interest me at the time. I thought you'd like to know." John went to the door and flicked his butt outside. On the way back to the register he said, "I won't come through here on my run for a few months. That's too long to wait. If old man Silver gets a six-case order from me with a couple of dispensers, he'll let me deliver 'em when I'm workin' Yankton next time. That ain't so long to wait. And I got time to get all the scoop on her. What's her name?"

"Marilyn," he murmured, knowing he'd just been taken by another Sioux City salesman. He signed the lease for a towel and toilet paper dispenser, then signed the $126.00 order for six cases of something he knew would lock him in with this peddler for as long as he worked. Watching the red glow of his taillights

14

leave when the wind let up, he saw the white Woodbury County license plate — the same kind he had seen parked at the Shamrock Motel. He felt like bending over and puking on his floor. The cot behind his oil drums at the back of his garage would have to hold him now. He needed to lie down until it passed, for once again a salesman from Sioux City had taken what he held dear. This time it was his money and a white-hot conviction.

Floyd spread his knees apart so the glove box door didn't bang into them when his dad removed his half-pint bottle of cheap vodka that was nearly empty. His father had been laughing out loud and coughing since they'd left Mission. Heading west on 18, Floyd listened to him mumbling out loud about how he duped that tight Czech with a little bull. "Boy, is he ever gonna get a story! He better be there when I deliver," he cackled, then slugged back the rest of the vodka without appearing to swallow, letting it flow down his throat like a siphon. He screwed on the cap to his empty bottle, rolled down his window, and tossed it across the roof into the ditch on Floyd's side while doing eighty under an azure-brown summer sky. He lit a non-filter, cupping both hands around his match while steering with the inside of his right thigh. Many times his son wanted to grab the wheel when they veered onto the right shoulder or over the center line. His dad seemed bent on lighting his stick before taking the wheel by hand.

"We gonna stay in a Custer motel, Dad?"

He answered no silently with his head while inhaling his smoke deeply. Afer exhaling he explained in his flinty voice, "Gotta work Pine Ridge. Heap big bucks on the rez," he smiled.

"But there's no motels in Pine Ridge," Floyd countered.

"I know that. You let me handle that stuff."

Floyd nodded yes while looking straight ahead, thinking how

he'd love to jump into that cold blue water at the Custer Inn like he did last summer. And he was thirsty for a pop iced with those crystal ice cubes with the hole clear through.

"We'll stay tomorrow night in Custer ... then head back Sunday. Okay?"

Floyd bobbed his head yes, keeping to himself how he didn't want to be stuck in some hot, abandoned room all by himself just so his old man could make an extra forty bucks off of Silver by getting a bogus motel receipt for two nights in Custer.

Amidst the children's laughter, Laura Bird decided to let them do it one more time — then nap time for one glorious hour. Walter would take his hour-long lunch during that time, and they would share a lunch he had made them at home. They would eat at a table in one corner of the old church with thirty children sleeping on resplendent mats made by a family member. These mats were lined along the gray floorboards behind the big fan that Walter had fixed.

The children chanted slowly in unison, "One! Two! Three!"

Josie and Dennis each held the inside biceps of the other's right arm while lying flat on their backs, head to feet with their hips adjacent to each other, about to Indian leg wrestle. Each right leg went up ninety degrees and crossed at the calves. Then Josie won by pulling Dennis's leg toward her left, once again winning the daycare's applause.

As soon as the children were sleeping on their mats, Walter came in with their lunch in a large paper bag that Dennis had colored the night before. There was a snorting black stallion with the Black Hills behind him on one side of the bag. On the other side was a beautiful white mare grazing under an orange moon. Walter called it their feed bag. Even taciturn Laura laughed at the name.

The next day, Friday, would be their last day together. Saturday was the day Granny Tenna was expecting them in Macy. It had to be Saturday, because early Sunday morning

Josie would be baptized in the oldest church in Nebraska. It had all been arranged by Granny, who told Laura on the phone that the terrible sins of Josephine's mother and father would be washed away in a single moment under God's roof. "I would not have it any other way," Granny insisted.

Walter gave Josie four quarters, saying, "Strong Legs, why don't you buy your cousin a cold pop, huh?"

When Josie's smile exposed her missing front tooth, Laura had to go over to the pulpit area with her back to the room until her upper body stopped convulsing from her sobbing.

Dennis hustled out the church's front door, catching up with Josie before they reached the grocery store. "You wanna get cold?" he asked.

She wasn't sure what he meant, but she followed him to the narrow breezeway between the smokehouse and the store's back door. They tramped over flattened cardboard grocery boxes that were still damp after getting soaked when grocer Ned Clouda had hosed off a side of beef delivered to him that morning from Rapid.

For Native American Ned Clouda, now slicing bologna behind his meat counter, these two kids were about the only kids in town to wear shoes on his pine floor, which was covered with sawdust and toe imprints up and down his three narrow aisles of sparsely stocked shelves.

Josie liked the red ribbon the stout, middle-aged grocer had bunching his ponytail. Dennis was sensitive enough to wait until Clouda's arms stopped rolling the slicer's blade forward and back, forward and back, until the last slice of meat piled onto the others on the white locker paper. "Could we please go into your freezer, Mr. Clouda?" he asked politely.

Ned wasn't about to allow a couple of kids into his walk-in freezer, but the little girl with the yellow eyes who had lost her mother by such a cowardly act was irresistible — quiet with eyes averted to the floor so he could have a look at her relaxed mouth and jawline that should have been tight with rage. The full-blooded Oglala removed his blood-stained white apron, cranked a handful of Gojo onto his palm at his sink basin, then used a paper towel from his stock.

"Come," he said to the kids. He punched open his freezer door and made sure there were no knives or other objects that could harm them. "I give you five minutes," he gestured with his iron-brown hand. He flipped on the light and left them alone in the sub-zero atmosphere with a few hundred pounds of beef hanging in a row on meat hooks at the far end of the freezer.

Josie's arms and legs immediately goose-pimpled. She was wearing one of Dennis's white sleeveless t-shirts and her blue cotton shorts that Aunt Laura had hemmed from a pair of pants she had worn to school once or twice a week last winter. Dennis made her giggle when his whole face smiled while inhaling the cold air with his eyes closed.

"Enjoy this, Josie. Be cold now," he smiled. She watched him being cold. Her goose-pimples increased when she thought about leaving him soon. He had talked her to sleep every night — at least he had thought so. But she was the one to stay awake listening to him breathe, trying to read his mumbling lips in the dark when he dreamed.

Now she laughed at their fogging breath and their goose-pimpled skin. Dennis — the full-blooded boy who had been permitted to paint their bedroom wall with his drawings of mountains, wildlife, and plants — opened his arms, inviting his best friend to share his body heat. She stepped close to his chest with her elbows tucked against her sides while looking down and shivering. He held her to him. She forgot the cold and stopped her impulse to shiver. This was unconditional and pure, and she would cherish this memory for years to come.

19

* * * * *

Floyd could see Pine Ridge on the horizon. Nothing but yellow arid grasslands separated the station wagon from the reservation. He was hot and bored from watching his old man find long nose hairs with his thumb and index finger then yank them out painfully. Sometimes two or three would be pulled simultaneously and examined closely by the feckless driver, then dropped onto the dividing hump on the wagon's carpetless floor. Floyd would watch for a gust of dry wind to send them his way, cringing and turning his face quickly to his window, firing his mind with thoughts of good things ahead.

Just when the Pine Ridge Reservation boundary marker flashed by, John began to thump his dusty dashboard with his right hand, imitating an Indian war drumbeat. Continuing his obnoxious pounding he laughed after barking, "Heap big bucks in Pine Ridge!" Then he turned those six words into lyrics while banging on his dashboard drum. He got only a courtesy laugh from his son.

Floyd could see the bleakness of Pine Ridge getting closer and resisted his urge to complain about spending the night there. He thought about his dad's only two calls on the rez. The first one was the grocery store, which was just ahead. He was happy to see the same pop machine standing to the left of the store's dusty entrance. It was sun-faded to a watermelon red, and the usual several-dozen bottlecaps were strewn before it.

The old paper man put out his stick in his ashtray overflowing with butts, popsicle sticks, and gum wrappers, after they parked near the store's front door.

"Wanna pop?" he asked his son.

"Yeah," he said, knowing well that his dad had never paid for pop in a machine in his life.

Just when he thought this would be an easy one for his dad,

Floyd could see they were being observed from the curb as he walked up to the hot Coke machine a step behind his father.

Dennis and Josie were standing together, each holding an empty green twelve-ounce Coke bottle. Dennis the artist had his eyes on the old salesman as he whispered to Josie, "A traveling salesman. See his old car and old sales bag? I'll bet the bottoms of his shoes are worn too."

Josie smiled, squinting from the sun while watching the teenaged boy standing close to the salesman's right side, as if shielding him.

"See the salesman's wrinkled pants and shirt?" he whispered.

She nodded, her eyes still on Floyd when they saw the skinny salesman feign putting change into the pop machine's coin slot. Then they heard the bang, bang, banging of the salesman striking the right side of the machine as if he were trying to get it to take his money.

"He never put in his money," she whispered to Dennis.

Dennis remained quiet, hawk-like, observing every detail and move made by these strangers. Floyd peeked over his dad's shoulder and self-consciously knew the two kids near the street had seen it all. It was so obvious. He felt guilt instantly. His father couldn't feel a thing.

Josie felt his guilt and shuddered as he followed his father into the store. She thought he was cool the way he leaned against the pop machine and ran his fingers through his hair. Then before going into the store he turned to them and snarled at Dennis with a boy's scowl, saying when his father was inside, "What are you looking at, kid?"

She realized he was talking to Dennis, who flinched back and remained a passive onlooker. Even though she felt afraid of him, she was drawn to something powerful he had. Then from twenty feet away from her, he looked right into her golden eyes and said, "Yer eyes are like the sun. Ms. Sun," he said.

"Miss Sun?" she lisped, not believing she just spoke to him.

"No ... Ms. Sun ... Mizz," Floyd said again. "I like yer eyes. I've never seen that color of eyes before ... 'cept on a cat," he laughed.

Dennis started to move away, his sandals making dust-poofs in the gravel road for Josie to follow in her bare feet. She had unconsciously removed her sandals and swirled her toes in the hot dust around her.

"Aren't yer feet hot, Ms. Sun?" Floyd smiled.

Josie blushed. He thought it beautiful the way she picked up her sandals and stepped onto the shade about six feet closer to him at the edge of the storefront. Dennis joined her.

"How old are you, Ms. Sun?"

"Nine," she said,

"Well, when you get to be fifteen like me ... you know a pretty girl when you see one."

Now Dennis was blushing too.

"In about ten years I'll look ya up. Okay, Ms. Sun?"

Dennis couldn't believe his cousin was nodding her head yes, as if she'd remember this moment and expect his call.

How could she forget? He had to be the most handsome young man she'd laid eyes on in these parts. When he ducked inside the store, she knew this was her first crush, and she knew it would last a decade. It was something good to have now that she was without her mother's guidance to diminish it and take it out of her mind over time.

This would be the fourth time on this run that they got a free soda. Clara Clouda's square Oglala face was tight, like the cracked vinyl on Deason's dashboard, when she nodded at the paper man before returning her attention to her crossword puzzle. She had heard him banging within a minute of seeing his car drive up.

"Chief in back?" John asked.

She grunted without looking up as Deason's wrinkled pant legs crossed the breeze-path of the blue floor fan blowing toward her husband at the back of the store.

Floyd's timing was perfect. He had stepped between them so his father could speak with his son in the middle. The paper man had trained his son from the time he was seven to stand between him and any Indian when he's getting free pop, since no Indian can turn down a father with his son in between them. It was beautiful! It made John smile at Clara with Charlie riding his hip. "Clara, I almost forgot. I just lost two quarters in yer pop machine again. Is it workin'?" John smiled.

Yes, his big, quick smile was back — between a father and his son. In that instant, Floyd knew that he too would be a paper man, but only after his father died or quit. John had told his son that he would inherit his route when he could no longer manage it. He would teach his son the fine art of prospecting and selling until his son was old enough to go to work for Silver. Then Floyd would work as a delivery driver until John decided to give up his sales route. Floyd remembered his dad telling him, "You watch me and learn everything you can. You'll be reselling half of my orders when you deliver, and you'll be establishing yourself in this territory until I quit. Then you'll take over where I leave off."

Floyd snickered between Clara and his dad. "Dad, I'm thirsty."

"Clara, would you please give the boy two quarters while I go see the boss? Thanks."

Floyd stood frozen between the breads and salad dressing remembering the secret "stash" he'd brought with him. Clara looked him up and down like he was a thief to be despised and remembered — like his father.

His first step toward her was weak when he saw her appear to will her mouth to turn down like a brown rainbow. He kept coming. She waited until he stood across from her counter. She had seen the paper man's son come into her store since he was five years old. He was cut from the same cloth as his father, and now he was being trained in his same deceitful, crafty ways.

"Maybe you should give me five dimes," Floyd grinned.

She did, then gave a bit of a smile — but not much.

"Hey, Chief! 'Bout ready for that locker paper?"

Clouda closed his freezer door behind him, not happy to see this shyster. He called the paper man *wasichu,* meaning White Man or "be-watchful-what-next."

"Gotta good buy on eighteen-inch white, Chief."

"Got plenty from last time didn't order," the grocer frowned, pointing back to four rolls of stacked eighteen-inch, white-colored locker paper. That was the remainder of the ten rolls f.o.b. when Clouda only ordered five rolls because Deason said he'd deliver them in his car the next time through. Clouda went back to string-tying hamburger and bologna, hoping the salesman would leave.

"How ya fixed on sawdust? Got some hickory left?"

"Got plenty."

Sometimes they just don't bite, John said to himself before asking the grocer to wrap him a half-dozen slices of bologna.

Josie and Dennis were sitting on the bottom step when Floyd came out of the store. Both turned to watch him go over to the pop machine. He could feel their stare as he self-consciously dropped in dime after dime. He pulled the Coke out of its hole and felt his hot blush at the back of his neck heighten with the cold glass bottle in his hand. There they were. On him. Those yellow-gold eyes that had seen it all. Then he glared hard at the

24

Indian boy with her, who had to be submissive when John came out with his bagged bologna and a loaf of white bread.

"Time to eat, Floyd Harvey!" John barked.

Josie watched them from the step as they sat in their hot car chewing their triple-slice sandwiches like the hungry dogs she'd seen in garbage cans. They gulped the Coke down in two or three swigs. After she memorized the Iowa license plate, she saw the old salesman light a cigarette and then pick his teeth with the matchbook. Dennis had taught her "to see." She could see that the salesman's eyes were small, blue-black, and set way back into deep sockets, creating shadows like a cavern you couldn't see into from the outside. She watched him smack his lips, then purse them for a deep drag that appeared to disagree with him coming and going. It looked to her as if he would die soon. Then she saw his son looking aloof out his window.

At least he has a father, she thought. *And they resemble each other.* She thought of being baptized in Macy. "Baptize," she murmured.

Josie watched them drive away, thinking she'd never see him again. They were like so many tourists she'd seen stop at this shack of a store for a pop, a candy bar, and a look at their map. She pointed to the station wagon's cloud of dust that led to the Tribal Agency building where Walter worked. Dennis ran inside the store and bought them some sourball gum with their change. They waited for the dust to settle before crossing the road.

* * * * *

The Agency was the central place for the Lakota people to get aid. Walter Bird was the paper-pusher who got things done for his people: food, shelter, clothing, and medical assistance. He was a progressive Oglala, willing to wade the channels necessary to make things work in the white man's system. The building itself was not much more than a stucco flophouse — a place where battered families could spend the night on the floor until the drunken husband or boyfriend could be apprehended and put in the jail a block behind the Agency.

Floyd trailed his father outside the Agency's front door. He held his breath to stop from smelling the dirty diapers and sour milk in bottles littering the lobby waiting area where a dozen Lakota mothers and their young sat listless and malnourished, sharing a small floor fan. He stayed on his father's heels down a short, narrow hallway after passing a full-blooded Oglala secretary on the phone at her cluttered desk.

John ducked into a storage room, flicked on the light, and surveyed cases of his product, occasionally kicking boxes to gauge their contents. He started writing up his biggest order of the run, using up a second page on his order pad. Floyd saw his father's twitch under his eye flickering and quivering more than usual. Then they crossed the hallway and entered Walter's unmarked office.

"Hey, Chief!" John barked.

Walter dropped his pen onto his cluttered desk. "Paper Man!" he stood and smiled.

"You remember my boy, Floyd?"

Walter shook Floyd's hand, smiling at the boy and recounting, "You were here last summer, weren't you?"

Floyd nodded and sat quietly next to his father across from the Tribal Chairman. *An Indian can't turn ya down when yer son's between the two of ya,* Floyd ruminated.

While Walter was telling John about his problem getting some crazed rez woman into the VA Hospital in Hot Springs, Floyd noticed the school pictures on the desk were those of the Indian boy and Ms. Sun at the store.

"Got a price increase comin', Chief. I gave ya the old prices and dated the order for next quarter," John said.

Walter was the opposite of his forefathers. Sioux were known by whites to be dominating, volatile, arrogant, and dangerous a century ago. When Deason showed him the order he'd written, Bird scanned it then signed the bottom of each page without question, except, "Is there anything I can do for you, Paper Man?"

"You still have that room in the back of the church?" John asked.

Walter nodded yes.

"We could use a place to crash tonight."

Just then Josie and Dennis came running into the office, breathing hard from laughter and running.

"Dennis, go to the back room of the church and show my friends how to turn on the water under the sink. They are staying there tonight."

Josie and Floyd looked at each other fearfully for different reasons. Floyd knew these kids knew about the pop scam. Josie knew that room at the back of the church was loaded with spiders — the kind that bite you in your sleep. Even the most desperate locals wouldn't stay in that room in the summer.

Walter walked his guests to the Agency's front door with Josie and Dennis already outside waiting in the shade of a scraggly pine near the road.

"If my father knew they cheated Mr. Clouda, he would not let them stay in the church," Dennis declared to his cousin.

"Maybe he knows ... and that's their punishment," Josie said.

Dennis smiled at her witty remark, knowing what a creepy place that was at night.

John told Floyd to walk with the kids to the church and that he'd drive the car over. Floyd stayed quite a few steps behind them in the ankle-deep dust as they walked to the church. Nothing was said between them until they entered the front door of the church.

"There's no locks on the doors," Dennis said to Floyd as they walked into the now-empty main room where broken stained-glass windows were covered with plywood.

A narrow hallway led to the back room. Dennis stopped at the second bathroom that was hardly used and showed Floyd where to turn on the water for the sink. Just then John came in and said, "We'll use the john in front. Keep the water off. Hell, I don't know why he wanted us to use this one."

Dennis pushed open the back room's creaky door. Josie was standing behind the visitors, not about to go one step further. John walked into a faceful of invisible cobwebs that she could hear spreading and clinging to the salesman's face and hair.

"Holy criminy! How long has this room been closed, for cryin' in the night?"

An old, stained, queen-size mattress lay bare on the dusty floor near the center of the room. An overhead bulb hanging at the end of a cord looked burned out. Josie stuck her hand inside the doorway and tried the light switch; it was burned out. She saw Floyd scanning the room's ceiling corners for spiders. "A burning candle keeps the spiders from biting at night," she said.

Floyd looked down at the young girl smiling with the missing front tooth. "How do you know?" he smiled.

"My mother told me," she replied.

"You don't look Indian," Floyd said.

"I'm part," she said.

"Get the flashlight outta the glove box," his father told him.

"That won't work. It has to be a burning candle," Dennis said.

Floyd and John stood staring at each other for a few moments until John finally blurted out, "I don't want ya burnin' down the place over a few spiders." Floyd knew that meant his old man was going out drinking soon.

Dennis tucked away in his mind the old salesman's remark

about "burnin' down the place.

The kids followed Floyd outside to the station wagon. Dennis stood back while Josie curiously peered in through the car's back window as Floyd was hunting for the flashlight under the front seat. She could see cellophane packages of white urinal and stool blocks, loose quarts of Silver's bowl cleaner, and brown plastic coffee cup holders scattered about twelve-ounce mop heads. The folded-down backseat never held passengers, and the once-painted cargo area, its surface worn to the bare aluminum, had carried and delivered ten thousand cases of paper and janitorial supplies.

Josie looked down at the Iowa plates. "Where's Woodbury?" she asked Dennis while pointing to the rear plate.

"It's a county," Dennis said.

"I know that. Where?"

Floyd handed Josie and Dennis each an empty pop bottle he'd found under the front seat and said, "Sioux City."

"That's not far from Macy!" Josie exclaimed.

"Macy, Nebraska? The Indian town?" Floyd asked.

She nodded yes excitedly, happy to finally meet someone who knew the place she would soon call home. "What's Macy like?" she asked.

He looked at Dennis before answering, "Mostly Indians live there. It's kinda small ... out in the country ... with lots of hills around it. I've been there lots of times."

"Is Sioux City a big Native American city?" she inquired.

Dennis laughed then quieted when Floyd looked his way again as if he didn't much like Indians. He thought the boy was laughing at her lisp when she said "Sioux City."

"No. There's some there, but that's just its name. Seems like there's more in Macy."

John came out of the church, his walk noisy and disjointed,

as if announcing his presence. His collar and the front of his shirt were water-spotted after splashing his face in the main bathroom's sink before using an excessive amount of his dispenser towels to dry his face. "I'll be back later," he told his son.

"Dok sa," Dennis replied.

"What's that mean?" John asked.

"See ya ... later," Dennis smiled.

"Dok sa," John smiled in return. He climbed behind the wheel of the station wagon and headed south on Highway 87 a couple of miles to Whiteclay, Nebraska, where the sale of booze was legal.

Floyd's pale-blue eyes watched his father's dust until it settled, oblivious to the two children observing how he handled his aloneness. Josie identified with the young man from Sioux City who had been dumped in Pine Ridge — alone in the world until his father's return. *At least I have Uncle Walt, Aunt Laura and Dennis,* she thought.

But that was going to change soon. She felt the young man had "something" that she would need when she left Pine Ridge, yet that "something" was far away from her knowing on a conscious level. She could only feel it as something terrible that was coming her way and to be dreaded fearfully.

Floyd walked aimlessly toward Ned Clouda's store, then he suddenly stopped to count the small change from his pocket before turning back to the kids standing like statues in front of the church. He wanted to call out to their gaping mouths, "Where can I get a candle?" That's what the man driving to Whiteclay would have done, and that's exactly why he kept quiet. Standing in the middle of the street, he realized he was his father's legacy. The thought was repulsive to him. Even his own name was repulsive to him: Floyd — his drunken father's middle name. He decided right then and there that he would break free of the mold his father was trying to force him into. This summer he would adopt his middle name, Harvey, as his primary name. It was safe and new — and it bore no relation to his father. Floyd stood for drinking, cheating, gambling, separations, and loneliness; but Harvey knew that it also stood for a great salesman and the only person in the world he loved or cared about. But he had to separate his own identity or be doomed to take his father's place and follow his father's self-imposed isolation in the manswarm. Alone. Endlessly alone.

Harvey clenched his teeth, ignoring Josie and Dennis while looking at the summer sun still high in the sky, trying to gauge the time before darkness overtook the town. How long could he walk these dirt roads? *Nothing but darkness ... and spiders for me,* he thought. He shook the flashlight in his hand, hoping the batteries would last through the night. He walked away from the children, crossed the road and cut through an empty weed-choked lot, and headed for some hills to the northwest where he could escape the dirt-laden places made by some of the poorest of Americans.

"Do you want to follow him?" Dennis asked Josie.

"No. He doesn't want company now."

It took over three hours for the sun to go down on Harvey. Each ten-minute span seemed like an hour to him. In the church's back room, he found an old rag and whipped apart every spider web he could find. For an interminable time the darkness wouldn't come. It was during that period of waiting to see how dark it would be that he thought of the girl with the golden eyes. His mind drifted back to a time when he was on a local run with his dad to Macy on the Omaha Indian Reservation. His father had been trying to collect on an old invoice from an Indian customer, who had called the paper man *"Iktomi."* A few miles north of there on the Winnebago Reservation, the boy had asked a friendly Native American what "Iktomi" meant because someone had called his father that Indian word. "Iktomi," the man laughed, "means *spider* ... the trickster ... weaving its web and trapping its prey."

Harvey turned on his flashlight and stood it on end on the floor at the head of the damp mattress. Its beams formed a yellow circle of light on the ceiling that cast a giant black shadow around it. *It's not a candle,* he thought to himself several times while keeping his eyes alert for "the trickster" who was out there watching, hungry, ready to bite when his prey fell asleep.

* * * * *

The paper man's son from Sioux City brought it all back. She had shut it off since her mother's death. She closed her eyes while Dennis snored at the bedroom ceiling. Her mother would creep into her room and walk ever so quietly to her bedside and kneel at her head. Sometimes Josie would be awake and pretend to be sleeping if she knew her mother had been drinking or was depressed — or both. Her mother would tuck in her covers and stroke her little girl's forehead and whisper, "Sweet dreams and snazzy squirrels." Then a kiss would come. Every night of her life, if her mother wasn't out all night, held the same ritual.

"Sweet dreams and snazzy squirrels," Josie whispered below the noise coming from her cousin's slack jaw. Again and again she moved her lips, saying it until she cried for her mommy. "Why, Mommy? Why?" she bawled, her pillow wet behind her ears and her head tossing back and forth. Then she thought of him in that dark spider room, alone with no blanket or pillow. *Alone ... alone ... oh, how alone he must feel,* she thought.

One-light shanty houses, June bugs, and ten million chirping crickets lined her short walk on the dirt road about an hour after midnight. Her blanket and pillow were tucked under her chin and covered her body from her neck to her knees. If she saw the salesman's car, she would turn back knowing the boy was not alone. She could see that the back room's tattered window shade had a dim glow behind it. The moon was nearly full above his window and had a bluish tint she'd never seen before. At the front of the church she could see that the salesman's car was still gone.

She knew the inside of the church as well as she knew her Uncle Walt's house, for this had been her daycare too. But her sandals made such a racket on the wood floor with every step

33

that she stood disoriented in the middle of the large room, unable to recall where the light switch was. By the time she remembered, she was too frightened of the dark and the thought of the boy's father coming in. She stood frozen in the church, thinking back to the dinner-table conversation earlier that evening.

Dennis had told his parents about the paper man's scam at the pop machine. Walter cut off a piece of his steak and showed his son how greed could be explained in "old days" by a person keeping the best piece of the buffalo meat. "Back then," Walter explained, "the piece that had the most fat on it was the best piece. Fat was important in helping our ancestors survive the cold winters. *Wasin icu na* means 'fat takers' ... or greedy. You see that, son?"

"So the paper man is a fat taker?" Dennis returned seriously.

"Like taking the biggest piece of pie and leaving the small piece for a friend," Josie said. Walter laughed and nodded in agreement while chewing his piece of meat.

"Why do you buy from him, then?" his son asked.

"His paper fits only his dispensers ... ya see? Those things that hold the towels and double rolls of toilet paper. Besides, nobody else bothers to stop or call on us." After a slight pause he added, "I feel very sorry for that young man ... sleeping alone without a blanket or pillow on that old mattress."

"Why don't you take him a plate and bedding?" Laura asked.

"Not while his father's around. I don't want to do any favors for the paper man's son."

His wife understood what he meant. She had seen it a thousand times on the reservation — parents ashamed by charity getting even more drunk and violent.

Through a crack between the window and the shade, Harvey gazed at the moon feeling the weight of his sadness. He lay fully clothed — shoes and all — curled up on the dirty mattress with his face toward the door. As he was letting the sadness and loneliness take him over, a very soft knock at the door startled his restive heart.

The door slowly opened and he shined the flashlight's weak beam on those yellow eyes. He could see the space of her missing teeth when she spoke from the doorway with her blanket and pillow covering most of her. Her hand trembled on the doorknob. "This is for you. It will keep the spiders off you," she lisped, extending her offering to him.

Ripples of joy raked up and down the back of his neck and all around his skull. The part of him that was Floyd was lost — or, at least, stuffed inside that cardboard tube of a dozen urinal cakes in the station wagon. He stood, smiling. His flashlight pointed down to the gift then back to her face. When he took the bedding, he saw the candle fisted in her hand.

"Thanks," he said in a hushed, deep tone coming from way down inside himself. That was where Harvey spoke from — a place closer to the heart.

"You burn sage too?" she asked, lisping the last two words adorably.

"What?"

"I smell sage," she said.

He realized she must have smelled the pot he had smoked over an hour ago. "I smoke it," he said.

She laughed at the notion.

"No, really. It helps me relax," he said.

"I didn't know people smoke it," she said.

"Yeah. I'll show ya."

She followed him to the bathroom next door after he put her bedding on the mattress. Then he lit the candle, holding it near his chest in the bathroom.

"There's no light in here," he said. He reached for the tiny dispenser key on the ledge above the rusty medicine cabinet.

"Here, hold this a second," he said as he handed her the burning candle.

She held the candle while he unlocked the towel dispenser with the key. He removed a folded baggie that was stashed inside the cabinet. "Don't tell anybody I keep this here, okay?"

She nodded innocently and watched him take a little pipe from his front pocket after pinching out of the plastic bag enough to fill the bowl of the pipe. He lit the bowl and inhaled deeply. He started to hand her the pipe but pulled it back when he looked into those gold eyes that were so young and innocent. Suddenly aware of the innocence he was violating, he quickly pulled the pipe back and said, "Nope ... yer too young to smoke ... what'd you call this stuff?"

"Sage. My uncle burns it in our house every morning to clean the air. He says it gets rid of bad spirits."

"Bad spirits, huh? Yeah," he snickered, *That's why I smoke it ... to get rid of bad spirits.* He took another hit from the pipe and held it in his lungs for a long spell before exhaling. "Don't tell your uncle I smoke sage. He'll think I'm crazy."

She watched him return the "sage" to the dispenser, lock it, and return the key to its hiding place. He took the candle from her hand when he saw wax dripping down close to her fingers. He blew out the candle and handed it to her saying, "Don't burn yer fingers. I might burn the place down with that. You better take it back."

When he brushed by her as he exited the bathroom, he caught the sweet scent of the strawberry shampoo she used on her hair. In the doorway of the back room, he thanked her for the pillow and blanket.

"Sweet dreams and snazzy squirrels," she said while walking away, then he could hear her footsteps running through the dark main room. He stood there until he heard the front door close behind her.

Her strawberry fragrance lingered on her pillow as he lay in the dark room covered with her blanket. For a few moments her pillow's aroma overcame the smells of old dust and mildew on the room's wallpaper. He thought about "snazzy squirrels" and why she would say that. *What is a snazzy squirrel?* he wondered before feeling guilty again for smoking pot in front of her. *That was stupid,* he scolded himself. *She's too young to see that.*

As Harvey dreamed under the warm blanket while still fully dressed, his father was insensate from cheap whiskey, driveling on to indolent Indians hunched over on barstools with Silver's urinal blocks, mop heads, and bowl cleaner piled on the bar to pay for his shots.

Nearing her bedroom window, Josie thought of that "big bunch of fear" she felt when he took the bedding from her. She would later learn, however, that it was not her fear she was feeling, but his. His fear was shaking her legs under her bed sheets and wool bedspread. The teddy bear she now used for a pillow absorbed the pulsing of her heart at her throat a thousand times before she slept. She had made it back safely from the darkness, and yet she had quaked and trembled as if feeling her own loss and aloneness for the first time on her last night in Pine Ridge.

By 7:00 the next morning, the station wagon was not parked in front of the church. *Maybe it's not even back yet,* Josie thought.

Her clothes and belongings were wedged between her and Dennis on the floor and backseat of the Bird car. By 10:00 they were already 180 miles east of Pine Ridge. Walter's stolid sixty miles per hour — fifteen below the legal speed limit — fueled their unbroken trance. Josie turned back to the rear window and looked deep to the western horizon. Her mind was quiet about her experiences there. She knew she would return someday as a big success, and these three people who had always been her family would always be in her life.

She could see Dennis was drawing something for her on notebook paper. He was keeping it concealed from her for many miles now as Walter and Laura debated their route to Macy. When she had heard one of the roads would take them through Sioux City she exclaimed, "Let's go through Sioux City!"

"Okay. Lakota City it is," Walter laughed.

It was the biggest city she had ever seen! It was much bigger than Rapid City, Walter had informed his gaping niece. When they crossed the narrow-lane, noisy Combination Bridge that connected Iowa to Nebraska, Josie could see the massive city auditorium in front of the Missouri River. It was the biggest building she had ever seen. Even though all the windows were rolled up, they could smell the stockyards two miles further down river.

"What's that smell?" Dennis asked.

"The stockyards," his father answered.

"What river is that, Uncle Walt?"

"The Missouri River. The 'Mighty Mo,'" he smiled.

"It's big, isn't it?" Josie lisped while looking back at the river's course.

Walter and Josie then noticed how sad Laura looked after crossing into Nebraska. "Will you visit me?" Josie asked her aunt while leaning forward.

"Of course we will," Laura said, unable to turn and look at the little girl she wanted to adopt. "You know we will always be in your life. We are family," Laura continued.

Josie saw her uncle's hand go over to his wife's lap, covering her hands and massaging them tenderly. Laura had always felt Josie was already adopted after the ceremony they had for her in the old church. *Hunka'pi,* the "making of relatives" or adoption into the community. But Granny Tenna called that meaningless. She told Laura the girl would be properly baptized in a real church — *Ini'Kagapi,* or "life renewal." Granny Tenna had explained, "It is a purification and cleansing of the girl's body and soul after her mother's cowardly deed."

Heading south on Highway 77, they drove through the green hills around Homer that resembled the sloping grasslands north of Pine Ridge. As they coasted past the poor Native American town of Winnebago, not a soul was walking or driving about. They passed a closed roadside café called Dingbat's that had its front door removed from its hinges.

Walter pulled into a grubby Sinclair station for gas at the south end of Winnebago. He checked the station's one restroom to be sure it was clean and vacant before the kids used it. He found it was an extension of the mechanic's shop. Oil and dirt were smeared everywhere, the floor was caked with dried greasy footprints, and the filthy sink only dripped cold water. Then he noticed them on the wall — Silver's roll-towel dispenser above the sink and the double-roll toilet paper dispenser next to the stool. Both dispensers were empty with black-finger-printed replacement rolls sitting atop them. There were also spare toilet paper rolls sitting on the grimy toilet's tank. Walter grunted to himself how far-reaching and obscure the paper man's territory was before telling the children they'd have to hold it until they got to Granny Tenna's place.

They left Winnebago with five more dollars worth of gas in the tank instead of the usual fill-up. They got on Highway 75 that curved east, then followed the eastern edge of the Nebraska border where undulating hills were green-gold with thousands of matured corn rows kept salubrious by the rich soil so close to the great river.

At a bend in the road, they could see the river's swirling currents and whirlpools at their highest intensity. Walter recalled a Santee foreboding legend telling of nearby hidden caves and treacherous caverns at the bottom of the river — a place where the bones of drowned victims are stored, their whirling spirits ever pulling down loved ones mysteriously never found downstream.

The Bird vehicle passed a roadside marker: Omaha Indian Reservation. Without warning, a second marker just past the first had an arrow pointed to the right for Macy. Making the abrupt, sharp right, the road led downhill into a valley of poverty akin to Pine Ridge, except there were many more trees in Macy. That was the biggest difference — trees. Mostly oak and elm. Their shade, however, covered the same one-story, clapboard, shanty houses.

Josie saw the Macy General Store. It too had a pop machine

outside near the front door. The only difference was that the two middle-aged Indian vagrants sitting on their haunches against the storefront would not have been tolerated by Mr. Clouda.

Walter parked next to a rather large vacant lot where a group of dogs played and sniffed freely. "I'll go into the store and find where her house is," he said to Laura.

Josie followed Dennis out of the car and studied her new home. An old, one-story school across the road covered all grades. Behind the store was a community center converted from an old gym, where now a meat locker shared its space. Behind that were the Macy jail and police station. Across the lot was the Omaha Tribal Agency, a cement-blocked, busy little spot where several rusted-out, late-model cars were parked — some abandoned on blocks.

"This is Macy?" Josie said, disappointed with her surroundings.

"There's a post office!" Dennis pointed behind her.

She didn't bother to look. The sight of her uncle returning caused her to hope somehow there had been a grown-up mistake and she would make the drive back to Pine Ridge with the Birds. He stood beside his niece looking at the same desultory things that made Josie's dreams of a better place vanish before he got directions to Granny Tenna's house.

"There's a lot more trees here," Walter said to Josie. "I'll bet they're really beautiful in the fall. What do you think, Josie?"

She felt like crying with her Aunt Laura, who was now holding the side of her head with her elbow resting in the open window of the passenger door.

"Is that my new school?" Josie asked.

"I believe so," Walter smiled. He tried to find something positive to say about the worn-out school that was spray-painted black and blue with graffiti, but he turned away from the subject and told the kids that Granny's house was just around the corner behind the school.

There were four parallel two-block stretches of unpaved, embowered residential streets on the south end of Macy. Most of the dwellings could have been bulldozed into scrap for more value than their appraised worth. Walter and Laura Bird were relieved to see the little lavender one-story Tenna house with white trim on the corner of the block. It was obviously the most well-kept house in town. The explosion of color caused by carnations, daffodils, geraniums, and violets between two violet-colored plum trees all mixed together tight against the house and its short, white picket fence. But they all fell to the background, subdued by the five-foot-two-inch aura of Ellen Mae Tenna, Josie's mother's grandmother. They all sat fixed on her from the car while her brown, hawkish, full-blooded Teton eyes smiled from her tiny front porch.

"That's her," Laura said to Josie. "She's your great-grandmother."

"Great-grandmother," Josie repeated.

"Just call her 'Granny Tenna,'" Laura said.

"Dennis, help Josie with her things," Walter said as they started getting out of the car.

Josie noticed how Granny's movement was so different than most women her age — smooth strides and quick feet were down her porch steps and over to greet her guests like an impatient cat. Granny made eye contact with Walter and Laura, saying their names. She stood two feet from her great-granddaughter, whom she was seeing for the first time. Josie's likeness was incredible and destroyed the old woman's deep breathing for a moment. "Josephine Ann Tenna ... you are the spittin' image of my daughter, and your eyes are the same shape and color as my mother's were."

They were both happy to be together. That so pleased Laura that her face ran wet with tears for most of the first hour of their visit, which included the unpacking and putting away of Josie's things in her new room. That's when Laura asked Josie what happened to her pillow and blanket. "I must have forgot them," she told her aunt without explaining her late-night escape out her bedroom window.

Granny's small house was filled with lush green plants, framed Native American oil paintings, and rigid antique furniture. Every color existing on earth were displayed in weavings, floor rugs, and baskets full of flower arrangements. Laura and Walter knew that Granny was known by her people as "Woman of Space Between." While sitting in her small front room with sparkling crystals all around, the Birds felt the mystery of her legend. Josie's mother would often recount her visits to this place when she was a girl, keeping Walter and Laura enthralled with stories of the healing powers of Granny Tenna.

Laura changed her mind about attending Josie's baptism. At first the plan was to get out of Macy soon after dropping off her niece, but now she was curious about the ceremony. Plus it would make their separation more gradual if they were to stay the night.

Granny was delighted with the company and spent the evening talking about the importance of Josie's baptism in the morning. She brought out the silk dress she had woven for Josie to wear. Josie went into her new room to try on the dress, first putting on the flesh-colored slip under the gold, violet, and cinnamon-red dress. She looked at her reflection in the bureau mirror and smiled big for the first time in a very long time.

When she came out into the front room to model the dress, Granny had lit a half-dozen yellow candles; she then sat in her chair telling the meaning of her creation to the gaping Birds.

Dennis the artist sat mesmerized between his parents on Granny's thin-cushioned oak sofa. As Granny spoke, Josie mysteriously moved gracefully around the room, unconsciously fluid and enlivened.

"It is not the colors or the fabric that make this such a beautiful weaving. Like reading a poem or a good book, it is your vision of what you see between the lines that gives it form and energy," Granny explained.

It was the transformation in the Birds' little Josie that had this Pine Ridge family captivated. Her shoulders were straight and back, not drooped forward as if burdened. Her smile was broad and beautiful. And her legs glowed in the candlelight like two of the gold flames flickering on the burnt-orange walls now following Josephine Ann Tenna's new shadow in her new home.

* * * * *

The old church fifteen miles north of Macy was of no concern to Josie. It was that bundle between them on the front seat of Granny's car that held her attention. Granny explained it was wrapped in black, red, white, and yellow cloths — the colors of all peoples. This intrigued her enough to keep her eyes off Walter's Crown Victoria following close behind — and to keep her mind off the fact that they would return to Pine Ridge without her shortly after the ceremony.

The church, built in 1860, was the oldest church in Nebraska. It was a small structure out in the country that had been moved from Dakota City to a piece of land near Homer. It had originally served as a territorial courthouse for pioneers living hundreds of miles away on the prairie on their isolated homesteads. The Birds and Josie felt a kindred spirit with the pioneers of old, having traveled over four hundred miles to visit the old structure.

There was no talking after the car doors closed and they approached the one-room church. Josie was wearing her special dress. Granny carried the colorful bundle up the wooden steps as if it were a newborn baby. Josie followed behind her. She could smell the burning sweetgrass of purification wafting out through the tall windows that had been opened a half-hour earlier, letting in no wind and a few flies. Kerosene lamps hung from the ceiling down the aisle. Josie thought of the paper man's son for an instant and how this smell was similar to the stuff he put in his pipe.

The heat inside was oppressive. Six rows of wooden benches made only for a smaller race lined each side of a narrow aisle. An Indigenous minister dressed in a stiff black suit stood at the front near a podium and makeshift altar. Off to the right was an organ covered by a tarp. The minister's face was pock-marked with deep scars, giving him a sinister and mean appearance that contradicted his soft voice and manner.

There were no other people in church, except for the minister's wife who placed an eagle plume on Josie's lap after introducing herself. She said, "This is to affirm you are loved. It's been done for centuries when a tribe or family adopts a child. The eagle feather gives you power to prosper in a white world, making it possible to do good for all Indigenous people."

The woman sat behind Granny and Josie in the second row of benches across from the Birds. Dennis sat next to the open window watching a bee circling just outside the window, intoxicated by the burning sweetgrass. He began to draw this scene in his mind, capturing even the rough grain of the floor and the bowed legs of the minister standing before the gathering. He noticed how the light in the room changed his cousin's hair to an auburn gold and the way her face tilted down submissively, as if she wanted badly to believe in this power of the feather that rested in her lap. His dark eyes colored the fine wood of an antique cupboard against the left wall.

On the floor in front of the minister sat a large aluminum tub filled with water. All wondered how cold it was — especially Josie. The energy in the room and the bundle on her lap told everyone this was Granny's show.

Dennis had never seen his parents sweat this much. His father kept wiping his brow with his forearm, then his son would imitate him, badly wanting to test the water in the tub.

The silence was broken when the man in black and his wife began singing a traditional chanting that soon encompassed the six directions. The minister and his wife were directing their voices to Grand Mother Earth, Grand Father Sky, Where Sun Comes Up, Where Sun Goes Down, to the North, and to the South. Josie listened to the chanting and could hear Granny mumbling Lakota to the bundle.

Behind them appeared a tall, middle-aged Native American man with prominent cheekbones. He stood near the back under a hanging rope that led up to the belfry. He was wearing a black suit that was even stiffer than the minister's and which was too short for his angular legs and arms. He pulled on the rope, ringing a dull bell six times.

The minister stood before Granny. Smiling, he leaned down and embraced her, saying, "Granny Tenna, I love you." She kissed his scarred cheek and they talked low in Lakota. Granny introduced the minister to Josie and the Birds as Reverend Little Stand, then the group approached the tub. Reverend Little Stand looked at Granny to see if she was ready, but she was meditating in Lakota and holding Josie's sweaty palm. The group waited and watched as Granny opened her eyes and handed Josie the bundle, whispering her instruction to the girl to take it up to the minister.

The bundle was lighter than it appeared. After giving it to Little Stand, she stood next to the tub while he lit a concealed braid of sweetgrass that crackled and burned and smoked up the room, purifying the altar and ceremony participants.

Walter and Laura knew that Josie was holding "The Pipe" in that bundle — a sacred pipe with a heavy red califate bowl and a thirty-two-inch stem. Granny knew that this pipe had not been used in thirty-five years, and that this made this situation proper with *Wak'an*, the Universal All. As the minister unwrapped the pipe, she bowed her head instinctively. She looked up from her silent reverie of the pipe's last use as Reverend Little Stand prayed in Lakota while raising another pipe from the podium to Granny's pipe, holding the pipes bowl-opposite-bowl to form a cross. She watched him address the six directions with Granny's pipe and return it to the altar before speaking to the Sky. "Father in Heaven, we are gathered here today to baptize Josephine Ann Tenna in Your name, Your Son, Jesus Christ, and the Holy Spirit. Let this be a beginning of a long and happy life with You. Amen."

Next, he balanced Josie on the rim of the tub, holding her hands and moving her backwards slowly, just as pioneer Christian proselytizing sects had done in that very building to save souls. Slowly back, further and further, she plunged into the cold water, her buttocks hitting the bottom of the tub. As Josie emerged from the water, Granny stood up, applauding, and rushed over to her, draping the pipe wrappings over her shoulders. "Was it cold?" Granny asked, laughing.

Josie nodded yes, shivering as Granny kneeled and patted her lower legs dry with a cloth. Granny removed a tiny vial of clear liquid from her side pocket and poured its contents onto her rough, brown hands before rubbing the potion vigorously over Josie's throat and shoulders. "It smells like candy cane," Josie giggled.

"Yes. It's peppermint!" Granny laughed. "You will smell like a candy cane while it soothes your nerves."

Laura and Walter smiled at each other, seeing that their Josie was in caring hands. They felt good about leaving her with the Medicine Woman from Macy.

It was Dennis who started to cry at the Bird vehicle when he hugged his Golden Eyes goodbye. Her special dress was dry, and her hair was clumped and damp when a curl from her bangs tickled his ear. "I'm glad I'm here," she whispered to Dennis. Dennis could only nod, then watch her from the backseat when his father pulled away slowly from the country church.

Crossing the Combination Bridge into Sioux City, Dennis found a page of his big-ruled notebook paper on the floor of the backseat where Josie had been sitting. He flipped the page over and saw the drawing with red crayon of two intersecting hearts with the words neatly printed below in Josie's handwriting "Josie and Dennis forever." He began to cry again without his parents noticing, tucking his small, quivering chin into his chest while keeping his eyes on the city's skyline that so captivated his cousin. She had moved close to this big city and was already happy with her change.

He held her hearts between his left thumb and forefinger — his drawing hand. He would live without her. She had made Pine Ridge so interesting and fun. He had been challenged to create things to do and say because he hated to see her sad. It was his way of keeping his beloved cousin from "going south," his father's name for depression.

On the drive home he began to see images and colors swirling through his mind's eye aloof on the yellow prairie grasses covering his backseat window. He compared Josie's journey to Macy with the "going south" of his people — the government's herding of Native Americans to reservations in Oklahoma.

Just then a tingling sensation waved up and down his left hand. He went to the coloring box and began to feverishly draw on the flip-side of Josie's drawing. From his rearview mirror, his father could see his boy in his creative state — his head down, the skittering of his crayons moving on paper, and his absolute abandon of reality. Oblivious to any sounds or distractions around him, he switched from color to color without pause or inspection — lost in his art.

Walter nudged his wife to see their son at work, sharing a look at each other in their proud way for having begun saving for their son's education at the University of Denver, a highly rated school that many Native Americans attended.

It was when nearing Yankton that Dennis proffered his drawing over the front seat between his parents' shoulders. "I drew this for Josie."

His mother's head tingled when her eyes beheld her son's creation of Josie standing alone on Sheep Mountain Table in the Badlands, her mystical dress made by Granny Tenna clinging to her skin, its tone replicated by blending colors. Josie's hair was the auburn gold he saw in the church, alive in the wind of the *mako mika,* known as Badlands. Native legends tell of the Badlands being formed when the *Wakan Tanka* made a cataclysmic storm as tribes from the western mountains threatened to invade the plains, leaving a barren path where nothing has ever grown. Josie's figure was perfectly drawn, but it was her facial profile he had captured the best — her intelligent nose which was slightly curved down from a bend at its middle, her brow was flat and wide around her golden eyes and partly covered by her hair, and her chin was small and defiant. It was her to perfection. "My word, Dennis! I believe I will frame this one," his mother beamed. His father agreed while looking back and forth from road to drawing several times.

On her first night alone without the Birds, Granny tucked Josie in under the covers in her new bed and told her, "Sweet dreams and snazzy squirrels." That's where her mother had gotten it! And Granny now referred to her as Josephine instead of Josie, as if she had grown up and were more respected somehow. She felt the chamomile Granny rubbed on her eyelids after she bathed, warming them into a soothing, slumbering melt-down.

Then sleep. Deep, deep sleep that was so far removed from her loss in Pine Ridge. For this first night in her life, she would dream of those snazzy squirrels because she had the safe harbor she'd longed for. These squirrels would be the color of lavender that covered Granny's house. Granny called it a "healing color." And these lavender squirrels would prance and scurry from limb to limb above the roof lines of the shanty one-story houses on Granny's street.

This was the first dream she remembered in such vivid colors — the oak and pine trees with their ash-gray bark and tiny grooves, the dirt road cinnamon-like after a cold rain, and the sky a vivid azure blue that startled her awake. She stirred in her strange and cozy bed. A moment of fear passed, and she soon desired to return to her dream.

* * * * *

As the months passed, Josephine noticed she was changing. Her missing teeth were beginning to come in — finally. She saw the difference Granny's potions and herbs were making in her body and her mind. Day after day and night after night the colorful dreams kept coming. She slept good in her safe place so close to the river she could feel its escaping moisture when it floated in her bedroom window from the breeze coming off its west bank.

50

He was breathing hard for ten minutes after reaching the ledge three hundred feet below the summit of Harney Peak, the highest point in the Black Hills and the highest point in North America east of the Rocky Mountains. The cabin his father had bartered for was now out of view. At three in the morning, Floyd had heard his father's car park outside the cabin. When the car's door failed to open and then close, he knew he had to go out and help the old man into the spartan cabin that he had gotten for free, except for an extra case of garbage bags in exchange for a bogus twenty-five-dollar room receipt.

Breathing normally again, Floyd's chin rested on his raised knees as he clasped his hands across his shins. The spasms under his eye were firing. He believed it was because of his dad's cigarette smoke that covered every inch of space in the station wagon, their studio apartment, and their rooms on the road. Even his jeans held the humid stench of tobacco smoke as he raised his head to breathe the fresh air. He was thinking of two things that bothered him: his clothes, which were faded rags that fit him like hand-me-downs, and the café in Newcastle on the first day of their run to the Black Hills.

Floyd had been at a table finishing his cheeseburger when a waitress came over with her glasses dangling from her neck by two black strings that looked like shoestrings. She had a cupcake with a tiny burning candle in its center on a plastic coffee saucer. It was raised too high for him to see it all. She sang "Happy Birthday" as he blushed sitting at the table in the middle of the dining room with three or four of the locals smiling at him. It wasn't the attention that turned his face crimson; it was the lie. His dad had told the waitress it was his boy's birthday. He did this often. But this time was one of those rare calls when the paper man wasn't getting his way with the owner, who was long overdue to give him an order.

"I'm covered this trip, John!" the café owner told his dad from the kitchen grill above his sizzling burgers, saying it loud enough that the whole joint could hear.

"C'mon, George ... yer usin' that store-bought TP instead of my dispenser rolls. I know ya are!"

"Take 'em out then! I got too many complaints about that one-ply in yer dispenser."

"George, yer gonna plug up yer commode with that paper! Septic tanks won't handle two-ply in these parts," the paper man explained.

After a long pause, Floyd could hear his father mention other product he had heard a thousand times — garbage bags, urinal blocks, paper towels, floor soap, paper cups, napkins. Only more silence from his old customer. The paper man saw only negative head-shaking while the café owner flipped his patties. From time to time he would scrape the excess fat forward into a grease catcher that would be emptied into a five-gallon lard bucket and used later to make a treat topping for his five mongrel dogs at home.

At their table he was finishing his birthday dessert when his father sat down hard and lit a cigarette as if it were the end of the world. Then the order came in a breaking whisper, "Cotton candy him."

Young Floyd's chewing stopped before he swallowed the last bite of his cake. "No, Dad ... I don't want to."

The impatience in his father's eyes so early on his run was

further evidence that the changes in his father since his parents' divorce were permanent. When they were together, his dad would never lose his cool over such trifles, giving him a cold, Hitler-like stare that told him he'd better do as he was told or else catch hell in the car.

He wiped the crumbs from his lips, got up, and walked to the back of the café. Once inside the men's restroom, he hesitated before carrying out his orders. Floyd knew "cotton candy" was never done to a regular customer. It was reserved for the deadbeats who wouldn't pay their bill or the cold bastards who never gave his dad an order.

He went into the stall and latched the door behind him. Silver's double-roll toilet paper dispenser was empty, carved with obscenities and initials. The store-bought roll was on top of the dispenser, and two more rolls were yet inside the four-pack wrapping on top of the toilet tank. He thought of not doing it. He could say he did it. Then he picked up the roll of puffy two-ply and began unraveling it, wrapping it into a huge wad around his hand. When it was cotton candy size, it was thrust into the toilet bowl then flushed before a hasty exit.

A blanket of scudding clouds passed in front of him about a hundred yards off. Right after the clouds moved past him, he knew it was a sign to start identifying himself as Harvey. *No more Floyd ... never again,* he resolved to himself. His father's life didn't work, and from now on he would not go by Floyd.

"Harvey!" he cried aloud. Then he stood and repeated his cry, putting his whole being into it. "Harvey!"

Early one beautiful Saturday morning in October of 2000, Harvey's mile-long walk to the Silver Paper Company from his studio apartment was alive with anticipation that he would be delivering in Macy that day. He had been there a few times but was either too busy or too insecure to look her up. *Did she get her pillow and blanket?* he wondered to himself. He didn't just hope he would see her that day — he resolved that he would. The thrill of seeing her again was in his gait as he tramped downhill on Jackson Street, his feet barely touching Sioux City's wet October sidewalks.

Albert Silver paid him $200.00 a week and bought his breakfast Monday through Saturday for delivering his product six days a week. After completing his Saturday deliveries, he was given the company van for his personal use until Monday morning. This walk on Saturday was his payday: cash and wheels!

Silver Paper was on lower Jennings Street in an old furniture warehouse that Silver shared with a wholesale tire company. Trains roared noisily on both sides of Warehouse Row, and salvage yards were plentiful throughout the area. In this almost ancient part of town, the streets were still covered with old red brick from the early 1900s.

Harvey's father had died of liver cancer at the beginning of the year, two weeks before Harvey's nineteenth birthday. Still trying to break free of the stigma of John Floyd Deason, Harvey had put his name in print as surviving son, Harvey Deason, in his father's obituary column. For nearly two years he had watched and listened to his father's atrophy while living crammed together in the same dumpy apartment. He'd heard that constant nagging cough that brought up black bile that stained the handkerchiefs cluttering the floor near his father's bed just eight feet away from the very uncomfortable sofa on which Harvey had to sleep.

As Harvey turned east on Third Street, he could hear his employer's '85 mud-splattered, forest-green LTD coming his way from behind him after his morning post office run. He crossed the street and waved for the 80-year-old Jew to stop. This would happen two or three times a week, only when Harvey wasn't late for work. It was always the same routine. Always. He opened Albert Silver's heavy passenger door and flopped onto the front seat.

"You hungry?" Silver asked with one of his stubby, unlit cigar butts stuck in the right corner of his moist mouth. His open ashtray overflowed with butts he would sort through and chew on before breakfast.

"Yeah," Harvey answered.

"Where's yer jacket?" Albert barked.

"I forgot it."

"It's gonna get down to fifty degrees later today!" Albert exclaimed.

They turned left at Court Street and parked in front of the Court Street Café where young Deason would often get his only meal for the day. But what a meal! Four pancakes, two eggs, a huge helping of fried potatoes, two sausage links, toast and jelly. Greasy but good.

"Nothing to drink?" Silver asked.

"No. Fills me up so I can't eat as much," he said while shoveling bite after bite into his mouth as if there were no tomorrow.

Albert chuckled so that he dropped the scrambled egg sitting on his toast back onto his plate.

"Hi, Albert," an old crony barked from his counter stool.

Albert waved, not knowing who the man was, quipping to his delivery man, "Whoever that is."

"He probably worked for ya," Harvey said, not missing a beat with his chewing.

Silver shrugged his sloping shoulders and hunched over his plate, his bulbous nose still sniffling from morning congestion. One of Albert's giant clown feet was angled out into the aisle as if anxious to leave. He was. The early morning before work was always his rush for the day. No man loved his work more than Albert Silver. Seven days a week he'd be at his cluttered office, happy to be away from his nagging wife, Esther. He didn't have to work; he was well off. The old man just loved to sell his average daily gross of two or three thousand dollars a day in paper and janitorial supplies.

"Don't you ever eat at home for God's sake?"

"Not much," Harvey answered while smacking down the last of his pancakes. "I'll have popcorn or cereal at night once in a while. A couple times a month the cook at the Y gives me a meal for taking out his garbage."

"What's that guy's name?"

"Ollie."

"Ask him if they need any TP or towels for my cabinets, will ya?"

Harvey nodded his assent.

"Huh?" barked Albert, wanting to affirm his delivery man's nod into clarity.

"Yeah. Yeah. Okay," Harvey said.

Silver got up from the booth with their ticket. He slouched and shuffled his skinny dinosaur legs under baggy, gray slacks up to the register, going over the tab with his white head craned into his sunken chest and occasionally glancing up over the top of his black-rimmed, mail-order glasses. They all knew him. Countless truckers had hauled his freight, transient laborers unloaded boxcars of his paper, and warehousemen knew he wasn't union. His manual laborers were equipped only with two-wheeled hand-pulled dollies and back-breaking jacks. If it had a motor, it wasn't at the Silver Paper Company.

The two blocks to his Jennings Street office and warehouse was covered by the worst road in the city — a mix of sunken brick and cement that was so pulverized by time and labor and traffic that it was too far gone to repair. As was his usual custom, Silver parked the nose of his LTD an inch away from smacking into the loading dock that spanned the front of an old five-story warehouse bordered north and south by railroad tracks. The north side of the building's visage housed the office of the tire company that sold mostly to farmers. Their office was in perfect order, always warm and cozy in the winter, cool and inviting in the summer. Stacks of blackness and the overwhelming smell of rubber permeated the first floor, leaving only narrow walkways wide enough to maneuver a cart of tires or a floor jack pulling a pallet of Silver's product. Albert Silver's chemical cleaners were stored in the damp dungeon of a basement 600 feet away, where it never got below freezing in the winter and stayed at sixty degrees even on the hottest summer days.

At the south end of the building, Harvey followed his boss up the four wooden steps onto the cement loading dock, passing Silver's rattletrap unmarked white delivery van that was backed into the dock to keep anyone from breaking into the back double doors that were held together by a piece of oily old rope.

The office light was on behind the glass of the second entry door. Silver led them into the office after unlocking the first door that had a cardboard sign taped to the glass identifying the office as that of Silver Paper Company. The office was the most cluttered of any business on earth, as Willard, the peevish sixty-year-old bookkeeper, pecked away on his old black Remington manual typewriter with his short, chubby fingers. He was busily updating the faded yellow index cards that had to be half a century old. Willard resented working on Saturdays.

"Good morning," Willard said coldly to the boss.

"Morning," Albert mumbled, putting the mail on Willard's cluttered desk.

"Good morning, Harvey," said Willard a little more cheerfully.

"Good morning, Willard."

Harvey liked Willard because he was the first to start calling him Harvey. In a few seconds, the time it took to look up to the big wall clock that showed 8:00, Harvey thought of the poor bookkeeper at his cluttered desk, drowning in literature, sample products, and assorted office supplies. The story about squat, little Willard had been told to him by Albert one day over lunch at a nearby hamburger joint. It was a story that everyone had heard about — everyone, at least, who had worked for Albert for any length of time. In 1986, Silver's accountant found that Willard had embezzled about $80,000.00. Instead of sending the Milquetoast to prison, Albert had him working off the debt since then, without pay. Albert told Harvey, "See, I figured lightning wouldn't strike twice. What else was I gonna do? He'd worked for me for twenty years."

Stacked waist-high across a support beam spanning the twenty-foot-by-twenty-foot office was a dusty patchwork of thousands of colored brochures, catalogs, price lists, and samples of product lines Silver carried or took orders for. The old man had an uncanny sense for finding any certain piece of literature he was looking for without wasting much time in the hunt.

The black, rotary, multi-line telephones in the office rang out. Albert answered the one on Willard's desk and began taking an order for Radlin Packinghouse, scribbling while standing slouched over a yellow order pad. Harvey walked over to the other desk behind the support beam and saw the other phone surrounded by dust-laden cups and literature, samples of toilet paper and towels, and ashtrays overflowing with chewed cigar butts. Then his eyes went to the hundred-year-old floor safe in the far corner. He always wondered what his father had Silver storing in there for him. He knew it was something to be given to him only if he decided to be a paper man. Whenever Albert would clear off a chair to sit in front of the safe as he retrieved some document or his petty cash kept in a small tackle box, Harvey could have easily peered over his shoulder to snoop. But no. He always turned or looked away. He hoped it was money, but his dad never saved a dime in his life. Harvey would wait.

Between Willard's pecks Harvey could tell this phone order was a big one and trouble was coming his way.

"Monday okay?" Silver asked his customer.

Harvey crept closer, saying behind his boss, "No, not today. Monday. Tell 'em Monday."

"Ya gotta have it today?" Albert whined. "Hold on." Albert put the phone receiver to his sunken chest and turned to his delivery man submissively, pleading with his magnified eyes. "It's Radlin Packinghouse. They gotta have it today. Can't ya deliver it before the country?"

Harvey's jaw tightened and he shook his head yes, knowing this would ruin his appearance if he saw her in Macy. Harvey went out the back door, slamming it behind him after picking up his country orders in Willard's basket.

As he made his way through the blackness of tires, he smirked at a memory from earlier in the summer when he was unloading a boxcar of toilet paper with a transient worker sent over from the shelter. Albert had asked him where the man was.

"In the bathroom," Harvey said.

He watched the old man head for the bathroom along this dark aisle, stumbling onto an empty tire cart and coasting ten feet before stopping. He followed his mumbling boss to the bathroom door where Albert pounded and yelled, "Hey! Come on! Sit on your own time, for God's sake!" Then he shuffled off, mumbling and grumbling and hiking his baggy slacks stained with cigar juice up over his big belly and shifting his glasses on his nose with his head bent forward.

Now Harvey raised the wooden gate to the elevator and saw the elevator's floor half full with his stacked and marked product. He slammed the gate shut and rode to the fifth floor. Each floor was darker than the one below it. The fifth floor stored the sixty-inch rolls of kraft paper Radlin ordered every month. The green two-wheeler he pushed out of the elevator was cold without the gloves that were in his van. He reached up and pulled string after hanging string every twenty-five feet, each turning on a sixty-watt bulb to light his way.

He was mad. These five-foot-tall rolls weighed eighty pounds. He twisted and rolled on end two of the giants onto the silver blade of his two-wheeler; then he let the balanced weight of his load rub dirt and dust on his shoulder, ruining his chance to look clean for the girl with the golden eyes.

The rattletrap ride over potholed roads and railroad tracks in the Stockyards District always irritated Harvey because he hated loud noises. And here it was: The most dreaded of deliveries was on him as he reached the perilous entrance to the very bowels of hell known as Radlin. The hundred-foot-long driveway was a forty-five-degree down-sloping nightmare. Since the van's muffler was gone, he had trouble hearing. He had to get out of the van, leaving it in neutral after pulling out the emergency brake that would barely keep the van from rolling on level ground. Then he'd squint into the black hole, listening for that red, square-boxed gut wagon to come roaring up out of the blackness with another load of animal waste. No sound. Go for it.

He jumped behind the wheel and saw the memory of that crazy gut wagon driver who loved scaring him back up the driveway every chance he could. Down, down, down, slowly in neutral, his foot squeezing the last threads of brake lining while grumbling how cheap his boss was for not getting a good delivery van ... *with all the money he's got!*

His six-hundred-pound load was shifting forward, even though he had positioned everything just right from a dozen previous terrorizing drops here. Down, down, down, darker and darker, until he could see that chipped-toothed weasel wearing his blood-splattered white hard hat and smoking his cigarette. As usual, he had his thumb stuck in his front pocket while his deep truck box was being filled with greasy, splattering, slimy hog and cattle guts, bones, brains and blood. The disgusting slop never failed to get on Harvey's hair and shoulders when he wheeled Silver's product through the narrow passageway and over huge water hoses right under the hole that was filling the wagon. Then he had to balance those giant rolls of brown paper up the slippery, uneven concrete ramp that led him into the noisiest place on earth — Radlin's slaughterhouse.

He was breathing hard already and sweating from toting two rolls at a time. His choice was to either maneuver 160 pounds worth of product at one time or to make twice as many trips past the filling gut wagon. The steady stream of rotting waste easily could have been halted by that devil simply pushing the red button that started and stopped it all. The fresh blood of a thousand head streamed through three-inch hoses that he had to arduously wheel his cart backwards over as he made his way across the slippery floor. Each jolting bump onto the floor dug the 160-pound load deep into his shoulder. And if he dropped it, all hell would break loose. Those dead-faced men in white smocks and hard hats would see him fail, and they'd laugh and carry on while watching his every step from behind the foreman's glass window. It was bad enough having to confront them to get a signature for the delivery without giving them any additional fuel. They'd always say, "More s—t paper" (even though most times toilet paper was not delivered). It was their laughter that bothered him most. He hated thinking he was so comical to watch doing his job that these desultory dough boy butchers could be heard laughing hysterically above the maelstrom.

The indignation burned into his face as he got his second load. He hunched his head into his shoulders to diminish the noisy memory of his father's final few months as a paper man, as Harvey drove him to his customers and prospects in the city and saw them laughing at his father. They had to know he was dying. He face looked skeletal; his eyes sunken and more fearful. And they too would laugh at his main line — toilet paper. It was a brutal, disrespectful kind of laugh that had to have chipped away at the very bone that showed more and more through his papery skin. Could Harvey ever be a paper man? No. No! NO!

His second load was easy. The anger about his father gave him enough strength to pull his load with ease over nylon hoses and slick floor drains after passing under the gut wagon's source — that damn twelve-inch-diameter hole spouting its grease-slopping slime of entrails until the box was half full. The spots on his best delivery shirt were adding up to a grotesque mosaic.

He would be a mess after five more trips to the cage where his load was stored.

God, I wish I was stoned, he thought.

Off went his royal-blue, long-sleeve shirt for his third load, stashing the shirt carefully folded over the back of the van's driver's seat. *That bastard!* he thought to himself after the gut wagon driver shut down the spout on purpose after seeing him remove his shirt. This threw him off, though, because other sounds that the gut spout drowned out were now audible: animal hooves tramping close together just above his head with their sickening bawling just before their shot to the head, and the butchers' knives being sharpened as swiftly as the whooshing steam from overhead pipes.

"You lose yer shirt?" the foreman barked from his desk when signing Silver's delivered order. It was there again. Again and again he feared it until it choked out any good thing that might have happened earlier. Floyd Harvey Deason kept his mouth shut. He was not a paper man. He would not say something clever or self-deprecating to secure a sale or make a bigger one. So he said nothing. A grunt from him said defiantly, *You will not own me or matter to me; I delivered your paper, did my job. See ya.*

The rope was wound tighter on the clanging back double doors. The two-wheeler would fly at it from the engine revving and the rpms he had to have to climb out when he hit the incline on his four bald, mismatched tires that hadn't seen a front-end alignment in five years. And watch out for that weasel returning with the gut wagon and backing down into the pit! He cared nothing for Silver's van except the hope of nailing it if it dared challenge him.

He started breathing normally again in the October sunlight, still bareback and perspiring heavily after that God-awful drop into hell. He rolled over a dozen bone-jarring railroad tracks on the quarter mile drive back to Silver's warehouse. Then her memory came to him in the sweeter air upwind of the stockyards. The girl in Pine Ridge. The memory of her in the doorway of the old church with her blanket and pillow stayed with him on the loading dock as he filled Silver's rusty, cancer-riddled van with the stacked country product. He wheeled it effortlessly from the elevator to the dock's iron lip that had rusted into a mauve color that matched the brick of the seventy-year-old warehouse.

He only knew this girl by the name he had given her — Ms. Sun. She had to have a real name, and he was determined to get that before he left Macy. Whatever her name, he wished she were older. She had to be only fourteen or fifteen now, he surmised.

His thoughts were interrupted as the office door squeaked open and the shuffling slouch of Silver came toward him with flailing arms and his cigar in his hand.

"How many cans of oil did you take, for God's sake? Huh?" he demanded while craning his massive head over the last stack of product that would cram the cargo area to the last cubic inch.

"Three," Harvey answered.

"Three! Do ya drink the stuff, for God's sake?"

"I need it! This junker burns oil like gas! You said you'd get me a new van last summer." That got him off the subject.

Silver handed him an old invoice from his files. "This guy's owed me 480 bucks for locker paper for four years. He's no good! See if you can collect it."

"Twenty percent if I do?" Harvey smiled with his back to Albert while tying the van's back doors with extra revolutions.

"Ten percent," Silver barked.

"You gave my old man twenty!" Harvey countered.

Albert's voice softened, "If ya can get it all, twenty."

"I need some lunch money," Harvey said stepping up to the empty dock.

Silver pulled out a wad of cash from his front pocket and handed his driver a five-dollar bill, mumbling while gritting his mulchy cigar butt between his front teeth. There was a visible smile from the crusty Jew above his flabby jowls. With a hint of love and compassion in his voice he said to Harvey as if talking to his own son, "Ya got plenty of gas?"

Harvey nodded yes, knowing the last gas receipt was only a day old. "Yes," he reiterated while closing the van's driver's side door that only opened from the outside.

Even softer Silver said, "Stop in tomorrow. The warehouse needs to be straightened up."

"On Sunday?"

"Yes. I'll be in at eight," Albert said.

"Okay. See ya tomorrow ... later than eight."

From his cracked side-view mirror he could see the hump on Silver's upper back was more obvious in that yellow, camelhair sweater. As the old man made his way back into the warehouse, he picked up his pace a notch upon hearing his office phone ringing. Harvey fired up the van and looked over at his full clipboard of invoices vibrating on his hot engine cover, then across to the passenger side that had no seat, its space now wedged up to the windshield with product except for a small gap allowing him to see his passenger side mirror.

His first two drops were to South Sioux City liquor stores across the Combination Bridge. He was delivering three weeks' worth of sales made by Jake Rutman, the most cynical, negative, rotten bastard that anyone could imagine. Even Albert was intimidated by him. He remembered Albert telling him that Jake's customers gave him orders just to get rid of him. Harvey's dad told him his customers were afraid to say no.

At Emerson, Nebraska, a tiny village off Highway 35, he delivered a case of Lava soap and two cases each of dispenser toilet paper and towels to an old machine shop. Then he delivered a case of napkins to a café. Twelve miles later in Wakefield he had one drop at a co-op elevator. Thirteen miles south and west of Wakefield was Wayne, a much larger town, where he made eight deliveries within a mile of each other — collecting checks, cash, and signatures with no problems. He then went southwest to Pender, another smaller farming community, where he made a drop at a co-op. A hatchery in that town took two hundred pounds off his dry, rear axle when he unloaded four fifty-pound drums of sweeping compound. A nearby hotel took a case each of Silver's bowl and glass cleaners. He made two more drops in Walthill and then headed to Winnebago, the reservation town just before Macy, that would get the bulk of his cargo.

Sourpuss Jake had three customers in Winnebago: the police station, the grease-pit gas station, and the Winnebago Tribal Agency. The last one was the big one. They had ordered for the school and their new building five cases of dispenser towels, five cases of dispenser toilet paper, two cases of bowl cleaner, three cases of glass cleaner, and ten cases of 33-gallon garbage bags — all of which Jake priced twenty percent higher just because he could. His father had cheated the Indians in similar fashion before Jake took over his territory. Harvey had overheard Jake telling Silver, "Who cares? They don't pay for it ... the government all but wipes their asses anyway!" Even squeeze-a-buck Albert would wince at the prices Jake charged his Indian customers. The old man justified sending in the invoices because usually he'd have to wait three or four months before getting paid by the government.

Highway 75 rolled and banked under a cloudless October sky

two miles north of Macy. The tops of trees were now yellow and auburn, but he noticed none of them. He couldn't remember if he had told her back then that his name was Floyd. *Still, she's too young,* he thought as the van's driver's side window slipped on its track. He had to raise it with one hand while steering his misaligned junker with the other.

At the Omaha Indian Reservation highway marker, he pulled over to the shoulder anticipating that the van had run low enough on oil that it would sputter and choke for minutes after turning off the ignition before finally dying. He gouged his metal oil spout into a can of Silver's oil, using a blue windshield towel to lift off the oil-soaked cap under the raised-up engine cover. The engine compartment was hot and steamy from a thousand cracks and engine leaks. No way was he going to enter Macy spewing black smoke, so he poured in all three quarts before checking his fine brown hair in his wobbly rearview mirror.

Entering Macy was like driving down from the lip of a bowl. He let off the accelerator to keep his muffler from blowing out the tiny valley town where she could be living. On his left was the school she probably attended. On his right he decided to tackle business first, parking in front of the old town auditorium where the steps leading up to the front doors were littered with empty beer cans and cigarette butts. He looked down at the $480.00 total on the old invoice on his clipboard and then at the name Bob Kozak. A thousand times he'd watched and heard his father collect on old debts. Three things his dad told him were necessary, the same three things any good salesman has: speed, surprise, and resolution.

He came in fast. The deadbeat locker owner was there behind his desk, surprised and knowing the young man with the clipboard had found his man. The chess match began. Would he close? Kozak waited to hear the young man's approach as he sat up straight with both thumbs tapping his desk. His glassy blue eyes were swimming in debt and lies — dead eyes in deep sockets.

Harvey quickly changed into Floyd. "Mr. Silver told me to get a check for this." Floyd watched Kozak's eyes not denying the debt, and a devilish smirk at the corners of Kozak's thin upper lip cracked in places below each nostril until Floyd surprised him again. "I'm headed for the Walthill Cattleyard ..." Floyd paused purposely to watch the rat's blink and flutter at the words coming from this kid. "You know Joe Forche ... the owner of the cattleyard. He told me to see you here and collect this cause he used to work for Mr. Silver. And he said he'd just take it off his account with you if ya didn't pay it."

Floyd's pale, teal-blue eyes stayed on Kozak as his father's words rang inside: *Keep yer mouth shut; close him with silence.*

Kozak kept silent too with thumbs yet patting his desk and thinking with bovine eyes that were dead and cold. Then he opened his front desk drawer, pulled out a ledger checkbook, and wrote out a check for the figure Floyd's hand placed in front of him. He couldn't look up at Silver's man when he handed over his check and heard the clipboard's spring open then snap down on his collection.

"I'll let Mr. Forche know it's paid," Floyd said when walking out.

From his office window, Kozak watched him drive behind the auditorium to the Macy police station. He wanted to pick up the phone and call his client in Walthill just to see if he'd been hoodwinked. He didn't. He could only watch him from afar and know he'd just been handled by a young pro. He smiled, shook his head, and went back to work.

The thrill of his twenty percent was not what electrified him. He bounced his two-wheeler out of the cargo area and loaded two cases of toilet paper onto its blade, pushing and then pulling it to the mud-rutted front entrance of the station. She had brought his father's confident side out of him: Floyd. He had simply remembered seeing Kozak's truck delivering meat to his Walthill account. Yes, it was something his old man would've done; but it wasn't in his heart to do it until he thought of her living in the same town with that snake. He imagined all things nice around her — not this.

"It's Paper Man from Superland!"

It was now Floyd who smiled back at the Indian policeman as he deftly maneuvered his cart through the door.

"How do you say 'paper man' in Indian?" Floyd asked.

"*Mni huka ska* ... for white paper," he said after thinking about it.

Floyd could see Indian inmates celled in a few barred cages behind a one-way glass door. He handed the policeman his invoice on his clipboard to sign after dropping Silver's toilet paper in the usual corner by the drums of sweeping compound yet unopened from February, the last time he was in Macy. He remember delivering them in the snow and thinking about her then. Now he was here again. *Find her,* Floyd told himself.

"There was a young girl from Pine Ridge that moved here five years ago. She has gold eyes. Do you know where she lives?"

The policeman blinked a quick smile from behind his desk. "That's Granny Tenna's girl."

"Do you know her name?" Floyd asked.

He shook his head no while pooching his lips out, then he inserted a toothpick between his jagged lower front teeth, saying, "She lives in the lavender house behind the school."

"Thanks." As Harvey turned to leave, it was Floyd who spoke again. "Next time you order, tell Jake you want it delivered on Saturday only, okay?"

"Sure. Saturday. See ya, Paper Man."

"See ya."

He had one more drop — this time to the Macy Agency — before he would go to the lavender house. It was a blur of a delivery. He couldn't remember off-loading at the Agency two minutes after he'd left. He only knew that he had to be Floyd to go through with this because of that nagging fear of not being remembered ... or welcomed.

The energy to get to this moment — on her dirt street, closing in on the lavender house — was leaving Harvey and going into Floyd. She was the only person in the world who had really seen Harvey, vulnerable and scared, that night in Pine Ridge. *I'll just thank her for the pillow and blanket and ask her if she found them where I left them,* he thought as he parked in the street across from the lavender house.

He wasn't sure what lavender looked like until he saw it. It was striking and alluring against the rundown shacks around it. A fleet of big, puffy clouds zoomed overhead, casting a cool shadow over Macy as he reached outside his window and squeezed open the van's door handle.

He stopped at the gate of the picket fence that had been painted by Granny the past spring. There were ripe, orange pumpkins visible in the dirt section at the front corner of the house near a bed of dying veronicas. It was Harvey now, clearing his throat and shining the white rubber front of his new tennis shoes on the back of each calf of his faded jeans. Perspiration was cool and sticky against his skin under his best shirt. No turning back after knocking on the front door.

"Ma'am ... I'm Harvey Deason from Sioux City. I deliver for Silver Paper Company." He turned and pointed at the old van. "I was in town deliverin', and I wanted to say hi to yer granddaughter. I met her in Pine Ridge a long time ago."

"She's not here," Granny said coldly. She could see the boy's disappointment in his eyes. Good eyes of a workin' man, she knew. "She's at the school having a dance class."

"Oh ... okay ... uh ... maybe I'll stop and say hi." Granny's square jaw jutted out while nodding yes to the polite young man with good eyes. She closed the door before he could say thank you and goodbye.

* * * * *

Could that be her? She's so tall now, he thought to himself. He watched the girl with the golden eyes in black ballet tights from outside the gym entrance in the Macy school. Poised on the gym floor, she and two full-blooded Indian girls her age were holding onto the floor of the small stage while their instructor, watched them. He watched the girls standing on their toes, moving and bending gracefully with their arms flowing down then up, over and over again. He could see she was by far the most graceful of the trio, her hair longer and more golden now and tied in back with a purple ribbon.

"Very good, Josephine!" her teacher called out. Her voice echoed in the dark room where only a lamp burned from a table on the stage in the windowless gym.

Josephine must be her name, he assumed. He repeated her name to himself, mouthing it quietly, while focusing on her white ballet slippers pointed toes-down and supporting her slim figure on the dark hardwood floor.

Then she broke away, alone from the others, spinning and moving gracefully without sound under her. Her neck relaxed to one side with her eyes closed in a trance-like meditation that stopped his breath and gaped his mouth. He stared at her long arms flowing up and over her head as her fingers dancing through a web of invisible blue-silver strands that encircled her and stayed with her every move. She was touching Harvey's left — that side of him that was feminine, sensitive, caring, and had

71

to be loved. She was saving him again.

Right there in the darkness, his eyes filled and drained all the sadness above Floyd's persistent order, *Be a man!* This was the same feeling he had wanted to recapture when she came to him in Pine Ridge. She had wanted nothing from him. She gave. He wanted to run to her now, take her away from this place, and protect her from a thousand things that can ruin a girl's life — a thousand things that can make her bail out and settle for something or someone far less deserving of her.

Her eyes slowly opened as she stood still, balancing straight and tall with her breathing heavy and low from her center. He felt somehow she needed him. Or was it his aloneness craving a fantasy? *No,* Harvey told himself, *she could bring us together if she loved me. Why her? She's too young for me.*

He knew these images would haunt him night and day over a million stops in greasy spoons and repair shops and slaughterhouses throughout the upper Midwest. This moment, soon to be only a memory, would sustain him and last him through the stale comings and goings of a thousand nameless ciphers he would encounter, all wanting to know him and take his mind and time away from this. Those nameless men with vacant eyes. Those nameless men breathing the same air as him. Those nameless men swallowing egg whites and tepid milk in their cafés before going back to their crippling dependency on meaningless work where he would deliver to them a thousand times. Over and over he washed his eyes over her in order to save Harvey, all without breathing.

"Very good, Josie!" her instructor applauded.

Josie! That fits her! Josie. He said it a hundred times to himself so he'd never forget her name for as long as he lived. *Josephine ... Josie ... yes, that's her.*

He thought of backing out — just leaving without being seen when the class ended. The girls went over to the far end of the stage and began pulling jeans, sweaters and shoes over their tights. He could see her bending, lifting each leg into each pant leg, her back thin and supple. *Her jaw line is well formed for only 14 or 15,* he thought.

Now the girls were coming toward him, walking side by side, unaware of the stranger in the doorway. He could duck out of view as Harvey would — relaxed and content and untouchable from harm. Or ...

"Hi," Floyd exclaimed, causing the Indian girls to pause and give Josie the lead.

She couldn't see his face until she got closer, then she smiled to expose her beautiful teeth upon recognizing him. "Paper Man!"

Harvey blushed. Floyd was fighting the fire spreading over Harvey's face, and that old twitch fired under his eye too obvious for those gold eyes to miss. He could tell she was not the quiet little girl he'd met in Pine Ridge. His image of talking to a shy girl vanished in the doorway shadows as his tenable head-fire shut off his hearing and let Floyd go. "You remembered me! Remember in Pine Ridge when you gave me the blanket and pillow?"

"Yes! What are you doing here?" she smiled.

"I remembered you saying you were moving to Macy. I was deliverin' here and ... I ... I asked about you. I went to your house and yer grandma said you were here."

"Is your father with you?" she asked.

"He died a few months ago."

"Oh," Josie paused.

"That's okay. He's better off dead ... the way he suffered, I mean."

There was an awkward pause as the two Indian girls stood back waiting for Josie.

"Is your name Josephine?"

"Yes. Josie Tenna." She extended her right hand, handshaking while looking at him and waiting to hear his name — unusually mature and confident for a girl her age. He was admiring her lips, full and protruding from her beautiful big teeth so straight and white. He was self-conscious smiling at them.

"Harvey. Floyd Harvey Deason is my name. I go by Harvey."

The girls passed by them heading for the front door.

"You like Macy ... better than Pine Ridge?" he asked.

"Oh, yes. Much better than Pine Ridge," she said.

They awkwardly moved toward the front door. Outside the school door the wind had picked up, blowing gusts of swirling dirt low across the road in front of them. His eyes were averted away to the western hills covered by tilled cornfields that sloped into jagged ravines where seasonal rivulets emptied into the river. Now his mouth was as dry as those rivulets. He felt tight and self-conscious — as if Harvey were unlikeable and so obviously unsure of himself.

"Maybe I'll see you again next time I'm in Macy." His calm, easy demeanor belied the words begging to be released from deep inside him: *I'm alone! How do I get out of this?*

She smiled into the neck hole of her sweater, thinking how skinny his legs looked compared to his broad shoulders. "Goodbye, Harvey," she smiled as she turned to join her giggling friends who were making jokes about his van.

He watched her dance away from him, a playful pirouette in the October air. She was giggling and happy to be alive, free from self-consciousness — away, away from him on the dirty cracked sidewalk to join her girlfriends who were still laughing at the van and whispering things about him.

When he slunk to his van he couldn't see her; she had vanished behind the school's west wing that was spray-painted with blue, black, orange and yellow non-salacious graffiti. *I could have said more,* he brandished himself.

"Damn!" he thumped his steering wheel hard with his palm, not knowing if he'd ever see her again. His muffler was blowing out the valley behind him as he turned south onto Highway 75 with only three deliveries remaining.

Josie told her friends during their walk home that he was someone she had met in Pine Ridge. One of the girls remarked that he was cute, but it was shrugged off by Josie. She had never felt any real interest in boys. But when she got home and Granny inquired about the nice young man with good eyes, Josie could feel her face reddening and was strangely embarrassed by talking about him.

"He was there ... watching us dance ... out of nowhere ... there he was." She told Granny about how he had two names. She couldn't recall which one came first — Floyd or Harvey. Then she said, "He goes by Harvey, his middle name. That's it!"

Josie recalled to Granny the time she saw him at the Pine Ridge store and how his father, the paper man, faked losing his money in the pop machine. She told her how she had felt so sorry for him sleeping alone in that spider-infested room in the old church, and how she brought him a pillow and blanket the night before she'd moved to Macy.

Granny kept asking questions about the young man while she made their peppermint tea with honey in her spotless kitchen as Josie sat at the little table for two. "He likes you. I can tell. His body is off-balance in a big way, which ages him beyond his years. He is already an old soul. He needs to change his diet or he will lose his hair ... and his belly will hang over his bird legs."

Josie laughed into her first sip of the hot, soothing tea, then smiled her affirmation to Granny's offer of a cinnamon stick.

"Bird legs," Josie repeated, laughing long and hard at having noticed that very feature about him as he was standing outside her school.

Josie may have given the paper man's son from Sioux City about one percent of the thought he was spending on her. Granny kept her busy painting her collection of miniature ceramic figurines — a thousand little creatures onto which the girl from Pine Ridge was allowed to brush, splash, pour, and spackle a polychromatic carnival of colors. They would line the windowsills facing a color wheel of annuals: violet and lavender phlox, yellow and red pansies, orange marigolds, orange and red-violet zinnias. The flowers were a festival of warm, vibrant colors in black loam beds or ceramic pots lining the peaceful lavender house that Granny called "The Healing House."

Yes, Granny was a safe harbor for her Josephine. She had no patience for drinking, fighting, and jaded Red Brothers who recklessly drove by, or passed out drunk near her house, or spent the night in jail for indecencies. After one young liquored brave threw a beer bottle in her yard, Granny followed him home on foot. She knew him from years before when she had served as the school nurse. When the drunk young man opened his door, there was Granny demanding an explanation for littering on the piece of earth God so graciously allowed her to live on. Within minutes the man was in tears, promising to come by and get some ginger and dandelion root from her to begin his inner cleansing. After only ten weeks on her potion, the sobered-up young man had cleaned up his act, joined the Army, and eventually got his high school equivalency diploma. Upon returning home on leave, he gave Granny a set of six-dozen glass-lidded pewter jars from Germany in which to store her many herbs.

The little jars were still in her kitchen, sitting alphabetized on her kitchen counter on a four-tiered shelf Granny had made from barn wood that Josie had found on the old Broad Tree farm across from the pond where Granny gathered her red clover in the summer. Josie stood staring at the shelf Granny named "Herb" and remembered the scene when she spotted the piece of wood. It had been nestled in a thicket of flaming dragons that were a dark raspberry color under the clouds but then exploded to a bright crimson when bathed in sunlight. She chuckled to herself as she remembered carrying the board with Granny at one end and herself at the other, and how they laid it across the backseat of Granny's old '72 Ford with one end of the plank sticking out the passenger-side rear window.

Josie's thoughts quickly returned to the paper man's son, Harvey, and his old, rusty van parked outside her school. His hair was now much longer and a fine, light brown that reminded her of someone or something, but she couldn't quite remember what. She thought about the way his small, red mouth opened just a bit when he spoke — the same way she used to speak before moving to Granny's and getting ground blackhaw and boneset, natural muscle relaxers, in her morning oatmeal.

How long was he watching me dance? she wondered. Then the thought was gone. Her self-consciousness about such trifles had bothered her to no end before coming to Granny's. Now her grades in school were nearly perfect. She was different. He was just passing through again. *How lonely that must be,* she thought. His eyes were the same — nice yet sad.

She found herself thinking about him again at bedtime. She had trained herself to put the day behind her and ruminate about the day ahead and her plans for it. No more wasted energy on the past, Granny had taught her. Then she prayed for him to find the same kind of peace she had been blessed with in Macy.

Four days before Christmas, Albert Silver bought a new white delivery van with no front passenger seat. The old van was scrapped for fifty bucks at a salvage yard across the street from Silver's warehouse. Albert told Harvey he would be allowed to take the new van home every night so it wouldn't get vandalized. In reality, though, Silver wanted to encourage Harvey's growing interest in selling his lines and supplies in the country.

One Sunday in mid-January found Harvey sitting in Albert Silver's office. The scene never changed. Old man Silver would hunt for a certain invoice, wetting his thumb several times while rifling through the pile until he found the one he was looking for, all the while mumbling incoherently. Then he'd stumble forward with his sunken chest and his massive head craned forward, make a notation on the paper, and drop it into Willard's basket. Peering above his glasses without blinking his cloudy pale-blue eyes at the young man seated at the other cluttered desk, he'd shake his head in disgust and bark at Floyd that he should get a haircut.

"Albert, please don't call me Floyd anymore."

"Well, I can't get used to calling you Harvey. Floyd's always been yer name! Who do you think you are ... John Wayne, for Pete's sake?" He then would slouch back to his pile of steel baskets holding hundreds of invoices.

A few grumbles came and passed as Harvey's eyes followed the worn, colorless carpet through a narrow path between piles of literature and unopened sample boxes of soaps, brushes, shop towels, paper cups, and urinal blocks leading to Albert's antiquated desk. On the wall behind the desk loomed an old, dark, dusty painting that had probably been hanging there for close to a half century. And there beneath the painting sat the cold, gray floor safe. It was always there — a constant physical reminder of his father's legacy to his son. It kept him here. *He was even withholding in death,* Harvey thought. A million childhood ghosts were locked away behind those four-inch steel doors, all waiting to withhold again. Anxious to say no to the paper man's son. Eager to turn him back to Sioux City just as they had his father. Thousands of faces that had rejected the father ten million times — in blizzards or stultifying heat or perfect weather — now waited to devour the son.

He sat staring at the safe's combination lock, his breathing shallow and his back teeth clench more and more when he thought of the territory. He thought of the roads, the myriad faces, and the storms ahead of him. They had killed his father because he was one of the weak ones who chose to drown his anger drink by drink, rejection after rejection. It was Floyd who saw from a boy's view a father stuck in that awkward space when a prospect turned him down. He watched his father's dry throat swallow his loss before retreating from the battleground. He saw the eyes of the rejecter screaming, "Get out! Intruder! We do not like you or else we'd buy from you! Crawl back to that sewer city you came from, you loser!"

Floyd Harvey Deason ended his reverie and got up from the creaky swivel chair. He had to get away from the red coils of the portable heater near Willard's desk that were chapping his lips and making his scalp itch. He felt trapped and closed in until he reached the fresh winter air on the loading dock.

The cold north wind seemed to blow in a new thought pattern. He thought of the girl he knew would be a beauty. And in Macy, of all places. But she would never be his beauty. "The pretty ones are taken young around here," his dad had told him. His shabby, colorless clothes he always wore made him laugh out loud at himself. So did the thought of him trailing behind his shuffling boss through the dive café on his way to his free breakfast. They all knew Albert Silver down on lower Fourth Street. There were transients who broke their backs unloading a boxcar for him. There were shabby owners of shabby businesses who bought his second-rate supplies because they were cheap. There were secretaries and waitresses more than half his age who'd be the recipients of a wink and a smile and a suggestive comment. "She doesn't have to worry about me," Albert would confide to his young protégé, "at my age I'm all talk and no action."

Harvey spent the afternoon thinking about his move to salesman. He would stay out in the country, preferring that to calling on Silver's Jewish business cronies who never bought big. Just paltry courtesy sales for the old man. Those knowing eyes and brooding lips would size him up as just another sucker for Albert, knowing there was always someone willing to work for minimum wage to fatten Silver's wallet. Yes, to them he was just a token delivery boy and not a "chosen one." He was a nameless cipher. In the country he could escape to Floyd and get away from the city vultures.

He also felt he had to get away from the stacked cases of toilet paper on downtown sidewalk elevators. He was embarrassed by the scores of pretty girls, all dressed up for work, who had seen his public display of twisting and pulling and lifting ten thousand rolls of toilet paper. Not only that, but if one of those stacks should ever fall, creating a two-ply tumbling avalanche toward the river, it would be all over evening news for everyone to see. The last thing he wanted was his face all over the evening news.

With the great toilet paper sidewalk calamity still playing itself out in his mind, he drove down Jackson and parked near Sam's Bookstore on lower Fourth. Dirty books only. Sam, a mean-looking elderly Jew, was at his register looking out his front window when he saw "Silver's boy" walking by coatless on a cold day.

Harvey passed two dive bars, a sleazy motel, and a hamburger joint called the Greek Kitchen. He decided he would get his mind off the young girl in Macy by stopping in there for a bowl of hot soup after buying a winter coat. The pretty Greek waitress who would serve him was only a couple years older than him.

"It looks good on you! So why don't you buy it?" Harvey looked at himself in the waist-length wool navy coat. The tilted floor mirror must have been distorted because the ugly Jewish sales clerk, Aaron, even looked good in the reflection. He could feel Aaron at his back, touching his shoulder and pretending to check the fit, craving to grab a feel from any male customer that came into his store. Aaron made a living pushing his cheap clothing stock on naive youth. "You look great in that. It really is you. You should have that!"

The lies were delivered behind big, yellow, chipped teeth entombed in a snarling, leering mouth. His thick glasses tripled the size of his rheumy, shifty, black-brown eyes. Harvey stepped forward in angry stupefaction. As he felt that conniving Milquetoast's hand leaving his shoulder, his back shuddered under the new coat. Harvey could not buy the coat right now, but Floyd could.

"I want you to charge this to Albert Silver. He'll send ya a check this week."

Aaron was caught off guard. He knew this was Silver's driver, but he was no relative. If this wasn't okay with Silver, he'd never see his money for the coat.

"I'd better call him to make sure," Aaron said. His eyes stared at Floyd from behind his frog-like lenses, waiting for the young man to balk or walk out without the coat. He only saw confidence. He only saw Floyd.

Aaron left Floyd on the sales floor and went to his back room where he found Albert's home phone number. He hoped he would answer. Floyd could hear Silver's voice resonating off the clothing salesman's giant ear after he told the old man his driver wanted to charge a coat to him.

"How much is the coat?" Albert barked over the receiver.

"Forty-two ninety-nine ... plus tax," Aaron said.

"Did he drive down?" his boss snapped.

Floyd yelled out from the sales floor, "Yes, I drove down!" knowing he'd promised not to drive the new van except to work and back.

Aaron was glad to give the receiver to Floyd when Silver asked to talk to him. Floyd took over: "Just tell him I can charge it so I can get out of here!"

When Floyd handed the phone back to Aaron, he could hear Albert mumble, "Send me the bill," then he hung up.

The receipt Aaron had him sign before leaving the store was balled and sweaty in his new coat pocket by the time he entered the spicy smells of the steamy, warm Greek Kitchen. He could see her long brown hair up in a hairnet. The back of her tall, 24-year-old, full body was bent forward scrubbing a deep pot at the sink behind the cook's porthole window. Floyd disappeared the moment he saw her.

He sat at a counter stool with his new coat on and buttoned. He wanted to twist his stool from side to side to catch her eye.

Her name was Beth. He'd heard it a thousand times when he saw her out dancing in clubs.

An old lady — a frumpy relative of the voluptuous Beth — stayed seated on her chair behind the counter. A transient drunk sipped his coffee at a corner booth, staring blankly at the wall in front of him.

"Ya want somethin' to eat?" the old lady frowned at Harvey.

"A bowl of soup sounds good." He wished he could summon Floyd now. But not with Beth around. He was always too timid to approach her table in a club to ask her to dance. He knew she dated older men with money and had plans to marry an already married man she was dating if he ever left his wife. He knew he was too late. *The pretty ones are taken early.* His father's words rang in his head as he watched Beth spin his clipped order slip towards her. She could see him and knew he was shy of her. She liked confident young men and older men who knew what they wanted and had money to spend on her. Beth was not beautiful — she was sexy and mature.

Harvey watched her as she brought his soup to him. Her eyes were on the brimming bowl instead of on him.

"Thanks," he blushed. *Too weak to even matter,* he thought. He watched her gorgeous, firm body walk away in that white apron. Her legs were naturally tan and strong. She could definitely keep a young man's mind occupied.

He ate his soup, even though it was so hot it burned the hide off the roof of his mouth. He thought about the burned flesh that was now a part of the soup he just ate — lost, just like Floyd. Even his sense of pain was numbed by her presence, leaving only his self-consciousness. He knew if Floyd would come out, she'd be animated, attracted to him, and standing before him listening to his every word. Walking out to his van, he felt the cold breeze on his skinny legs below his coat line.

* * * * *

Harvey's apartment, a small studio at 15th and Jones, was an old brownstone owned by an elderly widow. The place was completely furnished. The Deasons only needed silverware and plates after Harvey's mother split out of their two-bedroom apartment, taking even the roll of toilet paper from its holder in the bathroom. "A definite statement," John had called it after coming home and finding the place empty except for a dresser and a queen size bed. John had saved $150 a month in rent by taking the studio, but he spent more than that on extra booze after his wife left him.

The memory of his father's dying days were always there — the coughing up blood, the wasting away of muscle and bone, the labored breathing — producing terrible nightmares. It was Albert who stepped in and had his dying salesman sent to the VA Hospital in Omaha. Floyd drove to the hospital every weekend for six weeks, only to watch his father dying before his eyes. On his last visit, he stood at the foot of the bed and watched his father's blinking skeleton-like body look back at him from under starched sheets.

"Give me a stick," he garbled to his son.

Floyd lit the Camel and held it to his father's chapped lips for each slow and deliberate drag.

Harvey went to sleep dreaming of Josephine the dancer moving gracefully through the plains from Pine Ridge to Macy and weaving through a tapestry of color mile after mile along his territory. From Mission to Valentine, Bonesteel to Armour, Scotland to Menno, and to the Germans in Hartington, all who saw her were stunned by her golden eyes when she danced along their glowing main streets. She was headed for a home he could not see, dancing away from him, slipping out of his view, and

84

finally gone. He was left with only empty, dull, gray streets and the disappointing reality of impecunious, strident prospects complaining about the weather and economy while shaving his father's prices down to ten percent over Silver's cost. He then found himself cold and hungry, wearing wrinkled clothes and sleeping in a cheap roadside motel bed without breakfast money.

He awoke from his dream and felt for his legs, making sure the wrinkled pants were not there.

He got out of bed and paced his front room. He knew she was too young. Untouchable. *She'll dance away from me to a younger man,* he thought. Floyd would not rescue him. This was Harvey's dream.

North on Highway 75, Harvey cruised out of Hinton and headed for Merrill in Silver's LTD with an old, brown cowhide sales case next to him on the front seat. It was his first day in the field as a paper man. Albert had told him that morning that those two towns had old customers who hadn't been called on in years.

"Suggest things," the old man had instructed his new salesman while lumbering along his dock. "Show 'em your product card. That's what a good salesman does. Suggest right down the line with them. See? 'How ya doin' on can liners? Glass cleaner? Bowl cleaner? Towels and tissue paper?'" As Harvey opened the heavy LTD door to tackle his first day as a salesman, the stale cigar smoke nearly made him hurl his breakfast.

"I need some lunch money," Harvey quickly yelled to his tight-fisted boss before he had a chance to disappear back into the warehouse.

"You got money! Don't ya carry any cash on ya, for crying in the night?" he grumbled while returning to the dock's edge and handing Harvey a five. "Bring me back a receipt," he barked.

"I will."

Although that exchange had been repeated daily for several years, that particular morning it sparked a memory in Silver as he watched Harvey drive away from the dock. Near Christmas about fifteen years prior, Silver had answered his office phone late in the afternoon while Willard pecked away on his Remington.

"Silver Paper."

Through the lousy phone connection, Albert could hear in the background the sounds of a noisy bar and a loud jukebox. He put the phone to his chest and said, "Willard, wait a minute, please." Willard stopped typing to listen. "Who is this?" Albert barked into the receiver.

"Floyd Harvey Deason," the seven-year-old voice answered matter-of-factly.

"Where's your father?"

"He's here."

"Where?" Albert demanded.

"In South Dakota."

The wise old man knew the boy was being coached by his father in the background. Silver listened.

"My dad says it would be a feather ... in his hat ... for sales ... if you would wire him ... fifty dollars for expenses ... to stay out a couple more days."

Albert puffed out his chest and stood with his back arched markedly after swiping his cheap glasses from his ears. "You tell your dad he can stick that feather up his ass and fly home!" Down went the receiver, giving Willard a start.

As Silver chuckled out loud at the memory, his new salesman was deep in his own reverie. It was summertime in Spink, South Dakota. Harvey was five, unable to see over the dashboard where his dad was going on the long, long gravel road after leaving Iowa across a one-lane wooden bridge.

"This is the smallest town in South Dakota," the paper man said, smoking his non-filter down close to his pursed lips before flicking it into the dirt cloud behind their dust-covered station wagon.

Harvey remembered tilting his head back to see this wonder. "Where?" the wide-eyed boy asked. He recalled his father laughing all the way into the Spink General Store, which also served as the post office, locker, and gas station. It was the only commercial building in town.

George, the seventy-year-old aproned owner, was sprinkling some of Silver's oil-based sweeping compound on his beautiful cherry wood floor, using a scoop from his peanut barrel. Harvey remembered how he stood back out of the way but was able to see and hear every gesture and word his father said after George, the Jew-hater, waved off any offer to buy anything from that Jew in Sioux City.

"George, ya know ... I'm 'bout out of gas, and I don't have a dime on me," the elder Deason pandered.

"Don't that Jew you work for pay yer expenses?"

"It's not enough, George. He won't cover three meals a day ... or even two. And if I have to drive extra miles to call back on a customer, I'm low on gas and money." The paper man was appealing to the grocer's hatred of Jews, and the boy knew it. "I didn't leave the highway to call on ya for Silver. I'm here to trade ya a case of garbage bags for a tank of gas. An under-the-table kind of deal," his father grinned. "See, George ... if ya give me a receipt for the gas, I can get it back from Silver. We all make out ... 'cept for the old man," he grinned again.

A half-hour later, the two Deasons entered the larger town of LeMars with a full tank of gas and a receipt wedged above the visor of the old station wagon.

Gun shy in LeMars — a town his father always said was tough to sell — Harvey cruised for the right prospect instead of parking at the first business and "walking the line." The main business district appeared cold to him.

Too much retail, he complained to himself before getting back on Highway 75 North, rolling past fertile Dutch farmland yielding as good as any soil on earth. His first call was at a roadside gas station, but the owner was away on a tow job. Harvey bought a pack of cigarettes there and smoked two by the time he had turned west off of 75 to work the tiny town of Maurice.

Parking outside a lumber yard and facing his first prospect, Harvey felt dizzy from the smokes. Employees and customers were nearby, listening to every word as Silver's fledgling salesman's hand fumbled for and dropped the product card. "My name's Harvey ... with Silver Paper Company in Sioux City."

The middle-aged lumber yard manager was sensitive to the young man's anxiety. "How's Old Man Silver doin'?"

"He's fine," Harvey smiled.

"His office still look like a tornado hit it?"

"Yeah," Harvey's smile broadened.

"I 'member one time I was in there and he found an invoice under three feet of buried paper. Then he gave me a tiny cup of port wine that nearly got me drunk. Yessir ... he's a character, that guy," the lumberman recalled as he picked up the product card from his counter. He studied the items and asked, "How much ya get for five-pound nail bags?" That was an item he knew Harvey didn't have on his list.

"I can call Mr. Silver collect, and he'll give me a price," Harvey squirmed.

The manager pushed his phone over to Harvey and said, "Find out about ten-pound bags too."

Leaving Maurice Harvey lit a cigarette and smiled at himself in Silver's rearview mirror. He'd made his first sale as a paper man — two thousand nail bags that only added up to a thirty-dollar order. But it broke the ice.

When he returned to the office at 5:00 that afternoon, Harvey still had only the Maurice order for the whole day. He knew he'd made the mistake of working Sioux Center and Orange City, where Dutchmen were known to be parochial and tight with strangers.

"Those Dutch wouldn't spend a nickel to see Christ walk across the Missouri," Silver grumbled after slow-dropping Harvey's order in the warehouseman's basket. "Did you suggest things?"

"Yes! I went over everything ... towels, TP, cups, garbage bags ... bowl and glass cleaner. Everything!"

As Albert sat before his floor safe dialing the big tumbler, Harvey lit a cigarette nervously. After opening his heavy safe door, Albert turned to him and shot out, "When did you start smokin' so much?"

"Today."

"That's no good for ya. Look what it did to yer old man."

"You smoke cigars!"

"I don't inhale 'em. There's a big difference."

Harvey watched Silver's long, slow reach into the back of the safe, where he pulled out a folded garment bag wrapped around his father's legacy."

"Here," Silver said.

Harvey took the torn garment bag and carried it back to the swivel chair. He placed it on the floor between his legs and opened it after Albert slammed his safe door shut and spun the tumbler. From the garment bag he pulled his father's worn, butterscotch-colored, handleless leather sales case. It was smoothed on each side where it had ridden the paper man's hip for three decades in every type of weather. "It's Charlie!" he exclaimed to his boss who was now seated at Willard's desk. "I wondered what happened to him!"

Harvey started choking up, but Floyd held back from letting

go a flood of emotions that the case carried for Harvey.

Albert watched with his legs crossed in a room hazed with their smoke. He watched him open the old case. The main pocket was empty. Charlie's inside zipper pocket had been sewn several times in the course of three decades. Harvey felt a bulgy envelope inside and pulled out a bank envelope holding fifty $20.00 bills inside a tri-folded letter. The letter was not addressed to Harvey or Floyd and had been dated a year before the old man's death.

Dear Son:

I know I'm dying. I want you to have this money when you start selling. Kind of a good-luck gift. Charlie was my only possession that meant anything to me. Always there. True blue. Charlie was my trusty sidekick.

I certainly don't expect or want you to be a paper man and end up like I did. You know what I mean. I just think it will mean more to you than anything else I have, you know?

You've been a good son. I enjoyed our times on the road together. Sure would have been lonesome without you there on those long summer runs.

I'm sorry about your mother and hope you can forgive her someday. That was my problem. Sorry.

I love you,

Dad.

Floyd was doing his best to keep Harvey from crying, even turning away from Silver's stare and facing the dusty wall. *Sorry.* It was that word that quivered his chin and brought back the old spasm under his eye, twitching like it used to when they were on the road together.

Albert thought about how the dying elder Deason had him take out twenty dollars a week from his paycheck the last year he worked in the city.

Floyd won the battle of emotions. "Would you keep this in the safe for me?"

Silver looked at the envelope of money extended to him. "Why don't ya put it in the bank and draw interest on it?"

"I'll spend it."

Albert took the envelope and counted the money, then he had Harvey sign a slip of paper verifying the amount and kept it in the envelope with the money. After closing the safe again, he turned and saw Harvey filling his father's legacy with the contents from the cheap sales case he'd given him that morning.

"I need some pens. I can't write orders without pens."

"After today, one pen would last ya a year," Albert laughed. "In Willard's drawer." The old man watched over Floyd's shoulder, seeing what he was taking out of the drawer. "Whaddaya have there?" he muttered.

"Pens! Whaddaya think I have?" Floyd snapped.

The old man slouched away, his wet cigar butt jammed in the corner of his flabby mouth as he picked up Harvey's sole invoice from the day and put it atop a pile. "You'd do more business if ya got a haircut. Where ya goin' Monday?"

"Onawa."

"I'll see if I have any old statements you can collect."

"Make me a list of Onawa customers, will ya?"

"Call on everybody!" Albert barked.

"I wanna know who has dispensers and who's bought from ya. Arm me!" Floyd demanded.

"Yer old man used to say that ... arm me."

"That's right. And don't forget to pay me."

Monday morning Floyd hit small farm towns south of Sioux City on his way to Onawa. He worked them like a tornado disguised in new clothes and a short haircut. He left no prospects untouched: isolated grain elevators, one-pump gas stations, general stores that had been standing since the turn of the last century. Any small business that had a door, Floyd went through it. Most had never seen a paper man. They were too small for lazy salesmen to bother with when they lived on commission. Floyd's orders were small — mostly in the twenty- to thirty-dollar range — but consistent. Then he'd pop an occasional hundred-dollar order.

Charlie bolstered him. It was like having his father riding on his hip. The first few calls in Onawa were tense, using furious amounts of energy. His pitch was short. "Hi. I'm Floyd with Silver Paper in Sioux City." He'd flash the product card. 'How ya doin' on TP, towels and garbage bags? I'm deliverin' Saturday."

"Yer TP is too thin and too rough ... like sandpaper."

"I've got soft TP too ... but you guys want cheap prices so ya get cheap paper. I've got two-ply. It's more money. The cost is still below Charmin because I've got twice the paper on a roll. Ya got to look at the number of sheets per roll to really compare."

One case here, one case there. By the time he'd walked Onawa, he knew he had at least twenty orders inside Charlie.

He timed it right so he was back in Silver's office by five. In the fast-falling winter darkness, he watched Albert thumb through twenty-one single-item orders at full markup, plus two checks totaling $150 he'd collected from deadbeats.

"You did good," Albert whined with his cigar firmly ensconced in the corner of his mouth. "Did ya suggest things?"

"Yes! Yes! But I sure learned a lot today about that. I'm gettin' the hang of it."

"When yer gettin' an order, tell 'em yer gonna be deliverin' ..."

"I do!"

"How 'bout some deodorant blocks? Can liners? Try some of our bowl cleaner or glass cleaner? See? Suggest things."

The old man was right. Harvey had been so relieved to get a sale that he'd walked out of the customers' stores without pushing. It took too much gumption to ask for more. *Better leave while I'm ahead,* he thought. And they'd picked up on it right away, one after the other. He knew they were just testing him by giving him small orders at first.

"Where're ya goin' tomorrow?" Silver asked.

"Mapleton."

Tuesday was better. Mapleton, a picture-postcard town in the splendid Loess Hills, was ripe for the picking. Two and three items began to appear on every other order for Charlie and Floyd.

"Speed, surprise and resolution are the three things you need to be a paper man," his father had taught him. "There's no appointments out here in the country. Keep movin'."

In Mapleton he could see the bucolic eyes of his prospects matching his restiveness at once. They were consumed by Floyd's energy and confused by his tight jaw and serious lips. But his eyes were what closed the deal. Not their color or their size; they were small and had little light. Floyd's eyes were even hard to see up close. It was their look. Deason eyes were trained to look deep into a prospect's eyes. It was another tool his father gave him.

"Blink first ... look away ... and ya miss yer target. You may not have a smile on yer face, but the eyes gotta be on 'em."

Floyd knew his father never worked the territory this fast. Sixty, then seventy, prospects a day brought forty orders for Thursday and Friday to Albert's lap. On Friday, Floyd's first $250 payday, he overheard his cranky boss tell a will-call customer at 5:00, "I've never had a salesman who could sell starting out like a house on fire. That kid can sell. You remember John Deason? He's John's son. Sells more than his old man did when he started sellin' for me."

When Silver paid him in cash, he made Floyd sign for it. "Want some wine?" Albert asked softly.

With a dusty paper cup in his hand, Floyd waited for those dinosaur legs to lumber over to the back warehouse door to fetch a bottle of red port from its case under the coatrack. The blue-green veins on top of his pouring hand and his curved yellow fingernails were all Floyd could see as the burgundy liquid came within a quarter inch of the paper rim. Before he put his lips to the cup, he saw the wobbly, off-balance step of his happy employer as he returned the bottle to its case in slow motion.

Albert had no son to inherit his business. His only daughter was busy raising her family in Florida. This was why he returned to Willard's chair and plopped down hard on the bookkeeper's seat cushion and spoke out of character to his hotshot salesman across the room.

"I got nobody to leave this business to. You stick around ... and this'll be yours someday."

Floyd winced as he swallowed the wine he'd swished cheek to cheek, then replied cynically, "All this?"

"We do some business here," Albert said smugly. He shifted back with his legs crossed and put his lighter to the longest of a half-dozen cigar butts in the ashtray he'd set on Willard's desk.

The alcohol in the wine hit Floyd fast. After looking at the stack of three-dozen orders to be delivered on Saturday he shot back, "How many times did you offer this business to my father?"

Silver was cool but brusque, "Yer father drank too much and chased the wrong women."

Floyd got up and went over to the wine case to refill his cup. He knew the old man was referring to his mother, and he knew what was coming next.

"After yer mother ran off with that plumbing salesman from Kansas City, yer father went downhill ... drinking more and more."

Floyd knew his next move would bring Silver out of his chair.

"Where you goin' with that?"

Floyd pretended to put the wine bottle in Charlie after pouring his refill, just to antagonize his crusty old boss. "I wasn't going to take your wine," Floyd laughed.

"That's enough wine for you," Albert said as he dropped his head and stared at Floyd over the black frames of his glasses.

"Starting now I want to put fifty bucks of my pay every week in the safe," Floyd said.

If that's what my hotshot salesman wants, no problem, Albert thought as he lumbered over to the safe again.

For over three years Silver opened and closed his safe on Friday for Floyd, who now sported a beard and longer hair. Floyd had managed to get sourpuss Jake upset by calling on his Nebraska accounts more and more; he was supposed to work only Iowa and South Dakota and some distant towns that Jake never reached.

Young Deason was now in his prime for energy. Maybe it was the sweet spring air or the beautiful May morning that sidetracked Floyd to drive twenty-two miles out of his way at the front of his upper Nebraska run to Niobrara, Valentine, O'Neill, Red Cloud, and Chadron. She would be about eighteen now — nearly out of school.

"Josephine," he said aloud. Silver's van was jammed with product to the passenger-side windshield. Floyd had become a master at peddling product off of his van — toilet paper, towels, antifreeze, garbage bags, bowl cleaner, glass cleaner, and deodorant blocks. Silver loved it! Not once did Floyd come back from a cold run with any product left in the van.

He parked in front of the Macy school hoping she'd see his newer van. New walking shoes and clothes covered his filled-out body. *She'll see a confident Floyd this time,* he thought as Charlie rode his hip into the school's front door. His stride was purposeful into the principal's office.

The assistant principal, a white woman from Pender, smiled at the young salesman with the neatly trimmed beard and clean, shoulder-length hair.

"Hi! I'm Floyd with Silver Paper Company in Sioux City. Jake's the salesman who calls on ya. Here's some extra keys yer janitor wanted for the towel and tissue dispensers."

She took the tiny aluminum keys he handed her. "I'll be sure he gets them."

"Thanks. Oh, by the way, when does the next bell ring?"

Glancing at the clock she answered, "In about five minutes."

"An old friend of mine from Pine Ridge goes to school here. She's prob'ly a senior by now. Josephine ..."

"Yes ... Josie Tenna. She's in class now."

"Can I say hi to her real quick when the bell rings?"

"She's in the library ... in study hall. It's the last room down the hallway to your left."

"Thank you."

He walked fast toward her class. But before he realized it consciously, he was that coward Harvey again. His heart beat faster — much faster. He worried about his first words to her now, versus Floyd who would never waste his energy on such trifles. Speed, surprise, resolution. Each word he repeated a dozen times before he stood against the wall near the marked library door.

To bolster himself, he started thinking about his big sales in the territory. The grouchy old butcher at the locker in Avon said he wouldn't give that tight Jew in Sewer City any business, but he'd turned the prospect into a ninety-dollar sale after telling him an anti-Semitic joke he'd heard from Silver. The old spinster secretary in Winner wanted toilet seat covers for her own use and accepted ten thousand when he delivered them. The welder in Anthon could not say no and bought anything suggested. The vet in Custer ...

Just then the bell rang above his head, scaring him even deeper into Harvey. He hated this feeling of no control and wanted to put his fist through the wall behind him. His new duds were now merely covering those insecure tensions that flexed and pulled, straining every nerve. Then came that twitch again under his eye just when the library door opened and the students poured out. Most of them were Native Americans, quieter than the white students he'd seen a thousand times in a thousand schools scattered throughout his territory.

They all stared at him as they passed by. Harvey was all there; his back was tense and his knees were weak. His self-talk replayed an old, dusty record that he didn't want to hear. *What am I doing in this place? She's too young for me. I should be on the road on my run. Run! Yes! I should be running away from this kind of situation when I'm seen as* him, *that despicable coward who should be living at the Y or under a bridge.*

Just then she came out and passed by him without seeing him. She was chatting and laughing with a girlfriend. He watched her walk away. *She's so beautiful,* he thought. Her hair was thicker, with more of an auburn tint, and tied back in a long braid with violet and gold-colored ribbons. Beige knee-high socks and the hem of her goldenrod dress concealed her long, graceful legs, which moved away from him in a narcotizing motion. When she was finally out of sight, he went down the dark hallway on weak bird legs, petrified that she might see him walking by her next class.

He left his product card with the assistant principal. He wrote on the back: *Passing through and just wanted to say hi, Josie. Harvey, the paper man.*

She had taken away Floyd and turned him into Harvey, cowering in the shadows like that wimpy motel owner near Mitchell — a man with palsied hands and voice whom Floyd detested for his weak will. He had let pushy Floyd take advantage of him by foisting a case of cheap one-ply toilet paper on him and trading a night's stay by lying that he was broke.

Harvey's legs barely carried him to his van, enervated and tight with trembling yet strong enough to hit the accelerator hard and bolt the van up the hill and out of Macy. He grabbed a cigarette butt in the ashtray as he made a sharp left out of town. *She's growing into a beautiful woman and I'm still that scared rat she saw in Pine Ridge,* he scolded himself a hundred times while barreling north under the beginning of a May shower.

Over one green hill, then another, then another, it was easy to settle back into Floyd as the isolated farmhouses passed with the agrarian prairie landscape. This was his territory. His confidence returned.

At a hilltop gas station and café, he bought a pack of Salems because they only sold the two brands that the owners smoked. The fat woman behind the counter was French-inhaling a Camel non-filter, blowing smoke down from her wide nostrils over her upper lip darkened by a visible black mustache.

"I have a great buy on some garbage bags that fit that can," Floyd pointed while lighting his first Salem and getting instantly light-headed.

"How strong are they?" she inquired.

Floyd reached into Charlie and pulled out a folded, caramel-colored bag, saying, "Try to tear it."

She pulled on the bag, stretching the plastic until it tore.

"That's plenty strong for beer bottles and chicken bones," he smiled.

"How much?"

A case is $18.50 for 250 bags, or about seven cents apiece. They're twice that much in the store. I got two cases for thirty-five bucks with me. Can I bring 'em in?"

Now shut up! Floyd's dad was screaming inside his head.

He took another hit, keeping his eyes on hers, though she was looking down to his black-and-orange product card thinking of what else she needed.

Keep still, son, his father's voice reminded him.

"Yeah, I'll take the bags."

"Gotta good buy on some TP that won't plug up yer commode."

"Is it that cheap stuff ya poke yer fingers through?"

"So ya double it up. It's got twice the paper per roll as store-bought," he smiled.

"How many in a case?"

"Ninety-six rolls. I can only let ya have one case, though. The rest is sold."

"Okay," she said.

He drove away with his fourth Salem lit. He was happy and dizzy since he'd unloaded four cases of antifreeze with the bags and toilet paper at a cold call. When he was two-wheeling his loaded cart in to his new customer, he found himself thinking about her again: how she brought out Harvey — that unconscious sensitive side that was disjointed and stunted from his materialistic America that promised him wealth if he could sell.

After a half-dozen calls to gas stations, cafés, and grain elevators on his route, his usual zest and animation were gone. All he could think about was his failure to confront her. He breathed a little easier since he'd sold enough product to have a clear view to his passenger window. A beautiful stretch of desolate prairie led him toward O'Neill, but he only consciously saw a few approaching vehicles and a couple dead skunks on the right shoulder picked apart by birds. What usually was a panoramic display of wonder to him — the striking eastern Nebraska countryside — became a blinking, dead stare on the centerline. He began to formulate a plan to return to Macy at the end of his run, but he had to put Floyd behind the wheel and stuff Harvey under a ton of antifreeze.

101

The broken yellow centerline lulled Harvey back in time. It was in the early days when the elder paper man was healthy and laughed a lot, spending time and energy to instill in his son the tricks of his trade that had made him so successful; words that would be a part of him for as long as he lived.

"When yer on the road, keep yer mind on the next town and how you want it to be," the paper man said as he flicked his cigarette ash out his wing window. He'd look over at his son after he'd made his point to see the boy nod, then he'd return his focus to the centerline. "I try to imagine their faces glad to see me when I enter their businesses. Do you remember the three things?"

"Speed ... surprise ... resolution," the boy said with his eyes also on the centerline he'd watched habitually for a hundred thousand miles.

"Exactly!" his father laughed. "Don't waste yer time and energy thinkin' 'bout the town behind ya. They'll see it on yer face ... and know yer not all there. Use yer mind to work for ya. That's the only plannin' I do. Make yer mind work for ya."

His father's laugh came back to him. It was all Floyd behind the wheel driving for O'Neill as he came out of his reverie. Floyd was ready to punish O'Neill for Harvey's cowardice. And he did.

The town never knew what hit it. Floyd was a selling tornado that dropped in from Sioux City with Charlie riding his left hip and his right hand free to shake his prospect's hand. By 2:00 Floyd had already made ten calls, gobbling up seven sales, and diminishing his cargo markedly. A bar, two cafés, a gas station, a feed store, and a century-old brownstone hotel were hit without warning. Damages: $460.00 in less than three hours.

Heading west on Highway 20 toward Valentine, the harsh-looking, stark-gray bluffs and craggy ravines reminded him of his favorite run to the Black Hills in two weeks. He ruminated over his failure in Macy and resolved to return there at the end of his run. His plan began to manifest itself as he looked ahead, just as his father said it would. Thinking about it motivated him to tackle call after call, town after town. It was the perfect excuse to see her again, whether she was in school, at home, dancing, or wherever he found her.

Floyd had his first meal of the day at 5:15 p.m. in Ainsworth. He had sold nearly all of Silver's antifreeze at a co-op service station in Bassett. As he shoveled bite after bite of tasteless diner food into his face, he wished she were with him to see and share in his glory. Out here in his territory he was somebody — not just some cipher in the city known as Silver's delivery boy.

After eating, he decided to continue west 150 miles to Chadron so he could wake up in his new territory in the morning. The air smelled of rain on rocks, fresh and biting to his nostrils as his eyes wandered across the rim of the highest bluffs just to the west and north. He knew if she were with him at that moment, he would take her to romantic places where they could be alone together. *An abandoned homestead would be perfect,* he thought, and he knew of hundreds of them in western Nebraska.

With a quarter of his cargo remaining, Harvey took over the wheel. "There!" he said aloud, pointing to it with his eyes. A craggy old oak tree was standing alone about thirty feet off the highway, its branches yet ash-gray from winter. The massive roots lay exposed, heaved out of the earth by hundreds of freeze-and-thaw cycles. Harvey pulled to the side of the road and sat staring at the tree.

On that desolate stretch of Highway 20 where ten thousand souls have cried over hurts, pains, and solitude, it was safe for him to let go and cry here. He reached under the van's seat for the battery-operated CD player he'd bought one Christmas. The song was ready — the song he'd played six times on six runs over this same stretch of road in the past two-and-a-half years. Each time it let out his pain. Gary Puckett and the Union Gap's song "Woman, Woman" came out of the tiny speaker. Harvey sang along for as long as he could until his bawling and howling drowned out Gary and splashed the agony of that day and his father's lingering memory over his steering wheel.

The day after his mother had left them for that plumbing salesman, young Harvey could see on his father's preoccupied face the look of anger and hurt mixed with the numbing realization that he would be raising their son alone. The grief and anger on the paper man's face was too shocking for the boy to look at. This same road had been their first run together after his mother had left. His father had chosen it because of its desolation. He had seen this isolated oak tree, and it seemed to indicate to him that lonely days and nights lay ahead for both of them. His dad had stopped to get a half-pint of whiskey before noon. Never had he known his father to drink before his last call in the territory.

The bottled tension of those days taught Harvey to cry when he could. It felt good to let the pain out — washing down his face, diminishing the pinch between his eyes, and transforming his face once the song was over. Blowing his nose into the blue windshield towel he carried in Charlie he screamed, "Why did you hold on! Why, Dad? Why!"

* * * * *

The next morning he woke up in Chadron in the same little dive motel his dad liked. Floyd let Harvey call on the first half-dozen prospects that day, and the last call was the clincher. Harvey entered Marlene's Beauty Shop, a two-station closet on Chadron's main drag where Marlene worked by herself. She was changing a small waste basket liner filled with hair and using a paper bag from the IGA. Her snow-white hair was up in a giant bun, and her eyes were red from hair spray and a toxic green eye shadow that made her look like a lizard when she blinked. This time Charlie was riding Harvey's right hip. Harvey tried to remain relaxed and slow-paced versus the frenetic Floyd since his help from Gary Puckett. Marlene's customer shot him a sourpuss look above her magazine from under the pink hair dryer.

"Hi," Harvey smiled.

"Hello," Marlene countered with a half-smile.

He broke the first rule his father taught him when he said, "Can I talk to you for just a minute ... if yer not too busy?"

"I've got a few minutes. Whatcha got?"

Harvey handed her his card and let his eyes follow hers when Floyd would have scanned the room: a plastic grocery store bag in the waste basket, the obvious streaks and smudges on her mirror, a shelf which would perfectly hold a case of his two-ply, and a full ashtray inviting him to ask her to share a smoke. They were all there, and Harvey ignored them until it was too late for Floyd to save.

"I don't use this stuff by the case," she said as she handed Floyd back his card.

Yes, it was too late when Floyd shot back, "I've gotta glass cleaner with our name on it that'll leave no streaks ... the best glass cleaner in the world. Truck drivers swear by it. If you'll try just a half case, I'll betcha you reorder a case next time I'm in town."

"No. I got plenty of glass cleaner 'round here. What I need is someone to do the cleaning," she cackled until Harvey returned a courtesy laugh. "No, sir ... I don't need a thing."

Before noon, Floyd had wrested control of the situation and

had sold the last remaining cases of antifreeze to a Sinclair station and two dozen round urinal blocks to a bar his old man used to frequent. All afternoon Floyd made up for Harvey's wimpy calls, cussing his sensitive partner all the way back to the motel.

The Shamrock Motel was one of his dad's favorite haunts. He always asked for room number eight. So did Floyd, after swapping the room for a case of one-ply toilet paper with the same red-faced Irishman who had spent many an evening at the local tavern with his father. "You want a cash receipt for this?" the motel owner asked after Floyd wheeled in the toilet paper.

Harvey shook Floyd's head no. "Just give me a receipt in exchange for the TP."

Sunday morning at 9:30 they stood under the storefront's awning at the corner of Fourth and Pierce, smiling at each other and waiting for a passing May shower to let up a bit. Granny Tenna had a magenta canvas bag hanging from her shoulder that carried a couple dozen herbs she had mail-ordered from New Mexico. Josie was thinking about Dennis, who had enrolled in art school in Denver for the summer.

"We may as well go for it," Granny smiled after opening her crimson-and-black umbrella. Josie nodded her agreement, and they stepped off the curb sharing the umbrella that Granny held. Josie, a head taller than Granny, hunched down in her yellow windbreaker and denim jeans, giggling as they splashed and dodged the puddles along their six-block walk to St. Vincent's Hospital. They were on their way to see Granny's sister who was recovering from surgery.

"You know what, Granny?" Josie asked.

"What, dear?"

"You know how you showed me to breathe from my center?"

"Yes."

"I find myself doing it more and more during the day, but I don't when I sleep. I'll wake up sometimes holding my breath. How can I breathe from my center when I sleep?"

"Keep telling yourself that you breathe well during sleep," Granny laughed.

Crossing Jackson Street on the fringe of the lower Fourth

area, the streets were lined with dive bars and obscure brothels. A vagrant Native American man approached them from a bar's entrance in the rain with his hand extended. "Got any spare change?" he mumbled.

"Not for you!" Granny snapped, causing the man to jerk back his hand and slink off-balanced into his dark hole. He hiked up his pants with the back of his wrists, and his fingers were crooked and flexed cruelly in five directions.

A half block later they heard footsteps running up from behind them. Granny was ready to jab the vagrant's eye out with the end of her umbrella when the runner said, "Hey, Josie!"

Josie couldn't believe her eyes. "Paper Man!"

Harvey walked with them explaining how he was having breakfast when he saw them. "I left without payin'," he laughed. "They know me. It's okay," he quickly added.

"Where's your jacket?" Granny asked.

"Oh ... I left it. I'll get it later ... when I pay the bill. What brings you to Sioux City?" he asked Josie while walking next to her, trying to make those gold-colored eyes look up at him.

"Granny's sister had surgery this morning. We're going to spend the day with her."

"Mind if I walk with ya? It's not exactly a safe part of town." An awkward pause met his question until Josie's eyes met his and she smiled.

"Why didn't you park at the hospital?" Harvey asked.

"Granny won't drive in Sioux City," Josie replied, knowing what the next words out of Granny's mouth would be.

"I won't drive in this God-forsaken place! It's a madhouse! People turn in front of you left and right! And all the one-way streets! You don't know if you're coming or going in this God-forsaken town!"

"We took the bus," Josie smiled.

The rain was pouring down on Harvey's uncovered head, and

Josie noticed his hair was longer. "We need a bigger umbrella," she laughed.

"Or smaller heads," Harvey said, hoping to get a laugh. Finally, Josie did burst into laughter, relieving Harvey after an interminably quiet five or six steps.

"This isn't the best place to be walkin'," Harvey said. They turned uphill and headed north on Jennings Street where Granny's pace slowed considerably. Harvey thought of his "plan" and held off using it until they were within a block of the hospital. "I'll be makin' my Black Hills run through Pine Ridge soon. Anything you want me to deliver ... a message or somethin'?"

"You're going to Pine Ridge?" Josie asked.

"Yeah. I usually go three times a year ... or at least twice a year."

"I wish I could go. I would love to see Aunt Laura and Uncle Walter."

"What about that boy? What's his name?" Harvey asked.

"Dennis. He's a big boy now," Josie laughed."He's going to art school in Denver."

Josie could see Granny watching his shallow-chest breathing when they stopped to rest at the end of the block. The old woman reached with her right hand and placed her brown palm flat on Harvey's chest. "You breathe way too high. Your breath should be coming from your belly." Granny poked his stomach with her stubby thumb, continuing, "It will calm and energize you. Be aware of your breathing." But then it was as if she were dismissing him after her tip when she said, "Thank you for your company."

"What time does your bus leave," Harvey quickly asked.

"At 6:15," Josie smiled.

"Look ... it's s'posed to rain all day. I can pick you up at 5:30 and give you a ride to the bus depot. It's way too far to walk if it's raining."

"That would be nice," Granny said warmly.

After walking with them to the hospital's front entrance, Floyd cussed himself for not giving them a ride in the van from lower Fourth. Now he had to walk back to the restaurant alone, soaked. *At least I'll see her again,* he thought. He was amazed that he had seen her just minutes before and talked to her — so close to her beautiful face. If he hadn't been looking out of the café window, he'd still be in there drinking his coffee and picking at cold eggs.

His father had always talked about the window of opportunity. "Timing. It's all about timing," he'd told him. "The pretty ones are taken early."

As he drove to his apartment, he realized he had no place for them to sit in his empty van. On top of that, it was a mess; he knew he'd have to clean it up. Knowing Albert would be tinkering with invoices until noon, he went into the Silver Paper Company. Long ago he'd stopped going to the office on Sundays, telling Silver he needed a day away from it.

The bumper of Silver's LTD was parked in its usual place about an inch from the dock. He had no choice but to be Floyd, or he would be in for an embarrassing ride to the bus terminal. The office door was locked. Albert always locked his doors on Sunday, ever since a vagrant robbed him of his wristwatch on a Sunday in 1984. He knocked on the door.

"You fall outta bed?" Silver grumbled after unlocking his door.

"I ran into the girl of my dreams today. I'm giving her and her grandma a ride to the bus depot today at 5:30."

"She pretty?" his boss grinned while looking at Floyd over the top of his mail-order specs.

"No ... she's beautiful."

"She from Sioux City?"

"Pine Ridge."

"Pine Ridge?" Albert asked quizzically.

"Yeah. But she's been living in Macy a long time," Floyd answered.

"Macy? She an Indian?"

"No ... I don't know. Maybe part. But she's terrific. She's a dancer."

Albert scoffed, adding cynically, "Dancer! She'll dance away with yer money if ya don't keep yer pants on."

"She's not that way. I gotta put a case of TP in the van so they have a place to sit when I give 'em a ride."

"Yer not goin' to Macy with that van!" he railed while following Floyd out the back door into the dark warehouse.

At twenty-five-foot intervals, Floyd would reach up, find a string dangling above his head, and yank on it to illuminate a 60-watt bulb which barely lit the path from twelve feet above the floor. The damp chill of the warehouse gave Floyd stiff, jerky movements whenever his wet shirt rubbed against his flesh.

As he rode up the elevator shaft, he ignored his annoyed boss who insisted on badgering him.

"What're you getting, huh?" Albert growled at Floyd.

"Don't worry about it. I'll sell it Monday!" Floyd shot back. From the fifth floor, as he exited the elevator, he could hear the shuffling sound of Albert's dinosaur legs scraping away from him until the back office door slammed shut on its dry hinges. The weight of Silver's very best two-ply rode his shoulder onto the elevator. Then he two-wheeled it through the office since the warehouse door was padlocked until Monday morning.

Albert was hot on Floyd's heels to the dock. He watched his top salesman jump to the ground with an old household broom and open every door of the van. Then he swept out the dust and dirt from a thousand towns in his territory.

"I need fifty bucks of my money," Floyd yelled to the dock.

Silver watched while Floyd positioned the huge case of his best toilet paper in the van's front passenger area.

"Fifty! What for?"

"Just get me the fifty bucks, will ya?"

Albert turned to go into the office.

"Wait!" Floyd called out. "Give me fifty .. And take it out of my check next Friday. I don't want to touch my money."

Albert muttered something with his unlit cigar dribbling juice down the corner of his mouth while digging into his baggy pants until he pulled out a wad of cash. He must have had close to a grand in hundreds, fifties and twenties. He handed down a fifty to Floyd. "Ya takin' her dancin'?" Albert smiled. His cloudy blue eyes — old slits of mischief — ripened from five decades of seeing it all a thousand times.

"My dad used to tell me about a window of opportunity ... the timing it takes ... Good luck, he called it," Floyd smiled.

"Yer father climbed out of many windows after getting lucky," Albert laughed. He shook his head at the boy's foolishness that he secretly envied. "She must be some girl," the old man grinned.

"She is! She's got gold-colored eyes, Albert! No ... really. Have you ever seen gold eyes?"

"I've seen enough of 'em," he shrugged.

"I tell ya ... I'd marry this girl. She's a catch. I get all excited when I'm around her. And she's not doin' anything to make me feel this way. It's some kind of ... chemistry. Pure beauty must do that to men."

Albert muttered something and turned to go back to his office as Harvey finished cleaning the van's dash and motor cover with a rag he used to check the oil level. Glancing in Albert's direction, Harvey noticed a $50 bill lying on the dock where Albert had been standing. Although he never really thought about keeping the money, Harvey knew he'd never miss it or even know that he'd dropped it.

"Ya dropped a fifty on the dock behind ya," Harvey said.

He turned around picked up the money, mumbling a "thank you" before turning an emotional 180 as if humbled and embarrassed.

Harvey followed him to the office, staying close behind his boss in case he fell down the dock steps. After signing for the case of toilet paper and the advance, Harvey turned down the old man's offer of lunch, explaining that he had too many things to get done before picking up his visitors from Macy.

* * * * *

At 5:30 he'd been parked for ten minutes in the emergency parking zone. Fearing he'd be caught combing his hair in the rearview mirror, he got out and stood outside the hospital entrance in his best jeans and favorite short-sleeved plaid shirt. His hair was as styled as he could get it, and his nerves had been calmed by an hour-long soak in the tub. But it was the deep breathing from his belly that made him realize he would have to make some changes to get a girl like Josie into his life.

It was Harvey who stood outside the hospital waiting for his guests. He had Gary Puckett stashed under his seat, ready and willing to help if needed. Floyd was left at home, going down the drain with the bath water.

She was changing him fast, returning him to a ritual he had done faithfully for six months after his father died. With every low and deep inhalation, he imagined tiny white crosses flowing in his bloodstream sent from his heart. When he exhaled, tiny black pitchforks were pushing out — cleaning his eyes and soothing his muscles, and relaxing his jaw and mouth to a contented countenance he so craved.

"Hi," Josie smiled as she exited the hospital. She noticed the difference in him right away and for the first time felt a chemistry between them.

"Hi," he smiled back. "Where's yer grandma?"

"She's waiting for her sister to get her evening meal. She wants to add some herbs and minerals to her diet."

"You wanna wait in the van? I can play some music while we're waiting," Harvey offered.

As they made their way to the van, Harvey wondered if his feet were even touching the ground. He opened the van's passenger door and explained, "I made a passenger seat that should be big enough for both of you."

Josie laughed after lifting up the end of the bath towel draped over the box and examining the box of toilet paper.

"It's our best two-ply," Harvey smiled, nearly choking in embarrassment. He loved the sound of her laugh — loud and healthy and natural. She continued laughing after sitting on the makeshift seat.

"It's comfortable," she said grinning at him.

"My boss is Jewish. He won't put a seat in. He says he can get more product delivered this way."

"Granny says that the Jews own Sioux City and won't let it grow."

"She's right about that. So many young people move away after high school. A lot of them say the same thing."

"I thought Sioux City was big until I went to Omaha. Have you ever been there?" she asked.

"Oh, yeah. Several times."

"I'm going to college in Lincoln this fall," she added.

"Really?"

"The University of Nebraska. They have a top-notch dance program there. Granny and I walked around the campus in Lincoln. The campus alone is bigger than the entire town of

Macy!" she laughed. An awkward silence followed before she remarked, "Where's your radio?"

"My boss bought a van without a radio. I have a portable CD player, but I just remembered I need batteries."

It was a lie. Gary Puckett wasn't right for her. She was way too mature for "Young Girl." Besides that, he thought his tiny CD player would sound cheap — like his boss. "You cold?" he asked.

"No, I'm fine, thank you."

When she turned to see if Granny was coming, he could smell the sweet fragrance of flowers coming from the curls in her golden-red hair. He said the first thing that came to mind. "I'm moving to Omaha or Lincoln too."

"You are?"

"Yeah ... I'm going to start my own paper company. That area would be bigger and provide more territory for me."

He couldn't believe he said that. Floyd had just crawled out of the drain and found him. But she made him say things without thinking. He was willing to move to a strange city on a whim. Floyd was now trying to take over completely.

"Yeah, I'm lookin' forward to a change. I was thinkin' Lincoln or Omaha."

"It's funny how I first saw you way back in Pine Ridge, and now you'll be close to where I go to college," she said.

"Yeah ... kinda weird," he said.

Even Floyd could not look into those eyes for more than a heartbeat. He had been overpowered by her when she came to the church in Pine Ridge, and those feelings came rushing back to him as he sat mesmerized by her.

Just then Granny came out of the hospital with her ethereal bag of remedies strapped over her shoulder. He watched the way Josephine gracefully moved off the case and out of the van without a sound. The waft in the air from her motion sent him a sweet breeze he would call "Josephine" — an alluring, seductive scent that was as rare and precious as these very moments he could be so close to her.

Granny said nothing about sharing her two-ply seat with Josie. They were both accustomed to seeing poverty and the makeshift adaptations that were prevalent on reservations.

Harvey drove slowly to the depot. The silence was killing him. He knew he soon would be saying goodbye to her, not knowing when, if ever, he would see her again. His palms were sweating on the steering wheel when he turned into the depot's parking lot.

Josie was having the same thoughts about seeing him again. She had never been on a date with a boy in her life, but for the first time she felt she was ready. "When will you be in Macy again?" she asked.

"Oh ... in a couple of weeks or so," he said, looking deep into her eyes and hoping her question meant she wanted to see him again. "I'll go into the depot with you ladies to be sure yer bus is on time."

The terminal was stuffy and occupied by a couple dozen people with dirty luggage at their feet. Granny recognized some Native Americans from Winnebago and Decatur. Harvey sat in a row of polychromatic plastic seats, leaving an empty yellow one between himself and Josie as Granny checked on their bus at the ticket counter. As hard as he tried to think of something clever to make conversation, nothing came to him. He was afraid to open his mouth; he couldn't risk her not liking Floyd when she apparently liked Harvey. "Looks like the bus will be full," he finally said.

Her nod and knowing half-smile was too much for Harvey to take. He couldn't leave her in this place only to be sandwiched into a bus. He wanted to rescue her from this and spend more time with her since he could have to wait ten thousand hours until their next meeting.

Granny returned from the ticket counter and sat between them. "Our bus is about fifteen minutes late," she said.

Harvey could see that every eye in the depot was staring at Josie. A drunk-looking Indian man using the pay phone was looking right at her while talking into the receiver. Harvey decided to summon that side of his personality she hadn't seen since Pine Ridge. He'd risk it now or else he'd watch her dance away from him — again — on her way as she grew and matured and expanded her life into big-city Omaha or Lincoln while he withered and died a thousand times in the country, punishing himself for not trying.

Floyd stood up and looked down at them as if they were prospects. "Hey! I got an idea. Skip the bus and let's go to Macy in my van!"

The ladies looked at each other in stupefaction. "But they won't refund our tickets," Granny blurted as she held up the tickets.

"I'll handle that," Floyd said, then he confidently walked toward the bulbous agent behind the counter after swiping their tickets from Granny's hand. He saw the same scarcity mentality that ruled his territory and had destroyed his father. *Why not take my free ride and let the refund go?* he thought to himself. *You're getting home faster and without all that riffraff. How much can half a round-trip ticket to Macy set ya back, anyway?*

As he neared the counter, Floyd knew what to do. He'd seen his dad do it a hundred times. "Hi. What's the manager's name?"

The fat man looked up from his crossword puzzle, desultory and put out by another slug riding the bus. "John Reeves," he frowned.

Floyd handed the man a tiny, aluminum towel dispenser key. "Yeah ... John wanted me to bring ya this extra key for yer towel

117

dispensers in the john. It fits yer towel and TP dispensers. I told John I'd drop this by tonight if I could drive my friends to Macy. He said I could get refunded their return tickets."

The agent took the tickets, examined them, and looked into the pale blue eyes of the closer. He had Floyd sign for the twelve-dollar refund.

"Thanks," Floyd said. "Be sure to give him that key."

"I will."

Josie had been watching him since he walked to the ticket counter. She noticed his light step and the way his neck craned forward slightly as if he were an animal on the prowl. It was something she remembered seeing in his father that day in Pine Ridge. It was attractive to her — like a man at work without fear. It was a level of confidence she wasn't used to seeing on the reservation.

"He did it," Granny whispered to her. "By God, he did it."

Floyd smiled at Josie when he handed Granny her refund. Josie smiled back and asked, "We don't have to ride back on the bus?"

"Let's go, ladies," Floyd said.

The two ladies shared a seat on the toilet paper case with Josie sitting beside the warm engine cover and Granny sitting next to her by the door. Harvey was careful not to accelerate or brake too fast during their drive to Macy. He wanted to play "Young Girl" on his CD player, but the timing was all wrong.

Josie listened intently to him as they drove the flat stretch of Highway 77 to Homer. He talked about the beautiful hills surrounding Homer, the nostalgic Homer schoolhouse tour, and about the iron-rich water pouring from a rusty spout in these hills for over a century. "It's good and cold too," he added.

"We should see that schoolhouse, Granny," Josie said.

"Yes, I've been meaning to tour it, "Granny answered.

118

Floyd saw his chance. "How 'bout we all tour it next weekend?"

"That would be fun!" Josie exclaimed.

"Yes, that would be nice," Granny resounded.

Harvey jumped at Granny's invitation to stay and have some tea when he parked in front of her lavender house. At last he was free to be the more relaxed Harvey, the gentle young man who could be patient and enjoy every moment.

The house smelled of ginger from the fresh ginger cookies left to cool on top of Granny's gas stove. Josie lit a series of vanilla-scented candles in the small front room and carried one to the kitchen table. Then she lit two more on the windowsill above the sink. Granny and Josie happily watched the young man eat four cookies with his cup of juniper berry tea. They didn't tell him the cookies were laced with licorice root and devil's claw. They giggled and chatted about him softly while he was in the bathroom. "Imagine the toxins that boy must have inside him," Granny said.

Josie only nodded in agreement, but she told Granny with her eyes that she liked the paper man from Sioux City.

"You like him ... I can tell," Granny said.

Josie smiled, then blushed, then giggled out loud.

"He is rather handsome," Granny whispered. "And polite as can be," she added.

"I couldn't believe it when he said he's going to be moving to Omaha or Lincoln," Josie whispered.

"I predict you two will be friends a long time," Granny smiled.

"Just friends?" Josie wondered out loud.

"Yes, Josephine. You will dance away from him to live your dream," Granny smiled knowingly. "He's not capable of loving or of being loved."

"How do you know that? He's young. He could change, ya know," Josie shot back, surprised by her own words.

Granny's smile lines were always there, little creases going up her temples like friendly webs of wisdom. So many years ago she'd had another life and another name. Clair Lin Morgan grew up on the Pine Ridge Reservation. She was a very intelligent girl and taught herself to read the newspapers stuffed in her hole-ridden shoes. After getting pregnant at the age of fourteen by a man thirty years her senior, she decided she wanted to be as healthy as possible and raise a healthy baby. As often as she could get to Hot Springs, she would visit the library and read everything she could about diet, nutrition, and natural healing.

Eventually she got at job at the VA Hospital in Hot Springs as a nurse's aide. One patient in her charge was heavily addicted to morphine. Clair gradually replaced the woman's morphine with black cohosh and feverfew. Although her patient had been making great progress, one night the woman committed suicide by diving head-first from her window on the fourth floor of the hospital. Clair had informed her supervisors of her herbal intervention just the day before the woman took her last flight. The hospital never had to reveal what had happened, but Clair was advised to move out of state and keep quiet to avoid prosecution.

Clair and her daughter — Josie's grandmother — moved to Mankato, Minnesota, for a year, then she heard from a friend about a house in Macy she could live in if she made some repairs to it. The only thing she didn't repair was the foundation.

Harvey, Josie and Granny toured the old Homer schoolhouse with Granny staying so close to Josie that there was no room for flirting. Were it not for the fact that there was no phone in the Tenna household, Harvey would have called Josie every week. He began working eastern Nebraska in order to visit Josie once a week after she graduated from high school. Granny went bowling and to four movies with them before she felt she could trust Harvey to be alone with her beautiful great-granddaughter.

* * * * *

They laughed for the first thirty miles on their way to Yankton. It was their last evening out together before Josie moved to Lincoln to start her freshman year at the University of Nebraska. They hadn't so much as held hands yet, concentrating instead on building their friendship. Major life changes were on the horizon for both of them, and the fears they had that these changes could destroy a romantic relationship before it even got a chance to start kept them both distant. Josie wanted to work and study hard and eventually live her dream of dancing professionally. Harvey was mustering the courage to go off on his own as a jobber and buy product from Silver.

Josie had brought along an inflatable plastic seat cushion that Granny had given her to sit on. It made a croaking sound on the case of toilet paper that was so hilarious to them that she left it in place, both of them enjoying the laughter halfway to Yankton until she finally tossed it into the cargo area. She had noticed before that Harvey's skin below his eye twitched now and then when they were in the van. At first she thought it was nervousness because she was with him, but now she knew the source.

"That smell is what causes your eye to twitch," she said.

"What smell?"

"See? You're so used to it you don't even notice it," she laughed.

"What?"

She reached behind her to the floor in the cargo area and grabbed a bag of deodorant blocks. Holding them to her nose, the mothball aroma was so pungent she knew it had to be affecting the paper man's nervous system. Then she noticed several more bags of the blocks behind his seat. She put the bag of blocks she was holding on the engine cover between them. "Get rid of those ... and you'll get rid of your twitch."

"But I sell a ton of those," he replied.

"Is it worth it?" she smiled.

After thinking for a moment he said, "I'll get rid of 'em ... and see if that's it."

He watched her raking up all the urinal blocks in the van before tossing them out her window. Floyd laughed, pulled over to the shoulder, and opened his back and side doors. He then continued down the road, airing out his van at seventy-five miles an hour, with the two of them laughing the whole time.

"Have you gotten new batteries for your CD player yet?" she smiled.

"No ... not yet."

He watched her reach into a back pocket of her denim shorts, her long, tan, muscular legs together all the way down to her leather sandals. *Keep your eyes on the road and your mind on your driving before you make this your last date ... permanently!* he told himself. She radiated a natural sexiness that made Harvey feel more like a man than any other woman ever had. She wore no makeup. Her thick auburn hair hung just below her shoulders. Her blouse was silky with gray and orange butterflies of different sizes floating above a mauve-colored rope belt that Granny had made for her. Her breasts were barely noticeable when she twisted her torso to check her other back pocket with her other hand. He thought her most attractive feature, though, was her healthy glow, starting with those golden eyes that had such a wide light and were surrounded by a large area of whiteness.

She handed him four batteries.

"Thanks," he said. He reached under the seat and handed her the CD player and the batteries. "I only have one CD with me. It's in there."

She popped open the cover and smiled to herself before seeing that he was blushing. "Who's Gary Puckett?" she asked.

"He's a little before our time," Harvey said, keeping his face turned away from looking at her.

After she loaded the fresh batteries he realized she was pressing the "play" button. *This probably was a bad idea,* Harvey thought as "Young Girl" began to cackle over the player's tiny speaker. Gary sang about the young girl on his mind: "My love for you is way out of line ... better run, girl ... you're much too young, girl."

Unbeknownst to Harvey, Gary and his band were doing in three minutes what this paper man had only dreamed for the past decade; Josephine Ann Tenna was falling in love for the first time. Although it was not unlike the infatuations any girl can have, she knew this was not just a girl's crush. She looked out her passenger window at the poverty in all directions as they cruised through the Santee Indian Reservation. Gary's lyrics

123

continued: "Beneath your perfume and makeup ... you're just a baby in disguise. Get out of here before I have the time to change my mind ..."

By the time "Young Girl" ended, she was still facing the van's passenger window. Harvey clicked off the CD player. She remained silent, unable to turn to him. Josie had been having dreams recently about one of the Seven Rites of the Sacred Canunpa that Granny had taught her during her first year in Macy. It was the *Auric'a Dowampi* — "Girl into Womanhood." *This is it,* she knew. She was moving ahead to that space where a girl gives her worldly flesh and all else that is private in these material days. Yes, Josephine was knocking. Not loudly, but just enough for the girl to curiously open the door and see she was being invited to play.

She hadn't cried in a long time. Harvey kept looking over at her, then back to the road a dozen times over the next quarter of a mile. She now knew so clearly and understood her young mother's aloneness in Pine Ridge and the exultation of being on a date with a traveling salesman. *Perhaps,* she thought, *I have been prepared for this moment — a moment that can sideswipe my heart and leave me aching and hurting.*

"Josie ... you okay?" Harvey asked quietly.

She nodded yes, sniffing up her tears.

"What's wrong?"

Silence. Then she covered her face and hunched forward on top of the toilet paper case, scaring the hell out of him. He pulled over and parked on the quiet shoulder, then he got out and walked over to her side of the van. She moved over to her left as far as she could on the box so he could sit next to her, but she kept facing the driver's side so he couldn't see her face. He climbed in and sat next to her, keeping silent for several moments. "I thought you would like Gary Puckett," he said sheepishly.

She laughed a little, then more until they were both laughing hard and long. A livestock truck whooshed past them at eighty miles an hour, rocking the van and startling them. Their eyes met, and each noticed joy then fear reflected in the other's eyes. They knew they both felt the same thing sitting on that shoulder. He didn't press her why she was crying; somehow Harvey knew not to ask.

"Hold me," she whispered.

She leaned into his shoulder just as another truck sped by. He buried his face into her thick, sweet-smelling hair with his right arm across the front of her and holding onto her left shoulder, gently pressing her to his chest. They were quiet together for several minutes, breathing together and embracing.

"I breathe better now ... like Granny said to," he said.

"Uh-huh," she said softly.

He told her about the crosses and pitchforks and how it really relaxed him in a hot bath, but then how he would always "lose it" after his first call on a prospect. She understood but said nothing. She turned Gary's music back on, and they continued to hold each other as they listened to the music.

She wanted him to kiss her. She kissed him. It was a wonderful surprise, better than Harvey or Floyd had ever imagined. She tenderly and slowly kissed his chin and down his neck. After some fifteen minutes of just kissing, Harvey was beginning to wonder what he should do. That side of him that was Floyd wanted to press her now and relieve the stabbing pain in his groin. But Harvey, with every fiber of his being, wanted to protect the innocence of this angel in his arms. In an unprecedented momentary victory, Harvey won.

They held hands all the way to the Red Steer's parking lot in Yankton. Sitting across the table from each other in a secluded black-vinyl booth, Harvey confessed to her how his physical desire for her was painful for him, and it was taking every ounce of his self-restraint to not find a way to relieve himself.

"Granny would know what to do for you," she said.

Harvey courtesy-laughed and added, "Yeah ... she'd shoot me."

Harvey returned her to Macy at midnight. They held hands all the way from Yankton and committed to seeing each other exclusively. When he walked her to Granny's front door, she pulled him inside where they kissed among Granny's flickering vanilla candles, while Granny's low-belly snoring continued without interruption from behind her bedroom door. "Paper Man ... I love you," she quietly whispered.

At three in the morning, crossing the Combination Bridge into Iowa, the same pain returned. Over and over he thanked God for the best night of his life. He knew he would have to move to Omaha or Lincoln to be near her when she went to school, or he would lose her. Even the horrible stench of the stockyards was sweet to him, and it confirmed in his mind that the time had come to make his move — his biggest move.

* * * * *

Silver knew it was coming. Eventually they all did it. "You stick around here and I'll cut ya in on the business," he said.

"No, Albert. I want to buy product from you at ten percent over cost and make my own money," was Floyd's adamant response.

"Yeah! Off my customers," Silver snapped.

"They're not yer customers," Floyd shot back.

"They're my cabinets for God's sake!"

"And I put 'em in! Nobody else would've! You'll still get ten percent off everything I sell."

Albert sat low in Willard's chair, his face flushed.

"What's wrong?" Floyd asked.

"I don't feel so good," the old man said.

Harvey went over to him and told him to take some slow, deep breaths. He did, whistling air up his nostrils. "That's it. Don't worry ... it'll all work out," Harvey assured him.

"Yeah," Albert muttered. The loss of his best salesman weighed heavily on his ever-sloping shoulders — along with the $500 weekly profit he enjoyed after paying Floyd's salary and expenses. Yes, Albert knew this was coming. Floyd was a much better salesman than his father.

Floyd followed Albert down the steps of the dock. Bolstered by the port, he could hardly contain himself as he thought about his date with Josie later that evening and telling her of his break with Silver Paper Company. He would use The Paper Man as his new business name.

"I'll have to get my own delivery vehicle," Floyd said to Albert as he managed the last wooden step.

"Rome wasn't built in a day," Silver said.

Floyd opened the heavy, rusty-hinged LTD door for his tired boss and watched him as he sat down hard on his cigar-burned driver's seat. "Can you help me get a van so I don't have to touch my savings?" Floyd asked.

"We'll see," Albert mumbled, then he picked out a dry cigar butt from his jammed ashtray. His lips were flexed wide, indicating he was ready to leave.

The wine gave Floyd even more spine than usual. "No, Albert. That's too vague. I need to hit the road with product. I'll need a van Monday."

"I'll call 'em Monday. I gotta get home ... my wife has a headache."

Floyd watched the old car bounce over the railroad tracks

and potholes before pausing briefly at the stop sign. *My own business,* he smiled big to himself. The rush of going into the fall on his own with the most beautiful girl in Siouxland was a dream come true.

Josephine

In May of her sophomore year at the University of Nebraska–Lincoln, Josie danced by the classroom window that looked out to the street where Harvey would be parking. She led the Advanced Creative Dance, and this was her last class of the day. Three dozen muscled, thick-legged farm girls from all over Nebraska and Wyoming were enrolled in the class. They were very strong young ladies — used to hard work and bearing the toll that four markedly different seasons in the Midwest takes on their figures and light complexions.

They all knew her as Josephine. Only her two roommates knew her last name or called her Josie. In dance, however, she only went by Josephine. It was part of a plan brainstormed by Floyd one night after a date when they were parked on a deserted country road. As Josephine, she could be the dancer she knew she had the potential to be but that her secret doubts and inhibitions prevented her from being. Just like Floyd could sell ice cubes to Eskimos, but Harvey could barely manage to sell water to a man dying of thirst.

Josephine led her classmates by staying lost in the dance many levels deeper than anyone else — but not today. Harvey was picking her up as usual this late Friday afternoon. He was living in Omaha, which was forty miles away. It was close enough to see each other on the weekends, but far enough that they were each able to concentrate on their respective tasks during the week.

Granny paid Josie's tuition, room and board at Holly Dorm on campus. Josie knew her funding would come to an abrupt halt if she were to live with Harvey, so she stayed focused on her studies and occupied her mind with her plans to go to New York and make a name for herself on Broadway. Even though Josie really loved Harvey and longed to sleep in the same bed with him every night and wake up in the same house with him every morning, the words she'd heard Granny say a hundred times rang in her ears: "If you live with a man, you marry him or else you are just his whore."

The girls knew their class leader was the most beautiful and talented of them all, and they knew she was crazy about the Paper Man — but most of them couldn't see why. One time after class Josie overheard one of the girls having a conversation with a faculty member. "I really don't see what she sees in that guy. He's obviously quite a bit older than her ... and way too cocky and arrogant. Plus, I hear he's a real sneaky guy to do business with ... a borderline crook." Josie just smiled to herself after hearing the conversation. She knew the girl had only seen Floyd, but Josie had been dating Harvey for two years, and it had been the most fun she'd ever had in her life. He had a fancy apartment in Millard on the western edge of Omaha, which he had gotten just to be closer to her. And he had a new van and plenty of money — which he spent on her.

Josie's alter ego, Josephine, was as dark and foreboding as Harvey's alter ego, Floyd. She had the consistent, negative reminder of her mother's promiscuity and drunkenness. She knew the emptiness of growing up fatherless. They were always there, pounding on her heart, vying for her attention and demanding that she expend her energies nursing her hurts and living in a past she could never change. The two of them, Floyd and Josephine, were two solipsists captivated by their own reality — no more self-involved than any other couple with material goals, but far more talented.

Floyd's van was new and white with black printed lettering on both sides: The Paper Man/Paper and Janitorial Supplies/Free Delivery. Silver had paid for the new van with his top jobber paying it back by adding $75.00 to every order when he picked up every Monday morning in Sioux City. And Floyd's confidence was soaring. Business was great and he had Josie.

"He's here!" she wanted to squeal. Every fiber of Josie's being begged her to bolt out of the class and smother him with love, but Josephine remained poised and in control. She had heard him coming. Everyone could. He had the van's windows down and was blaring "Lady Willpower" from the stereo. Her classmates muttered to each other how corny it was, but each in her heart coveted the Paper Man's romantic nature. He did this every Friday, and her eyes welled with tears every time at the same moment in the romantic ballad: "Lady Willpower, it's now or never, give your love to me; one thing you can be sure of ... I'll take good care of your love ... if you will let me give you mine."

All the girls waited for the tears and teased her about it. She was Josie to him — not Josephine, the serious dancer who was bound to make it big one day. They would watch her run out of the class with her gym bag on her shoulder, again emotionally swept away by that toilet paper salesman.

Floyd had worn a full beard since November, but Josie preferred him clean-shaven. He turned down the stereo's volume. He smelled his fingers for any residue of cigarette smoke because he knew that soon she would be kissing them. Floyd had worked that week in northwest Iowa — Dutchmen and Germans. Tight country to peddle anything, but he did well considering it rained three out of five days since loading product

131

off Albert's dock. He reviewed in his mind the places he'd been during the week. A waitress in Sheldon he'd been casually flirting with for three years bought a case of toilet paper. A beauty shop owner in Sibley traded him garbage bags for a haircut. He'd met his quota with quick sales in Rock Rapids and Rock Valley. He'd tried a new sales approach in the resort town of Spirit Lake that streaked him to seven sales before he got a rejection. Then he laughed as he remembered the mechanic in Pocahontas who had a pet monkey that peed on the floor every time he heard a car horn. After laying on the van's horn to see what the monkey would do, Floyd sold him two drums of sweeping compound, two cases of garbage bags, a case of one-ply toilet paper, two cases of towels for the monkey, and a case of bowl cleaner.

Just as Josie opened the van's passenger door and hopped onto the "real" passenger seat, "Young Girl" began playing on the van's stereo. They locked eyes, smiling, as they always did when they reunited on Friday. Before they ever touched, each had to communicate to the other through only their eyes what kind of week it had been and how they felt about the other. No words — only eyes.

When the song was over and the CD stopped, Josie looked into Floyd's eyes and gave her accounting. "Sales were good. Rough driving weather. You smoked a lot." Then her voice faltered; she could see the strained dark blue in Floyd's eyes vanish as Harvey took his place. "You missed me. You were faithful. And," she laughed, "you want me naked."

Harvey took his turn. He began with the left eye of Josephine. "You pushed yourself this week ... physically exhausting yourself in the dance. You want something ... a bigger venue to show your talent to the world." Then he moved to her right eye, pausing to see a softer gold color that was all Josie. "You missed me. You were loyal to us ... no wandering.

There were times when you thought about Dennis and how he was doing in art school. You want me to hold you."

He was right on the money. They sat looking at each other while leaning closer and closer until their noses touched, then their lips touched without kissing. "I love you so much," she cried.

"I need all of you pressed close to me," he whispered.

She continued to cry, kissing under his eyes and down to the hair on his chin. "I have to go to my room and shower," she whispered.

"No ... I'd rather have you this way ... all sweaty and spent ... like me," he smiled.

He started the engine and headed northeast out of Lincoln toward Omaha. She watched him smoke a cigarette and blow his smoke out his open window without getting the van filled with second-hand smoke.

"Harvey?"

"Yeah?"

"When are you going to shave?"

"I shaved this morning."

"No ... your beard."

He blew out a cloud of smoke and thought about it before answering. He was having fun with it because she was not nagging him, instead giving him the space to be creative.

"I'll make a deal with ya ..." he said playfully.

"Yeah?" she smiled.

"You help me unload this product tonight ... and I'll shave it off tonight."

"Really?" she exclaimed, putting her arm around his neck while glancing back at the remaining product. "Well, come on, Paper Man ... is this as fast as this thing'll go?"

Floyd parked at the back door of a roadside biker bar outside of Waverly. His red two-wheeler stood empty with its blade facing the open storage room door behind the bar. He sat on a case of toilet paper in the storage room writing up a bogus order on a blank invoice form when a waitress walked in on him.

"Hey," Floyd said without skipping a beat, "I've got an order that ... I forgot her name ... the day bartender?"

"Marti," the waitress said.

"Yeah! Marti! She ordered this stuff over a week ago. Who's workin' tonight? The owner?"

"The night manager, Junior," she answered.

Floyd made his way through the crowded establishment and showed his bogus invoice to six-foot-four, three-hundred-pound Junior behind the bar.

"Who ordered this s—t?" Junior barked.

"Marti," Floyd smiled.

Junior glared into Floyd's eyes then down to the invoice. Just as the super-sized bartender began shaking his head no, Josephine came in the front door, slamming the door behind her. She was barefoot, wearing tight cut-offs and a very form-fitting little tank top.

Floyd and Junior stood mesmerized — staring at her as she put change in the jukebox and moved gracefully to the dance floor. Floyd could see the effect she was having on every man in the bar. Josephine began dancing to Steppenwolf's "Born to be Wild." Floyd was as lost as Junior in the erotic swirling motion of her hips as her free-flowing arms moved through the air as if there was no space between them. He was so lost, in fact, that he forgot to collect from Junior at the right moment and had to wait for the music and Josephine to stop. Junior stood frozen except for his tongue moving behind his lips like a Saint

Bernard anticipating a meal. Floyd knew he couldn't interrupt the bartender's salivation or he'd mistime the close and lose the sale. He just waited. It was beautiful.

Halfway through the performance Floyd realized his beard was not the only thing he was going to lose; she was forcing Floyd to hold onto her.

After the song and raucous ovation, Josephine walked over to the end of the bar opposite Floyd and Junior. She sat on a barstool with her long legs crossed and winked seductively at the numb bartender.

"Ninety-six ninety, Junior. Will ya pay me for what Marti ordered so I can get outta here?" Floyd said.

It worked. Junior went to his register to get Floyd's cash so he could wait on the beautiful dancer. When Junior finished counting the money out to Floyd, Floyd said, "She's got gold-colored eyes, Junior. You ever seen gold eyes on a woman ... or anybody?"

"No ... I ain't."

"Well, you'll never see 'em now," Floyd said.

Junior turned and she was gone.

"Thanks, Junior," Floyd waved with his cash before leaving out the back way with his two-wheeler.

Floyd and Josephine laughed for a mile down the road as they headed for Floyd's apartment in Millard, just west of Omaha's city limits. "You were terrific, Josephine! See ... you were the distraction — the edge — I needed at that moment! It was perfect!"

She reached over and pulled on his beard. "And you shave this off tonight ... Floyd!"

He resisted telling her how the entire bar was mesmerized by her and that she should dance professionally. He knew she wasn't conscious of her performance — she had simply been lost in the dance in order to move his product. She was in love with both sides of the Paper Man. He needed only Josie, her soft feminine side that balanced him. Harvey could see the crisis he was facing with her. But could he stop the warrior Floyd from chopping his way through it, stifling her to make himself even more powerful and controlling and manipulative?

* * * * *

The treeless rolling hills and deep ravines surrounding Millard were lush green on Josie and Harvey's early Saturday morning walk to Mom's Café two miles south of his apartment. They were both famished for the best country breakfast in the entire Omaha area. By the time they reached the restaurant, their appetites were ravenous.

As they devoured Mom's buttermilk pancakes, sausages, eggs and biscuits with Mom's special sausage gravy, Harvey decided to let Josie know how easily she could make it anywhere with her looks and talent. "You should think about striking while the iron's hot ... you know, while you still have it all," he said.

She could feel him pushing her away and sensed that he felt as if she had betrayed him or cheated on him — something that hurt him to the deepest part of his core.

"Why are you doing this?" Josie asked.

"Because I want you to reach yer dreams."

"We would lose us," she said.

"I don't want to think about that. If I don't let you go, you'll resent me and eventually just go anyway."

Their walk home from Mom's was a blur compounded by indigestion. The two warriors were out, tramping back to his apartment tight-jawed and proud. Neither noticed the natural beauty around them — the colors, the birds, the flowers and trees

— that Josie and Harvey loved and appreciated. The lone weeping willow fenced behind the front yard of an isolated Victorian house went by them without mention. The previous fall they had named the tree Granny because of its enveloping branches. The Willow Granny was a touchstone for Josie; its jutting roots gave her a warm feeling of family that usually came when Harvey's soft hand slipped into hers. But not this time. Floyd walked two steps ahead of her.

Now she kept quiet about the Sacred Canunpa rite, The Changing of Worlds. "No death ... only a change," Granny said. But this, she knew, meant the death of Harvey and Josie. The rites of Josephine and the dance-away lover Granny had foretold was manifesting into reality, splitting the lush green countryside into a nauseous specter for Josie.

* * * * *

Floyd had taken the lead in the relationship, forcing Josephine to follow her dream. He punished his prospects with a vengeance, selling anyone with a heartbeat his toilet paper at cost if they bought three cases of garbage bags at a fifteen-dollar-per-case markup. Since he only made nine or ten bucks on a case of toilet paper anyway, it was a perfect and profitable lead-in.

All week in the territory he thought about her. Although she had planned to spend a month at Granny's, he tried his best to convince her that she should spend her summer in New York or Chicago. She could work part time as a receptionist to pay her expenses. He knew in his heart he would support her — even if he lost her. His nights on the road were so long that his energy waned. He started drinking a beer or two before bed to help him sleep; but after the second beer he'd see his father in the mirror, then he'd shuffle off to his motel bed dejected and lonely. His morning calls were far from animated and lacked the vibrance he'd normally exhibited.

The following weekend Harvey took Josie to Macy where she broke the news to Granny that she was spending her summer in New York. "The best dancers are there, and maybe I can earn enough money to pay for my next semester in Lincoln."

Granny liked Josie's reasoning. She knew this would get her granddaughter some exposure to another culture, instead of simply getting indecently exposed down some desolate country road with the Paper Man.

From his van Harvey watched the emotional goodbye between Granny and Josie in the driveway of her lavender Macy home. He knew in his heart that the girl of his dreams was going to be away for a long time.

* * * * *

Harvey's beard was full again by late July. He was planning on moving back to Sioux City in the fall, even though he was still getting two or three love letters from Josie every week. As he lay on his bed, he tossed her balled letter to the ceiling then caught it again. He was trying to read between the lines of her most recent letter:

> *Dearest Harvey,*
> *I love you! Things keep moving so fast in NYC. Here's a payment of $50.00 on my rent you so generously covered during my first two months in the Big Apple.*
> *I'm in line to audition for an off-Broadway musical next Tuesday at 6:00 a.m.*
> *I took that part-time waitressing job you*

didn't want me to take, sweetie. I know you told me never to work where there's alcohol, but I just hate taking money from you. And Granny can't send much since she said she's saving for my next year in Lincoln. I'm sorry to disappoint her, but I can make a lot more money here and have enough left over to visit often. My big break is coming, sweetie, just as you always said it would.

Everything is so hectic and unreal here. Thousands of talented girls have come here to dance, sing, and act. (Some do it all.) I exercise every day (faithfully) to be ready for my break when it comes.

I know you must be terribly lonely without me to turn to. But, baby, I am with you all day and really with you at night when all alone. You too? I must get to bed early — and dream of you.

All my love,
Josie

"Why am I losing sleep over you? Reliving precious moments we knew ..." Harvey clicked off Gary's song "Over You" and went to sleep thinking of his young girl, so far away in the manswarm. He could not keep her from her dreams any more than he could keep his mother from chasing hers.

Yes, she will betray me, he whispered inwardly. *It will come in a letter one day. She will be stolen from me,* he cried inside, *and I'll be alone again.* It was just a matter of time.

Time: that relentless, manmade enemy of youth that squeezes the heart and stops it from singing in the new dawn. It robs us minute by minute, hour after hour, day after day. It chokes the life out of the sweetest dreams of yesterday into a miasmic swelling of pain and loss. The scarring of love lost would be picked and festered, but seen only by the heart.

Harvey would heal. But Floyd was in trouble. That feminine side she knew as Harvey — that side of him she fell in love with — would hold the light of love in his right eye through a thousand towns and back roads. It was his left headlight, where the boy Floyd lived, that would dim and flicker and withhold energy to his whole being.

Through summer and fall he slogged through each day. He peeked in tavern storage rooms, ducked in and out of grimy restrooms, and paced or stood impatiently while waiting to pitch a prospect who had the nerve to be on the phone or waiting on a customer. All without the chance of returning to her. He had nothing to work for but the trail of the paper man — the legacy his father left him. As he lay on foam-cushioned motel beds throughout the week, he would cry out to his absent father, "I know how you felt! I am lost like you!" Sleep was elusive. When he did sleep, it was a half-sleep that only sustained his muscles and bones, leaving his spirit unmoved. And his spirit remained unmoved, even after a good sale to a faceless cipher who would forever remain a stranger.

The Homecoming

Her flight was late for its arrival in Omaha on that cold December 22nd. He was bearded and nervous. She would not see the same Harvey Deason she had left more than six months ago. His face had hardened noticeably under his disguise. His best jeans and favorite blue flannel shirt looked inferior to him now. The van was greased and loaded for their trip to the Black Hills. Their plan was to spend two days in Macy with Granny, then two days in Pine Ridge with the Birds, then on to the Black Hills — just the two of them together for four days. He knew this was his last chance to compromise her dream of making it big in New York. She had not gotten her big break, but she was addicted to the manswarm and its specious promise of stardom to those who persevere.

He knew she had betrayed him. It was a visceral feeling he'd gotten from her letters. More than once she had mentioned a rich, handsome, forty-year-old Italian playboy and his Park Avenue penthouse. She talked about dinners and lunch dates but always added that he was "just a good friend" — a good friend who bought her expensive clothes to wear for her auditions. Perry was his name, and he was a well-known, big-shot art dealer. Josie had "befriended" him under the premise of jump-starting Dennis's career as a credible artist. But the Paper Man hated competition. And the Paper Man hated any man who would woo away a good woman from a hard-working territory salesman, like the way his mom had been so many years ago.

Perry represented the same kind of contemptible competition as the cutthroat butt-wipe jockeys who would slip into Floyd's territory and undercut his prices by five bucks per case on toilet paper. With two tiny plastic adapters, they could make their fifteen-hundred-sheet rolls fit on Silver's dispensers.

"Yer gonna drop me for a nickel a roll?" he'd appeal.

The response was always the same: a helpless shrug and a blank stare. Oftentimes Floyd would yank his dispensers from the wall, insisting they return the aluminum dispenser keys to him. Before leaving he would add his father's memorized diatribe: "I've been comin' here for all these years ... in all kinds of weather ... loyal to you, deliverin' yer order myself, bustin' my ass haulin' product to you knowin' you might be low. And you drop me for five bucks? That's the trouble with this country! There's no more loyalty to the little guy." Just as his father had, Floyd would make his exit feeling better, but still betrayed.

The haggard faces of the passengers from Josie's plane came up the tunnel ramp. He had to see her before she saw him — before her beauty had a chance to fool him. Floyd kept his distance so he would be able to furtively read her loyalty to him. It was an invaluable tool his father had taught him to use to read his prospects' moods. His father would assess the prospect and mumble to his trailing son, "No money." "Easy." "Be quick." "A talker." And he was right ninety-nine times out of a hundred.

She must be at the back of the plane, he said to himself as face after face came toward him. Floyd thought of the scores of times he'd picked her up after her class on Friday as he sensed her coming into view — her movement, her scent, her voice, the way her body felt next to his. He felt his jaw tighten and his teeth clench behind his beard as an image of her with Perry flashed through his mind. Betrayal. So bitter was this image

142

that it squeezed his eyes smaller and left his hands and feet clammy with sweaty toxins. With less than a minute before his instincts told him Josie would emerge from the tunnel, Floyd summoned Harvey at the penultimate instant he had to have him. The buried, neglected Harvey loosened his jaw, gave him his breath, parted his lips, and relaxed his blue eyes. Harvey produced a genuine smile that reflected his happiness at being released from the ruthless hold of the prospector Floyd.

Harvey blinked away Floyd's fear that Josie may be wearing the fancy clothes Perry had bought her. *They're only clothes,* Harvey smiled to himself. Just then she appeared, wearing the faded jeans and flannel shirt he loved. He felt a spark as she caught his eye from the back of the ramp. He inhaled deep from his center — a neglected good habit she'd taught him — just as she began to hurry with her carry-on bag draped over her shoulder. Her hair was full and flowing, but a little shorter. She slowed to look at him, and he could see her golden eyes shining; even more fire was emanating from them. She loved him. He could see that. She stopped close to him, and his blue eyes began to drain tears with hers.

"Hi, Paper Man," she smiled.

"Hi, Ms. Sun."

His chin quivered under his ash-brown whiskers. She let her bag hit the floor. They embraced before kissing, a long kiss tainted with tobacco and breath mints.

They drove up Highway 75 from Omaha to Macy. Just outside of Macy, they parked on a hill overlooking the little town. Harvey put in his Boz Scaggs CD and played "We're All Alone." He cut the engine and they listened to the lyrics. They looked deep and hard into each other's eyes and read each other's souls. When the song was over, he turned off the stereo and they faced each other.

Josie went first, verbalizing her assessment in a breaking whisper through choking tears: "You have been so lonely ... you were worried about me and thought many times you had lost me. You've been loyal ... and you love me," she cried, seeing his tears stream along his nostrils into his light moustache.

His turn came and he wiped his face with his sleeve. He looked deeper into the gold — like the prospector who knew the mother lode was there as no other could believe. She watched for the words he was forming, seeing them rise and then fall again in his throat. She could see through her veil of tears the face of the young boy she had first seen in Pine Ridge so many years ago. It was smaller, clean-shaven, and craned forward as his father's had been.

Harvey could see that Josie's face had turned into the little girl that came to him in the middle of the night in Pine Ridge. It was smaller and etched with pain that he could see so clearly now. He began to convulse and breathe higher in his chest. Then he saw in her eyes the same sorrow and unhappiness he had seen in his mother's eyes. His chest heaved and his head became dizzy. His ears rang a dull, deep tone he had only heard twice before: when he found out his mother left and when his father died.

Josie was letting him stay with it. She knew he was resolving pain that had to come out. She wanted so badly to rescue him from his past, but she allowed him to stay with it — whatever he was going through — until his voice was again the young boy from Pine Ridge. His words came out soft, stammering, and forced, as in a boy's voice: "You've seen a lot. You've ... missed ... me too. You have been ... you were with ... someone."

Josie lost it. Her upper body dropped left to her side, sobbing, as when she had broken down in tears on their way to Yankton. They were a boy and a girl alone in the darkness. He listened to her cries bouncing off the van's engine cover with his forearm supporting her head. He felt the pressure of Floyd behind his eyes, knocking hard to confront her. Floyd's knuckles were pounding faster and faster as if punishing her with guilt for betraying him. *She screwed you, you sap,* Floyd resounded to Harvey, who was trying his best to stay in control. Again Floyd's voice boomed, *She did not wait for you! She will always compare you to that Italian. She's going back to him again.*

He rolled down his window to breathe and lit a cigarette. Then he pulled at her shoulder for her to sit on his lap. She did, wrapping her arms around his neck, crying on his throat. He could feel her warm tears turning into cold drops of water as they ran down under his shirt to his belly. It was then that he noticed he was not aroused to be with her. Just by being so close to her, she had kicked Floyd's ass — that side of him that wanted to punish her and take only her flesh.

"I still love you, Josie," Harvey whispered.

"Only one time, Harvey. I swear. I was drunk and so lonely," she cried into his ear. His head beat with a steady five-alarm pain. Too much bad news to comprehend; his biggest fear now realized. He said nothing while holding her and listening to her whimpering contrition.

On the way to Granny's they were quiet, silenced by the storms raging in their heads. She worried about what this would mean to him. He knew he was now being punched and pounded by Floyd's ego showing Harvey images of a stranger having all of his Josie.

He dropped her off at Granny's as snow started to fall in big flakes. He told her he'd be back after getting cigarettes at a convenience store in Winnebago. "Plus," he added, "it'll give you a chance to be alone with Granny."

He drove on auto-pilot all the way to the Kwik Stop. He couldn't remember turning on his windshield wipers on the four-mile drive there and was barely aware that snow now blanketed the earth. *The whole thing has to be a dream,* he kept saying to himself. He began inhaling crosses and exhaling pitchforks outside the Kwik Stop after lighting a non-filter from his new pack — the brand his father smoked.

He walked slowly down Highway 77 toward nothing. He didn't think he could ever forgive her — or face the red-hot issues of his mother's betrayal. He screamed into the night, "This is how my father must've felt!"

He lit another cigarette with what remained of the first one. He turned onto a snow-covered, unpaved road that was lined on either side with shanties, junked cars, and overflowing garbage cans. The speckled blackness surrounding him turned the white road before him into a movie screen of images — images of Josie and of his parents: Sleeping between his parents when the furnace didn't work; falling asleep on the couch with Josie in his arms while watching a movie together during a blizzard last winter; the terrible look on his father's face after he'd pawned his wedding band; touching Josie's fingers in church when Granny turned to greet someone behind them; the sickening scene of a dark-haired Italian man entering his woman ... and enjoying it ... both of them.

The last image dropped him to his knees in the middle of this residential road in Winnebago, vomiting his last meal and spilling his guts on the side of the street, bringing up the sounds and pieces of a thousand rejections and memories in all those lonely towns. The movie continued to play in his head as he dry-heaved in the dark: looking out the window of the train he and his father took to Chicago when Grandma Deason died; the tiny towns of Lennox, Parker, and Irene, South Dakota, which were so close together but peopled so differently that it left his father bewildered on a barstool at 5:00 p.m.; his father hiding product and then using up half a roll of dispenser towels after washing his hands in a grimy gas station john; the buxom beauty shop owner in Pender he watched his dad flirt with; the empty dresser drawers in their stuffy studio apartment after his mother left, which he would open while his father was out drinking to try to catch his mother's scent; the black-and-white photo of his mother holding him on her knees when he was three.

His heaving echoed down the Winnebago street. Then Floyd hit him for all he was worth. *Enough of this!* Floyd screamed, bringing the bandy-legged warrior to his feet while gripping Harvey's wounds of torpor in the left hand that always held Charlie. He carried Harvey back to the van with enough anger in each step to level Winnebago into dust.

Nakota Hills! Floyd screamed. Again, but louder, *Nakota Hills!*

Floyd started to run, dragging the weaker Harvey behind him. Floyd, his face hotter than July, would take her tonight in that sacred place just across the river in Iowa. The whites named it Loess Hills, but Granny told Josie its real Lakota name was *Mini Sose,* River of My Life, long before the white man came. Granny told her of the sacred burial grounds on raised platforms throughout Nakota Hills, and how the Lakota people would leave their dead exposed so Nature would pick them clean, leaving their bones scattered throughout the hills. Granny always stressed that the area had to be respected.

It has to be respected! Floyd yelled near the van, repeating her exact words.

He remembered walking with Josie in those beautiful hills one October. He remembered how they'd found a perfect place to make love, but Josie would not do anything in that sacred place unless she were engaged or married to him.

All the way back to Granny's house, Floyd wanted her. He

would take her in the sacred hills and leave the crying to Harvey later. "Yes!" he exclaimed, exhilarated by his plan. *This is the only way to keep her from returning to New York,* he thought to himself. *But what if she's pregnant? I have to find out when it happened.*

He was still worrying hard about that possibility when he turned the van onto Granny's street. The little houses were decorated with red and green Christmas lights, except for the white bulbs strung along Granny's fence.

After peppering Granny with all the fast and furious things she'd experienced in the City and her determination to make it big there, Josephine heard the van's engine outside the house. She could tell by the robust knock it was Floyd who came in the front door.

"Merry Christmas, Granny," Floyd beamed from the doorway as Josie and Granny sat on her small, hard sofa that was covered with a shocking orange blanket Granny had made. He looked down at the bed on the floor Granny had prepared for him. Only Josephine's reddened golden eyes could see that Floyd wanted her. It tempered her warmly and she became excited to see him this way. When their eyes met, Granny knew her guests would be leaving her home before long.

"How are you, Paper Man?" Granny smiled while scooting forward to stand.

"Don't get up!" Floyd laughed as he walked over to the couch and sat between the two ladies. He hugged Granny and kissed her.

"You've been smoking," Granny laughed.

"Yes! And I loved every puff," he said enthusiastically, provoking a big laugh from Granny. The old woman was happy to see him so alive, instead of the polite gentleman who once returned her great-granddaughter home with her sweater on inside-out after a prolonged "good-night" on the front porch.

"How's business, Harvey?" Granny asked.

"Oh ... I've got twenty grand in the bank," he boasted, even though he only had eight.

"Well," Granny smiled, "good for you."

"Granny, how about if we catch up tomorrow at breakfast. You gonna make yer French toast with blueberries and bananas that I love?" he smiled.

"Why, I s'pose I could," she laughed.

Floyd stood and took Josie by her hand. Looking into her eyes from arm's length he said to Granny, "We're going for a drive."

"I'll leave the door unlocked," Granny said as she watched Josephine turn into her little Josie before her eyes.

"We won't be late," Josie smiled.

"Yes we will," Floyd laughed.

They could still hear the old lady laughing after Josie kissed her goodnight and the door closed behind them.

Josie was silent until Floyd turned the van south on 75 and passed their favorite parking spot.

"Where are we going?"

"It's a surprise."

"What happened when you went to get smokes?"

"Oh ... I did some thinkin'."

"About what?"

Floyd thought for a minute then said, "After this song I'll tell you."

They listened once again to the Boz Scaggs song "We're All Alone" — a romantic ballad Floyd had played a thousand times as he anticipated this very moment. It worked! He only looked over at her three times before he saw her crying.

"It was only once, Harvey," she said again. "I was so lonely, and I missed you so much. The whole time I kept my eyes shut tight and just imagined it was you with me. But when it was over, I felt such emptiness and shame and guilt. I was so afraid I was going to lose you forever. I love you now, Harvey, more than I ever have before, and I am still so scared that I will lose you. It is enough to make me want to give up my dream of dancing in the spotlight. I only want to dance for you now ... and with you. All the way here on the plane, I thought about how comfortable and contented I would be to be a big fish in a little pond with my Paper Man."

The song had made her want Floyd more than ever, and Floyd knew it. Boz had come through for him in a big way as he drove through Decatur, Nebraska, before steering over the little bridge to cross the river into Iowa.

"When did it happen?" Floyd demanded.

She stopped herself from coyly asking what he meant and answered directly, "In October."

She saw Floyd wince.

"When in October?"

"I don't remember."

"Was it late October, early, or in the middle?"

"It was early ... I think. Where are we going?" she asked with a hint of fear in her voice.

"Nakota Hills," he said, looking for her reaction.

"Harvey ... not there ... please."

"It's time. You'll either be with me there ... or ..."

"Or what?"

"Or you won't marry me," he said.

He was afraid to look at her. It was Harvey's side who was supposed to propose. He could not look at her. He kept driving for the hills, waiting for her to answer. Finally, he said softly, "Don't answer me now. Let me know there ... please."

While she sat quietly looking out at the darkness through the passenger window, her heart pounded in her chest for the man she loved and the future she anticipated with him.

As he headed up the western slope of Nakota Hills, Floyd played Gary's "Young Girl," then his romantic "Over You," then "Woman, Woman" — a torchy song about a man's heartache over fading love with the lyrical question, "Have you got cheating on your mind?"

Yes, Floyd was cruel. "Woman, Woman" had left Josie feeling so blue and spent that she cried with her head laid back over the headrest.

Floyd turned down a snow-covered dirt lane lined with glistening red oaks and parked at the end of an open meadow. "Josephine Ann Tenna, look at me."

She raised her head forward and turned to him with swollen eyes. As she looked into his eyes, she saw Floyd fading into the background and Harvey taking over.

"Josie, there is no past from here on. I forgive you. We both forgive you," he said with a smile.

She laughed, just as she had on their way to Yankton more than two years earlier.

"I know I'm not rich ... and I can't give you your dream of being a professional dancer. I can give you my devotion and my love, and I can work hard for you. I'll take good care of you for the rest of my life. I want to spend my life married to you, Josie. You are ... my dream."

His eyes welled with tears when he saw in her golden eyes the little girl in Pine Ridge who came to his aid, sustaining him in his darkness as no other ever had. He continued, "I want to get married in that little church in Pine Ridge where you came to me."

She could see his chin trembling under his whiskers. She wanted to rub his beard all over her flesh.

"I want us to honeymoon in the Black Hills. Will you marry me, Josie?"

"What about Granny?"

"No problem. She'll go with us. No selling. And I'll fly her back from Rapid ... and pay her cab fare from Sioux City to Macy."

"She can't ride in here," she said while looking back into the cargo area.

"You'll ride back there," he laughed. "I'll make it work ... and I'll make it fun for her. No selling."

She stared out the windshield. "It's beautiful here," she smiled, and Harvey noticed the peace that swept over her face and body.

She didn't say yes. She climbed into the cargo area and began preparing the sleeping bag Floyd kept back there in case he couldn't find a room while he was out on the road. Floyd put in the Boz tape, then turned sideways to watch her slowly undress while on her knees on top of the sleeping bag.

"Does this mean yes?" he whispered.

She extended her arms to him and flashed a sexy smile. "Paper Man ... what do you think?"

The van rocked until its lettering could easily be read in the dawn's early light. *There is no past,* she sighed inwardly after he fell asleep. She was wrapped around him inside the warm bag in the van. Charlie was on the floor near them, and she was in her territory in the sacred Nakota Hills. She could not sleep. *Josephine Deason ... Josie Deason ... Josephine Ann Deason ... Josie Ann Deason,* she ruminated. She kissed his neck, thrilled with the sound of her new name and confident her roommate in New York would send all her things to her. *And a wedding in the old church ... how romantic! Uncle Walt, Aunt Laura, and Dennis will be there. It will be so good to see Dennis,* she thought, swirling in a thousand girlhood images of so long ago. *Aunt Laura can do my hair,* she smiled. Again she repeated to herself, *There is no past,* then nuzzled against Harvey's back with her arm around his stomach. ·

She felt him breathing low and deep while curling tufts of his belly hair between her fingers. "Yes, I'll marry you," she whispered into his back. She thought of *Mini Sose*, River of My Life, before drifting off to sleep. "Sweet dreams and snazzy squirrels," she added softly.

The Indian grocer in Pine Ridge, who hated to see the Paper Man in his store, was caught off guard when he saw the fat taker approaching his meat counter without his sales case. The quiet butcher knew something was up, and his defenses went up immediately. Harvey stood facing him, but his focus was on the meat case.

"Hi, Chief," he said softly. "I want you to cater my wedding reception tomorrow. It'll be at the Best Western in Custer."

"How many?"

"How many what?" Harvey asked absent-mindedly.

"People."

"Oh ... I s'pose twenty or thirty ... yeah ... about thirty."

"What time?"

"Three ... yeah, three o'clock."

"You seem confused," Clouda smiled wryly.

"I've never done this before. I am confused, Chief. You remember Josie ... Walter and Laura's niece? The little girl with the golden eyes?"

"Oh, yeah! Yeah!" the grocer beamed. "Golden Eyes ... I remember her."

Harvey could feel his left hand cupped as if holding Charlie. He stopped Floyd from scanning the back wall where his customer stacked his locker paper. "Ya know, Chief, there are getting to be fewer and fewer lockers in my territory. The chains are buyin' in, moving into small towns. The locker is going to be extinct ... like whites tried to do with your people. You ever think about that, Chief?"

The grocer stopped wiping around his meat slicer and looked the salesman in the eye. Floyd had never before seen that look on a butcher in his territory. "Speed kills all people eventually. The whites will grow tired of it one day ... and slow down. Things will go 'round again. You want mixed cold cuts?"

"Yeah ... fine ... fine. And some dip with cheese ... and some chips."

"No pop?"

Harvey blushed at Clouda's double entendre, knowing his pop machine scam was no secret. "Yeah. Two cases of pop ... mixed. You want me to pay you now?" he smiled.

"Mr. Bird pays me."

"Walter?"

"No, his son. He called me this morning to order champagne for the reception in Custer. He told me to send him catering bill too."

Harvey thought about how Dennis must have been called in Colorado about the wedding. He wasn't due to arrive in Pine Ridge until later that evening — the day before the wedding.

As Harvey left the small grocery store, the smell of bacon curing in the smokehouse hung in the air all the way to the front of the old church. He looked around at the small town and tried his best to commit to memory every sight, sound and smell he was experiencing. *Soon a married man,* he thought. Things had moved quickly since they called the Birds from Macy the morning after their tryst in Nakota Hills. Granny had taken the news well, but not without ascertaining from Josie that this was what she really wanted. Josie's radiant eyes, glowing as bright as rain-drenched apples, gave her the answer. Floyd preferred Josie's answer in the sacred hills; but on the way back to Macy, she made her fiancé promise that they would remain celibate until the honeymoon.

Upon receiving the phone call from Josie, Laura began excitedly cleaning and decorating the little church. Now she and Josie were in Rapid City buying a wedding dress. Harvey still needed to locate a honeymoon cabin in the Black Hills, but first he wanted to go into that back room of the church where so long ago she came to him.

He passed the cluttered storage room that housed the day care's product. *No selling,* he reminded himself as he walked across the freshly cleaned pine floor that Laura had shined with Floyd's thirty-six-inch dust mop and floor cleaner. He could smell Albert's glass cleaner on the cracked, streakless windows on either side of the main room as it commingled with the sweet scent of sage Laura had burned to purify the air. *Gotta get Granny's plane ticket too,* he remembered.

Each step he took toward the closed door of the little back room took him back another year. *How far I've come to get here ... here with her. That little girl will be my wife tomorrow.* He stopped himself from opening the door, saying to himself, *The past is dead.*

He quickly walked away from the little room as he ran through the list of things he still needed: *Suit, dress shoes, haircut.*

By evening Harvey was clean-shaven. Over the course of three hours he smoked fifteen cigarettes in the parking lot of Custer's Best Western motel where he was staying. He smoked one, then another, not wanting to offend the health-conscious artist who would be sharing his room. He was proud of the fact he'd gotten everything done on his list with the alacrity of the Paper Man.

As he smoked behind the wheel of his van with the door

open, he listened to the song he had played when they made love in the Nakota Hills, Steve Winwood's "Talking Back to the Night." He became aroused with the memory, but it passed when he realized it was his father who made it possible to be marrying such a young and beautiful woman. Indeed, his father had given him his two greatest loves: Josie and his work. Thousands of lonely nights, spent for the prospect of orders from strangers, had finally paid off for him. So many times he overcame the grim jail of winter. Unlike his father, the loneliness did not consume him.

He thought of his mother's traits that had saved him — her aversion to drinking during the week, her disdain for idle conversation, finding humor during trying times, and her cleanliness and rugged constitution. He remembered one time asking his father what his mother was like when he first met her. He had asked the question in a Wagner café when his parents were still married. He could still see his father leaning forward on his elbows, his blue eyes lit up as they had been after he'd sold the Farmers and Ranchers Bank a three-hundred-dollar order. His voice was hushed to softness as he looked into each eye of his son — first the left and then the right and then both — saying, "She was like a picture I saw when I was about yer age. There was this beautiful prairie woman wearing a cotton dress. She was pumpin' water in the wind on her homestead. Her hair was covering one side of her face. She wasn't smiling or troubled. She looked so content just doing her summer chores ... for some lucky man who would return to her. When I first laid eyes on yer mother ... I saw that woman in the picture. And later she told me that I made her feel so beautiful that she thought we had met before."

The music had just stopped when a new Jeep Cherokee parked next to his van. The man with his dark, long hair in a ponytail got out and stretched gracefully with his back to the van. When he turned around and saw the van's lettering, he smiled big at Harvey. "Paper Man!"

"Dennis?"

Harvey got out of the van and stood still as Dennis came over to him, extending his soft, brown right hand. "Congratulations, Paper Man!" he said as his handshake transitioned into a heartfelt hug. "Do you remember me?" he asked as he stepped back from Harvey.

"Yes. Josie told me you were the boy with her when I came to Pine Ridge with my dad." Dennis's eyes were black and shining with a light Harvey had seen in Josie's eyes. His face was round but muscular. The two men were nearly the same height, but Dennis was more evenly proportioned with bigger legs and a much bigger and easier laugh.

"You ready for the big day tomorrow?" Dennis laughed.

"No," Harvey smiled.

Dennis's laugh was loud and contagious. Through the dark tinted windows of the burnt-orange Jeep, Harvey could see the neatly divided rows of covered oil paintings on canvases standing in the back. "That's my work," Dennis beamed.

"Yer a good artist. Josie says you were very good at drawing pictures when you were little."

Dennis smiled, thinking about Josie and how lucky this man was to be marrying her.

"I think she wants to see you tonight," Harvey added.

"I would like that very much, but I am too tired to see her. Besides, this is your last night to be a free man," he laughed. "We must go out and have a few beers before I go to sleep."

* * * * *

Dennis tied a small knot in Harvey's beige, cotton tie,

positioning it just right between the lapels of his new corduroy, forest-green sports jacket. He stepped back from the mirror in the old church's back bathroom to look at his whole outfit, including the beige corduroy pants and brown dress shoes.

"She said to get earth colors. What do you think, Dennis ... is this earthy?"

"Very earthy. You look like an earth groom," he laughed. "You have the ring?"

Harvey fumbled in his pockets until he found the tiny dispenser key. He unlocked the towel dispenser, opening the cabinet's lid to remove a velvet ring box. Dennis was amused with the Paper Man's hiding place. He handed the box to Dennis. The best man opened the box and examined his cousin's gold wedding band. "It's nice, Paper Man ... real nice."

The left-handed artist looked at his turquoise-banded watch on his right wrist. "You have at least three minutes to bail out," he laughed.

"I'm ready," Harvey said, breathing in deeply with just a faint twitch under his eye.

Dennis gave him a bear hug, saying, "You are one lucky white man."

"I know it."

There were about thirty people sitting on two rows of five benches on either side of the aisle. Granny sat on a front bench near the aisle and floor heater. She was wearing her finest traditional dress — a linen, ankle-length muslin of purple with specks of white interwoven deliberately between the spaces to represent Eternal Bonding. Laura sat beside her in her off-white ankle dress that she had worn at her own wedding. On the bench on the other side of the aisle was loyal Charlie — the worn, butterscotch, handless Charlie — flat and turned lengthwise, his mouth open toward the groom. To Floyd, Charlie represented his father being there. To Harvey, his mother's picture was zipped inside Charlie's side pocket, just as she had remained enclosed inside the heart of her paper man.

Dennis stood next to the groom in front of a sage-burning altar where the elderly Reverend White Horse from Lead stood piously. Dennis and Harvey turned to watch Walter's approach with the bride on his arm. Harvey glanced over at the open church window directly across from him. His van was parked just outside the window with its passenger door open, ready to provide the wedding song. He gestured with his hand to the boy inside the van, whom he'd paid five bucks to press the stereo button at this moment.

As the Boz Scaggs song "Isn't it Time" drifted in through the window, all heads turned to see beautiful Josie escorted by Walter at the front entrance. Her hair was radiantly styled high above her golden eyes that streamed with happy tears from Boz's love song. The bride's sheer cotton dress rose slightly with each slow step, exposing her black, laced, ankle-length shoes — the kind prairie women wore long ago.

Granny and Laura cried into their hankies as proud Walter Bird slowly moved his captivating niece toward the groom. As the song continued, she could see that it was all of Floyd Harvey Deason waiting, her Paper Man, known to the room as *Mni huha ska*.

His pale-blue eyes were on her, emanating light with every step she took. As she got closer her eyes shone bright with the golden light, knowing that she would take his name and get his heart and soul. Forever.

Walter followed Josie's lead, stepping with her only when the music moved her and not at some uniform cadence. Her head was bowed submissively to a bouquet of purple and white daisies in her hands, moving closer as the wedding song played on. As she reached her place next to her Paper Man, there was not a dry eye in the room.

Walter left her beside the groom. Facing each other they locked eyes as the song ended and exchanged vows and rings.

The champagne would have to be consumed off of the Reservation. Dennis had paid for the reception room in the same Custer Best Western. There they ate and drank, and Josie had her first chance to catch up with Dennis. They were standing by the wedding cake Laura had made while Harvey listened to Walter, Laura and Granny talk about relatives and friends they knew.

Harvey could see that his new bride and her cousin were close. He could see them hugging and kissing often, touching each other when they talked and laughed. Harvey wondered why he never saw such affection in his many divagations.

"Any immediate plans for any paper boys and paper girls, Golden Eyes?"

"Not now. It's too soon, Dennis. We haven't even had our honeymoon."

"That's why I ask you now," he laughed.

"I'll have to figure out who I am and who I want to be before I'll be ready to be a mother. I've given up my dream of making a name for myself on the stage, but I can't help thinking I'm destined for something big. And seeing that old church again and the poverty that surrounds it made me remember how our people are in such great need of help. My heart really goes out to them, Dennis. I want so badly to do something to help them."

"I'm glad that's important to you," he said with a serious tone. Then he lightened up as he remembered, "You know, I think back to that day when we first saw Harvey and his father. Remember the pop machine? To think you're married to that boy we saw that day blows me away."

"I know," she smiled.

"You look so happy, Josie."

"I am," she blushed.

"Now ... for your wedding gift. Wait here. I want you to see it first."

Dennis soon returned to the banquet room carrying a large covered canvas. He uncovered the painting in front of the light coming from the window.

"It's beautiful, Dennis!" Her gold eyes pored over the twenty-six-by-thirty-six original of the same old church which now glistened in oil. Next to it was the small grocery and the red Coke machine. The old station wagon was parked in front of the store. The plated title on the frame read "Passing Through." She saw his signature in the lower right corner — Thunder Bird, the name she had given him when she lived in Pine Ridge.

"The colors ... you captured it just the way everything was! It's perfect, Dennis." She kissed him before bringing Harvey over to see their gift from Dennis.

"That is really good," Harvey smiled. He stood staring at the captured likeness of himself and his father as Josie wrapped her arms around his chest. For so long Harvey was mesmerized at the realness of everything on the canvas — the summer light, his and his father's postures, the bologna-skin tires, even the burnt-orange rust spots that had pitted through the car's metal wheel wells from the winter slush.

Dennis was very pleased with their response to his work.

"How long did it take you to do this?" Harvey asked.

"A while," he smiled. Dennis Bird never talked about the details of his work. He was like most talented Native American artists — unable to take credit for his God-given gift, and not very adept at marketing or pricing his work. Thunder Bird was getting mentioned in gallery circles with the likes of other renowned Indigenous artists: Edward S. Curtis and his *Oasis in the Badlands;* Dana Tiger of the Creek Tribe Oklahoma and his watercolors, acrylics and gouache; the acrylic of Pima Tribe Arizona artist Urshel Taylor; the mixed mediums of L. David Eveningthunder of Shoshone in Texas; and Jerome Bushyhead of the Cheyenne. Yes, the *Nemi-neht* (Native American people) had a new genius named Thunder Bird.

"Thunder Bird ... how'd you come up with that name?" Harvey asked.

"Golden Eyes gave me the name," he smiled.

* * * * *

At sunset after their reception, Mr. and Mrs. Deason, still in their wedding attire, stood on the spot where little Josie had scattered her mother's ashes. The van was parked behind them with toilet paper streaming from its sides and rear that had been stuck to it with aerosol shaving cream.

Josie saw something down the Sheep Mountain butte near a wide ledge. It was the product of lightning striking grains of sand and turning them into a black-and-blue, three-foot-long solid tube. Harvey followed her down to it. She picked it up, examined it, and put it in the van's cargo bed.

"Nice souvenir," he remarked.

"Something to remind me of my mother."

He allowed her the space to walk back to the ledge of the butte. He could see her taking in the Badlands. With her mother's Indigenous blood beating from her heart, she saw the sun low in the west off her right shoulder. As she looked at the sun, her husband could see those golden eyes not squinting, as if her eyes were lost in a living father who still loved his little girl. She cried into the sun, still looking at its orange-gold light that was slowly turning her mother's people's Badlands into a polychromatic sight so beautiful that Harvey began to cry with her. He could see the little girl again.

She had told him of her mother bringing her here a week before her suicide, and how her mother told her that she could have her anytime she came here if she imagined these splendid wings of color the sun made near sunset. She told Josie these wings would carry her mother away one day, far away from her little girl. Josie remembered her sad mother looking into the sun like this near the summer solstice and saying proudly, *"Wi Wá yang wacipi,"* which translates into "Dance Gazing at the Sun." Josie knew its meaning then. She knew there is no death, only a change of worlds.

Her Indigenous roots now were beginning to move her arms, as if warming up for a Seven Rites ceremony of the Sacred Canunpa that Granny took her to every year. She began dancing The Space Between — that invisible fabric of space between wind and dust and light. Even though the snow had begun to fall, she removed her laced wedding shoes and lace stockings, and stood on her toes, swirling and spinning Harvey into a long space of lost breath where his heart supplied his air. He watched her on the wings of the evening, close to the edge, dancing while gazing lovingly at the sun. Her perfect profile and this dreamy scene would be forever etched in his mind, and he would see it whenever he thought of his own mother — free at last of her paper man's drunken loneliness. Maybe now he could forgive her because of his new bride.

He turned away from her while he smoked near the van's open door. If he watched her any longer, he would break down for sure in this phantasmagoria known as Badlands.

* * * * *

Their honeymoon cabin was nestled back in the woods — way back in the woods. Traveling alongside Sheridan Lake via a two-mile, circuitous dirt road north of Custer, they arrived at their cabin three-quarters of a mile from the base of Harney Peak. The stained cross-timbers of Black Hills pine gave it the feel of a small hunting lodge.

They parked about ten paces from the cabin's three-step front porch. Sitting in the van they stared at the picturesque little cabin framed by pine trees and a sheer veil of big snowflakes.

"You first," he said. He watched her scan the cabin and then the lake with her golden eyes yet swimming in champagne.

"It's been here a long time," she said.

"Yes," he agreed as he looked out the windshield at the red/black chimney.

"Your turn," she said.

Harvey pushed in the CD he had reserved for this moment. They listened to Boz Scaggs sing, "We're All Alone," as they held hands and drank in the beauty of their honeymoon spot.

When the song was over, Harvey kissed his wife's wedding ring and said, "Wait here." He carried two bags of groceries to the cabin, unlocked the door, swung it open wide, and deposited the groceries on the table inside. When he returned to the van, he lifted Josie right off the passenger seat and carried her into the cabin, kicking the door shut behind him.

Inside the cabin he carried his beautiful bride straight over to the soft, queen-size, four-poster brass bed in the far corner of the one-room cabin. He sat next to her as they looked across the cold room. There were two crates of firewood and a stack of logs on the grate ready to be lit. The tiny repainted kitchen had a small refrigerator and three-burner stove. There were a couple of white-chipped cupboards hanging on the kitchen walls and an unfinished pinewood table for two. The only other furniture in the cabin was a cobweb-covered rocking chair.

"Where's the bathroom?" she asked.

He got up from the bed and opened a latched door next to the fireplace. She could see the shower stall, sink and toilet in the little room.

"Candles will burn here," she smiled.

"Me too," he laughed.

"I W Y N," she said, lying back in her wedding dress.

Harvey smiled as he remembered the acronym they had created to express publicly their private desire for each other. "I want you now."

"Let me get the fire going," he said. Harvey quickly lit newspaper kindling in several places while watching her remove her prairie shoes. He left the cabin, and soon she could hear another Boz song, "You Can Have Me Anytime," coming from the van. He was already half undressed by the time he got the cabin door closed, but she waited to see if he wanted to remove her dress.

"You do it ... slowly," he smiled.

After making love for the first time as husband and wife, Josie lit a few candles amidst a crackling fire. She burned sage to purify the cabin that Floyd named Horny. The van's stereo filled their retreat with all the music they loved together. Clad in only wool socks, Josephine danced for her husband in the candlelight.

Lying in bed together, Harvey held his sleeping wife in his arms and whispered, "I can't believe you married me. You're too good for me, Josie. I'm afraid I'll never keep you."

He finally fell asleep at four in the morning.

The next day was colder but with no snow. They breakfasted at noon on the leftovers from their catered reception. As they were sipping tea and sharing a piece of their wedding cake in front of a roaring fire, Josie heard a whining sound coming from outside the cabin door. She strained to listen above the fire.

"Listen," she said.

Nothing.

"What did you hear?"

"I don't know."

"Prob'ly the wood."

Just then they both heard a whine and a little scratching at the base of the cabin door. They both got up in their pajamas and socks and went to the door.

"Stay back from the door," Harvey warned. "Heaven only knows what's out there that's looking for a place to warm up."

Harvey unlocked the door and squeaked it open a couple of inches. "Aw ... look, honey ... a puppy!"

A two-month-old Labrador/shepherd/greyhound mutt, a gold-black-brown mix of color, came right in the cabin whimpering from cold and hunger. Josie picked up the baby, snuggling it to her chest and kissing it on top of its square little head. Harvey ducked outside quickly to see if someone was out there.

"He must be lost," Josie baby-talked as Harvey locked the door.

"Boy or girl?" Harvey asked.

Josie raised the pup in the air. "It's a boy!" she laughed.

Harvey knew what was coming next. Josie took the puppy by the fire and fed him some warm milk out of her teacup. She looked at her new husband as if this was the greatest gift they could get.

"He prob'ly lives near here ... and his mother's looking for him," Floyd said while looking for his pants.

"Let him stay ... please, Harvey?"

Floyd took a deep breath and smiled, giving up his hunt for his pants. "Tomorrow we find his home ... right?" he said.

"Right," she agreed, slipping the pup inside her warm robe.

The next morning it was much colder, although the temperature in the Hills was still ten degrees warmer than in Rapid City. The Deasons began the day with a snowball fight and a new puppy they named Huck, naming him after his floppy-eared, cartoon lookalike Huckleberry Hound. But Josie thought it was short for "huckster" because he was such a smart little guy who already knew how to get his way. Huck was their wedding gift from God — at least to Josie's thinking.

Leaving their honeymoon nest, Huck rode on Rocky's cargo bed, falling down with every turn while exploring his new home. The dog had brown eyes, a square nose, and a tail that curved up. He appeared as if he'd be a big dog by his big paws and chubbiness. Already the Deasons were a family of three. Floyd thought it took the edge off of not having any kids planned.

Over breakfast in a Custer café, Josie told Harvey he could train Huck to work for him. She thought Huck would be a good companion for the Paper Man when he had to be out on the road.

"What about you?" he asked.

"I'll keep our home in order and be rested for your return. I'll work for myself ... but not you ... or anyone else."

"Yes, dear," he replied in mocking submission.

* * * * *

They visited the Birds and drove Granny to the airport in Rapid City. Then they saw the Crazy Horse monument, still under construction, and Mount Rushmore. Huck went everywhere with them. By the time they arrived at Floyd's apartment in Sioux City, Huck was already housebroken. Floyd made sure Josie wasn't watching when he swift-kicked the little huckster out of Rocky's side door after he peed on Floyd's sleeping bag at a rest area.

"No pets allowed" was the policy of the apartment Floyd

rented. It made a good excuse to move.

"But where to?" Josie asked.

"There's a farmhouse for rent in the Nakota Hills not too far north of Sioux City. We drove there one time ..."

"Oh, yes! I remember! It's so beautiful there!" she exclaimed.

Her enthusiasm gave way to apprehension quickly, though, as she pondered its isolation, knowing it may be an extreme change for her after her life in New York.

"I know it's isolated, Josie ... but Huck could stay with you sometimes. And you can go out in the territory with me whenever you feel like it. We'll make it work," Harvey assured her.

"I don't have a car," she said.

"I'll get one for ya. Let's just look at the place first ... okay?"

"Okay," she agreed.

"Rocky"

They turned west onto a gravel road for two miles before turning down a single-lane dirt road leading fifty yards into obscurity beneath a stand of big knotty-trunked, red oaks. He parked so they were facing the spot on the top center of the windshield where the sun was setting. She stopped herself from asking how he knew of these obscure places. She hated those possessive thoughts. Josie Deason reiterated that there was no past — only now. Granny had instilled in her the futility of clinging to the past. "Holding onto the past is like carrying around your eliminations and showing your old crap to everybody. It gets heavy fast ... and stinks like hell," Granny would laugh.

There was no farm in sight in any direction. He rolled down his window and said, "Listen." It was late January — too early for insects. The only sound to be heard was the rustling of the dead and dried oak leaves resistantly clinging to the trees in the lonesome prairie breeze. The exhilarating cold created an intoxicating aphrodisiac for the newly married couple. They watched the subtle, grapy bloom of dusk that looked as if it could melt the land around them.

They kept listening to the sounds of the prairie while breathing together unconsciously. She could always stay with it longer than he could. Soon Floyd would find her scent and turn to her. Her eyes would meet his, giving his heart and ego a shot of adrenaline and letting him know without a doubt that he was her only love.

He selected a song he had played all week on his run in anticipation of this moment. After putting the CD in the player, Floyd climbed in the back of the van and began to undress. He laid out the sleeping bag on the green patio carpeting covering the floor of the van. Josie sat on the engine cover and faced him while removing her top as the Classics Four song "Traces" began to play.

All the while the song played, they never touched each other. They removed their worldly covers while facing each other on cushioned knees, allowing the love in the music to purge them of the negative things life brings to good people. When the song was over, they fell into each other's arms and made love — a pure, joyful, passionate expression of what they meant to each other. An hour after parking in the secluded prairie grove, she was a softer Josie and he a more relaxed Harvey.

He turned on his side facing the van's side door. She was tight against his back, rubbing her slender leg down the side of his muscled calf. "It should have a name," she said softly.

"What's that?" he asked, perplexed.

"Your van. Our van. I feel like this is more than just a vehicle. It is a part of us ... a part of our family. It's like a private sanctuary far away from the pressures of everyday life. A place where we are free to open up and share our deepest and most intimate secrets with each other. A place where our love is free and flowing. It should have a name ... some kind of personification."

"Well, after what transpired here for the better part of the last hour, Rocky seems appropriate."

They both laughed until their sides hurt, but the name stuck.

Setting up Housekeeping

Late March brought inchoate spring. They had until the middle of April to move. The farmhouse for rent was encysted in a series of folds and hills covered with lush prairie grass. Josie liked it for its stark beauty and the fact that the modest farm buildings were far from the house.

Harvey had parked Rocky behind a hill a quarter mile from the farmhouse. He wanted her to see their new home from the approach of an artist. Huck was staying close, following them, sniffing and exploring with all the happy senses of a capricious puppy.

"He's a mama's boy," Harvey scoffed. "Watch this."

Harvey playfully tackled Josie onto a clumpy thatch of soft prairie grass and rolled them away from Huck's attempts to join them, whining and whimpering with their joyous laughter. Just then Harvey hushed her laughter, whispering, "Look."

She followed his eyes to the edge of a poplar stand where a deer stood frozen in motion, sniffing in their direction and giving them only a few seconds before vanishing. Harvey turned to Josie, kissing her nose and holding her face in his hands. "I will always love you. I still can't believe you married me, Josie. You could have gone back to New York, and I would still feel this way and see you here with me. I can't help but feel I will lose you someday ... because you'll grow tired of me. I don't have whatever it takes to keep you happy ... for long. I really fear it. And I know that fear like that can manifest into losing you. Keep telling me what to do, Josie. Please ... tell me if you know you are feeling you made a mistake by being with me. Please ..." he cried.

She cried her liquid gold tears onto his neck and into his beard, sobbing on his chest, repeating over and over, "I love you."

They made love right there — a convivial feasting and drinking each other in — as Huck capered and played in the cool March wind, chasing butterflies and new smells. On this sacred Nakota ground with the poverty grass holding them to its magnetic bedding, this was as splendid a scene as any man who ever returned to his prairie woman. At the well of life, in the wind with the deer, they were sustained by Earth itself. The manswarm was a million galaxies away with its myriad dead faces endlessly streaming past cold, stained buildings, obscured from the horizon and devoid of tenderness.

* * * * *

Rocky moved all their belongings to the two-story farmhouse in just one full load. Their new home had a gray barnwood exterior that was all but peeled and flaked away. The front porch was their favorite spot. It overlooked the hills and an eighty-year-old windmill. Nothing else. The kitchen was nothing but cupboards, a double sink, and an antiquated stove. Both tiny bedrooms were upstairs above the main room, not much bigger than Josie's old dormitory room in Lincoln. Just off the kitchen was the lone bathroom. It was large with a giant tub that had more rust stains than whiteness. The well water was iron rich and ran very slowly out of every spout. Josie vowed never to drink the water and made her husband promise the same. The old well pump outside didn't work.

Harvey and Josie had lunch with an impressed Albert on their first trip into Sioux City, then they went to the grocery store to get twenty gallons of drinking water and groceries. At the store, Floyd made his wife put back paper towels, toilet paper, garbage bags, and glass and bowl cleaner. "I've never bought that stuff in a store, sweetie, and I'm not going to start now," he said. By the time they started back home, Rocky's cargo area was loaded with food, twenty gallons of water and an old refrigerator.

They only lasted a month without a television. When Floyd came home tired, he wanted to watch news and weather and an occasional movie. Huck was starting to go out a day at a time with Floyd after the Paper Man had one of his veterinarian customers examine the dog and put him on worm pills.

Floyd used a leash as he walked Huck along downtown Hawarden sidewalks and crossed the streets. Initially, he secured the leash to a pole or tree outside his prospects' doors, but eventually he just left the leash untied. He studied his new companion: sitting, waiting patiently for him. Huck watched his master through the glass doors, making friends of passers by and barking for Floyd's return.

After lunch Floyd dropped the pup to the curb by his leash after rubbing his nose in the business the dog dropped outside his client's beauty shop. Floyd could see he had one smart dog by how fast he learned. Huck picked up on words and commands faster than any dog he'd ever seen. A stern "Stay!" was enough to keep Huck from budging for the entire duration of a ten-minute call without any leash.

"You hungry?" Huck barked more than once for yes. "You wanna ride in back?" One bark for no. Huck would sit on Rocky's passenger seat listening to Gary, Boz or Chris Rea. His favorite singer was Boz — always three or four barks in a flurry for Boz.

Each night when Harvey returned home at around six in the evening, he would excitedly tell Josie something new Huck did in the territory. "Huck goes into businesses with me now and sits beside me real quick-like. He stood on his hind legs and begged after a prospect turned me down! He knows when I sell somethin' 'cause he heads for Rocky when we leave the place ... without a leash!"

Josie was making progress turning the farmhouse into a cozy little home for two. She burned sage every morning at dawn to purify their space. She bought and arranged earth-tone area rugs for the living room and bedroom. She had giant floor pillows, cushions, and blankets made by Granny arranged into such a cozy nest on the living room floor that two or three times a week all three of them would fall asleep there and not stir until morning. During the week Mrs. Deason kept herself busy buying little things for their home, anxious to see if her husband noticed them when he returned home from work.

Twice a day Josie walked the hills, taking a different route each time, until after six weeks she had a pretty good feel for her surroundings. "The wildlife is incredible here!" she excitedly told Harvey one day. "I was talking to a biology teacher from Morningside College who was hiking with his dog. He said these hills have their own ecosystem. There are certain plant species that are found all the way to the East Coast, but they just end here ... in the Loess Hills, he called them."

"Did you tell him they were called Nakota ..."

"Yes! And he knew that too!"

Harvey knew that it was Floyd who wanted her living out here — keeping his young girl away from people and their ways that can ruin a good thing. *It's my own selfish fear,* he thought as he watched the way her eyes lit up after recounting her talk with the hiker. He recognized her unspoken and unmet thirst for interaction with other human beings. *Dad did the same selfish thing with Mom.* "You wanna go with me for a couple days while I work Pierre?"

She smiled and kissed him yes.

* * * * *

On the run to Pierre, Floyd worked Freeman, Parkston, Mitchell, Chamberlain, Presho and Vivian. Josie stayed in Rocky, reading most of the time and occasionally looking up to marvel at Huck's progress on the job. He was one happy dog with the Paper Man — detached from her and focused on his work, working without a leash. She could see he was Floyd's dog now, and she could see the big difference it made in her husband's work. His attitude had changed from a ruthless loner with territory to burn to that of a boss with a helper.

At times Floyd would get impatient with him, like when Huck trotted across Main Street in Kimball to investigate a dog in the back of a parked pickup. "Get over here!" Floyd barked. When Huck cowered back he wiggled down submissively, scooting up to Floyd's feet and looking up at his boss with sorry brown eyes as he took his smart and final tongue-lashing. "No!" Floyd demanded as he pointed at the other dog's vehicle. He then opened Rocky's side door and ordered him inside for his punishment — fifteen minutes in Rocky's cargo bed.

Josie noticed the most significant change in Huck. Instead of him wanting to be with her and nuzzling her for attention, the whining pup would get behind Rocky's wheel or stand up to look out the side or back windows and watch the Paper Man's every move. Before long, he was barking up a storm for his release, eager to show his master that he was ready to return to work and had learned his lesson for good.

Outside of Pierre Josie saw a little boy give Huck a bite of his ham sandwich. Big mistake! After failing to make a sale to the café owner, Floyd came outside to find his helper chewing the treat. Back inside Rocky for another fifteen minutes of whining and barking, crying to go back to work after excoriations and another lesson learned.

At a Pierre vet, Josie bought a case of premium canned dog food, and Huck's diet was improved considerably from the dry dog food and carry-outs from their meals.

On their return home at a stop in Canton, Huck started earning his keep. Floyd had his client at a shoe-repair shop outfit Huck an adjustable sales collar he would never outgrow. The collar was the same color as Charlie and had a velcro pouch under his neck that would hold product cards, a small order book, a notebook and a pen. The sixty-dollar investment in the collar paid for itself the next day when Floyd and Huck worked Rock Valley and Rock Rapids while Josie stayed home.

Floyd nearly burst into their small kitchen that night and excitedly recounted to his surprised wife Huck's first day as a salesman. Huck sat on the floor panting, listening proudly to every word, and waiting for Josie's response.

"Ya know what this guy sold today?" Before Josie could say anything, Floyd continued, "Three cases of garbage bags! Two cases of TP! And two cases of single-fold towels! To one vet, a grain elevator, and a gas station! Three sales. Two hundred bucks! He paid for his sales collar already! Two hundred bucks, Josie! I never sold two hundred bucks in a day that fast! You should've seen him, honey ... He would trot off on his own right after I said, 'Vet ... gas ... elevator,' and I'd follow along behind him. He'd stand up on his hind legs and beg for an order! He knew who the boss was! They'd take his card, they'd read it, they'd check off whatever they wanted on the card, and write it down on his order pad! Josie, can you imagine? Everyone in the place just watched and laughed! It was so much fun, Josie! You have to go with me and see it for yourself, honey! Can you go tomorrow?"

"Oh, I want to! But I got a call from Dennis today. He's stopping by tomorrow on his way to Minneapolis to a big gallery showing of his work."

"Really?" Harvey's smile belied his sudden apprehension. "What time?"

"He thought late morning. He can only spend a couple hours because he has to be there by seven tomorrow night. I thought I'd take him on a walk around the hills. He'll love it here."

"Great!" he smiled again. "I wish he could stay longer. Maybe on his way back?"

"I'll ask him," she smiled. "He's gonna call me from Beresford and I'll have him meet me at the Akron bridge."

"That's a good idea. He'll never find this place." He paused for a moment to think about the words he'd just said. *He'll never find this place.* Yes, he had hidden his beautiful wife from the outside world — away from any contacts and anyone who could steal her away. All so he could keep her for himself. "Why don't you go with him to Minneapolis ... so you can spend some time together?"

"You wouldn't mind?"

"I want you to be free to get away when you can. You can't stay here all the time." He couldn't believe the words he was saying. He wanted to hide her away from the world, keeping her under lock and key, shielding her from the predators he knew would one day steal her from him.

She kissed him and told him, "I love you."

* * * * *

The next afternoon after showing Dennis around the

homestead, the two cousins set out for Minneapolis. "You and the Paper Man have created a beautiful place to live," Dennis said.

"It really is," Josie returned.

"Do you get lonely?" he asked.

"Sometimes. Not really lonely ... anxious."

"Anxious about what?"

"Oh, just things. Like I miss having people around. I feel really isolated at times."

"How's married life treating you," Dennis asked. He watched her eyes light up under her brindle-shaded hair.

She laughed, saying, "I know I'm happy most of the time. I think he is. Did you know we have a dog? Yeah! Huck. He showed up at the door of our honeymoon cabin. He is so smart, Dennis. Harvey has him trained to sell for him!"

"Really?"

"Yes! He made him a sales collar. And he goes into businesses and gets orders!"

Dennis laughed, adding, "Sounds like the Paper Man is the smart one!"

Dennis filled his Jeep with gas in Worthington. While he was in the restroom, Josie thought about their long walk in the Nakota Hills. They'd stepped together on the wet ground that would soon be dry from the increasing prairie winds that blew predominantly out of the west and southwest. He'd stopped in his tracks to watch an owl swoop by before landing on the limb of an old oak tree. She'd watched him watch the owl as if painting the wise bird with his black eyes.

Dennis had spoken of healing the Sacred Circle. "Many thousands of years ago, the Great Mystery created and placed the four colors of people in the four directions of the earth. The people were to be caretakers of the Sacred Earth and the life forms on it ... living in unison with all of Nature. Over time some of our own kind began sowing the seeds of corruption. These *wasichus* began to domesticate naturally wild animals, till large portions of the Sacred Earth, and build towns and cities. They formed hierarchy powers of control over other Human Beings. They left behind the natural ways of hunting and gathering. Their corrupted behavior was the beginning of the Pyramid Belief. In this belief, Josie, success is measured by how much wealth one can acquire, how many fellow men one can control, and how many of the natural resources one can hoard and exploit. As time went on, the Pyramid Ones became very powerful, using science and technology to draw the peoples of the Sacred Circle away from Nature ... away from the Great Mystery. Most of the Children of Nature who wouldn't be led away by materialism were soon divided, conquered, and destroyed.

"Josie, now that we have entered the new millennium, there are few if any Indigenous Nations of the Sacred Circle intact. The Pyramid Belief has all but conquered the world. And they maintain their power by continuing and promoting division among the people. Josie, it is now time to turn the tide of greed. Each one of us as individual members of the human race needs to examine ourselves and research the natural ways that our ancestors were given by the Great Mystery. As we work our way back, there is one very important thing to remember ... the people are not the problem, but the system is ... the Pyramid System. All people are members of the family of the Sacred Circle. We must get our share for our people. And I have a plan to do it, Josie."

As they climbed back into the Jeep, she started talking about the dreams and musings she'd had since moving to the Sacred Hills. She told Dennis how she'd wake up in the middle of the night and prowl the hills while Floyd would sleep, not knowing where she was going. "I feel like I'm being led in the dark by ... something outside of myself, Dennis."

Dennis paused with goose bumps and ripples of visceral knowing racing up his temples and out the back of his head. Then he said, "I've had the same thing, Josie. But I've also had a vision ... and I have a plan that I know will work."

She looked at him. Dennis waited for her to verbalize her interest in his plan. Sharing this vision with her required her commitment to it. More importantly, he needed her participation in it. But he knew it was risky, and he was not about to force this on someone who wanted to remain safe and uninvolved in the greater things of life. He'd never told another soul about it, and he waited for her to say something.

Josie knew Dennis well enough to know that finding out the details of his idea meant she would have to give her allegiance to the cause. How great a risk would she be required to take? What would it cost her? And would it mean sacrificing her marriage to Harvey? She'd discovered that whenever she told her husband about her dreams and cravings, his fear of losing her overwhelmed him and he quickly changed the subject. She learned to keep these things to herself rather than endure the rejection of her husband. Would she have to choose between Dennis's plan and Harvey? She was not concerned about Floyd. The Paper Man would always be there. But, oh, the thought of losing Harvey!

Dennis and his plan could bring her the greatest gift — the fulfillment of her dream to do some great thing, not just being the wife of the Paper Man. She pondered again the thought of losing Harvey. Waves of childhood emotions swept over her as she remembered the key events of her life that led her to where she was now. Then the clarion realization hit her that being the isolated wife of a paper man was not going to help her fulfill her dream. "Tell me about your plan, Dennis."

I'm Losing You

In early June, Blair, Nebraska, was worked thoroughly until the last roll of toilet paper had been sold from Rocky's cargo area. Huck had his job down pat. He would work the prospects on the fringe of the business district or isolated vets and grain elevators. Floyd had been told by a Norfolk veterinarian that his mutt was one-quarter greyhound. The dog was fast and could easily handle all of the perimeter businesses in the time it took Floyd to work the central business district.

Josie began accompanying Floyd on some of his selling trips so she could distribute Dennis's colorful brochures to local galleries and frame shops.

"Huck's got greyhound legs," Floyd blurted to her as she climbed into the van. He looked down Main Street in the direction Huck would return from but couldn't see his four-legged salesman yet. "Ya know that annual mutt race they have every August at that dog track in Council Bluffs?"

"Yeah ... Isn't that always the last race of the season?" Josie asked.

"Yeah. I'm entering Huck in it next week."

"Don't they charge five hundred bucks to run in that race?"

"Yeah. But the payoff, Josie ... Last year the winner got ten grand! I'll risk five hundred for a twenty-to-one return."

She waited for him to ask her how she did for Dennis after her cold calling on prospects. Not a word. Ever since she went with Dennis to that showing in Minneapolis, she had been his

182

agent and business manager — promoting Thunder Bird, a name she'd created from the stories and legends they'd heard when they were children in Pine Ridge. Walter had recounted legends about the Big Birds with the enormous wings flying high in the warm winds from Mexico on the summer solstice. The legend warned that the Big Birds could swoop down on children who were not watchful and carry them off into the Big Sky, only to drop them on the rocks of the sacred Black Hills and feast on their remains.

"How'd it go for Thunder Bird prospects?" Floyd finally asked as he sat behind the wheel watching for Huck.

"Okay. They may order a piece or two. Except I had to guarantee them if they didn't sell," she sighed.

"His work is good enough ... you won't have to buy them back. These people want everything on consignment or some guarantee of some kind," Floyd stated with an air of disgust. "Let's get some lunch."

Huck was standing upright on his hind legs with his sales pouch around his neck, begging to a laughing group of ten farmers in the Blair co-op elevator.

"Hi, Huck. Whatcha sellin'?" the elevator's manager laughed.

Huck barked once for his prospect to take his product card from his pouch. The man did, scanning the card aloud and entertaining his customers: "Let's see, here ... Toilet paper, paper towels, garbage bags ... There ya go! Garbage bags! I can use a case of those." As the buyer checked garbage bags on the card with Huck's pen, Huck barked twice while his customer scribbled on the order pad. "All right, then ... I'll take two cases."

With a quick kiss on his customer's face after he returned the order pad and pen to the pouch, Huck pranced to the door and wagged his tail for someone to open it for him as the farmers laughed even harder. As soon as the door was opened for him, he was gone.

* * * * *

It was disconcerting to Floyd to have his wife spending two of the next three weeks on the road with Dennis. On her first night back home after a week in Denver galleries, she could see the understanding eyes of Harvey change into the predator salesman eyes of Floyd. Lately she had been making love to Floyd instead of Harvey, leaving her with a cold feeling that she was just another customer. The understanding and compassionate man she fell in love with had for now been sacked by Floyd.

On Saturday morning after completing her gallery tour with Dennis, Josie sat on Rocky's passenger seat with a stopwatch in her hand. Through the side-view mirror, she watched Floyd and Huck walk back from the van about fifty yards. Huck was wearing his black-and-white racing jersey with #8 on both sides. Huck's floppy ears drooped over the strap of the racing muzzle and his snout was covered by the racing headgear. As Huck sat patiently on the road facing Rocky's back bumper, Josie could see Floyd checking his clipboard of statistics on Huck's previous runs. Huck remained sitting on the road as Floyd returned to the van.

"Isn't it too hot out for him?" Josie asked.

"One more run and we're done. Don't start the time till I honk. Ready?"

"Yeah."

Rocky took off, spitting dirt clods and dust as Josie watched Huck in her side-view mirror. Floyd kept his eyes on Rocky's

184

speed and odometer. Then as Huck's ears rose, Rocky honked, signaling the fur-covered salesman to chase the white cardboard bunny taped to Rocky's bumper.

Floyd's excitement was contagious. "Come on ... come on! Faster, Huck! Faster!" he exclaimed, while Josie watched her baby running like crazy and closing in on them.

"Stop!" Floyd yelled, cuing Josie to click off the stopwatch. Rocky slowed, letting Huck wind down after his run. "What was his time?"

"Thirty-six and two-tenths."

"Great! A record! That's almost two seconds off his best time! Last year's winner was only a second faster."

They went to the back bumper where Huck was standing and panting heavily. Josie knelt to him and removed his muzzle and jersey before hugging and kissing him. When she poured Huck a bowl of water in Rocky's cargo bed at the open side door, Floyd lifted Huck into the cargo bed and happily watched him lap his water.

"Ten grand, baby," he said to Josie.

Josie smiled, putting her arms around his waist and pulling his hips to hers. "Fifty-fifty," she smiled.

"That's right," he smiled back, kissing her on her mouth quickly and without passion.

She held back from saying the things that bothered her. *You don't kiss me like you mean it. You don't make love to me — you take me. I want to go to Chicago for three weeks with Dennis because I'm his agent and it would mean big bucks from international galleries.*

It was both Harvey and Floyd who knew she was too young and beautiful to hold for long. The lure of the manswarm with its money and fame was like a toxic cesspool he was wading in. He knew it would soon swallow him whole.

When they returned home, the three of them sat on the front

porch with the sun high over the western hills. Floyd looked into the golden circles that were no longer his Josie, but now Josephine. "I'm losing you."

In the past, Josie would have come to him as in Pine Ridge and soothed his fear again by holding him and telling him it wasn't true until he believed it. Then they would have made love. Afterwards, he would ask her while pressing her flesh to his, "Are we okay?" She would assure him everything was fine while kissing his beard deep into his skin. And again they would make love.

Now the eyes of Josephine were looking into his. She was living her dream again. This was the Josephine that betrayed him and let the manswarm devour his Josie. She would not answer him in her usual quick way. Her loyalty was to The Plan she could not discuss with anyone but Thunder Bird, her client. Her slow response was curt and abrasive.

"We've discussed this already at least a hundred times. Dennis is getting a name for himself in the bigger circles. I'm his agent and business manager. He's giving me twenty-five percent of every piece sold. I have to get a computer to get organized ... and you won't buy it. So I hope you win your race."

She went inside the house, slamming the door behind her. Floyd looked down at Huck and said calmly, "No pressure, boy. Just run. Don't think about that crap. Just run."

Huck laid back and whined, raising his front leg and exposing his short-haired belly. Floyd rubbed his belly with his shoe bottom, back and forth, thinking how his time with Josie was up. In order to keep her, he had to learn to live with Josephine or be doomed to his father's aloneness. *Huck will help with the loneliness,* he thought as the dog's hind leg pedaled excitedly from his master's massage.

They did their own thing for the summer — Josephine accompanying Dennis on a tour of galleries throughout the country while fleshing out the details of his plan, and Floyd working his territory and training Huck for the big race. But his wife's independence and loyalty to Thunder Bird bothered Floyd tremendously, and he took it out on his customers.

He had just popped a couple of quick sales in Newcastle, Nebraska, when the town's noon siren blew and wound down, bringing in farmers and small business owners to the town's only café, the Cornhusker. He tossed his faded red two-wheeler through his van's open back doors, the clatter of it hitting the cargo floor diminished by Rocky's indoor-outdoor carpeting. Floyd's blue eyes got even smaller and impish looking as he carried Charlie into the Cornhusker while Huck made a few calls.

It had been four months since he'd last entered the busy little café that smelled of the pork tenderloin special written in chalk on the menu board above the back counter. There were the same two young waitresses working like gangbusters to feed and serve their four-dozen regulars. He parked his bones on the last empty stool at the counter and squinted into the kitchen where he could see the back of that bastard who only bought from Jake, Albert's cynical Nebraska salesman. Floyd had purposely taken a dozen customers away from the grouchy salesman and sold product to twenty more.

"He doesn't work for me!" Albert had snapped at Jake. "He's on his own!"

"Yer sellin' him the paper for yer dispensers I put in, you old codger!" Jake railed.

Each time the argument ensued, Silver would shrug his round sloping shoulders and laugh inwardly at his top-jobber's audacity. Finally, the surly salesman with the black horsehair mustache would storm out of the office, cursing all the way down to his car.

Floyd was pulling the hairs at the tip of his covered chin with his left hand, the hand that had carried Charlie into the Cornhusker and leaned him against the counter's base on the floor. He knew the impish little deed he was about to pull might get him banned from Newcastle.

He took Charlie into the restroom and slid the door latch before seeing Silver's towel and double-roll paper dispensers. The dispenser key — always in Charlie's inside zipper pocket, unlocked the toilet paper dispenser. Both rolls fit snugly and unobtrusively at the bottom of the spacious sales case, and Floyd closed the now-empty dispenser.

Floyd grinned like the devil as he ate the pork tenderloin that Bohunk in the kitchen made him, and he watched as a farmer in overalls, a banker in gray polyester pants, and a scrawny-necked mechanic headed for the restroom.

When Floyd was ready to drive out of Newcastle, the café owner peered out his front window at Rocky's vehicle lettering. It was when Floyd was picking up Huck on the highway that the Bohunk's teeth clenched from the complaints of his customers of "no corncobs in the john." To add insult to injury, on his way back to the kitchen the café owner stopped at the counter where the Paper Man had eaten and saw a dollar tip on top of his product card. He swiped up the product card from his counter and saw toilet paper circled in red ink. He angrily crushed the Paper Man's product card in his clenched fist while he fumed inwardly. This wasn't the first time he'd been duped and robbed by that Sioux City salesman. He went to refill his dispensers with his ulcer boiling mad, bleeding its toxic acid into his memory for next time.

She should be here, Floyd complained to himself as Salesman Huck was being led by a lead boy to the dog track's starting chute. He'd had it with Dennis and his career! Josie had already agreed to accompany Floyd on his upcoming Black Hills run and stay in their honeymoon cabin, but she wouldn't be able to return home with him. Thunder Bird had two important showings in Laramie and Cheyenne, and Dennis would pick her up at the Harney Peak cabin and take her to Wyoming with him. Floyd wanted to change her mind about going. *I'm going to give her an ultimatum — it's either me ... or Thunder Bird!* "Choose!" he murmured aloud at the track's front fence by the finish line.

It was the last race of the season. Each dog had to be between one-eighth and one-quarter greyhound. As the electric rabbit started moving and picking up speed on the flood-lit far side of the dog track, the big, rowdy crowd stood and cheered for their mutt to win. The chutes opened and Huck bolted from the #8 chute somewhere in the middle of the pack early in the 550-yard race.

"Run, Huck!" Floyd yelled. "Run!"

Huck was in fifth place with a lap to go. Floyd glanced at the twenty-five-to-one odds on #8 displayed on the electronic tote board. As Huck rounded the first turn, he ran too wide and ended up in sixth place on the back stretch.

"Run, Huck!"

Huck gained speed and position until he was in third place rounding the final turn on the stretch to the finish line.

"Go, Huck! Go!"

Huck finished third — out of the money. Only the winner took home the purse.

Floyd met his panting dog at the lead boy area. He removed his leash, muzzle and jersey before walking through the grandstand with him. "Maybe next year, boy," Floyd consoled the panting dog. With his head hung low from exertion, Huck followed the Paper Man out to Rocky where he was given a rare T-bone steak with his bowl of water.

While Huck enjoyed his treat, Floyd played Gary's song "Woman, Woman" with the lyrics, "Have you got cheating on your mind?" He played the song a dozen more times during his one-hundred-mile drive home. By the time he parked Rocky on the quiet lane beside his dark homestead, Floyd had convinced himself she would betray him. With Dennis. They were not full first cousins. She loved Dennis. Dennis loved her. And with Josephine building Thunder Bird's reputation as a top-notch artist, she was manifesting her dream to do something successful — all without help from her husband.

I'm too old for her, he thought as Huck loped up the porch steps. "Now or never," he would tell her on their run to the Hills. He looked behind him to the east before opening the kitchen door. He could see the blue-black outline of the Nakota Hills where Josie and Dennis had walked alone. Something happened then, Floyd knew, and he blinked his tired blue eyes and yawned at the moon's silvery sheen to the south.

The rooms inside were hot from the August sun broiling above closed windows. Floyd opened every window and turned on the floor fan in their upstairs bedroom. His back hit their queen-size bed in the dark. A hundred lonely towns flashed across the void of his bedroom ceiling: Bonesteel, Viborg, Oakland, Valentine. Deserted roads into Battle Creek, Pierson, Sac City, Early, and Sanborn followed suit. On and on they came. Then came the faces of his customers — faces that rejected him and faces that bought. All of them strangers. His life mimicked that of his father's, and he remembered the drunken words his father once uttered: "All of my friends are strangers."

Floyd always knew he would lose the best part of his life. It was happening now — out of his control. Harvey could stop this and save them, but he was battered from Gary's warning and not having her with him. And Floyd was battered from the hot, long summer — the meanest of all seasons for a paper man.

He longed for sleep to salve his aching heart on this breezeless night in the northernmost part of the Nakota Hills. She would have to save them now. Or he would let his "young girl" go and drive only the back roads until he healed. "At least I have Huck," he mumbled before falling asleep.

Saturday morning Floyd backed Rocky to the dock next to Albert's forest-green LTD. His order would be stacked on the elevator. On the other side of Albert's car, Floyd saw Jake's black Mercury parked in anger — its wheels turned sharply and angled in, as if he'd jumped out of it still running. Floyd's sandals, khaki shorts and wrinkled T-shirt felt heavy on his beleaguered body as he carried Charlie into the office. *It's time,* he said to himself as he entered Silver's office without fear.

Inside the office, Jake paced the soiled path from the vault to Willard's desk in a golf shirt and long knit shorts. The back of Jake's calves were muscular, as if softballs were wedged in either one. Albert, seated at Willard's desk, was in the middle of haggling with Jake over his expense account. Both men quieted and exhibited an abrupt change in attitude as soon as Floyd entered the room.

"There's the kid now, Jake! Tell 'im yer business," Albert whined. He lit a dead cigar butt from his ashtray and listened with his big ears as he puffed.

Floyd moved to the back of the room opposite the two men and took a seat by the back door while going over the order he'd called in the day before.

"I demand you stop calling on my customers!" Jake barked to Floyd's bowed head.

Floyd eyes met Jake's little black eyes behind his lenses. "What are you talkin' about?" he asked innocently.

"The Cornhusker Café in Newcastle ... and the crapper paper you stole outta my account's dispensers!"

Floyd stood and walked over to where Jake was standing. He stopped right in front of the sourpuss salesman — well into his "personal space" and much too close for the angry man's comfort. Jake backed away several steps as Floyd said, "It's free territory out there, old man. If yer customers aren't loyal, that's a sale for me. Some win ... some lose, Jake. But don't ever accuse me of stealin'. I don't like that."

Jake left fuming. As he watched from the window, Floyd laughed when he saw Jake back away from the dock just as a slow-moving freight train blocked his path. After a comical U-turn, Jake sped away with his jaw clenched tightly around a cigar butt he'd retrieved from his ashtray.

"How's married life treatin' ya?" Albert asked.

"It's okay," Floyd said, slumping onto a chair on castors.

"She still workin' for that Indian artist?"

"Yeah."

"You say they're related?"

"Cousins," Floyd said, finding it hard to hide his disdain for their relationship. He watched his supplier look down to his ashtray as he flicked his cigar ash with his little finger. He could see the words all over Silver's snarly mouth — unspoken yet loud and clear to Floyd. He had to hear the words. They had to be said by his old boss in order to see if he loved her. Floyd pushed on. "What would you do if she was gone all the time?"

The old man shrugged his shoulders and leaned back in Willard's oak swivel chair. The dust-covered window air conditioner blew cool air onto his wrinkled neck as he held his cigar close to his big black wing-tip. "She makin' any dough?" he asked.

"Yeah."

"She givin' ya any?"

"Any what?" Floyd smirked.

"Ah ... you let yer putz do yer thinkin' for ya. Like yer old man. He went downhill, ya know."

"Yeah ... she gives me money."

"Then let her make ya dough ... and quit whinin' about it, for God's sake." He muttered inaudibly when he got up and shuffled over to a stack of invoices he had to price for the Paper Man.

"Yeah, but I'm not seein' much of her lately. I don't know ... maybe I'm jealous of the artist ... not Dennis."

"Who's Dennis?"

"The Indian ... I mean, the Indigenous artist. Native Americans ... Indians ... hell, who knows what to call 'em!"

"What's her commission? Ten ... twenty percent?"

"Twenty-five. She's his business manager too. The money's comin' in. I saw her deposit a check for fifteen hundred in our checking account."

"You better start keepin' yer money here," Silver laughed.

Just then the outer office door opened, and in came a tall, quiet man who resembled a Viking with his unkempt, long blond hair and massive, high cheekbones. His demeanor was that of a volcano — ready to erupt if he got hot enough.

"You Joe Paul?" Silver asked.

"Yeah."

Albert submissively asked if Floyd would show Joe where the paper was stored on the fifth floor. "He's gonna unload that boxcar," Albert added as the two men headed for the door.

"I'm not helpin' with that car," Floyd protested.

"I didn't say that, for Pete's sake! Just show him where to put the stuff!"

"After I have a shot of wine," he countered.

"Have some ... I don't care. You drink wine, Joe?"

"Yeah ... some," he replied.

Floyd watched Joe closely. He'd been sent over before by the Labor Power office, a place loaded with transient day labor that charged area businesses eight bucks an hour for temporary help. Labor Power got two bucks of it, and guys like Joe got $6.00 an hour for eight hours of back-breaking work loading and unloading boxcars and trucks jammed full of product. Silver ordered twenty-five boxcars a year filled with cases of toilet paper, napkins, locker paper, cups and oil dry. Joe Paul's forty-eight bucks a day would get Albert's pallets filled with fifty-pound cases. Then with a manual jack, he would pull the pallet load halfway though the dark warehouse and onto the freight elevator. When two full pallets were on the elevator, he would hold his finger on the elevator button all the way up to the fifth floor, adroitly lining up the elevator's floor with the fifth-floor landing. Then he would pull his load to the right spot in the aisle amidst fifty thousand square feet of jammed product stacked five or six cases high. Floyd remembered seeing this man stack seven or eight cases high easily — the last case heaved overhead with the biggest pair of hands he had ever seen on a man.

He gave Joe Paul a paper soufflet cup topped with Silver's dry red port. "Ya have ta sip it. It's pretty strong stuff," Floyd advised.

Floyd watched him taste it. His big, cracked and calloused, dirty fingers held the rim of the cup to his pursed lips. Then Floyd took a sip and offered the man a kitchen chair pushed under the round table between the floor safe and Willard's desk. He tried not to stare or be caught watching him as Joe Paul sat straight as a rod with his jeans baggy and soiled from unloading trucks all week at a nearby baking company.

"You from Sioux City?" Floyd inquired.

"Yeah."

That was it. The quiet man slugged back the remaining half of the port in his cup. As he stood up, Floyd glimpsed the brown cotton work gloves sticking out of his back pocket below his ragged white T-shirt that was stained yellow around his armpits and neck. He stood awkwardly holding his empty cup in his giant paw.

"Break the seal and help him open that car, will ya?" Albert mumbled to Floyd while shuffling over to a pile of tools he kept on the floor beside the wine case near the back door. Silver handed Floyd a big pair of wire cutters.

"My stuff on the elevator?" Floyd asked.

"Yeah," Albert said.

"Can he help me load my stuff?"

"I don't care. Open that car first!"

Not a light was on in the tire warehouse. The smell of rubber was so powerful in the absolute darkness it was like walking through a stifling black hole. Gargantuan tractor tires stacked like donuts revealed themselves with each 60-watt lightbulb that Floyd turned on as he made his way to the dark freight elevator. Joe Paul was behind him a couple of steps, his ice-blue, almond eyes seeing deep into the darkness. Floyd stopped to lift the elevator's heavy wooden gate, briefly surveying his product for his Black Hills run. Joe Paul two-wheeled the Paper Man's product to the edge of the dock at Rocky's back door as Floyd loaded his cargo area. Not a word was said between them, even when Floyd took him up to the fifth floor and showed him where to stack the product from the boxcar.

Floyd tossed the seal into a coffee can; and with Joe Paul's strength of two men, they slid open the boxcar door to expose a full carload of toilet paper, towels and napkins from California.

On Sunday morning Rocky was loaded to the max when Floyd picked up Josie at the Sioux City airport. As they ate breakfast together in a downtown Sioux City restaurant, she animated about how well Thunder Bird's reputation was growing and how she was looking forward to their Black Hills run. He could see the changes she was making, and they were coming way too fast for him. She told him she had decided to become a vegetarian and had given up caffeine for bottled water and herbal tea. He listened to her excited voice go on about meditating with Dennis and reading Native American spiritual books. It was Josephine now breathing from her center. And she now wore her hair wild-like — ratted and teased back as if a born-again free spirit.

During their meal Floyd did a lot of nodding and grunting, throwing in a few comments to show he still had a pulse. "Oh, yeah?" "Really!"

When they got back home Josie said, "I wish we had a full day tomorrow to just spend at home around the hills." But both knew it was impossible. Dennis was meeting her in Pine Ridge on Saturday for a showing at the old church after spending Friday night with his parents. She volunteered Rocky to haul chairs from the Hot Springs Holiday Inn for the showing. She had expected to hear protests from Floyd about cutting short their stay in their honeymoon cabin, but there was nothing said.

That night Huck laid at the foot of their bed after they made love. They had waited until bedtime before lovemaking. It was another first that confused Josie. She was willing to let him park Rocky on some isolated dirt road in the hills and let Boz take over, but that was not there anymore. Josephine and Floyd clashed for control, and now sensitive Harvey wasn't appealing to her. Josie began to feel she was just too weak for the things that had to be done.

* * * * *

Late Monday morning after working Vermillion, the Paper Man was on his first call in Yankton when his wife did

197

something so shocking he felt as if he had been hit by a cannonball right in his center. As Floyd and Charlie pitched the redneck owner of the Super Chief station, Huck watched Josephine go into the station's one restroom with the skinny buckskin purse Dennis had bought her in Cheyenne. Floyd could instantly smell it seeping in from the cracks in the stucco and plaster behind him. His jaw tightened like that of a lumberjack sawing the oldest rings on a redwood. *I'm losing her,* he thought as he continued to pitch his prospect, who was apparently oblivious to the sweet smell of pot coming from his restroom.

He worked Yankton for an hour before checking into the Yankton Motel, one of the dives he'd stayed in many times with his father. He didn't mention the pot, even though he could smell it on her.

Josie sprawled out on the musty queen-size bed and watched television while Floyd worked Yankton in a foggy stupor. His mind wasn't focused on his prospects. A thousand times in the next four hours he caught himself thinking of the life she and Dennis lived far away from him. *Half-cousins,* he warned himself a hundred times, until he realized he was selling only the minimum orders he used to get when he first started selling. Even Floyd didn't feel like suggesting, pushing, and adding to his sales. It was as if the entire afternoon had been taken over by the pushover Harvey.

"Okay. I'll bring ya in a case. No problem," said Harvey plaintively to a service station owner. *You wimp!* screamed the stifled Floyd to the lackluster Harvey.

When Floyd got a chance, he'd punish his weaker side by slamming his two-wheeler into Rocky's cargo area. Once he struck Huck, causing his sidekick to whimper in pain while cramming himself into Rocky's cargo bed with only a couple feet of space to spare. "I'm sorry, Huck. I'm sorry," the remorseful Harvey assured the dog. Huck kept still, gingerly lying against a case of 1,500-sheet one-ply toilet paper — Huck's biggest seller until now.

Then Floyd had a plan. "Okay, boy. One more call. Here's what yer gonna do ..."

Immersed in hot bath water in the long, deep, pink porcelain tub, Josephine thought about her Paper Man and how they'd made love in this tub on several previous runs. This was Floyd's favorite room. She admired his work ethic and independence — the ruthless predator with the skinny legs. She began to cry as she thought about the plan she and Dennis had been conjuring. It was coming to the point in Pine Ridge when she would tell Floyd Harvey Deason goodbye and commit herself to building a better future for her people.

She thought back to the Super Chief restroom earlier in the day and felt a twinge of guilt at what she'd done. *I have two good reasons for doing it,* she justified to herself. But the truth was she knew right from wrong, and the heaviness of her guilt and shame robbed her of any exoneration she thought she deserved. Remembering back to her childhood, she recalled how Floyd and her mother had both been seductive forces in her decision to dabble in "smoking sage." On a trip to the Badlands with her mother, the two stood on the same spot where Josie would eventually leave her mother's ashes. "Josie, when I was pregnant with you, I was hooked on morphine from painkillers they forced on me in the VA Hospital. All I did was pray for you to not be affected by the drugs. You are healthy ... and I am depressed, honey. I don't know what to do," she'd cried to her young daughter.

It was several months later when Josie found herself in the old church that night with Harvey. She had seen him smoke his stash — that magical smoke that seemed to help his loneliness.

She remembered how his fingers were so long and slender and clean; so different from the rough hands on characters she'd seen on the reservation. Then she remembered seeing the guilt on his face as he realized what he was doing. "Yer too young for this. I don't know why I ever showed you my stash. I guess I just wanted company."

She knew she'd fallen in love with him right then and there, and the scene had been burned into her mind for nearly a decade as she waited for him to come back into her life.

Floyd and Charlie entered a crowded Yankton tavern with Huck trailing. The bartender could not see Huck, but the customers were petting him as he sat placidly adorned in his sales collar. Floyd placed his product card on the bar and said with confidence to the bartender, "Remember last time I was in and you wouldn't buy 'cause you thought my garbage bags were too thin? Well ... let me show ya somethin'."

Floyd reached into Charlie's side picket, whipped out a goldenrod-colored 33-gallon garbage bag, and snapped it open. The Paper Man backed up a few steps so his prospect could see Huck climb inside the open bag. With the dog inside, Floyd lifted the bag into the air and displayed its strength to the amazement of a dozen onlookers. "Look! His nails won't even puncture it. Can I bring ya in a couple cases?"

"Sure," said the grinning bartender above the laughter of his customers.

The motel room's window air conditioner was humming obstreperously. It was after midnight when she heard him come in. The room smelled of sweet pot, but he was nearly drunk and paid no attention as he sat in the dark on the end of the bed to undress. Huck's belly hit the cool tile in the bathroom.

"Did you eat?" she asked.

"I had a loosemeat in the bar. Did you eat?"

"Yeah ... I walked a couple blocks to the pizza place."

"You had pizza?" he asked, startled.

"No. A big salad."

Floyd balled his socks and tossed them, then slipped under the covers naked. He scooted next to her bare back with his back to hers. She said nothing. Within a few minutes she heard his snoring and couldn't get to sleep.

Josephine dressed and walked the quiet Yankton streets behind the motel. She thought about the plan and how it would be afterwards. *As long as nobody gets hurt,* she reminded herself. Continuing her walk, she mused about their honeymoon in the Black Hills. She laughed aloud when she thought of him carrying her into the cabin while Rocky played Boz. She wanted that again.

* * * * *

Tuesday morning they had breakfast in a Yankton pancake house before heading west on Highway 50. On their way to Armour, Josephine knew things were cold between them. She had gotten up first and showered right away. He showered soon after, not mentioning a word about anything. *Could he know?* she worried. *No ... no way,* she assured herself.

They were closing in on Armour when Harvey thought about the pot he'd smoked in front of her in Pine Ridge long ago. "You must've started smokin' pot when I showed you my stash in Pine Ridge. I'd left some in the cabinet, and you got my key and smoked some."

"No ... I left Pine Ridge early that next morning," she said, then she remained quiet on Rocky's passenger seat.

"You smoked in Macy?" he asked.

"From time to time, yes," she confessed.

"With yer friends?"

"Yeah."

After turning off from Highway 281 into Armour, Harvey took over as he turned from Main Street onto a gravel road heading west out of town. He parked Rocky on the side of a hill between a cornfield and a set of railroad tracks and shut off the engine. Then he turned to Josie and said, "I'm sorry."

"About what?" she asked.

"For gettin' you started with the stuff."

"Harvey ... I would have sooner or later. You're not to blame."

He put in Boz's "What Can I Say?" and they sat in silence listening to the song. As soon as it was over, Josie spoke first. "You are my only true love. You don't have to say anything," she smiled.

Harvey got out and quickly slid open the van's side door. "Huck! Work the whole friggin' town!"

Huck excitedly stood up and jumped out of the door. As Harvey put his sales collar on him he said, "I'm gonna make love to yer mother now. Get!" Huck took off like a shot, anxious to bring back orders. For an instant, he reminded Harvey of how he used to do the same thing for Albert.

Josie got out the sleeping bag after Harvey closed Rocky's side door from inside the cargo area. She wanted him more than ever, knowing it may be their last time together for a long while.

After they made love, Josie cried while he napped. *Couldn't he be in on the plan?* she wondered. But no. She recalled Dennis snapping at her when she suggested it. "He's our ace of hearts. The Paper Man cannot know," he'd said when he dropped her off at the airport Sunday morning. She thought again about how much she loved her Paper Man and longed to have the passion they'd had when they first got married. She gently shook his shoulder and said, "I W Y N, Paper Man."

Harvey turned toward her and wrapped his arms around her again.

Huck made three sales in Armour and returned to the van. Occupied with sniffing the ground between the van and the railroad tracks, he didn't seem to care that the doors were still closed and Boz was still serenading the preoccupied couple inside. As the ground began to rumble from an approaching train, Huck heard the crunching of gravel from the van's tires. In Harvey's eagerness to be with his wife, he didn't realize he'd put the van into neutral instead of park.

As the rumbling train approached and the van inched down the hill toward the tracks, Huck barked a warning to Harvey and Josie. Caught up in their passion inside the van, the two were oblivious to the world outside. Suddenly, they heard the train whistle just outside the van's rear door, along with a muffled whimper from Huck. Without taking time to dress, Floyd instantly threw open the side cargo door and searched feverishly for Huck. Behind the van he found him — his body wedged beneath the back tire of the van, preventing it from rolling into the freight train.

As the last car of the train lumbered down the tracks toward Nebraska, Floyd braced his feet against the tracks and was able to push the heavy van forward a couple of inches. He yelled for Josie to set the emergency brake, and he carefully picked up Huck and set him in the cargo area. After quickly dressing, Floyd drove to the town's only vet as fast as he could.

Harvey and Josie watched anxiously as the vet examined Huck. "Looks like a couple bruised ribs. No signs of internal bleeding. I'll take a couple x-rays to be sure, though."

"Will he be okay?" Josie asked.

"He's young and will bounce back pretty quickly. Should be good as new in a couple of days. I can't for the life of me figure out how he got pinned under the van, though."

Harvey and Josie looked ashamed. "It's my fault, doc," Harvey said. "He was sleeping under the van, and I'd left it in neutral instead of park. When the train came by and shook the ground, the van started backwards. It was all my fault."

"You're too hard on yourself, honey. It was a mistake," Josie said softly

"Well, he's a lucky dog. He'll be fine," said the vet as he walked out of the room.

On their way to Platte, Harvey told Josie how proud he was of their dog.

"Why don't you tell him?" she said.

"He hears me ... don't ya, Huck?"

Huck weakly barked twice for yes.

War Path

Tuesday night they spent the night in another old nest of the Paper Man, the Plainsman Inn in Burke. Then on Wednesday they continued through Gregory, Dallas, Colome, and then on to Winner on Highway 18. Huck was already showing improvement, jumping in and out of the van and accompanying Floyd on his calls in Gregory and Colome.

By Wednesday night, Josie had returned to Josephine, and so had Floyd's jealousy of her relationship with Dennis. He thought if he joined her pot smoking and welcomed it without criticism, he could hold on to her. But the pot was only her smoke screen for the breakdown dead ahead. He could feel her slipping away again — as if the closer she got to Thunder Bird, the further she was from him.

After working Winner that night, they stopped at the Winner Motel for the night. No lovemaking — she was tired and had a headache.

By Thursday morning, Floyd threw Harvey out of Rocky and was ready to punish Wagner. He knew this was only a warm-up for the massacre he had planned for Pine Ridge — that dump in the Badlands that had brought him Josie, only to leave him with Josephine.

* * * * *

Thursday evening in Pine Ridge, Josie was having dinner

with the Birds while Floyd slept in Rocky with a headache. He planned to say what needed to be said to her on Friday after he emptied Rocky's cargo van and he'd won his own personal victory over Pine Ridge. But for now he would rest long and deep.

Friday morning's August sun shining through Rocky's windshield had Huck whining to get outside. Floyd groggily got up — nude in his sweatbox — and rolled down the front windows. Huck jumped out the passenger-side window and began sniffing around the reservation where dogs roamed freely. Huck wasn't wearing his collar. Floyd had given him the day off for covering for him in Armour.

Floyd squinted hard at his small, bloodshot blue eyes in Rocky's rearview mirror. No shower. No brushed teeth. He would wear his snarly beard as his war paint. He donned an old baseball cap and did what his father did over two decades ago when they were closing in on Pine Ridge. He remembered it as if it were yesterday.

The station wagon was clogged with soiled bags of bologna sandwiches and black bananas. The stench of old Camels permeated the air, and the nicotine had long since yellowed the glass and upholstery. Father and son twitched from the fumes of the four dozen urinal cakes they'd been inhaling for four days.

"Heap big bucks in Pine Ridge," his father said. Then the laughing old man began thumping the cracked and dusty dashboard with his yellow fingers, imitating the sound of an Indian war drum rising, beating and then falling in volume. In a high-pitched frenzy the old man said, "Pine Ridge! Better than a four-year fargenzinger! Yes, sir." Thump-thump-thump-thump ... thump-thump-thump-thump.

"Dad," the young Deason inquired, "What's a four-year fargenzinger?"

The old paper man stuck his right hand into his wrinkled shirt pocket for another Camel and lit it before answering with his cynical mouth pooched out, "Son, a four-year fargenzinger is that ... perfect place ... or ... that woman you return to every four years. Yer both just so glad to see each other ... that only good things can happen to ya. That's Pine Ridge ... the big fargenzinger," he cackled. Again he pounded the dash, laughing this time as his son joined him on the dashboard.

"Fargenzinger," Floyd mumbled after sliding open Rocky's side door so violently that Huck heard it some three hundred yards away. He grabbed Charlie, then he honked Rocky's horn once.

Soon Huck came running up to his master, his ears perked and confused why he would be summoned on his day off. Floyd scribbled on the back of a product card and stuck it folded under Huck's flea collar. "Give this to Josie." Huck paused as if to ask why. "Never mind. Go!" Huck high-tailed it for the Bird house.

Floyd eyed with contempt the old church where he was married, as if planning to destroy it. The stage was set for a record day. Walter would be the key.

"The key," he snarled out loud. He remembered that night in Pine Ridge over a decade ago when he had mistakenly showed his stash in the dispenser to little Josie. Then his mind was flooded with a thousand negative thoughts about Josephine and Thunder Bird smoking pot together, laughing and having a ball while he blistered and begged in his territory — standing up to the manswarm town after town, mile after mile, one endless lonely night after another.

Floyd pinched down his cap, slammed Rocky's side door, and dug his heels hard into the gravel with every step in six directions until he saw his old prey. He waited restively outside the Pine Ridge grocery until the games began.

Walter was leaving his house after breakfast when Huck started barking for Josie. It was already too hot for the morning. Humidity had rolled up from the Nebraska panhandle and stuck to every living thing like fresh road tar.

"Huckster!" Walter laughed. "Are you hungry, boy?"

Josie came out the side door from the Bird kitchen wearing wrinkled khaki shorts with a lavender halter top and sandals. She knew what Huck was telling her and took the note from his collar, which simply read: "Meet me in front of the store."

She took the short way, waving goodbye to the tribal chairman on his way to work. She remembered this walk on the same ground when she carried her pillow and blanket to him that night in the church. She pondered the irony of the situation: If she hadn't gone to him that night, she wouldn't be Mrs. Deason now. Nor would she have such a smart dog as Huck. Behind her she heard Thunder Bird's Jeep turning into the Bird driveway and parking on the spot where her mother spent her final moments alive. Should she make one more plea to her client to spare her husband? *NO!* she scolded herself.

She reiterated to herself her devotion to the plan as she stepped in fresh dog dung on the north side of the old church — right in the same spot where Rocky had played their wedding song. *Bad omen,* she thought to herself. "Shoot!" she muttered, aware that Huck was letting his boss know she was coming. Floyd could see her scraping the bottom of her sandal on a culvert near Rocky. He ducked back around the corner of the storefront where Huck sat panting by the old pop machine with his pink tongue hanging from one side of his slack jaw. He could hear her sandals crunching gravel underfoot.

"Go to the back door and stay," Floyd ordered Huck. As she neared the front corner of the store, she heard pounding on the pop machine — the same war drumbeat he and his father imitated so obnoxiously. She stopped, invisible and waiting.

Charlie, tucked against his left side, was sweaty on both sides when Floyd entered the little store. She listened for the door to close behind him, then watched through the front door as the Paper Man got his bogus refund from the grocer's wife after leaning his face close to her small fan on the counter. Then he headed for the back of the store and waited for Clouda to come out of his walk-in freezer.

It was too hot outside, so Josie slipped inside and stood under an air conditioner dripping cool water onto the front entrance. Floyd knew she was listening to him from the far aisle. "Hey, Chief! Brought ya two cases of towels for my dispenser."

"Don't need any. Roll lasts me long time."

"The old man says two cases or yank the dispenser. He thinks yer buyin' towels for it in Rapid."

"How much a case?"

"Thirty-six bucks," Floyd said, his pen already writing up the order. He knew his wife was listening.

He's onto something, she worried. *Why is he cheating this passive man at this particular moment? How much does he know?*

As she followed him out of the store into the sweltering heat, Floyd bounced his two-wheeler out of Rocky, loading two cases of towels onto its blade. He would deflect her as only the Paper Man could. He wheeled around and faced her. "I am not the coldest place in this town," he scowled.

"That was pretty cold," she said as she followed him to the grocer's back door.

"Sometimes ... you step in it, Josephine."

"What are you talking about?"

He stopped in the breezeway between the smokehouse and the back door where Huck waited, panting. "Remember when you told me about how you and Dennis took baths together?"

"We were just kids!"

"And sometimes ... even now you said you share a bed with him in motel rooms."

"You think I'm screwing around with Dennis?" she laughed.

"After this Indian pays me ... I want you to go into his freezer with me ... where it's cold. We can't talk in this kind of heat."

She waited and watched him collect from the grocer for his brutish over-charging. "Chief, mind if me and my wife step into yer freezer and talk privately for a few minutes?" The grocer grunted passively. Then Floyd audaciously asked, "Got any scraps for my dog?"

He gave Floyd big T-bones with strips of red meat visible on the bones.

"Thanks, Chief."

As Huck enjoyed his treat and the Paper Man and his wife disappeared into the freezer, Clara Clouda walked up to her husband and asked, "Why do you back down to that fat taker?" Her demoralized husband simply shook his head and walked back to his meat slicer.

Inside the freezer Floyd had Josie's back against the grocer's apron hanging on the closed door. He'd pulled up her halter top and was trying to kiss her exposed breasts while holding her elbows against her sides. She was repulsed by his facial hair scraping her cold chest and tried to push his face away from her skin with the side of her head.

"No! Don't!" she insisted.

He continued kissing and fondling her roughly until she'd had enough and pushed him away by thrusting her upper body into his. Then she adamantly pulled her top back down.

She had never refused him before. But neither had she ever

seen this creature before. His eyes were mere slits of blue-blackness. He was like a shark — emotionless and ready to eat her heart out without blinking. The smell of his fetid morning breath was so repulsive she nearly gagged when he pressed his mouth on hers. How different this was now, in here, compared to her embrace with young Dennis the day she first met Harvey.

Floyd and Charlie followed her out the back door, dragging his cart toward Rocky as Huck chewed on a T-bone in the breezeway. Josie was headed back to the Bird house when Floyd yelled to her, "I need ya to cover for me in the community center."

She stopped akimbo, then followed him over to the van. "Why are you cheating these people?"

"I don't know what yer talkin' about."

At Rocky's open side door she violently grabbed Charlie and ripped out his order pad from the side pocket, pointing to Clouda's bogus order. "Look! That man didn't order these paper towels! At thirty-six bucks a case? It's double the price you charge anyone else!" She shoved Charlie and the order pad at him as he stacked three cases of toilet paper onto his blade.

"They don't pay for it anyway!" Floyd snapped.

"That's bull, Floyd! That man pays his bills!" Josie was hot on his heels as he wheeled the toilet paper toward the center's front door. "You can't deliver stuff they didn't order!"

"There's a price increase ..."

"Price increase my eye! You only pull this crap on reservations! You can't cheat them just because the government pays for it!"

As he strenuously pulled his tottering load up the old church steps he said, "Keep it down, will ya. If I don't stock 'em, someone else will. Why all this sudden altruism for the poor Indians? You want nice things. I'm workin' my territory to get them for ya." He waited in vain at the church door for Josie to

211

open it as he balanced his product on his cart. Finally, he opened it himself.

"Your territory? You picked up this scam from your old man! That drunken fool did the same thing! Like father ... like son!" She followed him into the storage room that was already jammed and cluttered with Silver's products. "See? Look at this place! They don't need any product!"

He dropped his blade and pushed it against his product. "Look! They're usin' my dispensers!"

"Albert gives those to you for free! I've seen you charge Indians twenty bucks apiece for those dispensers, and I've seen you give them away to your white customers!"

"How do you know?"

Because you laugh and brag all the time about the easy money you make in Pine Ridge, Winnebago, Macy, Santee ... You rob these people blind!" Josie kicked over the newly stacked toilet paper and added, "I'm going to the Agency and turn you in!"

As Josie turned to leave the storage room, Floyd grabbed her arm and pinned her against his product. "Listen to me! There's an edge I need out here! This isn't art! It's much easier to have yer Thunder Bird sign a check, isn't it?"

She fought to get him off of her, but he pressed on. "Tell me you don't use yer charm on clients ... to get a sale."

"Let me go!"

"How's that different, Josie? Huh? Tell me!"

She finally punched Floyd in the chest, pushed him away, and stormed out of the hot storage room.

Huck watched Josie run out of the community center with Floyd in hot pursuit, dragging his two-wheeler behind him. "Where you goin'?"

She headed for the Agency but then turned back in the direction of the Bird house. "Any place to get away from you!"

Huck whined near Floyd as the Paper Man squeezed the back of his throbbing neck before angrily tossing his cart into Rocky's cargo area. He had one more drop — the Agency. This would be his biggest sale. He turned to see Josie disappear out of sight. Huck wanted to climb inside Rocky for a nap. "Stay with her," Floyd demanded. He watched the dog trot across the church lot.

Walter took the two-page order from the Paper Man's trembling hand. Before the elder Bird could say anything, out of Floyd's mouth came the specious words he'd heard many times: "I dated it for the first of October so you can put it on the next quarter. Four of the cases are in the center."

"Paper Man ... that storage room is jammed with back-orders now."

Chief, I got it all in just fine. The savings is real ... with Silver's price increase comin'. I'm doin' you a big favor, Chief."

Walter signed his order pad on both pages and noticed how anxious the Paper Man seemed. "Everything okay?"

"Josie's really upset with me."

Rocky's cargo bed was empty as Floyd paced in front of his open side door after honking for Huck to return. Soon the reluctant watchdog was sulking back toward Rocky with his head bent low. If a dog could feel guilty, Huck was in big trouble. The Paper Man was hotter than the August sidewalk and in no mood for insubordination. He blocked the side door. "She still there?"

Huck whimpered and circled in front of Floyd, scooting his rump submissively to Floyd's leg and angering his master further. "Get in!"

After Huck hopped inside Rocky, Floyd drove to the Bird house. The Jeep was gone and so was Josie. Huck rode on his belly in the empty cargo area, fearful of Floyd.

Floyd drove to the on-ramp of Highway 18, but he pulled over to the shoulder and cut Rocky's engine before reaching the highway. He got out and walked over to the sliding cargo door, opening it slowly. He remained outside the van as Huck lay against the back door, wary of Floyd's calm demeanor.

"Where is she?"

Huck's quiet, brown eyes moved up then down as Floyd's anger rose.

"She leave with Dennis?"

Huck remained quiet. Floyd stepped into the cargo area and slammed the door shut behind him as Huck whined fearfully. Moving closer to the cowering dog he said through clenched teeth, "Which ... way ... did ... they ... go?"

Huck whined and backed as far as he could into the corner, turning his head away from Floyd. "You don't know?" Floyd barked. Moving closer to the dog he said, "I told you to stay with her! Where'd she go?"

More whining ensued from the dog as Floyd stepped up to him, hovered over him, and craned his neck down in the dog's direction. "Huck!"

After more whining and whimpering, Floyd lost his cool in the hot van and raised Huck off the floor by his flea collar. As Huck yelped, Floyd shook him furiously in the air, roaring, "Don't you lie to me! Don't you ever lie to me!"

Huck's flea collar snapped and Huck went tumbling to the floor. At the same time, Floyd heard Josie's wedding band clink against the back door. Floyd, breathing hard and perspiring heavily, picked up the ring, opened the side door, and stepped outside to face Huck's trembling body. "You wanna join her? Come on! You can go with her! Come on!"

Huck shivered and cried in the far corner of the van. As he panted in Floyd's direction, saliva dripped from his slack jaw.

Floyd slid his full water bowl to him and said before slamming the side door, "The friggin' both of ya can go to hell!" Then he climbed behind the wheel of the van, popped open the glove box, threw the ring inside, and slammed it shut. He left Pine Ridge in a cloud of peeling dust.

Doing eighty-five miles an hour into Custer got him a speeding ticket that didn't help Huck, either. Floyd decided not to get their honeymoon cabin as he'd planned. Instead, he checked into the same Custer motel room he and his dad used to stay in.

Floyd sat with his chin in his hands at the foot of his queen-size foam mattress, thinking about Thunder Bird's showing the next morning in the old church. They could get someone else to haul their friggin' chairs.

Huck lay on his belly on the cool bathroom tile, somber and quiet and occasionally snorting out a breath above the roar of the room's air conditioner.

The Holiday Inn delivered their chairs just in time for the Thunder Bird showing. Josephine looked strikingly beautiful in the powder-blue cotton dress that Dennis had bought her in Boseman. Laura had woven Josephine's hair into a multi-layered braid that enhanced in the eyes of each client her Indigenous bloodline.

Josephine Ann Tenna got as much attention as Thunder Bird's five-thousand-dollar oil painting *Tracking the Strays,* depicting a herd of wild horses being corralled by Apache braves in an Arizona canyon. *Montana Goldmine, Stagecoach, Superstitions, Sacred Hills, Lead at Sunset* and *Badlands* all were displayed on individually lit tripods arranged in order of price behind Josephine and Thunder Bird, who stood at a makeshift podium on the center's small stage.

Foppishly dressed prospective new buyers and old clients were seated on the rented chairs marking their preferences for originals and prints when the quiet room was startled to life by three FBI agents in bullet-proof vests coming in fast through the front door. The lead agent further stunned the room by brandishing his badge and saying in an authoritative tone, "FBI! We have probable cause to believe there is illegal contraband on these premises. This is a search warrant."

Like vultures the other two agents began cutting and slicing into the back side of Thunder Bird's works. Walter and Laura walked in just when an agent found an ounce of marijuana stashed behind *Sacred Hills*.

Laura cried when Dennis and Josie were handcuffed and whisked away in a government car. Thunder Bird's work was confiscated, stacked in a federal van, and soon followed their creator and agent to the Rapid City Federal Building.

Dennis's carefully orchestrated and long-awaited plan would have worked. A fire in the community center's cluttered storage room was ripe for a big insurance payoff with Thunder Bird's valuable oils coloring the ashes with plenty of green for a new center. The Paper Man would have borne responsibility for over-crowding the supply room with accelerants, and the Reservation would have obtained insurance settlements from both the policy on the center and the Paper Man's umbrella policy. Walter and Laura knew all about the plan. Walter was proud to have his talented son and niece united for this worthy cause, but Laura was apprehensive. "Nothing can go wrong," Dennis had told his worried mother the night before.

As Walter and Laura sped out of Pine Ridge headed for Rapid City, Walter had faith that this whole mess would be explained and all would be well.

"His career was going so well," Laura cried. "What was he doing with this scheme to raise money for a new community center?"

The following night in his honeymoon cabin, Harvey sat alone in the shadows weighing his options. He had been the one to destroy the careers of Josephine and Dennis. She would not get a chance to grow into something better without him. And if he was the one to get her started, he would be the one to end it. Harvey's guilt convinced him that everyone knew it was his hand that planted the pot. But it really didn't matter what anyone else thought; the divorce papers would put an end to Harvey and Josie.

* * * * *

Josie was to serve six months on the Pine Ridge Reservation under house arrest, helping the Birds with the Agency and daycare. Dennis was sentenced to spend a year in the Pine Ridge jail.

By mid-October Harvey had moved out of their homestead in the Nakota Hills and into a studio apartment in Sioux City, where he and Huck settled in for an early winter that promised to be long and lonely. All of Josie's belongings had been shipped to her with no explanation of why he'd set them up so cruelly in Pine Ridge. He knew it was a rotten thing to do, uncalled for, and much too vile to apologize for.

In December Harvey began writing his estranged wife letters that he never mailed. He even composed a contrite letter to Dennis which was also never sent. Egoistic self-preservation prevented him from sending anything that could implicate him in a federal crime. The divorce papers stayed inside the envelope in a bureau drawer where he kept his mother's photo face-down on old newsprint.

By Christmastime Floyd had been working every other day. He was deeply depressed and slogging around with a head cold he'd been holding onto since Thanksgiving.

From the time Dennis was incarcerated, Laura and Josie faithfully cooked and delivered three meals a day to the sullen Thunder Bird. He was down, painting dark landscapes, leaving most of his meals untouched, and hardly speaking a word for days at a time. But a breakthrough in Dennis's mood and demeanor came on the day before Christmas Eve. The Pine Ridge Police Chief, Arthur Drinkwater, delivered a note from Dennis to Josie at the daycare. He told her he had "imagined whiteness." From that moment, he was more prolific than ever with his paintings, cranking out a new piece about every ten days.

Josie practiced meditation from her old bedroom in the Bird house. In a letter from Granny around Thanksgiving, she'd been told to imagine whiteness with her eyes closed. "When you can see only whiteness," she wrote, "you have brought your mind and spirit together for a higher purpose that will be revealed to you before springtime." During that time Josie realized she'd been competing with Dennis since childhood. When he announced he had imagined whiteness, she tripled her "sitting time," meditating until her hips ached.

It was in January's early darkness when her golden eyes opened with an awareness that skipped her heart out of rhythm and sent her out into the snow to the Pine Ridge jailhouse in only a t-shirt, jeans and sneakers. When she reached Thunder Bird's cell, he was waiting for her. His hands were trembling on the bars, unable to let go of what he'd "seen." They had seen it together. It was as if the two of them, focused together, had been given an early vision months before Granny's springtime prediction. "Paint it," Josie said, "and I'll take care of everything else."

This time they had a shared vision; not some half-hearted plan that might work. This time only Walter would have to know — eventually. Aunt Laura's maternal paranoia would be kept out of it.

The flu hit Floyd hard, sending him to bed for a week. No food. No water. He just lay in bed and replayed every memory he had with Josie. Huck's food bag was dumped on the floor and he drank out of the toilet. The sick Paper Man let Huck out three times a day; otherwise, the dog was on his own.

Floyd's legs were losing muscle, atrophying at an alarming

rate. He lost twenty-five pounds during a week of sweating and shivering under blankets that all but covered a dead man. He would pee, flush Huck a fresh water supply, then go to the mirror and see the ghost of his father's shrinking head and greasy hair looking back at him.

After the long week of suffering, he touched his hot cheekbones with both hands and realized he could die soon. His pants were so cold and baggy on his legs that he put on a second pair. Two pair of socks, three shirts, a wool cap, and a coat clothed his weak frame as he walked to the hospital nine blocks away. Huck was left whining inside their apartment. The snow was a foot deep. His head was bent down and forward to the uphill whiteness that made night become day. Every street corner was counted until he stumbled into the emergency room. More than once the fear of the hospital expense to come nearly reversed his course back to his apartment.

The IV needle pricking his skin then entering a vein on the top of his right hand was soon delivering needed fluids to his dehydrated body, while at the same time draining his bank account some six hundred dollars. After a blood sample was taken and a prescription filled at the hospital's pharmacy, Floyd left with the doctor's advice to drink plenty of fluids.

Restepping in the deep tracks he'd formed earlier, he made his way home. *How self-destructive I've been,* he scolded himself. Not drinking water or feeding himself the cans of soup in his cupboard could have cost him his life. He knew he had hit bottom. *But now I'll rise,* he told the whiteness step after step. "I will not die," he said aloud.

The Separation

On Valentine's Day Floyd came into Albert's office to load Rocky for the week. It was a cold Sunday.

"Jake died yesterday," Albert said.

"Good," Floyd muttered.

Silver dropped his lenses and looked at his depressed jobber.

"At least now I can call on his customers," Floyd added.

Albert had spent the morning sorting through Jake's accounts and finding the oldest invoices. He handed them to Floyd and said, "Collect these."

"Ten percent?" Floyd asked.

"Yeah," Albert grumbled, watching Floyd head for his supply of motor oil under his coat rack. He saw the unkempt salesman take two quarts from the case and tuck them against his side.

"How many you have there, for God's sake?"

"What do you care? I collect on yer old accounts for ya. Why do ya always nickel and dime me for two lousy quarts of oil when I collect on yer deadbeats and spend over a grand a week for product?"

"You hear from yer wife?" the old man changed the subject.

"No ... Why should I?"

"You sign yer divorce papers?"

"No."

"I see ya didn't shave, either," Silver quipped, referring to Floyd's beard. "She was too young for ya. You need a woman

221

more yer age."

Floyd sat down amidst the clutter and torpor as Silver went over to Huck and patted his head. He felt like telling the old man the truth about what happened in Pine Ridge and how sorry he felt for doing such a stupid thing that ended his marriage and ruined a young artist's career. "I still love her," he droned pathetically.

The old man sat down hard on Willard's swivel chair. He could see the pain on the face of a good salesman — pain he had seen before. "I saw yer father go through this with yer mother. It ruined him. You have to let her go ... or you'll end up broken down and bitter."

"I've loved her a long time. A long time."

"You gave her a nice house and her freedom to work with that Indian painter. Things change, my boy. Things change."

Floyd stopped himself from confessing his deed then said, "I'll never find a woman like Josie again. That's what really bothers me."

"Sign the divorce papers and meet someone new. There's plenty of fish in the sea! You'll see! Move on. Things will change."

Later that night Harvey wrote the first letter to Josie that he actually mailed. Her attorney had sent him divorce papers, but he wasn't ready to sign them. "I feel there's a ray of hope for us, Josie," he wrote. "I can't explain it now, but things will change. Somehow."

A week later he received the letter back. He examined it carefully and knew she had not opened it.

* * * * *

By late March spring had really just begun when Rocky cruised into the valley of Macy playing Boz's song "Miss Sun" before parking in Granny Tenna's drive.

The craggy-faced old woman stood at her doorstep studying the Paper Man's haggard, bearded face. He had lost quite a bit of weight and his "good eyes" were dead with pain. She knew he was looking for words of hope that she may have heard from Josie, but she only said that Josie's probation was over and she did not know Josie's plans. She noticed the poor fool was still wearing his wedding band.

"Did she say anything about me?" he asked.

After shaking her head no, she watched him walk away without the usual zip in his step. He appeared middle-aged to her.

Granny said nothing about how her Josephine had changed dramatically in Pine Ridge when she had visited her two weeks ago — and how much the Paper Man's deed had changed her Josephine's life for the better.

Floyd spent the day in a fog making a couple of collections for Albert and calling on Jake's customers. All the while he was haunted by the look in Granny's eyes that told him Josie wanted nothing to do with him. The image of never seeing her again was real and enervating. Even Huck could see that his partner was lost and not into selling product with the improving weather stripping the countryside of the bleakness of winter. Upon seeing a chain of pearl-colored clouds moving from the west, Floyd decided to stay away from his Black Hills run until he heard from her.

By the end of each workday, he had developed the habit of buying a quart of beer for his night alone in his apartment — a habit he'd developed over the long winter. At night Huck would stay away from the apartment, prowling the neighborhood just to get away from his scowling, lovesick roommate. He preferred sleeping outside their apartment to watching Harvey get up several times during the night to smoke and pace their tiny quarters.

* * * * *

By late April Josie had her hair cut shorter than she'd ever had it. She was driving the Jeep into Hot Springs every morning at six to work out at the YMCA, taking two or three of the local girls with her to run the treadmill and swim before dropping them at school back in Pine Ridge.

She was beginning to sell Thunder Bird's work again to tourist shops in Custer, Rapid City, and Lead. The little money she made provided her food and gas and art supplies. Dennis was as prolific as he'd ever been, filling canvas after canvas with vibrant colors and energy that had to be stored on every inch of wall space in the Bird house.

One morning Josie went to Thunder Bird's cell after Laura left her son's breakfast and clean laundry. She stood silently by his cell door for ten minutes while he painted under a bright light with the back of a large canvas to her. It was the piece that would catapult him to his greatest glory. He'd spent his meditation that morning on this, his biggest project.

He put down his brush, exhaled deeply, and smiled before walking over to his agent and business manager. He took her hand and kissed it. "It's half ready in my mind's eye," he smiled.

She smiled back at him, seeing the old light in his eyes and the return to youthfulness his face had undergone of late. His jaw was more relaxed and the lines around his mouth and eyes diminished.

"We can do this, Golden Eyes. It will work. But it must be big."

"No one gets hurt," she said.

He agreed with his eyes before saying, "You still love him?"

She looked down to his clean-swept concrete cell floor, then back to him. Her eyes were a relaxed golden fire as she said in a whisper, "He's out of me now."

Dennis took his smooth, dark hand and placed it on her cheek. "When?" he asked.

"There's so much to do," she said.

He handed her a list of names and phone numbers on a folded piece of paper from his shirt pocket. "These people will help us. Some have money. Some have skills. We can trust them."

She put the paper in her pocket without looking at it. She smiled and leaned forward, kissing his smooth brown cheek, then left quickly.

Dennis went to his open cubbyhole window made of lead mesh. He could see far out to the hills north of the reservation. There swayed the tall green-black prairie grass where he and Josie used to go when they talked about their dreams. They never spoke of true loves, happily ever afters, or having children. Usually they talked of traveling to new places, having money to eat in good restaurants, and wearing nice clothes. Above all, they wanted good health. They had seen too much poverty and illness on the reservation to settle for just surviving.

He tried to smell the air outside his cell, breathing in deeply with his wide nostrils flaring and his onyx-black eyes closed. When he opened his eyes, he blinked and turned his head sideways to his canvas. Without Josie he could never do this. She was the touchstone for it all — everything that was coming. He carefully selected a brush and stood gazing at his canvas, ready to paint something great.

* * * * *

In Missouri Valley, Huck was calling on a vet when Floyd drove Rocky toward his last call for the day, Logan Locker.

The warm May air was lifting his spirit out of the dumps. He felt good. The night before in Denison, he'd met a twenty-year-old girl in The Corner Drugstore who had given him her phone number in Harlan. He thought he'd try to find her the following week when he worked Harlan — when he was in a little better shape. Little did he know at the time she'd given him the wrong phone number.

Harvey was coming out of the longest winter of his life. The winter nights had promised only a dolorous prelude to a wicked journey. He was creeping into the rural places where the cob and catalog were yet saved. These were tiny places — ancient specks on maps; scruffy villages and unincorporated burgs. Places where a lost traveler would pass through unremembered like a scudding cumulus cloud. Places where people refused to grow and failed to care that they didn't.

He noticed his prospects in these places seemed to agree on two fronts: Prepare for the worst; hope for the best. Always to his stupefaction, there would be the isolated grain elevator man, motel clerk, café owner, or eye-popping beauty who was completely content to be there. They would possess a happiness so genuine he would feel his life wasted and useless until his next sale. Their clear eyes, laugh lines, and easy smiles could not all be lying to him. Yes, he was living his father's legacy without feeling whether it was right or wrong for him.

During the winter he'd realized that without Huck he'd be lost. But without Josie he was unseen — a meaningless atom of blood, bones, sweat and prices. He knew for certain only one or two of the million faces bought because of him. It was forever the cost, the price on his tongue, and the held breath hoping for a sale.

"How much ya gettin for a case of them towels?" "What's a case of that glass and bowl cleaner go for?" "How many's in that case?" The queries were always immediately followed by the abeyance of abstract figuring and calculating. No matter how scrubbed and neat, clever or handsome he appeared, it always boiled down to "How much?"

It stoked him to jealously and madness whenever people like Dennis, the artist, would have no concern about money — versus Floyd's specious buoyancy that would soon die after every sale made. This quality in Thunder Bird had to be attractive to her. And it was. He just knew it. He would have to make drastic changes in his life if he were ever to keep someone like Josie. Or he'd have to settle for something he could never respect.

Yes, he thought, *these are the happy settlers — my hayseed customers and prospects who never spend a moment longing for what they don't have or how much credit they can get and use up.* He was in a field of their dreams, not his, he mused.

The sweat poured off him more at night when he slept — or, at least, tried to. It could be the coldest night on record, but his glands would gush from the stultifying fear of having to do something else with his life. Something other than being a paper man. It was his biggest fear. Bigger than losing her, he knew, for he was still in his territory doing the only thing he knew. He was little more than a professional walker with a memorized price list.

As he parked in front of Logan Locker, he thought of the Harlan girl again. Gone were the days when he could overcome his work by flirting with a country girl. Or flirting with the idea of having a one-night-stand just because of his youth. The energy he had left now was old — the smoldering embers of what a few years ago was a blaze that consumed every prospect in his path. His youthful beauty was forever lost. He was getting older and seeing fewer and fewer opportunities to bolster his manhood.

The past winter had done most of the damage to his looks. He was seeing the gaunt, dead face of his father more and more in the motel mirrors each morning. His beard was graying before his eyes, but shaving meant revealing a face tightly wracked with tension and pain. So he kept the beard.

Yes, he thought as he stepped toward the locker with Charlie under his arm, *I'm too old for her. Anyone can see we don't fit. She's going to get over me fast. I had my chance and blew it. Or did my chance just blow by?* he smirked to himself. *God, I wish I'd hit bottom and start improving on the way up! Or will I stay down here till I die ... like he did?*

Such was the typical self-talk of Floyd Harvey Deason in those painful days. *Only change can help me now. God, help me change.* He'd prayed that a thousand times a day, even while pacing his room at night and smoking till his fingers yellowed. He sang to himself Gary's mawkish song "Over You." *Why am I losing sleep over you? Reliving precious moments we knew ...*

As soon as the door to the locker squealed open and he walked through the door, all the self-berating anguish in his head stopped. The Shieldorfs, owners of the locker, were glad to see the Paper Man. They bought from him about every other time he stopped in. Arnie Shieldorf was missing his left thumb and laughed about it every time he saw the Sioux City paper salesman.

When young Harvey first began delivering in the country, he'd stopped at Arnie's locker to get directions. He had approached the young butcher who was slicing bologna with his left hand riding and pushing the slicer. Harvey's words had caught Arnie off guard: "You lose yer thumb slicin' bologna?"

Arnie laughed and answered, "Naw ... I shot it off pheasant huntin' when I was twelve."

Now when Floyd walked through the squeaky door, he said the same thing he always said when he greeted Arnie. "Hey, Arnie! Wanna go pheasant huntin'?"

Arnie laughed then unwittingly stole the wind from Floyd's sails when he said, "Where's yer pretty wife?"

"She's visiting her family in Pine Ridge," was Floyd's sullen reply.

When Floyd climbed behind the wheel of Rocky, he saw Huck trotting toward him some three blocks away. Floyd put in his Boz CD and played Huck's favorite song — the one that made him howl and get excited. He turned up the volume and noticed Huck running faster and faster toward him, his ears pinned back by his speed. This gave him an idea and began to lift his depression immediately. He stood outside by Rocky's left headlight and watched Salesman Huck run to him. *This could heal my emptiness over Josie and help replace the money I lost over the winter!* The idea thrilled him. It was all he had. Floyd was back. His music had come through again to save him, just as it had manifested Josie. He was determined to win her back.

As Huck came up to him panting with the order from the vet in his pouch, Floyd crouched down on his haunches to rub his loyal friend's ears and kiss his snout. "Good boy, Huck! Good boy!" Huck eagerly licked Floyd's neck, happy his master was alive again.

Floyd would have to figure out a way to lure her to see it. With music he could do it again, he knew. He laughed into Huck's face as he removed the sales collar. He smiled at Huck's order on the pad inside the collar's pouch — an order that would save his marriage. "Come on, Huck. We've got work to do!"

Huck jumped onto the passenger seat. Floyd replayed the song louder as they drove to the vet and delivered the case of towels Huck had sold. Floyd was so excited about his plan that he sold the vet a case of two-ply plus two cases of garbage bags and a case of Silver's bowl cleaner.

For eighty miles up Interstate 29 they listened to Huck's song, singing and howling together along the west side of the Nakota Hills. Green and verdant, the sacred hills posed a reminder of love once made.

* * * * *

Josie had to sit in Dennis's Jeep and use his cell phone to make her calls so Aunt Laura wouldn't know what she was up to. She went through the list in two days, setting up private meetings in obscure places. She eliminated some of the individuals on the list, but many proved solid choices to provide the help they would need. As long as she imagined whiteness, this new plan was all coming together. If she was hurried or thinking too much, the plan seemed impossible to pull off and the people impossible to trust. At one point her discouragement convinced her that she and Dennis would have to do it alone. It was too dangerous to trust anyone else. But Dennis pulled her out of it and got her to trust again, and she went back to working her list of prospects.

Dennis Bird had Josie bring him another blank canvas to start his work over again. He was having trouble creating what he wanted, and he knew it was tied in with Josie's confidence and success in working the list and the trouble she was having in bringing a team together. He never spoke of it to her. He just ordered another canvas. And another. And another.

A breakthrough finally happened for Josie when she removed the rusty towel dispenser in the back bathroom at the center and tossed it into the dumpster. Her smokescreen of anger vanished when she realized Floyd was jealous of her pot-smoking with

Dennis, and he had set them up for a bust rather than endure her abandoning him the way his mother had. She could see how he had thrown her away before she could do that to him. It all became clear to her, and her anger began to give way to understanding.

That night before the police chief returned from his dinner break, Josie told Dennis about her revelation with a half-dozen roaring-drunk Indians carrying on in the station's other three cells. She spoke directly: "I understand why he did it."

Thunder Bird listened to her with an open mind. He really could see it all through her eyes. After she spoke in depth about the Paper Man's parents and all the things he had told her about them when they were living on the homestead, Dennis asked her if she could still go through with their plan.

"Yes. It's not about him. I forgive him. I failed him once when I was pursuing my dream in New York. He supported me and never held it against me. I know that. This has to be done for Pine Ridge ... and my mother."

She didn't have to explain to Dennis. He always knew Josie had something inside her that was inexplicable and untouchable — a painful yearning to do some great thing for their people. He knew she wanted to make it big in the city and return a hero after doing some great thing that would show them all that her mother's suicide was good for something more than the ashes she left her little mixed-blood girl with the golden eyes.

Dennis was allowed one hour per day of exercise outside the jailhouse. The police chief let Dennis walk alone with Josie in the evening after Josie's day was done. He did this because of Walter. Walter had brought Chief Drinkwater into the plan, knowing his involvement would be crucial if they were to have a chance at pulling it off.

"Do you ever get lonely to have someone you can hold in your arms and wake up next to in the morning?" Josie asked.

Dennis laughed until they were past the store, then he stopped to look at a clump of orange-red lantana radiation growing near a rock twenty feet from the highway. "I could ask you the same question. I guess the longer I go without it ... the easier it gets."

"That's true," she laughed with him. "You know, I don't believe I've ever heard you talk about women, Dennis."

"I'm afraid of them," he laughed. "They scare the hell out of me. I had a couple of flames in school that soured me. I could never paint when a woman was in my life. Weird, huh?"

"Well ... you are a strange bird," she teased.

"You miss your Paper Man?"

"Oh, at first I did. Not now. I thought about going into Rapid and getting picked up in a bar when I got off probation. But it passed," she said with a smirk.

"You will see him again," he said.

"Yes."

"You may change your mind then," he laughed.

They turned back and passed by the store again. She noticed he was walking faster. Something had inspired him.

"You seem anxious," she said.

"Exercise, Golden Eyes," he laughed.

She marveled at his attitude change since the past summer and remembered what he had told her at Christmastime when she asked him about revenge. "Anger is one letter away from danger. He'll get his ... without my anger."

In front of the small jail she stopped and said, "So many things could go wrong, Dennis. In three months you can start over."

"My reputation as an artist was ruined by one stupid act. No gallery in the country will now spend the money my work is worth."

"But they must know you wouldn't stash a fifty-dollar bag of ditch weed in your painting and risk losing the sale of an oil for five thousand."

Dennis stepped close to her. "They don't see it that way, Josie. Now, look ... we've seen this long before that phony bust, haven't we?"

She stood still. As she recalled their drive to Minneapolis, she knew he was right.

"Maybe I want this more than you. It's my freedom that's been taken away ... for nine months now. I can't make a living with this over my head. I'm working to follow the plan ... but I can't do it without you."

She looked down the block to the old church where she was married. She was the one who had gone to him and let him have his hold on her youth. Now it was Josephine who turned back to Dennis. "Imagine whiteness," she said. She kissed him goodnight on his chin after saying, "Dok sa."

He watched her graceful, lithe body walk away from him knowing he had it now.

After Chief Drinkwater locked him in, he sat with his legs crossed under him on the floor. For ninety minutes his eyes were open in his dark cell, focused on the whiteness of his canvas leaning against his cot six feet away. He thanked Grand Mother Earth, Grand Father Sky, Where Sun Comes Up, Where Sun Goes Down, to the North, the land of green trees and snow, and to the South. After serving as a vessel of six directions for an hour and a half, oblivious to the endless snoring and scratching of his neighbors, he began to cry. He finally saw.

"Floyd ... it's six hundred bucks this year. I know last year was five hundred ... but we raised the entry fee to get a faster bunch of dogs to run."

Floyd rolled his eyes at the corpulent track manager of Bluffs Run. "Doug ... can't you get me a number 1 or number 8?"

"Floyd, I only got number 6. That's all I got left."

"That's the devil's number, Doug ... for cryin' out loud! Nobody's gonna bet on the devil to win!"

The track manager winked at Floyd, giving him a surprising response. "Maybe yer right, Floyd ... but better odds if ya win, right?"

Floyd smiled, saying, "You might have somethin' there. You'll take my check, right?"

"Cash only, Floyd."

"I've been sellin' ya paper ... for how long?"

"All right ... I'll take yer check," he said, rolling his eyes and popping a sunflower seed into his cherubic face."

While writing out his check, Floyd made his move that had to work or his plan would be ruined. "Can I bring in three cases of TP on race day?" The track manager started to get up from behind his desk. Right on cue, Huck stood on his hind legs at the office door, causing the man to smile and sit back down before he could check his supply in the storage room.

"Okay," he laughed. "Bring three cases on race day."

Out in the massive track parking lot, Floyd expressed his

relief to Huck as they climbed into Rocky. "That was a close one. Good job! Ya got number 6. It's only a number ..." He gazed into the rearview mirror at his full beard, which was covered with more gray than ever before. "God ... am I agin' or what?" Debating inwardly whether to shave, he finally remarked to his best friend, "I'll shave if ya win. Or ... it doesn't matter. No pressure, though."

Since late May the Paper Man had been getting into the best shape of his life — delivering cases by hand from Rocky, walking five miles a day versus two miles, quitting smoking and drinking. And he had received a note that Josie had mailed to Silver's office telling him she would be visiting Granny on July 15th, and that she wanted to talk to him.

Yes, there's hope, he told himself each day. *Or is she just going to hammer me to sign our divorce papers?* A combined sense of hope and overwhelming doom filled his days and nights with anxieties that tested his will to its limits. He was taking his frustrations out on Huck with grueling training on dirt roads morning, noon and evening. On the weekends, #6 Salesman Huck worked on his race as if the existence of both of them depended on it. Huck was a smart dog; he remembered the race from the year before when the training was less important.

On the morning of Saturday, July 15th, it caught him by surprise to see the Jeep in Granny's drive. She had wheels! There went his hopes of driving her back to Pine Ridge. *What are her plans?* he worried to himself as Huck followed him to the front door. Harvey was self-conscious of his beard and how he must look old and ridiculous. The night before he had left in his beard coloring formula too long, leaving it a chocolate brown that appeared obviously foolish in his reflection on Granny's glass front door. For an instant he lost the slick confidence he had managed to hold onto all the way to Macy. He was sniffing at a violet in a ceramic pot when the door opened.

"Hi," Josie said in a lukewarm tone, then she stepped outside to lavish love on Huck.

Harvey noticed her hair was short and redder — thick in the back and a dark contrast to the creamy skin of her bare neck. He avoided looking into her eyes to see if she was angry or if she had missed him. But as soon as she looked up at him with those golden eyes, his feet were heavy and clammy, unable to turn to her directly. He couldn't say anything. He'd lost his confident, powerful voice that had sold ten thousand orders.

"You two look good," she smiled.

"You ... look good ... too," he forced awkwardly. "How's Granny?"

"She's fine. Can we go for a walk?"

"Sure," he said tentatively. His heart was pounding so hard he thought for sure she could hear it.

She went to the Jeep to get her beige cap that shadowed her eyes. Her long, bare legs beneath her cutoff jeans were tanned and shapely. They walked with Huck trailing off down a dirt alley that bordered her old school. "Not much ever changes here," she said while raking her eyes over the school.

"How's Dennis?"

"Oh, he's doing fine ... considering."

"Yes ... that's good." Still no confession or apology came from him to free his tension. She didn't need one, it appeared.

"How's Albert?"

"Grouchy as ever."

Floyd decided to take the upper hand and broach the subject of their divorce. He had been carefully planning his approach for months. "An attorney advised me to wait a year before signing the papers. But that's not why I waited." They watched the ground before them as they slowly walked. He went on:

"Huck's race is the end of August. I — or we — want you to see it. Anyway ... if you ride with us on my run to the Black Hills after the race ... I'll sign the divorce papers when we get there."

She thought about it for a few steps before answering. "You'll sign the divorce papers in Pine Ridge?" she asked curtly.

He knew by the tone of her voice and her answer that it was over between them. He couldn't hear the thousand thoughts racing through his mind. "Yes."

"Why then?"

"It's what I want." He stopped himself from explaining.

She knew he was hoping they could reconcile their marriage and a long run would give him time to change her mind. He knew she could see his ulterior motive.

"Two beds?" she asked.

A voluble tightness pressed at the back of his neck, making him want to grab his throat. "Agreed," he said.

"And a case of two-ply for Dennis?" she added.

He snorted, not caring to hear why. "Agreed. Anything else?"

She noticed his wedding band on his left hand, then shook her head no as she kept her eyes straight ahead on the old Macy Agency she and Granny had visited several times.

"August 30th is the race date ... at the Bluffs," he said.

"I'll be there," she smiled.

He wanted to ask her about her plans for the future, but he felt sick to his stomach. She was too strong about it all.

They retraced their steps back to Granny's. When Huck jumped through Rocky's open driver-side window, she wanted to add a "no music" stipulation. But she could see he was hurting.

"See ya at the race," she smiled.

"Yeah," he said, faking the same smile he had all winter.

She didn't watch him drive away. Josephine had work to do.

By early August, Huck was as lean as Floyd. Rocky was parked in downtown Fremont, Nebraska, right in the heart of Floyd's toughest territory. Never in the thirty times he had worked Fremont had he left this overgrown town with more than a half-dozen orders. His father called Fremont "Skunkville" for skunking him more than any place he carried Charlie. Floyd's pitches were curt and abrasive in Fremont, just like his father's had been. After a dozen rejections, he would slap down his product card on the prospect's counter and say cynically, "I've still got that great buy on one-ply and thirty-gallon garbage bags that you've never bought from me."

He always got the same response — a negative shake of the head and a satisfied smirk to send this Sioux City salesman away without a word of explanation. Even bringing in Salesman Huck to beg didn't move them, causing even Huck to exit with his head hung low after his sad brown eyes had pleaded for the smallest of orders.

"Let's get out of here," he told Huck. "This is worse than Seward. These people are cold. Never again will we come here." It wasn't the first time he'd made that vow. And as in the past, they hit the smaller towns nearby for quick sales to bolster their confidence before the day was gone and word got out about Skunkville.

The gray was back in his beard, so he trimmed it short and got rid of the chocolate hairs bought at Walgreens. August was hotter and more humid than July. Each day he wore less clothing until a V-neck white t-shirt, shorts, and sandals were all that covered his sweaty frame. He started eating more to sustain the weight he was losing through his pores. His heart's anxiety over Huck's approaching race was beating off the added calories before the sun went down. Huck was getting a steak every evening just to hold his forty-two-pound racing weight. Floyd bought protein powder and vitamins, and he exercised faithfully every night to stay toned.

Over the course of the past year, he'd discovered his father's atrophy could easily be his — and he worried about it late into every night on damp bed sheets. The Paper Man started making calls only on regulars in order to conserve his strength. He had to be strong on his run to the Hills. It was his last chance.

The last week in August he drove to his apartment every night. The rooms on the road were sirens of his father's loneliness, wailing the grief of a life abandoned. How could he be trapped in this work — dead work that scaled away his old man's flesh to his very bones?

His dreams haunted him; quick dreams by the hundreds night after night of those specter faces of prospects in isolated grain elevators and feed stores, motels, cafes, grimy gas stations, body shops and machine shops, implement dealerships, all in a thousand places off of unmarked roads, emptying themselves onto his wet, twisted bedding.

Only his anticipation of the race kept him alive. He knew he was banking too much on his sidekick to rescue him, but not even God could stop him. It was the product of too many miles of aloneness without laughter that mixed his brains with the dust he made while leaving those places — places he would return to again and again in the night without sound, without the hope of glorious tomorrows with his beautiful Josie waiting for his return.

Floyd got his teeth cleaned on August 27th. On the 28th, he and Huck rested under a puffy, gray, overcast sky. It was cool and humid for late August. Huck would get two days of play near the old Deason homestead in the Nakota Hills. The old place was sill vacant. Driving Rocky there, Floyd felt healthy and relaxed.

It was Huck's favorite spot — overlooking the sacred hills on a bluff where Harvey and Josie would watch the sunset. Harvey was there for Huck. He had been careful to never talk about the divorce or that Josie would be there for the race, as if the dog were a child who might get confused and hurt his chances of winning.

Huck sniffed every dandelion and wildflower in the prairie grasses. His paws and snout had instinctively led them to this western edge of the hills where Harvey and Josie made love before watching the glorious prairie sunsets. Here — on the same spot, perched on the bluff — Huck and his friend sat side by side in the early afternoon. Huck was on Harvey's left, the side she said was all Harvey. Huck's nose ran with moist aliveness as he sniffed the sweet air and earth all around them.

Harvey said softly, "It's nice here, huh?"

Huck gave a single soft bark of approval while sitting close to Harvey's bare left thigh.

"I kinda wish we'd stayed here. It's really nice out here."

Huck put his head on Harvey's shoulder and kissed Harvey's ear.

"Somehow I gotta learn to be more like you ... and live in the moment. This livin' in the past and thinkin' ahead has got to go, boy. After the race I will ... I swear. I've just gotta change."

Huck followed Harvey's lead, lying back on the grass and closing his eyes. He put his head on Harvey's chest, and they both lay quietly breathing together. Harvey watched the gray clouds drifting to the north and felt the sacred ground under him. He and Josie had lay on this very spot, and it was here she ruminated about her days in Pine Ridge. He recalled the spartan daycare in the old church, the unboxed games and makeshift toys kept in the corner, his stash in the rusty towel dispenser, and then their wedding. He thought back to that spider-webbed back room and the innocent girl bringing a pillow and a blanket. He remembered the key he had shown to little Ms. Sun — the key that concealed his temporary diversion from the pain of watching the world suck the life out of his father. Yes, he had made her the innocent victim, destroying her dreams in the very place she came to him.

He began to cry, his chest heaving under Huck's warm throat. The dog's cry for the creature he loved brought Harvey's hands to caress the back of his short-haired neck. "I'm okay ... I'm okay. I love you too."

* * * * *

The Bluffs Run Dog Track parking lot was full for the season's last night. The track's giant marquis announced: Annual Mutt Also-Ran Handicap. Floyd parked Rocky tight against the track wall near the starting chutes at the far end of the parking lot. He looked at his watch and knew the tenth race was about to begin.

He left Charlie standing on the front passenger seat with Rocky's key in the ignition. The track's order for three cases of toilet paper was in his shirt pocket. In Rocky's rearview mirror, he finger-combed his hair and winced at his clean-shaven face. He removed a cheap bottle of cologne from the glove box and dabbed some on his neck and behind his ears. He had timed this ritual three times over the past month.

Behind the wall he heard the lead boys loading the eight muzzled and restive greyhounds into the chutes for the tenth race. Deliberately he opened Rocky's doors with the windows down, then he opened the back double doors and left them open. After loading three cases of toilet paper onto his two-wheeler, he stood on Rocky's rear bumper and double-checked the tote board across the track to be sure it was the tenth race. It was.

As the white electric bunny razor-zipped toward the chute area, he opened Rocky's side door. He wheeled his product toward the track's front entrance and wondered if she was there. The crowd's noise from the finish of the tenth race told him it was a full house. At the main entrance, the two uniformed security women recognized him, and one unhooked the chain for him to pass. He pushed and maneuvered his heavy load through the manswarm of gamblers with their beer cups and programs and averted eyes. When he reached the track office, he parked his delivery. After obtaining a signature from the track secretary, he pushed on with his load to a large storage room with a set of double doors. He knocked on the door. "Richard?"

"That you, Harvey?" a spooked, muffled voice asked from inside the storage room.

"Yeah. Open up!"

Harvey turned to see the eleventh race was about to begin. He was behind schedule! He parked his product in the storage room as Richard, a young alternate lead boy, started removing his black jeans and white t-shirt.

"You get me the twelfth race?" Harvey asked while undressing quickly.

"Yeah. But if you get caught I'm fired," Richard said nervously.

Harvey pulled fifty dollars from his big wad of bills and shoved it at the lead boy. "So what! It's the last race of the season!" Harvey could barely zip up the boy's tight jeans that were way too short for him. Then Harvey counted out twenty one-hundred-dollar bills and gave them to Richard before squeezing into the t-shirt. "Put that two grand on number 6 to win. Don't forget my cart ... and just press the play button in the van. After the race drive to the kennel area ..."

"Yeah, yeah. I know," Richard said.

After Harvey tucked in Richard's shirt, he put his shoes back on and snatched the black baseball cap from the lead boy's small head. Harvey pulled the bill of the snug cap low to conceal his eyes. As Harvey grabbed the doorknob Richard said, "Harvey?"

"What!"

"Good luck," Richard smiled.

"Thanks. And plug yer ears."

Lead boy Floyd hurried into the grandstand area, walking briskly through the crowd as all attention was focused on the results of the eleventh race displayed on the tote board.

In line at the betting window with a small suitcase at her feet, Josie circled #6 Salesman Huck on the program's twelfth race. She was dressed in shorts, sandals and a halter top, and she wore several turquoise rings on each hand. She took no notice of Richard at an adjacent window wearing her husband's baggy clothes. She handed the cashier a twenty-dollar bill and said, "Twenty bucks on 6 to win."

As the public address announcer was telling the crowd about the Mutt Also-Ran Handicap race, the final race of the season, Richard put the Paper Man's two thousand dollars on number 6 to win at the betting window. Then he ran through the crowd, rattling Floyd's two-wheeler toward the track's entrance.

Already sweating profusely, Floyd ran up to the other seven lead boys escorting their leashed assortment of mixed-bloods to the lead boy holding area. Floyd looked in vain for his friend's number 6 jersey and shouted, "Where's six?"

"He won't race," one lead boy called out.

"What?"

"He won't budge!"

"Stall as long as you can!" Floyd barked while running for the kennel. He entered the kennel building frantically, but then purposely relaxed as he neared the open kennel of number 6. Dozens of caged greyhounds yelped and whined all around them.

Muzzled and jerseyed Salesman Huck lay listlessly on his belly. His sad eyes looked up at his confused master.

"What's wrong?"

Floyd knew right off what was wrong. He clenched his jaw tight and tried to keep his cool. "Josie was here, wasn't she."

Harvey crouched down and spoke softly, "You know how we worked hard for this. I promise ... Josie's going with us to the Black Hills."

Huck's ears perked as he lifted his head and gave an inquisitive whine.

"Yes ... even if you lose she's going with us. Just like old times."

Huck stood, stretched, and bolted out of his cage with his leash trailing behind him, headed for the track with Floyd chasing after him. "Wait for me!"

The other dogs and their lead boys were halfway to the chute area when Huck and Harvey emerged from the kennels. The buzzing crowd watched as number 6 stopped at the fence near the finish line to be loved by the beautiful Josie.

Floyd ran up to them out of breath and angrily asked her, "What did you tell him?"

"I told him I loved him and missed him."

"Did you tell him about ... you know ... the papers?"

"Yeah."

"Damn! Did you tell him yer going with us on the run?"

"No, I didn't."

Floyd looked at the tote board's forty-to-one odds on number 6, then down to the chute area where the others were nearing. "Tell him, please!" he demanded in subdued anger.

A heckler called out from the crowd, "C'mon six. Hit the gate!"

"Yes, Huck. I'm going with you on the run."

Again Huck bolted away without Floyd, loping toward the

chute area with the crowd laughing at the older lead boy's short pants in humorous, stiff-legged pursuit.

Floyd put Salesman Huck in the number six chute while the lead boys ran down the track. He removed Huck's leash while the other dogs yelped excitedly. "Good boy. Stay relaxed." Then Floyd yelled out to Richard behind the wall, "Get ready!"

As Richard's finger trembled on the play button in Rocky, Floyd ran away from the chute area toward the finish line. The electric bunny started moving around the track. Josie nervously waited at the grandstand fence area by the finish line as the bunny closed in on the chute area.

Huck's ears perked up in the hot chute box as the Boz Scaggs song "Breakdown Dead Ahead" began playing loudly from Rocky's speakers. At the penultimate moment in the song, just before the lyrics begin, the bunny passed the chute area. The mutts bolted from their open chutes with Huck trailing the pack. Floyd and Josie cheered on their Huck as the music blared above the crowd noise.

Floyd's eyes followed Huck at the back of the pack on the first turn. "Make yer move, Huck! Now!"

On the track's back stretch, Huck made his big move, passing dogs and moving through jerseyed mutts. Closing in on the lead dog, he went through the last turn and headed down the final stretch. At the finish line, Salesman Huck won by two lengths! Josie and Floyd jumped for joy, and Floyd took off at a dead run to meet Huck at the finish line. Breathing hard as he closed in on Huck, Floyd shouted, "You did it, boy! You did it!"

The track's display board touted #6-Salesman Huck as the winner of the race. Josie watched Floyd remove Huck's muzzle and embrace him as the music stopped, then he removed Huck's jersey and handed it to a lead boy. As she ran to meet them at the lead boy area, Huck loped toward her. "You did it, baby!"

she said as she wrapped her arms around his neck and kissed his snout.

Floyd watched Josie with Richard's cap still low over his eyes. "You know where the kennel parking area is?"

"Yeah."

"Rocky's parked there. I want you to go with Huck out the back kennel gate, drive Rocky to the main entrance, and pick me up."

She handed him her winning ticket and watched him walk into the exiting crowd. Huck followed her toward the kennel area.

Richard was in the same track storage area nervously pacing in his underwear when there was a knock on the locked door. He let Floyd in. "Nice race, Harvey," he whispered excitedly.

"Tickets are in the case?" Floyd asked while undressing fast.

"Yeah."

After putting on his pants he gave Richard a hundred bucks. "Nice job, Richard."

"Thanks."

As Floyd turned to walk out the door Richard asked, "Harvey ... whatcha gonna do with all that money?"

"Save my marriage," he smiled hopefully.

After Floyd cashed in and signed the IRS paperwork, he exited the track and hopped into Rocky's side door, slamming it hard behind him. "Go!" he yelled at Josie's confused look from behind Rocky's wheel. She sped out of the track's parking lot.

Cruising north on I-29, Floyd laughed in the cargo area while smothering Huck with praise. "You did it, boy! You did it! I'm so proud of you! You finished this time, didn't ya?" After filling Huck's bowl with water from the van's small fridge, he handed Josie her winnings.

"That song ... where'd you come up with that?" she asked.

"That's his song!" Floyd laughed.

"How much did you bet on him?"

"A few bucks," Floyd smiled while climbing up into the front passenger seat. "You can pull over if ya want me to drive."

"That's okay ... I'll drive."

"I've gotta load product tomorrow. You stayin' at Granny's?" he asked.

"No ... I can get a room in Sioux City." After an awkward silence, she thought about playing some music but decided not to go there. *Too many memories in Rocky,* she thought to herself.

"Dennis will be getting out soon, huh?"

"Yeah."

It's time. Before the run. Get it out in the open and over with, he thought. "I'm real sorry for what I did in Pine Ridge, Josie," he said with sincerity. There was no explaining why and she asked nothing. Just more awkward silence. "I quit smokin' and drinkin'," he said.

"That's good."

"You look good, Josie."

"Thanks."

He turned on Rocky's radio. There was no more conversation until they arrived in downtown Sioux City where he started to give her money for a room.

"I'll get this one," she smiled as she held up her winnings.

"Pick you up at nine."

"Okay. And don't forget ... two-ply."

He courtesy smiled and nodded yes. Then just like that, she was gone with her suitcase.

On their way home, he talked aloud — more for his own benefit than Huck's. "That's okay. We'll see her tomorrow. At least she's goin' with us."

After doing his banking at eight the next morning, Floyd backed Rocky up to Silver's loading dock where his product was already stacked in neat rows. The case of two-ply toilet paper with "Dennis" written at the top in thick black lettering was loaded first tight against Rocky's driver's seat.

Albert came shuffling out of his office, scraping his size thirteen wingtips on the smooth concrete. "I saw in the paper ya won yer race!"

"Yeah. You should've seen his finish!"

Floyd continued loading as Albert petted Huck. "How much dough did ya win?"

"Enough to pay my tab with you."

"Ya still goin' on yer Black Hills run?"

"Yep ... on my way!"

"Ya gonna hook up with yer wife?"

"She's goin' with me."

"What?" Albert exclaimed with obvious surprise at the news.

"She's goin' with me!" Floyd repeated.

"You sign the divorce papers?"

"No ... she's still my wife."

"She's no good for ya ... too young."

Floyd barked back from inside Rocky, "Mind yer own business! I'll live my life and you live yours!"

"I'm tellin' ya ... ya better end it with her!" After a palpable silence Albert said, "You shaved that crap off yer face! Yer a good-lookin' man without a beard!"

"Get me a couple cans of oil, will ya?"

After picking up Josie at the motel, Floyd played Chris Rea's song "Working On It" as they crossed the Missouri River into Nebraska. Josie — in her cut-off shorts, t-shirt and sandals — was reading a novel. He could see her occasionally look out Rocky's passenger window at the Nebraska countryside, knowing this was the route they took to Yankton when she was eighteen.

Floyd's first call was at a grimy Jackson gas station. Josie looked up from her novel to watch him through the station's oil-stained front entrance handing his product card to the owner as Huck sat beside her on the driver's seat. A couple of minutes later, Floyd opened Rocky's back doors and retrieved a case of toilet paper, towels, and garbage bags ordered by the bearded, swarthy-faced station owner. Back inside the station, Josie could see the customer was dubious about the strength of the Paper Man's garbage bags. Floyd snapped his fingers, and like a shot Huck jumped out of the driver-side window and trotted to Floyd inside the station. Floyd held one of the garbage bags open near the floor and Huck climbed inside. Josie laughed out loud as she watched Floyd lift the bag off the floor with Huck inside to prove his product's durability. She quickly concealed her smile with her hand as Huck exited the bag and stood on his hind legs to beg for the order. Then it was the station owner's turn to laugh out loud.

In Ponca Josie bought a gallon of bottled water at the IGA while Floyd called on a half-dozen steady customers in town. Returning to Rocky, Josie listened to her Native Flute Ensemble CD as she sat meditating on the passenger seat. Floyd returned to the vehicle a short time later to find her in her meditative state. He circled Rocky and intently watched her quietly sitting

249

there, breathing deeply and slowly to the haunting music. She opened her eyes when he got in and started Rocky's engine. As they drove to Newcastle, he asked her what she was doing.

"Meditating," she answered.

"I've never done that. What's it do for ya?"

"It quiets my mind. I feel better afterwards ... more relaxed."

"Where'd ya learn it?"

"From Dennis. That's how he's able to handle his time. He says it helps him to create when he's praying for a vision."

"Can I listen some more to that music you were playing?"

She continued reading while he listened to her CD on their drive to Newcastle. She wanted to tell him about all the healing she had experienced in Pine Ridge, but she knew this wasn't the right time.

They had lunch at the Cornhusker Café in Newcastle after Floyd worked the main street businesses. The locals in the busy café stared at Josie as she sat alone at the table surrounded by their uncleared lunch dishes. After what seemed an eternity to her, Floyd emerged from the restroom with a big smile and Charlie under his arm. Jake's customer, the Bohunk café owner, intently watched Floyd pick up his meal ticket, leave a tip, then walk with Josie toward his register.

"Hold it right there, Paper Man!" The Bohunk's deep voice quieted the room. He pointed his accusing finger at Floyd as if he'd finally caught him. Floyd looked confused as he spotted two highway patrolmen in the quiet gawking lunch crowd, which only exacerbated Josie's embarrassment at the situation.

In a tirade the Bohunk said, "For years you've been comin' in here peddlin' yer cheap toilet paper! And every time you leave here, there's no toilet paper in the john!" Folding his burly arms in front of his greasy apron he continued, "I've always wondered ... why is that, Paper Man?"

Floyd looked flabbergasted. "What're ya sayin'?"

"Well, this time ... I've caught ya! See ... I wrote "butt-wipe thief" on my roll ... under the wrapper!" The café owner laughed at his ploy and haughtily added, "So ... if ya don't mind ... you can just open that bag of yers and show us what's inside!"

Floyd looked at Josie in complete stupefaction. She scowled at him, letting him know she did not at all like the kind of attention she was getting. Floyd addressed the room, still agape in mid-chew: "This is crazy! Do you believe this guy? He's accusin' me of stealing his toilet paper!" Seeing that the quiet faces were waiting for proof, Floyd emptied Charlie's contents onto the counter. There was no toilet paper.

In a panic the Bohunk exclaimed, "You hid it in yer clothes!"

Floyd smiled and raised his arms, willing to be searched. The Bohunk frisked Floyd and found nothing. Desperately trying to prove his case, the café owner walked backwards toward his restroom. "Just stay put!" he demanded.

He scrambled into the restroom and returned seconds later fuming mad. To the still-silent faces in the room he pleaded, "It's gone! The roll is gone!"

Floyd smiled big, remembering all the times this man had rejected him and his father. "I believe you owe me ... and my wife ... a sincere apology in front of all these people."

Josie tugged on Floyd's arm and tried to pull him toward the door. "Let's just forget it," she pleaded.

"Hey, I have an idea," Floyd said in mock inspiration. "How 'bout you pick up our lunch tab and I'll forget the whole scene?" Floyd's triumphal smile was big and broad.

The red-faced man swiped the ticket out of Floyd's hand.

"Thanks," Floyd said as he and Josie exited the café.

As they drove out of Newcastle, Josie finally broke the silence. "What was that all about?"

"He's an idiot. I've called on him for years and he's never given me any business." Floyd adjusted his rearview mirror to

251

see Huck panting in the cramped cargo area. "Good boy, Huck!"

Josie turned to see Huck with an individually wrapped roll of toilet paper between his front paws. Floyd reached back and picked up the roll, then handed it to Josie. She unwrapped it and laughed at the crude words printed on the roll.

* * * * *

They checked into a Yankton motel for the night, and Josie made sure they got a room with two beds. She went to the pool while Floyd sat on one of the beds in the room counting his sales. Huck, still clad in his sales collar, lay just outside the door to the room.

Shortly before sunset a middle-aged pizza delivery man pulled up outside Floyd's motel room. He walked up to Huck carrying a boxed pizza and squinted at the note stuck to the door. Huck sat up as he read the note aloud. "Leave pizza with dog. Dog will pay." He saw a five- and a ten-dollar bill sticking out of Huck's sales collar pouch. Setting the pizza box on the ground, he tentatively reached for the money situated precariously close to the dog's mouth. "That's thirteen dollars," he said in as gentle and soothing a voice as his shaking body would allow. After successfully retrieving the money, he started to give Huck the two dollars in change, but then decided not to. As he began walking towards his car, Huck growled. The guy froze in his tracks, then returned to Huck and stuck a single dollar in his sales collar. Huck growled again, and the man inserted the second dollar. "What ... no tip?" the pizza man asked. Huck barked no, and the man hastily returned to his car.

Floyd had changed into his bathing trunks by the time Huck scratched at the door to announce the pizza's delivery. He stashed Charlie under the mattress, slung a towel over his shoulder, grabbed his room key and the ice bucket, and left the

252

coolness of the room for the heat and humidity of the outside air. He took the change from Huck's pouch and picked up the pizza before heading for the pool. "Stay here," he told the dog.

Huck growled at Floyd. Turning back to the dog, Floyd softened his tone as he said, "I'm sorry. I forgot." He opened the pizza box and asked, "Vegetarian or sausage?" Huck barked twice for sausage. "I thought so," Floyd grinned. After setting a slice of sausage pizza on the cement for Huck he said, "Careful ... it's hot." Huck licked his hand. "Yer welcome. Uh ... give me some time alone with Josie ... ya know ... Thanks."

Floyd filled the ice bucket with ice and a couple of sodas before arriving at the pool. He watched Josie towel-dry her slim and toned body by the pool-side table. She poured some of her bottled water into a motel cup. He set down the pizza and opened the box. "Bottled water, vegetarian diet, meditation ... you've really made some changes," he smiled.

She courtesy-smiled before biting into a slice of vegetarian pizza.

"No ... I mean ... those are good things. You look good, Josie."

"Thanks."

An awkward silence filled the air between them as they ate.

"In some ways ... I guess Pine Ridge has been good for you, huh?"

She nodded yes while chewing, not wanting to discuss Pine Ridge.

"Look ... I was drunk that night. I know, I know ... that's no excuse. But I have regretted it ever since, Josie."

She nodded again, putting the towel over her shoulder.

"I wrote you several times ... but only mailed one letter. Did you get it?" he asked.

She shook her head no.

"That day ... I know I cheated those people in Pine Ridge ...

253

and ... I haven't done that since. Ever."

More silence from Josie.

"I just wanted you to know that I've made positive changes too since then ... and I'm really sorry for the whole damn mess I made."

Another nod.

"I don't s'pose there's anything I could do to make up for what I caused you and Dennis to endure."

After a long pause Josie said, "I know you are sorry. I forgive you. It's done now. The past is dead. I don't want to discuss that or anything else in the past."

Harvey nodded and watched her leave the table as she headed for the room; but before leaving the pool area, she returned to the table to pick up her room key.

"Is that all you're going to eat?" he asked.

"Yeah."

As soon as she disappeared from sight, Harvey dropped his slice of pizza on the table. His appetite was gone.

He swam laps until he was exhausted, then collapsed onto a pool-side reclining deck chair. He covered himself with a towel, then sank into muted congeries of cataleptic sleep. Late in the night he was awakened by Huck licking his foot. He gave his loyal companion the cold pizza, then returned to the room.

The air conditioner hummed in the darkened room — a room that had the haunting visage of loss that churned in his dyspeptic belly. It appeared Josie was asleep in the far bed. He removed his dry trunks in the dark and slipped under his covers quietly as she stirred.

Josie wasn't asleep. Her mind was fixed on the impending events in Pine Ridge, which she rehearsed again and again — searching for any details she might have missed. She wanted to get up and meditate her mind to the stillness that had gotten her through the most important time in her life, but she remained motionless and silent in the bed. She was in this room with her husband — the only man she had ever really loved. Josephine and Josie struggled for control under the covers. She felt the space between herself and Harvey was even greater than when she was in Pine Ridge and he was in Sioux City. This was the end of her marriage, and it was more real than she ever imagined, yet at the same time so unreal. This man who had once been the young girl's knight and rescuer was now a tired, aging man holding onto a crumbling way of life. He had no human friends, only strangers in isolated towns. And she was just another stranger.

She had watched his quick sales on this run with him. It was sad to watch, and it depleted her to a worrying girl along for the ride. Her thoughts turned to Dennis, so patient and strong. She wanted Dennis to hold her unconditionally. She knew an artist of his caliber would provide financial security for her one day. That was something Floyd Harvey Deason could never do in a million stops. She prayed for the loudest of dreams to take away the aloneness she was picking up from the man in the other bed.

* * * * *

On Tuesday morning the wind blew hot from the southwest. "The devil's breath" Floyd called it as they left the motel room in Yankton. Josie remembered hearing Walter call the wind the devil's breath, but she mentioned nothing of it to her traveling companion. She had half her normal sleep, so she felt tired and cranky as she climbed into Rocky.

"I know this great place to get breakfast," Floyd smiled.

"Fine," she muttered.

Sitting over his scrambled eggs and pancakes in a Yankton café, Josie watched Harvey sprinkling a white powder over his food. "What's that?" she asked.

"Protein powder. I've cut down on meat ... except chicken ... and the occasional sausage pizza."

"I noticed you left the spare roll of TP in the motel room," she said.

"Yeah ... I cut down on that, too."

"Since when?"

"A while," he smiled.

"I don't believe it!" she smirked.

"Yeah ... Really! I've prob'ly left the last twenty rolls. It's still kinda hard, though. I mean ... I still think about it every time I check out of a room. Habit, I guess."

"You've made some changes yourself," she smiled. She looked away from the wedding band he was still wearing.

"My biggest change is this run," he admitted.

"How's that?" she asked.

"I've given up you," he declared softly with a serious face.

After several minutes with no eye contact, Harvey broke the silence by adding, "I've thought about givin' up sales too."

"Your paper route?"

"Yeah ... but I don't know what I wanna do yet. I've thought about movin' to New Mexico. Santa Fe. I've heard it's really nice there. This last winter was way too hard on me."

"You could do this down there," she said.

"No ... this is a dead end. I've got to do somethin' diff'rent."

"You could go to school."

"No ... I don't see me doin' that. But maybe ... I just don't know. I'm confused."

"Confusion is a high state of being."

"Then I'm bein' really high these days," he laughed.

She laughed with him.

He said, "I know you don't want to discuss the past ... but I need to say how sorry I am for smokin' that weed in front of you ... that first time we met."

She nodded with a smile, resisting the urge to talk about her history with pot when she was a teenager in Macy.

"It really surprised me when you were smokin' when you were with Dennis on the road."

"We both quit that. He had to," she said.

"I've spent a lot of energy getting you into my life," he said. "That's why I've been so out of it since Pine Ridge."

She thought about her words carefully while finishing her breakfast. "It takes meeting someone else to move on."

"Have you met someone else?" he asked.

"No ... I've been getting to know me."

He wanted so badly to tell her how he always knew he was too old for her and that this would happen one day, but he kept quiet.

After a few quick sales in Yankton, they headed west on Highway 18. He worked with a fury in Tabor, Tyndall and Avon as Josie read and meditated to Native Flute Ensemble.

They got to Wagner shortly before noon, about an hour ahead of schedule. The Paper Man's first stop was a seedy-looking tavern. Parked in front of the tavern was an old, dirty pickup truck from Arkansas with two worn-out dirt bikes and a couple of sleeping bags in the bed. A shotgun hung inside the cab in the back window. Taped to the back of one of the bikes was a cardboard sign with crude lettering that made Floyd laugh out loud. "B H Motocicle Raly er Bust."

Floyd walked inside the bar. The owner was serving beer to two unshaven hayseeds sitting at the bar talking about how they planned to "score some babes" at the rally. Since the two men had come from quite a distance, Floyd decided not to tell them the rally had been a month ago.

"Got a great buy on a case of TP," Floyd said to the owner, who was ringing up the sale from the beer.

The older and heavier of the two rednecks snorted a laugh to the other and said, "Hey, Clyde. That guy's a corncob salesman!"

The younger man laughed and shouted over to the bartender, "Hey, barkeep ... Ask him to demonstrate his product fer me and Bubba."

Floyd turned to the bartender and said, "Ralph ... looks like ya got two big buttheads 'round here ... if ya need an extra case."

Clyde jumped up from his barstool and clenched his fists as he glowered at Floyd. Bubba slapped a hand on Clyde's back and told him to settle down, then both men returned to their beers. As Floyd finished writing up the order for the tavern, the two rednecks finished their beers and left the bar, with Clyde glaring at Floyd all the way out the door.

Outside the bar, the two rednecks saw Josie reading her book on the passenger seat in Rocky. Her long, shapely legs extended out onto the van's dashboard, and her round breasts were accentuated by the close-fitting halter top she was wearing.

Rocky's cargo door was open and the men were eying the few remaining cases of toilet paper. "I do believe we could use a case of that TP, Clyde," Bubba said to his younger companion.

Clyde eyeballed the case with Dennis's name on it and said, "Yeah. I see one right there. Says 'Denise' on it." After a gut-busting laugh he added, "Wonder what's wrong with her that she needs a whole case o' crapper paper!"

Josie quickly climbed out of the passenger seat and positioned herself between the cargo door and Dennis's case of paper. As Clyde started to climb into the van, both men froze in their tracks when they heard Huck growling behind them. Slowly turning around, they saw Huck with his teeth bared at them standing next to Floyd.

"You guys know you can get AIDS if a gay dog bites ya?" Floyd asked them with a serious look on his face. Turning to

Huck he said, "You know it's dirty pool to hide yer little secret by not wearing yer red neck kerchief."

The two rednecks backed away from the van about ten feet, then took off at a dead run for their pickup. After three unsuccessful attempts to start the pickup, it finally started with a loud backfire, and the two men sped away westbound on Highway 18.

Although visibly shaken, Josie couldn't help but laugh out loud once the two hayseeds were gone.

As they were getting ready to leave Wagner, Floyd flipped down Rocky's visor. Josie saw a worn three-by-five index card taped to it and leaned over to read it out loud: "You have to give up the way it is ... to have it the way you want it." Reflecting on the affirmation she said, "That's beautiful. Where'd you get that?"

"In a book I read about self-healing. Let things go ... go with the flow ... stuff like that," he said.

At a stop in Bonesteel later that afternoon when she went back to the cargo area to pour some water into Huck's bowl, she let out a sigh of relief that Dennis's case of paper was still safely in her possession. She smiled as she thought of the case of toilet paper she had sat on in Albert's van the time Harvey had driven her and Granny from Sioux City to Macy. Then she realized the fear of what she was doing and why she was there. The changes he was making and his pure-loving, confused eyes brought a dyspeptic knot to her belly.

Lost in her fears, she didn't hear the Paper Man coming up behind her with his two-wheeled cart. She nearly jumped out of her skin when he said, "Teach me how to meditate."

She looked down to the ground and saw Huck begging beside his master's leg. "Okay," she laughed.

Tuesday night, sitting in a Burke motel room, the Native Flute Ensemble played above the hum of the air conditioner inside and the patter of the rain outside. The room was dark except for a burning candle placed eye level on a chair in front of Josie and Harvey. They sat cross-legged on the floor with their backs to the wall, both staring at the flame without blinking. Harvey's eyes began to tear as Huck watched from across the room beside one of the beds.

"Don't blink," Josie instructed. "Look into the flame. It will cleanse the eyes. Breathe deeply from your center. Imagine your safe place ... where you are all alone. Let the tension go ... with each breath. Let go, Harvey. Now close your eyes ... but see the flame ... and breathe."

Outside the rain had stopped and the night was still. Josie turned off her CD player, and Harvey opened his relaxed eyes after meditating for forty minutes. His face appeared relaxed as never before. Josie turned on a lamp and extinguished the candle. Harvey's eyes looked lovingly at her, but she did not want to connect with him in that way. She poured herself a glass of water from her gallon jug and sat on the bed nearest Harvey.

"How do you feel?"

Harvey smiled but didn't move. "Relaxed."

"Look at yourself in the mirror," she said.

Harvey went over to the bureau mirror and smiled at his relaxed reflection. Looking at Josie's reflection on the bed across the room he said, "You learned this in Pine Ridge?"

She nodded her assent.

"From Dennis?"

Another nod.

Harvey swallowed hard into the mirror. His eyes began to run with long-held tears. His jaw was so relaxed he looked prognathous. "Thank you, Josie. I know you've taught me something that will get me through the trying times ahead. For some reason ... I always knew you would be the one who was good for me. Thank you."

He sat on the end of the bed and sobbed, letting go of his grief. She remained still and allowed him his space. He lay back on the bed, breathing from his center with his eyes open, and stared at the ceiling. He spoke softly in the voice she fell in love with. "I saw things, Josie ... that were all gold ... even my father. He was covered in a gold light ... like the color of yer eyes. I could see how I should go to Kansas City to visit my mother ... maybe see if I can reconcile my relationship with her. It will help me handle our divorce. It's all so clear to me, Josie."

"Why don't you call her?"

"Now?"

"Yes."

He got up from the bed, opened his billfold, and found an ancient piece of scrap paper with his mother's phone number on it. He dialed the number as Josie started to leave the room. "No ... please stay," he said.

She sat down on a chair near the door, thinking of the dreaded phone call she would have to make soon.

"Mother! Yes ... it's Floyd! Who else would call you Mother?" he laughed. "No ... everything's fine. I just called to tell you I want to visit you soon ... maybe spend some time with you ... and ... tell you I love you." His words choked out of him. "I stayed with Dad too long. I understand why you left him.

And I know it was hard for you to let me stay with him, but you honored my choice."

Josie's trembling hand covered her trembling mouth and chin as she heard his mother crying on the other end of the phone.

"I forgive you, Mother," he cried. "I've been carrying Dad's pain all this time." He cried as he listened to his mother.

"It feels good to tell you this, Mom. ... I'm in Burke, South Dakota, on the road with Josie. She's my wife, but we're getting divorced. We're friends, though. ... Yeah. ... I wish you could have met her. She's terrific."

Josie left the room, stopping Huck from leaving with her. She walked and cried at the full moon. If it hadn't been for her sentence in Pine Ridge, she would not have helped Harvey forgive his mother. Even Dennis would not be the polished artist with so many more incredible pieces if it weren't for his time served in that jailhouse. She cried for a quarter mile along the dark, wet, graveled strip of road running adjacent to Highway 18. It was plangently clear to her that all the positive changes she had made in her life were because of the Paper Man and his stash. It all made perfect sense to her. And she realized it was too late to stop what lay ahead of her.

She kept on the side road and realized she had not totally forgiven her mother. She thought this new plan with Dennis would be her way of forgiving her, but now she could see it was not the same thing. This brilliant scheme ahead would only stiffen her pride and not let out the real core of pain she always managed to dance away from. She was younger than Harvey, and she could see clearly that she had to do what he was able to do.

"But she's gone!" she cried aloud.

The scene replayed itself before her eyes as she continued crunching down the gravel road. The sickening feeling in the pit of her stomach and the knot at the back of her neck were just like they had been that morning she awoke to see the blue-and-white ambulance slowly drive away with her dead mother.

She began dry-heaving, bending over and vomiting on the road while gurgling, "Sweet dreams ... and snazzy squirrels. Sweet dreams and snazzy squirrels, Mommy!"

More pain came from her stomach to her throat. She knew she had to keep going with this to be truly free. "Mommy!" she wailed, letting out a groaning black bile that streamed down her chin and onto the gravel road.

Burping, spitting and more dry-heaving brought out virulent ululations that made their way to Huck's keen ears in the motel room. Huck began to pace nervously near the door and scratch at it. Realizing Josie had been gone for quite some time, Floyd opened the door and ordered Huck, "Go find her!"

Huck bolted in Josie's direction with Harvey in hot pursuit. His body felt considerably lighter as he ran. *So help me, if anyone is harming her,* he thought, *he'll be blown over as soon as I get there!*

Huck whimpered in confusion as he ran up to Josie and found her on her knees with her head bent low, crying like a little girl. He sniffed the wet ground in front of her.

"Josie!" Harvey called from a distance. He stopped running when he was about twenty feet from her. Through his heavy breathing he called out, "What happened?"

She put one hand up and waved at him as if to say she were fine. He could see her girlhood emotions on the gravel road when headlights from the traffic on Highway 18 passed in both directions.

"You sick?" he asked her as he stood over her.

"I'm okay," she groaned in a little girl's voice.

Harvey bent down to her and gently rubbed the back of her neck. "What happened?" he whispered. "Tell me ... please."

He helped her to her feet as she looked down at what she'd

carried inside for so long. He walked her back slowly toward their room. With his arm around her waist, he could feel sweat pouring off her as her head rode his shoulder.

"My mother," she groaned. "I forgave my mother too," she cried. She sobbed on his shoulder with Huck circling them in a concerned prance. As Josie's legs buckled, Harvey quickly placed his free arm underneath her and caught her halfway to the ground, scooping her up and carrying her like she was very special product. He held her securely as he made his way down the gravel road on skinny legs that suddenly had the strength they did on their wedding day. His arms curled effortlessly around the 118-pound frame of his wife — his most valuable treasure on earth.

He could have carried her a mile without stopping for rest. His foot kicked open the partly closed motel room door, and he gently placed her on his bed. A cool, wet washcloth that he retrieved from the bathroom was dabbed over her face and neck.

"I've got to shower," she moaned.

He stopped her from getting up and said, "Not yet. Rest a bit." After a short pause he whispered, "What happened?"

"It must've been because of your call to your mother. My mother ... just started ... coming out of me ... A bunch of emotions. God, it was so terrible. What did your mother say?" she asked.

"She was surprised. It was wonderful, Josie. Carryin' that crap all these years was killin' me. To tell her I forgave her ... sent this wave of emotions up my back ... down my fingers and out of my mouth."

"That's what I experienced. Thank you," she told him sincerely.

"I'll run ya a hot bath. Wow! I feel so ... energized!"

She came out of the motel bathroom towel-drying her hair in

clean clothes after an hour of soaking. She began combing her hair in the mirror when she saw him sitting in the chair meditating. His eyes were closed. His face was so relaxed that he looked ten years younger. She had never seen him look this good since she first laid eyes on him in Pine Ridge. Tension that had been constantly in his face was gone. The resolution with his mother seemed to put a healthy glow all over his countenance. He looked handsome again. Then she turned back to the mirror and saw her own eyes glowing as they did when she was a little girl. The light coming from her irises was markedly more visible than before. Her face was more relaxed now as she combed her hair back behind her ears. In the mirror she could see him open his heavy eyelids and watched as his eyes glowed with a sparking fire she had never seen before.

"Feel better?" he asked, again using that voice she fell in love with.

"Yeah ... much better."

He got up easily and came up behind her, looking at his reflection and then hers. "I can't do this anymore," he said.

"What?"

"Sellin' this way. It's so clear to me now, Josie. Peddlin' to these towns puts me in a place where I can't think of nothin' but movin' product. And it leaves me too tired to think of anything else that's better for me. I know this guy in Winner who will buy every bit of product in my van at cost.

She stood listening to him in stunned silence.

"If all my product's gone tomorrow ... will you go to the Black Hills with us if I have you in Pine Ridge by Friday?"

She thought about what was expected of her on Friday. Everything happened Friday. She could not show up early. "Yeah ... sure ... as long as I'm back Friday."

"Great!" he exclaimed as he clapped his hands together loudly. He paced the room with arms akimbo as his thoughts tumbled from his mouth. "I'll go south. Gotta get out of the Midwest. Better winters in New Mexico. And all this is from a little meditation! I have to make my move before all this wears off."

"You were ready for this change," she smiled.

"Yes! Ready for somethin' for sure." He hurried to the mirror and stood beside her. He peered at himself for a long time before their eyes met in the mirror. "If I changed my work ... would you go with me?" he asked.

"Harvey ..." She shook her head no at his reflection. His new eyes begged for an explanation.

"I can't ... I just can't," she said.

She left the mirror to sit on the bed with a pillow cushioning her back against the headboard. Something inside her was changing. Was it her heart? She could not let it reach her mind and her reason for being there.

Late into the night she was coming out of a dream surrounded by passive white elephants while hearing the enchanting "Summoning Wind" of Native Flute Ensemble — a haunting melody calling her home to rescue her people. Her golden eyes, yet dreaming, could see Harvey's father riding one of the white elephants with Charlie riding his side.

Dream interpretations were common in Josie's Native American culture. Granny and Walter gave meaning to many of hers. When she opened her eyes, she heard "Summoning Wind" low and soft and distant. It was coming from outside the room. She looked to Harvey's bed, but he was not in it. She slid out of her bed wearing an oversized t-shirt over her unsexiest cotton underwear, one of three pair Granny had sent her for Christmas. She called them "grannies." She turned the air conditioner on low and cracked open the window. Peering around the dusty motel curtain, she could see Harvey meditating from Rocky's driver's seat. She thought about how his music had been so much a part of her fall into love with him. Now it was her music.

Don't let him in! she said to herself. *But if I can forgive my mother ... And now he wants out of his way of life so much. Can I stop the plan?* she wondered.

Yes! Her resolution on the gravel road had just cleared the miasmic pool of pride to a running stream of options and possibilities. Yes, he was reaching even the mind of Josephine. Instead of no feelings and a willingness to adhere to the plan no matter what happened on this run, she now felt the cool air blowing up her shirt and an excitement for her husband she hadn't felt in a very long time. She put Friday and all its preparations behind her.

As she climbed over his bed to return to hers, she heard the music stop. Under her covers with her back to the door, she held her trained breath and listened for Rocky's door to close. But instead Gary's "Over You," began low from Rocky's speakers. She knew the lyrics: "Why am I losing sleep over you? Reliving precious moments we knew. So many days have gone by ... I get so lonely ..."

Josie's heart overwhelmed Josephine's mind with sentimental waves of emotions too powerful and loving for her tough counterpart to handle. She was all Josie.

He clicked off Rocky's stereo when Gary's song ended. This was his last shot. He knew she had heard it; he had seen the curtain crack open. He returned his closer to the glove box and thought about putting on cologne. *No, that's tacky,* he thought.

He was so elated to be all Harvey again that he gave Rocky's wheel a loving squeeze as he left. His left hand perspired, reminding him that Charlie was already behind the door — the door that was his most important in ten thousand. After closing Rocky's door quietly, he saw his faithful Huck resting in front of their room. He would not send his friend to beg for him. He would go to her alone. A man. It was his turn.

Seven slow, disparate steps revealed flashbacks shrouded in aloneness and exultation. He thought back to the days with his father on the road when he learned every lesson the old man had to teach about selling. Yes, the old man was right. A thousand times he was right! Every sale Harvey ever made to the butchers, grease monkeys, elevators and beauty shop owners on his route brought him goat-crying joy. He had learned from a master.

With his hand on the gold-colored doorknob, he remembered another flash of wisdom from the senior paper man. "Keep yer mouth shut after yer pitch." Gary had made the best pitch he had left, he hoped, as he pushed the door closed behind him. He kept his eyes focused on the ground until he looked up and realized he'd stepped into a dream.

The bathroom door was cracked open and the light was on, allowing him to see this second miracle with his new eyes. She was in his bed under the covers with her back toward him. She remained quiet during the sound of his clothes coming off. He got under the covers faster than he had in a long, long time.

That familiar dusty, musty scent that mixed together on his skin was intoxicatingly erotic to Josie. He pressed warm and close against her back as he put Charlie's arm around her. His wedding band lay against the bed sheet on fingers that flexed and relaxed inches from her face. She leaned her face into his smoke-free fingers, kissing and smelling them while her long legs slithered against his. Harvey's left hand moved her face gently toward him until gold met pale blue and his lips met hers. For two hours they made love. Nothing was said.

New Again

Wednesday. Glorious Wednesday! Always that midweek gauge for his weekly sales goal. This would be his last Wednesday in the field. The drive on Highway 18 seemed so dreamlike after their quiet breakfast. The ghost of his father was all but gone now, and he was making plans to visit his mother on his move south after he said goodbye to Albert.

He felt he could now overcome his crippling dependency on Josie and his work, and he stole a glance at her staring at the pages of her book. For the first time he saw the passing desolate, mud-spattered farms and homesteads and the raw land — the way a city tourist looks in stupefaction. *How can they live here?* he wondered. *Here ... so far away from anything new or hopeful.*

He could see what lay before him on these desolate scratches of human existence sprawled in every direction to the horizon. These were the places that had sustained him for nearly three decades of four separate and distinct seasons — covering his dash and brow with dust in summer, roiling his soul in winter, exulting his joy in spring, and dangling love's colors in the fall.

Yes, he mused, *I feel like an artist. I'm no failure,* he thought as he scanned the ditch-lined highway that he could drive blindfolded. *I have come through this an experienced man. A paper man. I've done things out here that perhaps one in ten million has done since this road was conceived.*

He knew what he *wasn't* going to do, and that was enough

for now. *To give this up ... is a victory!* he smiled to himself. He noticed a crow perched on a barbed-wire fence, balancing in the stiff prairie wind that blows incessantly across the plains. Forgetting she was reading — or, at least, pretending to be reading while lost in thought about Friday's impending events — he blurted out, "This must've been some place in the dust bowl days."

She only nodded and continued her pretense.

"I remember an old rancher out here who told me he went through it when he was a boy. He said that dust was in the air, the food, the water ... everywhere. I'll never forget that old guy."

By late morning he'd wheeled away the last of his product into the Winner General Store. Josie looked behind Rocky's driver's seat at the case of two-ply for Dennis. *I still have two days,* she reminded herself as her thoughts assailed her. She thought of Walter burning sage in the old church every morning before the children arrived, and how Dennis was so pleased with the painting he said was destined to be hailed his greatest work, and the Red Power she had so carefully handpicked, and all the money from Thunder Bird's sales since the bust — some twenty-two thousand dollars — all of it spent for Friday.

She dropped her head to her chest, pinching the bridge of her nose between her fingers. She could not summon Josephine's logic. Josie was here now. Last night's lovemaking had returned her to him, her husband, though nothing was said about calling off their divorce. Soon they would be heading for the hills to spend two nights in their honeymoon cabin. *Friday's going to be even harder after that,* she thought.

When they drove into Custer, Harvey remarked to himself how much happier Huck was with Josie around. He laid off his

271

old music, not wanting to relive a past that didn't work. He kept quiet about the events of the night before, allowing her the space she needed as he drove past the businesses of former prospects and customers. *They won't miss me,* he knew. *They'll buy cabinets from another paper man and continue on like the dust and wind that always blow out here.*

Josie only broached the subject once when they were leaving Winner. "Any regrets?" she asked.

"About what?"

"No more Paper Man," she said.

"No more Paper Man," he replied.

* * * * *

By the time they reached the cabin it was dark. Huck was exploring Mount Harney, his sales collar retired under Rocky's driver's seat.

The ash-filled fireplace was but a shadow in the candle-lit cabin. No honeymoon feelings arose before, during or after they meditated on the rug in front of the fireplace. Long after Rocky's stereo stopped playing her music, they remained in their quietude, breathing, letting thoughts come and go while seated Indian-fashion. Dennis had shown her how to keep her hands open with palms down on the inside of each bent knee, a place where the earth's energy had a pulse. He had told her, "When you feel your blood beating on your hands, stay with it. It's the heart of all Lakota people who passed on to the Great Father ... living again on Mother Earth."

She didn't share Thunder Bird's words about this with Harvey. She opened her eyes and saw him slack-jawed and even more relaxed than the night before. He could feel her watching him and opened his eyes. They sat looking at each other as they did in the beginning when she was eighteen.

272

"There's something going on in Pine Ridge," he said softly into her eyes. He could see her eyes change, then he continued as she stayed with her breathing. "It's some kind of storm ... like the sunset we saw in the Badlands when you showed me where you sprinkled your mother's ashes."

Her eyes changed again to those of Josephine the warrior. He was silent — waiting for her. Waiting. But Josephine was in the present. The sunset, the ashes, the Badlands that day when she was a little girl had taught her that no other storm could touch her. Anything that happened Friday would never be as bad as that moment when she shut down inside her aloneness, an aloneness that she'd carried until yesterday.

Now it was Josephine's turn. "Whatever storm is coming ... I will handle it ... and survive it ... loving you."

Harvey's eyes welled, then streamed, then stopped. He knew something was going to be final. He now had the strength to do what he'd been dreading for so long. She would do with it as she pleased. It was all up to her.

He got up from the floor and walked outside. She heard him opening the van door and then closing it again a half a minute later. When he walked back into the cabin, she recognized the envelope holding their divorce papers. He handed it to her, saying, "I signed them a couple days before the race ... when Huck and I went to his favorite spot at the homestead ... on the bluff."

She held the envelope on her lap without taking her eyes off of him. She said nothing as he left the cabin.

He had shown no trace of his sadness when he'd handed her the envelope. He walked to the end of the drive and onto the narrow path that led to the lake. He walked and felt the brush of the bushes against his arms and legs, guided only by the moon's light. There was no use in crying or hoping or pretending anymore. When he saw Josephine's eyes, he knew he had lost his wife. He would only give that envelope to Josephine. He had hoped it would be Josie who rode into Pine Ridge with him — and left Pine Ridge with him. But not now. He knew that whatever made her Josie was changed on that butte in the Badlands, and nothing she could spit out on any gravel road in his territory could change the storm coming his way.

Since calling his mother, he noticed it was much harder to feel sorry for himself. *That's good,* he said inwardly. *I've been beating myself up for too long, now.* Just then Huck came running up to him, pouncing his front paws onto Harvey's thighs, then turning and running ahead to the lake. Harvey picked up his pace on the path, removing his shirt.

"You wanna swim?"

Huck barked excitedly from the end of the rickety dock made of ash-gray barn wood, turning to get approval when Harvey's feet creaked and rocked their platform.

"Well ... go on ... test the water!"

In Huck went, dog-paddling a full circle before the sound of the splash was done echoing back from Harney's base.

"Is it cold?" he laughed.

He laughed for he knew his smart dog had barked once for no in order to lure him into one of the coldest lakes in South Dakota. He stripped and toe-tested the water.

"You liar!"

Harvey back-stepped a few paces, then ran off the dock flailing his arms and legs and screaming at the top of his new lungs. It was all so dreamlike to him as he swam and waded and splashed about in five-and-a-half feet of cold, black lake water from Harney. He wondered why he'd never taken time to run and jump into other area lakes, when this felt so exhilarating to him now. He remembered swimming with Josie in Minnesota lakes when he worked up there. *They were never as cold as this,* he recalled.

His thoughts turned to his new life in the Southwest — how far removed it would be from the upper Midwest. *Maybe that's why,* he thought. *Getting so far away from Josie and my territory will make it so much easier to start over.* But he knew he would miss their lovemaking. More than that, it was the feeling of carefree youth she gave him that he would miss most of all. He hoped he could find it again — somewhere. In the divorce papers she'd asked for nothing from him. Clean and final. His signature in exchange for her freedom. But not his freedom. Floyd and Harvey would have her in their lives far longer than the divorce papers decreed.

Huck dog-paddled up to him as Harvey dug his toes deep into the lake's sloe-black, muddy bottom — a place much colder than the surface temperature of the water. He listened to the chirping crickets and watched for more flickering fireflies, paying attention to the flexibility his belly now had. *That must have been because of the call to my mother,* he knew. *But what about my heart and mind?* Josie had filled the spaces that kept him going, spaces that encysted his aliveness. He wondered if he could survive such a devastating storm without this heart and this mind, and with no tools except his mouth that moved to the only kind of work he'd ever known.

I have enough money saved, he told himself. *But maybe I'm too old to start over.* Then he asked Huck, "Am I too old to start over?"

Huck turned to him in the water with his ears wet and perked, not sure how to answer. Harvey started to playfully grab Huck's tail and said, "Let's go."

Huck was shaking dry on the path ahead of Harvey when they reached a clearing where he could see the cabin. Rocky was gone.

Inside the cabin he found a note on the bed. "Be back soon. Don't worry. Josie."

He didn't worry about where she went. It was the blunt way she signed the note. "Love, Josie," would have given him some hope. Could she be thinking over the finality of the divorce now? Did she even open the envelope to make sure he'd signed the papers? He thought he'd better meditate.

* * * * *

Josie had been pacing the cabin interior, trying to think of a way to avoid Friday. Her time spent meditating brought no answer except that she still loved the Paper Man.

The drive to Pine Ridge was the longest one of her life. She intended to drive straight to the police station, but she saw a large number of vehicles parked near the old church. She parked Rocky on the grass on the north side of the church — the same spot where he'd played their wedding music.

Inside the front door, she was stunned to see candles burning in the main room with at least a hundred locals chanting while seated on the floor facing an altar of burning sage. She looked for Walter and Dennis, but they were not there. While walking behind the back row of full-bloods, she could see they all appeared to be Praying for a Vision — even some of the children.

Can they all know? she wondered. She left Rocky parked and ran to the Bird house. Both the Jeep and Walter's car were there. Lights were on in the house. Laura was sipping tea alone at the kitchen table, her hand cradling her head in her usual state of worried anxiety.

Before Laura noticed Josie, Dennis saw his cousin from the front room, where he and his father were chatting softly before an open map of Canada on the coffee table. Dennis came into the kitchen when Laura and Josie were embracing. He led her into the front room away from his mother.

Dennis asked, "What happened?"

"He quit his route."

"What!" Walter said in surprise as he sprang to his feet.

"Out of the blue ... he quit. He sold everything."

"The TP ..."

"It's in the van."

"Where's the van?" Dennis asked after looking out the front window.

"By the church. I drove it from the cabin in Custer. I told him I'd go with him to the hills if he had me back here by Friday."

Walter said, "Or he would have been here today?"

"Yes," Josie replied.

Laura appeared rattled as she walked into the room and said, "Is everything okay?"

Dennis quickly ushered his mother back into the kitchen. "Don't worry, Mother. Everything is fine. We just need to talk to Josie for a minute."

"I have to get back to my cell," he told his father and Josie when he came back into the living room.

They left out the front door. She walked between them, headed for the jailhouse. For an instant, she remembered Floyd telling her about "Indians" and what his father had taught him about "Red Power." It was Floyd who taught her about her people in ways that the white in her could understand.

"Why are all those people in the church?" Josie asked.

"Praying for the new center," Walter said.

"All those people? The children? They're not involved. They don't know ..."

"They know that a change is coming," Dennis said. "They

277

don't know how. Too many people ... too much talk going around. When it's over, they will say nothing." In an annoyed tone as they walked past the church he said, "Do you hear them now? No!"

"So he will bring you Friday?" Walter asked Josie.

"Yes. But ... it's really ... hard now ... for me ..." she said.

Dennis snapped, "You slept with him and made up!"

"Yes ... I did. He's still my husband. No making up. He signed the divorce papers."

"And you fell in love with him again," Dennis said, almost smiling at her. Thunder Bird knew that their plan would only have a chance at working if the Paper Man thought he had a chance with Josie.

She hesitated before answering. "Yes. He's changed. He's not a paper man anymore. I love him."

"How can you be in the plan?" Walter asked his niece.

"I just want to know if there's another way to do this without jeopardizing the plan," she remarked as they crossed the street near Walter's office.

"No!" Dennis answered for them.

With the jailhouse coming into view, Dennis stopped and gently placed his hands on her shoulders, looking into her worried eyes. "Josie ... strong Josie. What else happened?"

She softened and let the tears run down her cheek. "He's really changed, Dennis. I was able to let go of my mother because of him. I was doing this for her," she cried. "I don't want to lose him too."

"And our people?" Dennis asked sternly.

"I know ... I know. That's why it's so hard."

Dennis pulled her to his chest and they embraced.

"You will have to decide," he whispered. "If you go with him, we lose his motive ... and the plan will die. Let him come to Pine Ridge. You decide if you go with him."

She nodded yes on his shoulder, then she kissed them both goodbye and ran toward Rocky.

They watched her drive away and continued to the jailhouse. "You said this might happen," Walter said to his son.

* * * * *

She carried a full bag of groceries into the cabin. He was sitting on the bed, facing her as she emptied the bag onto the table.

"Peanuts!" he exclaimed.

She handed him the jar of peanuts when he came over to the table.

"Huck and I went for a swim," he smiled.

"Was the lake cold?"

"Very," he said.

He didn't ask her where she went. *That's another big change,* she thought. They sat at the table eating yogurt. Harvey mixed peanuts into his. He really was not concerned where she had been. Then he surprised her by saying, "I could take you to Pine Ridge tomorrow ... if you'd like."

"No. It's really nice up here. I want to hike the whole day tomorrow."

"I'd like to go with you," he said.

They slept without making love. He had talked humorously for an hour about the types of work he couldn't do and that nothing interested him. Her mind was balanced between engaging him in his brainstorming and weighing her decision about Friday. She was looking forward to the physical workout of hiking on Thursday in the hills — away from thought patterns that were creasing her brow and giving her a headache.

She suggested they meditate in bed, breathing together until sleep came. His eagerness to be still, leaving her flesh alone, only made it harder to calm the waves of thoughts coming and going in Josephine's mind. When she slept, her mind was wrapped in a series of bizarre dreams that sought to rival Thunder Bird's vision that created this plan.

* * * * *

Thursday morning after breakfasting on bagels and fruit, they followed a trail that circled the lake, off-shooting toward Harney Peak across the lake from the cabin. Under the shimmering shade of tall pines, Huck and Harvey led the way until they came to a fork in the trail.

"Which way?" Josie asked.

"It doesn't matter ... as long as we go together," he smiled.

For the first time since leaving their cabin to hike, her mind trailed back to the plan that was less than twenty-four hours from fruition. She now vacillated between leaving Pine Ridge with him or going through with the original plan.

For three miles they tramped along the base of Harney Peak when Harvey suggested they stop and meditate on a large, shaded boulder that faced the mountain. After twenty minutes of nothing but the sounds of birds and wind, Josie had made her decision: She would deliver him to Pine Ridge and stay with the plan.

Hunger set in by early afternoon when a thunderstorm turned them back towards the cabin. During a downpour the trio ran for cover, but none could be found. Thoroughly soaked, Josie and Harvey laughed all the way to the cabin.

As they rounded the corner of their cabin, Josie and Floyd stopped directly between the cabin's front entrance and Rocky's bumper when they noticed the old, dirty pickup truck with two dirt bikes in the bed parked next to Rocky. The two rednecks

280

from the Wagner bar were trying all the doors on the van to see if one was unlocked. The van held only two things of value — Dennis's case of toilet paper and Charlie, and every dime Floyd had was still in Charlie. As Clyde raised the butt of his shotgun to break out Rocky's passenger side window, Floyd yelled out, "Hey! What're you doing!"

Taken by surprise, Clyde quickly lowered his shotgun and aimed it at Floyd and Josie. "We came back fer our case of TP, Paper Man."

"And we'll just take that bag sittin' on top of it, too," Bubba added.

Before Floyd could take a step, Huck shot around the front of the van, leapt at Clyde, and bit him hard on the hand. Clyde dropped his shotgun and held onto his bleeding hand. Josie quickly grabbed the shotgun and had it trained on the two dirty men before fat Bubba could bend himself down to pick it up.

"Oh, God, Bubba! Oh, God! I got AIDS now! What am I gonna do, Bubba? I don't want to die this way! Oh, God!" Clyde wailed as he clenched his bleeding hand.

Josie shot out the windshield of the pickup, then pumped and aimed the gun back on the men.

"I suggest you two get out of here while you still have four inflated tires. My wife's an expert marksman," Floyd said as the men slowly backed toward their truck. They didn't even take time to clean the glass off the seat before jumping into the truck, burying the gas pedal into the floor, and heading for Arkansas as fast as they could go.

Still trembling from the drama with the unrelenting rednecks, the two hikers went into the cabin. Harvey held her close until she stopped shaking and both began breathing again from their centers, then they napped for a few hours.

As they ate dinner in front of the fireplace Harvey said, "D.H. Lawrence wrote about the sun's light in Santa Fe. He said it's diff'rent ... unreal ... fascinating. He wrote about nature like no other writer I've ever read. I read several of his books this winter without knowing what I was reading half the time. But when he wrote about Santa Fe's light ... it really interested me ... because I knew I'd have to get away to somewhere like that."

I'll tell him tomorrow, she thought.

In the middle of the night, Harvey thought she was asleep when he went outside to Rocky and put his wedding band in the glove box.

Rocky cruised off Highway 18 Friday morning. Pine Ridge looked like a ghost town as Harvey parked in front of the old church. They had said their goodbyes on their drive to Pine Ridge. She kissed him quick, saying nothing. Then she gave Huck a big kiss on his snout, saying, "Huck, I love you."

They watched her hurry with her bag toward the church, then detour to the Bird house.

The center was empty, as planned. Laura had taken the children on a field trip to Hot Springs.

Harvey loaded Dennis's two-ply onto his two-wheeler, knowing this would be his last delivery. "It's over," he told Huck from Rocky's open side door.

The Pine Ridge Chief of Police went into the cell area after telling his deputy to keep an eye on the Paper Man. "Call me when he's coming," he ordered. Walter was in the open cell with his son when the police chief came in. All of the other cells were empty. Speaking to the two men as if they were in charge the Police Chief said, "He's in town ... trying to deliver to the center."

Walter gave the chief his orders. "Call Big Bird. Tell him to fly."

The chief left the cell area as if ordered by a superior, for Walter outranked him as Tribal Chairman. And this was Walter's plan.

A painting was carefully wrapped with two blankets and leaned against Thunder Bird's cell wall. "She did it," Dennis smiled at his father.

"Yes," Walter smiled back.

On a blacktop road north of Pine Ridge, still on Reservation land, a group of Indian inmates stood near a police van parked lengthwise in the middle of the road. The van blocked any traffic from entering Pine Ridge from the north. The driver, a trusty inmate, received a call from the chief. "Pine Ridge Landing ... Big Bird flies."

"Okay, Chief."

As the other inmates cheered then quieted, the trusty switched channels on the radio and made another call. "Big Bird ... this is Pine Ridge Landing. Fly!"

Huck watched the deputy cruise past Rocky in his patrol car and park down the street as Harvey entered the center with his loaded two-wheeler.

Harvey found a note taped to the storage room door. "Storage Room Moved to Agency." He opened the storage room door. No product. The usually jammed storage room was empty. He wheeled the case of paper back to Rocky. Huck was gone, watching the patrol car from the shade of a scraggly pine tree near Walter's office.

After tossing his two-wheeler and closing Rocky's side door, Harvey wiped his brow and looked around for Huck. The humidity was high for early September, reminding him too much of the last time he'd been in Pine Ridge. He knew he was stalling, even though he was thirsty, as he walked toward the front of Clouda's store while digging for change in the front pockets of his shorts.

The old pop machine brought back the memory of the day he

met Josie. He squinted at the sun overhead as he recalled their talk about her going with him to Santa Fe.

"I need some time," she'd said. "If you write me when you get settled, I'll either come visit you ..."

He didn't want her to say more, so he interrupted her and said, "That's fine. See how you feel. No promises ... Okay?"

"Okay," she'd said.

Inside the store he got some change for the pop machine. He decided not to go to the back of the store and see his old customer. As he left the store, he smirked when he saw Clouda's wife watching him from behind her cardboard sign that read, "Cantaloupes 79¢ each." He couldn't blame her. He'd never, ever actually bought a pop there.

He gulped down his Coke and placed the empty bottle on top of the machine. Something was different about the place — Harvey could feel it.

Josie lay on her bed in the empty Bird house staring at the ceiling. Restless with anticipation, she got up and grabbed her bag to unpack it, finding the envelope with the divorce papers. To her gaping surprise, inside the envelope was a cashier's check made out to her for eighty-two thousand dollars. She quickly checked to see if their divorce papers were signed. They were. On the last page was a note.

Josie:

> *The race money is for you and Dennis. I'm sorry for what I did, and this is at least something to make up for some of the trouble I've given a great artist and his terrific agent.*
>
> > *I love you,*
> > *Harvey*

285

P.S. Love is Money.

She ran out of the house with the check in her hand.

Harvey walked through Walter's empty Agency. He hid in the open storage room when he heard approaching footsteps.

Walter took a seat behind his desk and began nervously tapping his fingers on the desk just when Josie ran into her uncle's office.

"Uncle Walt ... you have to stop this. He's given us eighty-two thousand dollars!" she cried, showing him the check. "It's the money he won at the race. We can do a lot with this!"

"It's not enough," Walter said.

"It's a start! With sales from the paintings we can still get it done!"

Walter shook his head and said, "It's up to Dennis."

Josie exited the Agency in a hurry.

Harvey walked out of the storage room and left the Agency unnoticed. He saw the patrol car driving to the little grocery store next to the center.

Inside the police station, Josie ran past the nervous chief and into the cell area, where Dennis was pacing in his cell. She showed him the check and Harvey's note with their divorce papers. He read them thoughtfully.

"See? He's changed! We don't have to use him now."

"That's a fine gesture ... but it's not enough. That won't cover what we need. It's too late."

"Dennis, I want out," Josie pleaded.

"Okay. Tell the chief to come here," he said.

When Josie returned with the police chief, Thunder Bird told him, "She wants to warn him."

Dennis brought out his wrapped canvas out of his unlocked cell and carefully leaned it against another cell's bars. Then

Thunder Bird grabbed Josie and locked her inside his cell.

"Dennis! Don't do this!" she pleaded.

Thunder Bird went into another cell with his covered painting and told the chief to let her out when it was over.

Walter greeted the Paper Man outside the Agency. Floyd was listening now.

"We can't handle any more product here. I didn't order that."

"Relax, Chief ... It's a gift from Josie. It's paid for."

Walter appeared to be thinking of a place to put the paper. "You can deliver it to the police station ... the storage room. You know where it is," Walter said.

As Walter was inwardly sighing his relief at seeing the Paper Man return the case of two-ply to his van, Harvey called out to the Tribal Chairman, fluttering Walter's heart. "Chief! I'm sorry for what I did to yer son. I just wanted you to know that."

Walter nodded awkwardly, his eyes fluttering with deception while turning his back on and walking away from the Paper Man.

Floyd watched one of his customers walk away. Knowing he may never see him again, he said, "You can find another supplier. I won't be coming back."

He watched the Tribal Chairman continue walking, not turning to converse with him. "Chief!"

Walter turned.

"You see my dog?"

"No," Walter said, continuing to his empty Agency.

Floyd looked around for Huck after closing Rocky's side door.

Josie escaped. Dennis forgot she had a set of keys on her at all times — something Floyd had taught her to do. She had a duplicate cell key that Uncle Walter had given her. Locked in the cell next to her, he was powerless to do anything to prevent her escape. The key to the cell wasn't his biggest concern, however; it was the keys to the Jeep that gave him the most concern. If his vehicle could be traced to the plan, it could diminish the impact of the whole thing.

Josie made a beeline to the Bird house and missed Harvey, still parked in front of the Agency. She drove the Jeep over to the center and saw the note on the storage room door. She knew they had changed the plan on her, because the plan had been to have the case of two-play blow up the old center. A dynamite charge was in the case of toilet paper for Dennis. The case of two-ply could only be detonated by Big Bird.

Floyd drove Rocky to his last drop at the jailhouse storage room as Huck watched him from his shady spot.

The chief's deputy was in the patrol car and had the other end of the blacktop road barricaded. He scanned the sky with binoculars.

The Indian inmate in the van watched the sky with his barricade of excited inmates. Then he too used binoculars and saw the small twin-engine aircraft approaching from Rapid City. Quickly, he got on the radio. "Chief ... Big Bird is coming!"

At the jailhouse, the chief hurried into the cell area and unlocked Thunder Bird's cell door. "Brace yourself," he told the jailhouse's only inmate.

Josie ran to Walter's office after checking the Agency storage room for the toilet paper. "Where is it?" she demanded.

Walter stood up from his chair behind his cluttered desk and said, "We changed the plan."

"Where!" she demanded with the envelope clenched in her fist.

"Josie ... it's not enough money. You can't stop this."

"Where!"

"The jailhouse storage room."

"No! He's given us eighty-two thousand bucks! We can sell his work without this now! Is he gone? Has he delivered it yet? Why the station?"

"Dennis is flying away," Walter said.

"Flying? Where?"

"Canada."

"Why?"

"He believes this will create a bigger demand for his work."

"When is the plane landing?"

"Any minute," Walter said more quietly.

"Where?" Josie demanded.

"On Flattop Road."

Josie ran out of the office with Walter on her heels calling out her name, but to no avail. She outran him and bolted for the Jeep, driving away fast toward Flattop Road. Walter hurried inside to his phone.

Floyd exited the police station's storage room after ceremoniously leaving the blade of his two-wheeler under his last delivery.

Dennis lay on his open cell floor with his mattress covering him and his wrapped painting flat against his chest.

Floyd stood by Rocky's open side door outside the jail's storage room and watched the police chief speed away in his pickup.

Josie sped the Jeep past the barricade made by the police van as she saw Big Bird directly ahead of her and closing in on his landing spot on Flattop Road. She put on her seatbelt.

Harvey scanned for Huck after his drop. He decided to play Salesman Huck's race song "Breakdown Dead Ahead." Huck's ears perked in the shade. He stood, ready to bolt at the same instant in the music as he did during the race. Huck, five hundred yards away, left his chute, racing for Harvey.

The police chief saw Josie speeding on Flattop Road in the plane's landing path. He picked up his truck's radio and ordered the deputy, "Take her wheels out! Now!"

The deputy quickly grabbed his scoped rifle and sighted her front tires.

The Native American pilot of Big Bird had a finger on an ominous red button when the police chief came in on his radio. "Big Bird ... we're clearing your point of landing. Stay with the plan!"

Huck was running like the devil toward Harvey's open arms at Rocky's open side door. The music blared from Rocky's speakers.

The deputy fired, blowing out the Jeep's front wheel and causing Josie to veer off the road. The Jeep overturned in a shallow ditch next to the road.

Harvey was caught in a slow-motion reverie as #6 Salesman Huck made his way through the pack at the racetrack, oblivious to the Jeep's horn sounding a steady warning from the north. At the very moment the plane touched down on Flattop Road, the red button was pushed as Huck was in midair. The case of toilet paper exploded, blasting open the storage room wall. Hurling concrete and floating bits of toilet paper soon covered the area in a thick, confusing smoke.

Thunder Bird quickly recovered from the blast and escaped through the gaping hole in the storage room wall that led to the outside. He ran with his protected painting through the smoke and debris as the song continued playing from Rocky's stereo.

Harvey was dazed, lying behind his driver's seat in Rocky's cargo area. His face was cut and bleeding from all the glass that had shattered out of Rocky. Above the music Harvey screamed out, "Huck!"

Josie was crying as she limped back toward Rocky from a quarter mile away. She screamed out above the music, "I tried to stop them!" Unaware that he was behind her, Thunder Bird intercepted Josie, dragging her back in the direction of the idling plane. She strained to see Harvey in the smoke-covered area around the jailhouse.

On his hands and knees, Floyd searched for Huck on the ground around Rocky in the thick smoke. Eventually, he found Huck's lifeless body. Huck had shielded Floyd from the blast and was killed instantly by the Paper Man's two-wheeler. He quickly carried Huck to Rocky's side door and gently placed him in the cargo area as the song continued to play. He scrambled for the driver's seat and sped away with no windshield.

Big Bird took off with Thunder Bird and Josie, who was still clutching the envelope in her fisted hand and sobbing uncontrollably.

Rocky's speedometer was buried as the nearly unconscious Floyd headed west on Highway 18 for Custer. His upper body was pelted by wind and insects as he spoke to Huck's lifeless body behind him. "NOW THAT WAS A TOUGH DELIVERY!" He noticed Huck's sales collar on the floor of the cargo bed and started to sob. "You'll be okay! Hold on, boy! We're gonna see one of yer old customers!" Hold on!" Just then Floyd saw Josie's gallon jug of bottled water and angrily tossed it out the window.

Floyd sped through Custer and reached the veterinarian's office. He carried Huck inside and gently laid him on an examination table. The vet examined Huck and asked, "What happened?"

"There was an explosion ..." Floyd said breathlessly.

Seeing there was nothing he could do for the dog the vet quietly said, "I'm sorry."

As Floyd left the vet's office with Huck's dead body in his arms, two Custer policemen crouched behind a patrol car and aimed their guns at the Paper Man. "PUT DOWN THE DOG ...

RAISE YOUR HANDS AND FREEZE!"

Floyd was handcuffed and put in the back of the police cruiser. As they drove away, Floyd watched the veterinarian carry Huck back into his clinic. In Floyd's head Native Flute Ensemble's "Sacred Spaces, Sacred Hills" played as he stared at the Black Hills out of the squad car's back window.

Big Bird flew low and north, headed for Canada.

On the street outside the Rapid City Federal Building, the pedestrian and vehicular traffic came to a halt as the crowd anxiously awaited the verdict.

"Well, it's getting close," the nightly news reporter said into the camera as he stood on the courthouse steps. "We just got word that the long-awaited verdict of Floyd Harvey Deason — the Paper Man — will be handed down within the hour. Will the government find him guilty of conspiracy? Or is he just an innocent toilet paper salesman who got duped in his own territory?"

Throughout the upper Midwest, business as usual was tabled as townsfolk, farmers, and former customers of the Paper Man sat glued to their televisions awaiting the trial's outcome.

"I've met that loser, and he's as crooked as they come. He's guilty for sure!" slurred a rheumy-eyed patron of a small-town tavern. The barflies seated around him stared at the big-screen TV.

"Nah! They'll let him off. He's lyin' to protect his wife," retorted a slightly less drunk stool-warmer next to him.

The bartender jumped up on the bar and waved a roll of toilet paper high in the air. "I gotta roll sold to me by the Paper Man right here goin' for ten bucks!"

"How do we know he sold it to ya?" shouted one skeptical patron.

The bartender unrolled a few sheets and poked his finger

through the nearly see-through product. "See? It's one-ply!"

With that, several customers surged forward hoping to buy a piece of local infamy.

The story was the same throughout the countryside. From the rural South Dakota farmer whose wife excitedly waved him in from the field to the small-town beauty shop where women in curlers scurried to the corner gas station with the only television on Main Street, people everywhere abandoned the task at hand to watch the verdict as it was delivered.

From the fifth floor conference room window of the federal building, Floyd Harvey Deason looked out on the crowd below. Some people were carrying signs that read: "Free Floyd — Paper Man Not Guilty." Others were chanting, "There is a reason you must convict Deason."

Harvey was wearing a suit and tie that belied his tumultuous past. He was alone in the room with his attorney, a young Native American man named Jason Running Bear, as they waited for the jury to finish its deliberations and return with a verdict.

"Floyd, she played you for a big fool. You're letting her and Pine Ridge get away with this!" Jason disgustedly advised him. "I know this judge, Floyd. He's tough. He'll throw the book at you and send you to Leavenworth till you're an old man if you don't tell him who set you up. Tell him she left you for another man."

"That's not true!" Harvey said angrily.

"Then tell him what *is* true, Paper Man. You keepin' quiet is not savin' yer ass in there. I've got nothin' to go on if you protect her. Look, Floyd, hundreds of witnesses saw her with you between Sioux City and Pine Ridge. Why are you protectin' this woman who divorced you and took off ..."

Harvey stopped pacing in front of the window and shot a look at Jason that warned him he'd better back off.

"Whether or not she's your ex-wife, when we go back into the courtroom that judge is going to convict you of complicity and withholding evidence in a federal crime. You're protecting Josie and Dennis for some ..."

Just then the bailiff knocked on the door letting them know court would reconvene in one-half hour and the jury would deliver its verdict.

Harvey turned from the window upon hearing Jason place a tiny paper towel dispenser key on the table and slide it in his direction.

"A friend of yours told me to give you this," Jason said quietly. Before Harvey could ask who gave him the key, Jason excused himself to go outside for a smoke.

Harvey picked up the key and ducked into the small private bathroom off of the conference room, unable to lock the door behind him. With a trembling hand he unlocked the antiquated dispenser with "A. Silver Paper Company, Sioux City, Iowa" stamped on the front of it. Inside was a paper bag containing a small MP3 player with earbuds and a note that read, "Listen and remember." He inserted the earbuds and began playing Steve Winwood's "Talking Back to the Night." Smiling to himself, he knew he had hope for the future.

Inside the courtroom, the federal judge was flanked by U.S. Marshals while seated at his bench. Harvey and his attorney stood and faced the judge, along with the prosecuting attorney. The judge scolded the prosecutor. "I've never seen so many loose ends where Prosecution failed to prove complicity!"

The scowling judge then turned to face Harvey. "And ... Mr. Paper Man ... in lieu of your contempt by using false claims of amnesia and your obvious complicity by withholding evidence ..."

Harvey swallowed hard.

The judge continued, "The jury finds you guilty, and you are hereby sentenced to serve four years in Leavenworth. Plus ... a twenty-thousand-dollar fine for damages." He turned to the bailiff and said, "Now get him out of here."

Harvey was stunned.

Outside the federal building, Floyd was ushered into an unmarked government car and whisked away from the crowd of protesters. Josie was wearing sunglasses and a brunette wig in the crowd, having heard the announcement that Harvey was found guilty and given four years. She watched the government car leave the area with the Paper Man en route to Leavenworth.

Later that afternoon at the Rapid City Regional Airport, Josie, still wearing the same disguise, boarded a plane destined for Minneapolis. Her portable music player was in her hand as Chris Rea's "Working On It" played through her earbuds.

Newspaper headlines throughout the Midwest read "Paper Man Guilty." All over the country, every newspaper ran at least a quarter-page article in the main news section about the now-infamous Paper Man.

The Paper Man boarded a flight to Kansas City, chained and escorted by U.S. Marshals.

In Minneapolis, Josie switched planes to one bound for New York City.

Arriving at Leavenworth, Indian inmates watched the Paper Man, now in prison clothes, being escorted to his cell by a prison guard. The cell door closed behind him with a deafening clank, and Harvey's future all but disappeared as the echoing sound died.

That night Harvey had on his headphones in his private cell. *The bed's pretty comfortable,* he thought. He knew this was his grieving time. He clicked on Gary's "Over You" and reflected on his memories of Huck — how he trained the pup to wait outside the prospect's door, walking him to the next call, Salesman Huck begging for an order with his sales collar on, training him to race, the race he won, and the race to save him at the jailhouse. Harvey buried his face in his pillow and sobbed hard inside his lonely cell.

* * * * *

The chauffeur held open the back door of a waiting limo for Josie. As he closed the door, Josie took a seat beside the handsome Perry Villa, the world-renowned art dealer she'd had the affair with before she married Harvey. She removed her sunglasses and wig, flouncing her beautiful auburn hair. Perry embraced her and kissed her playfully on her neck.

"Have you seen the painting?" she laughed.

"It's better than I imagined. Have you seen it?"

"No," she said. "Tomorrow. Are they all coming?"

"Yes. I had to turn away twenty people. Oh, how I loved it!"

Josie was alone in her penthouse suite as she lay in bed anticipating the events of the next morning. It would be the biggest day of her life. She thought about the Paper Man and how she was determined to get him out in less than two years. Then she let it go. Tomorrow.

The next morning, wearing a very formal and expensive dress, she stepped out of the limo. Josephine was on Perry's arm as they entered the luxury hotel. Several reporters hounded Perry with questions as the hotel security guards ushered them inside.

"Mr. Villa ... Sir ... What's on Thunder Bird's canvas?"

The press was kept out of the hotel by security as Josephine and Perry passed through the front doors. Inside, Perry could hear another reporter shouting out, "Mr. Villa! Will this be the most expensive painting you've ever sold?"

Josephine whispered to Perry, "I hope so." He smiled at her remark as they approached the hotel manager behind the registration desk.

"Good day, Mr. Villa ... Madam ..." the manager smiled.

"Have all the guests arrived?" Perry asked, obviously in control of the situation.

"All have arrived with their respective entourages, Mr. Villa."

"Have the painting sent to the meeting room at once."

"Right away, sir."

"And no reporters until after the sale!" Perry slipped the manager a crisp one-hundred-dollar bill.

"I'll handle everything, Mr. Villa," the manager said as he picked up the phone.

Perry and Josephine walked to the hotel elevator. Once inside, Thunder Bird's beautiful agent admitted to the famous art dealer, "I'm so nervous."

"Relax and breathe easy. Soon it will be done." Josephine stepped back to the elevator wall. That wasn't the first time he'd said those words to her. She removed her sunglasses and breathed deeply with her eyes closed.

In the Leavenworth dining hall, Floyd was in the cafeteria-style line with other inmates. A Native American inmate food server gave the Paper Man a larger than usual helping of food on his tray. As he carried his tray to a table, a roll of toilet paper unrolled toward him on the floor. An inmate yelled to the room,

"Roll out the white carpet! Here comes the Paper Man!"

The inmates roared with laughter. Floyd was not amused. He sat alone at a table.

An armored car was parked outside the New York City hotel service entrance, and two armed security guards carried the wrapped painting into the awaiting hotel manager.

Inside the meeting room, Josephine and Perry stood on a small stage near a podium. A few dozen expensive armchairs were splayed out before them. The armed security guards entered the room with the painting and placed it on a display stand on the stage near the podium. The halogen track lights directly above the stand illuminated the covered painting. The guards stood by to protect the painting as Perry nodded to the hotel manager that it was time. The manager hustled away as Perry walked away from Josephine to evade any questions about the painting.

Ten wealthy art dealers and their guests were seated quietly as Perry stepped up to the podium. Josephine stood next to the covered painting to assist with the unveiling as Perry addressed the room.

"Welcome, ladies and gentlemen. You all know the work of Thunder Bird. This being his most infamous piece, I suggest a two hundred thousand point of start."

Perry scanned the room confidently. The sober and attentive dealers did not object. "Very well ... let's begin."

Perry walked over to the painting. The room was darkened so that only the high-intensity lighting shone on the painting.

"Ladies and gentlemen ..." Josephine and Perry carefully lifted the cover from the painting. *The Paper Man.*

The room stirred. Josie was stunned. On the colorful oil painting was the Deason homestead. Josie, dressed in a sheer cotton dress, was pumping water into a pan at the well. The

Paper Man and Salesman Huck returned home on the distant dirt lane before the beautiful Nakota Hills sunset. Floyd was carrying Charlie on his hip, and Huck was wearing his sales collar.

The dealers stared at Josie, who was angry and self-conscious as Perry returned to the podium. Several dealers requested and were granted permission to approach the painting and examine it more closely. Josie looked down to the stage, avoiding their eyes on her. One dealer looked closely at the painting, marveling at the effect of the wind playing on Josie's hair. He removed a magnifying glass and focused on the tiny barbed wire fenceline in the background. He zoomed in on worn Charlie riding the Paper Man's left hip. He scrutinized the happy dog that looked so smart walking beside his pale-blue-eyed master — the veteran warrior returning home to his love.

After returning to their seats, the first dealer called out to Perry, "Three hundred thousand!"

The bids came from all parts of the room..

"Four."

Another dealer at the back of the room signaled five as Josie held her breath.

"Seven."

"Eight."

"One million."

"One point two."

The bidding paused, then, "One point five."

A dealer from Texas said, "Two."

There was a longer pause as Perry scanned the room for a higher bid. Just then, seated at the back of the dark room, a man dressed in a three-piece business suit with a braid running down his back stood up. The quiet Pine Ridge grocer, Mr. Clouda, was a plant at the auction. "Three million," he called out in a confident voice.

There was another pause until the Texas dealer bit. "Four."

After no further bidding, Perry smiled at the Texan. "Sold for four million dollars!"

Josie hid her elation as the dealers and their guests left the room, including Mr. Clouda. The Texas dealer shook hands with Perry next to the painting.

Wanting to protect Josie, Perry asked the gentleman, "Would you be so gracious as to allow the lady to leave for the airport before the press arrives?"

"Certainly," the Texan smiled.

Outside the hotel, reporters were questioning some of the exiting dealers as Josie hustled unnoticed into a waiting limo. The limo sped away for the airport.

* * * * *

In the Leavenworth recreation room, Harvey sat bored and depressed watching the TV news as Native American inmates played ping pong behind him. As a local news anchorwoman came on with a breaking news story, Harvey's heart leapt into his mouth.

"Earlier today in New York City, Native American artist Thunder Bird made news again. Still at large after his daring escape from his Pine Ridge, South Dakota, jail cell, his painting titled *The Paper Man* was sold for four million dollars, making it the most expensive painting ever sold by a Native American artist."

Harvey sat stunned as the Indian inmates cheered behind him.

"Thunder Bird apparently sold the painting for one dollar to his tribe while incarcerated. Floyd Harvey Deason — also known as the Paper Man — is currently serving a four-year sentence in a federal prison for complicity in this bizarre scheme."

Harvey was even more surprised to see Josie in the painting as the newswoman continued, "The woman in the painting is purported to be Josephine Tenna ... wife of the Paper Man."

"Ex-wife!" Harvey jumped up and screamed at the television set. He sat down, still stunned by the sale of the painting as Indian inmates patted him on the back, celebrating this dupe their people managed to pull off.

The first two years of his sentence passed slowly for Harvey. He settled into a prison routine as an inventory storekeeper, keeping the vast kitchen supplied for thousands of inmates. His nights were spent reading every book in the prison library, and he spent two hours a day in meditation — an hour before breakfast and an hour after reading before lights out.

Harvey had learned to escape in the words he read. A deeper level of strength and understanding came to him in his silent meditation, quieting his mind with practice until his busy mind slowed and stopped, reaching a level of supreme silence amidst the familiar sounds of captive men struggling with the desultory passing of time. Only the Native American inmates understood what the Paper Man was doing — speeding up his time by slowing his thought patterns.

After two years it was becoming clear to him that he could never be the Paper Man again. Time showed him he could not be free while roving from town to town, making a profit while blind with his fear of aloneness in the manswarm. Another place. Another sale. Another empty day. But the sad news had reached Harvey that Albert Silver had died in his sleep; and with the passing of his friend and mentor, so went his fear of not being a paper man.

After sixteen months in Canada, Josie too had discovered another layer of peace. She lived alone off of Huck's racing money in a cabin north of Winnepeg until it was time for her to return to Pine Ridge with her tribe's half of the four million dollars from the sale of *The Paper Man*. Perry's half of the sale was well worth his connections with Swiss banks — a safe place to keep the tribe's money.

Living once again in the little room she'd once shared with Dennis in the Bird house, she donned a hard hat and a pair of jeans and began overseeing the construction of the new community center. She worked with Native American architects and contractors to design the new center, and she took charge of the construction crews who demolished the old church and built a marvelous new facility that rivaled anything in any South Dakota town of that size. Managing the project from a construction trailer on the building site from early spring to late fall, she supervised every detail from handing out paychecks to having the final say concerning every construction phase of the modern facility. The finished Pine Ridge Community Center housed a library, daycare center, recreation room, health club with indoor pool, and even a machine that dispensed free purified water.

The youth of Pine Ridge were alive with hope and smiling faces when Josie and Walter cut the grand-opening ribbon.

The day after the grand opening, she finally completed the bargain she'd made with the United States Government. She had been given liberty to return to Pine Ridge to oversee the construction of the new center — funded solely from the sale of *The Paper Man* and without federal assistance — and Thunder Bird would surrender to U.S. Marshals at the Canadian border when the center was completed. In return for his surrender, she would not be prosecuted. Dennis made a deal with the feds that he would only have to serve the remainder of the Paper Man's sentence in Leavenworth.

Although Dennis arrived in Leavenworth in early December,

Harvey was not released until January second. For that month, Dennis was kept in a private cell far away from Harvey's cell; they never saw each other until Harvey's release day. As the guard escorted the Paper Man out of his cell for the last time, Harvey requested that he be allowed to see Dennis.

The artist was painting alone in his cell. He put down his brush upon seeing Harvey standing outside his cell. Walking over to his cell bars, Thunder Bird could see that the Paper Man's eyes were relaxed and new.

"How did you know to paint that scene of Josie pumping water in the wind?" Harvey asked him.

"I saw it in a vision."

Once the guard was out of hearing range, Harvey asked in a quiet tone, "Did Josie set up your escape?"

"She knew nothing about breaking me out. She thought the delivery was for the center. I changed the plan."

Harvey took a deep breath before asking his next question. "Does she love Perry?"

"No, Paper Man. She loves you. It was your silence that made this happen."

As Harvey turned to leave, Dennis said, "Sorry about Huck." He extended his right hand through the cell bars. Harvey accepted his handshake with a smile as nearby Native Americans cheered and said goodbye to the Paper Man.

Clad in faded jeans, his favorite blue flannel shirt, and a black dress coat, Harvey was escorted to the release clerk's window where he signed his release papers. Deason's pale-blue eyes watched the clerk open a manilla envelope and pour out its contents: some cash, a wallet and a set of keys. The clerk smiled as Harvey pocketed his belongings. "Good luck, Harvey."

Harvey nodded his thanks then exited the prison with the guard. Outside the building, they walked to the last gate to freedom. As the guard shook Harvey's hand he said, "I'm happy for ya, Harvey. Good luck. And ... don't come back."

Harvey smiled and walked away as the gate locked behind him.

The day was gray and cold and windy, but Harvey was alive with his freedom. At the end of the parking lot, he saw Rocky parked and waiting for him. He had no vehicle lettering and had been completely restored after the explosion in Pine Ridge. Harvey unlocked the driver's door and climbed behind the wheel.

He sat in the van shivering from the cold until he saw Charlie sitting upright on the passenger seat. Inside his worn sales case were the cremated remains of Huck in a sealed plastic bag, and his free and clear title was sticking out of the outside pocket. Harvey opened the glove box to slip his title inside and found his wedding band. He thought back to the explosion and couldn't remember putting his ring in there. He slipped the ring on his finger and wondered what had happened to her ring as he started Rocky's cold engine and listened to him idle.

He turned on the headlights, then the wipers, enjoying these simple things as if surreal and in slow motion. Then he remembered putting his ring in Rocky's glove box during the middle of the night when they were at the cabin. He presumed she must have taken her ring out when she had Rocky restored.

Shortly after *The Paper Man* had sold, Josie had written him a long letter explaining why things happened the way they did and how sorry she was that it had cost them both so much — especially the life of their beloved Huck. She revealed that Joe Paul, the transient day laborer who unloaded boxcars for Albert Silver, had been paid to place the explosive in the case of toilet paper that Floyd would deliver to Pine Ridge. Admitting that part of the reason for the elaborate plan was to get revenge for what he'd done to them by planting the marijuana in Dennis's painting, she promised him that she tried everything possible to get them to abort the plan after she found the check he'd put in with the divorce papers. Unfortunately, Dennis had changed the plan without telling her, and there was nothing she could do to stop it. She also told him she had placed twenty thousand dollars in his savings account to cover his court-ordered fine, and that she was having Rocky restored so he would have transportation when he was released. She ended the letter by giving him the news that Albert had passed away, adding, "I just thought you'd want to know."

Is she at Granny's now? Harvey wondered.

Looking down on Rocky's console, Harvey noticed a collection of CDs he'd played during their relationship — Boz, Chris, Gary, Steve. They were all there.

Harvey buckled Rocky's passenger seatbelt around Charlie. He turned on the CD player, and Chris Rea's rare fast version of "Josephine" began playing through the speakers. He'd listened to the song hundreds of times out in the territory and used to play it for Josie when they first started dating.

Rocky's tires burned rubber as he pulled out of the Leavenworth parking lot. By the time he reached the Iowa border on I-29, he'd played the song a dozen times. The Nakota Hills flanked Rocky's right side, covered in snow so lightly that Harvey saw the golden earth the whiteness could not cover.

Just north of Omaha, Harvey left the interstate and made his way to the Bluffs Run Dog Track. Parking near the grandstand area, he cut the engine and took the seatbelt off of Charlie. He hugged the sales case to his chest as if the ashes of his faithful companion could feel his arms and hear his voice. "I spent most of my time in there trying to forgive myself for playing your song in Pine Ridge." Tears streamed down his face as he continued. "The hardest part about being locked up ... was knowing that when I got out ... you wouldn't be there. I'm sorry for all the mean things I did to you ... and ... I miss you every day."

He stepped out of the van and made his way to the main entrance of the track. The place was deserted except for a maintenance man sweeping near the offices. Down on the racetrack near the finish line, Harvey knelt down and removed the sealed bag from the case. He opened the bag and emptied Huck's ashes into the wind, watching them float carefree across the finish line and continue on their journey to the Sacred Hills.

Harvey closed his eyes to picture his beloved companion running through the hills when he heard a puppy whimpering at his feet. He opened his eyes to find a pup that looked almost exactly like Huck when he had come to them on their honeymoon. As Harvey knelt down to pick up the puppy, from behind him Josie said, "I thought you might want a partner."

Josie looked fantastic walking toward Harvey as he still knelt on the ground with the new pup. She removed the divorce papers from her pocket and ignited a corner of them with a lighter, letting the ashes scatter in the wind. Once the papers were gone, she stood nervously twisting her wedding band while waiting to see if her husband would forgive or reject her. Harvey put down the puppy and took her in his arms, and the passion in their kiss erased all doubt about whether or not he still loved her.

"I W Y N," Harvey said.

"That's what I was gonna say," she returned with a smile.

Harvey took his wife by the hand and they made their way to the grandstand with the new pup loping behind them and sniffing everything in his path. As they passed by a garbage can, Harvey took his worn sales case and stuffed it firmly into the receptacle. "No more Paper Man," he said.

"No more Paper Man," she replied and wrapped her arms around his waist.

They took their time driving to Santa Fe, detouring first to Macy to say goodbye to Granny, then spending a week in Kansas City for a reunion with Harvey's mother. Josie proudly showed pictures of the new center and the faces of dozens of Pine Ridge children who were benefitting from all the amenities there. They enjoyed a second honeymoon along the way, and life had never been better for either of them.

Dennis was released from Leavenworth after nine months and was allowed to serve his remaining two years of probation in Pine Ridge. He lived in the Bird house and slept in the same room he and Josie had shared as children.

Free to be Josie and Harvey, the Deasons made a life for themselves in the new light of Santa Fe. They lived off of sales of Thunder Bird's art, went for drives in Rocky at sunset, and made love while their new pup — whom they named Albert — frolicked and explored the desert. He was a dead ringer for Huck, except that he was slower, barked more, and had bigger feet.

Lying in her husband's arms one hot August night, she remembered back sixteen years to the night she went to the boy Harvey in the church where the spiders were. How things had changed! The church was gone forever, as were Floyd and Josephine. Harvey and Josie had known love, betrayal, forgiveness, and reconciliation. The road they'd traveled to get to where they were was a hard and rocky one, but they would not be who they were without the people and events that had shaped their lives — the people they'd known, the lives they'd lived, the plans they'd made, and the things they'd accomplished. She relished the thought of how far they had come and the adventure of what was yet to be, and she gave a silent prayer of thanks that both had been able to forgive their parents. In a day or two she would give him the news that he was going to be a daddy soon, but for now she kept that secret to herself.

"Sweet dreams and snazzy squirrels," she whispered as they fell asleep.

Years ago when I first wrote the screenplay for *The Paper Man,* I had envisioned actor Jim Carrey playing my lead character, Floyd Harvey Deason. Unfortunately, since I'm an independent writer without an agent, it is impossible for me to get an agent or actor to read a script without any connections in the film industry.

Michael is currently living in Asheville, NC

But I have you. Yes, I mean you, one of my many readers.

Since 1999 when I first published *The Paper Man,* thousands of my loyal librarians who read my books agree (in laughter) that Mr. Carrey was born to play the "roll" of Floyd Harvey.

In fact, when I lived in Culver City, I was young and full of crazy ideas. I even thought of personally delivering a case of toilet paper with the screenplay inside of it to J. C.'s door ... but I didn't do it.

Now, with 2010 approaching, he may be too old for the part or too involved with other projects. So perhaps you, my reader, know of another actor I could consider to play the part. If so, put something on the internet about who you think should play this incredible character. And be creative! If I like your ideas (after you've e-mailed me the site) I will send you a personalized signed and dated copy of *The Paper Man.* But hurry - this offer is limited to the first 100 respondents.

I look forward to hearing from you.

mfrederick310@aol.com

Feedback to author:
Michael Frederick
14435 S. 48th St./Apt. 1138
Phoenix, AZ 85044